The exile[illegible] the dilemma. [illegible] elegant ball given in h[illegible] honor, she is stalked into a moonlit hedge-maze by a toweringly handsome man who then spirits her off to his so-called gentleman's club. Then he informs her that not only is her life in danger from an unknown assassin, but that he's there to protect her, whether she approves or not!

A spy for the Foreign Office, Andrew Chase, the dashing Earl of Wexford, detests playing nanny to arrogant royals. But the brazen and beautiful Princess Caroline takes his breath away, and the more he learns about this remarkable lady, the more she enchants him. Yet to save her life, Drew must reveal a shocking secret that could send Caroline's world spinning out of control . . . and risk losing his lady's love forever.

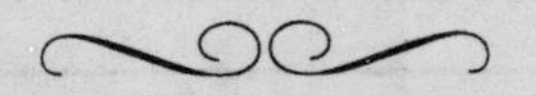

"Linda Needham creates the most dashing, romantic heroes I've ever read."

Lisa Kleypas

By Linda Needham

A SCANDAL TO REMEMBER
THE PLEASURE OF HER KISS
MY WICKED EARL
WEDDING NIGHT
HER SECRET GUARDIAN
EVER HIS BRIDE
FOR MY LADY'S KISS

If You've Enjoyed This Book,
Be Sure to Read These Other
AVON ROMANTIC TREASURES

A DARK CHAMPION *by Kinley MacGregor*
AN INVITATION TO SEDUCTION *by Lorraine Heath*
IT TAKES A HERO *by Elizabeth Boyle*
SO IN LOVE: BOOK FIVE OF
THE HIGHLAND LORDS *by Karen Ranney*
A WANTED MAN *by Susan Kay Law*

Coming Soon
HIS EVERY KISS *by Laura Lee Guhrke*

LINDA NEEDHAM

A Scandal to Remember

An Avon Romantic Treasure

AVON BOOKS
An Imprint of HarperCollins*Publishers*

This is a work of fiction. Names, characters, places, and incidents are products of the author's imagination or are used fictitiously and are not to be construed as real. Any resemblance to actual events, locales, organizations, or persons, living or dead, is entirely coincidental.

AVON BOOKS
An Imprint of HarperCollins*Publishers*
10 East 53rd Street
New York, New York 10022-5299

ISBN: 0-06-051412-4
www.avonromance.com

First Avon Books paperback printing: September 2004

Printed in the U.S.A.

10 9 8 7 6 5 4 3 2 1

Chapter 1

London, England
April 1851

"So, where've you stashed that princess of yours? You can't just keep her to yourself, old man."

"You know how bloody careless Drew is, Ross. He's probably gone and lost her."

"Sorry to disappoint you, Jared," Drew said, wishing once again that his meddling friends hadn't come to the duke's ball tonight. "But I have yet to meet the little virago."

"Andrew Chase, behave yourself!" Kate had been standing peaceably near her starry-eyed husband, but managed to look away from Jared long enough to give Drew one of her chiding scowls. "Princess Caroline is hardly a virago. I've met her myself; she's lovely."

"Begging your pardon, Kate," Drew said as he adjusted his neck cloth, "but I've never met a royal who wasn't a pain in the . . . trousers."

Ross laughed and whispered overloud, "Word around town is that she's stunning."

"Great." Drew snorted, not at all pleased to hear this. "Royal *and* beautiful."

Not to mention vain, arrogant, demanding. Bred in the bone.

"Husband, dear," Kate said, grinning up at Jared in that bountiful way of hers, hooking her finger into his lapel and drawing him closer, "if you and Ross had been paying the least attention, you'd know that the princess hasn't arrived yet."

Jared got that goofy look on his face again as he gazed down at his wife, lovesick and lusty. "My sweet, how can I possibly pay attention to anything else in the room with you wearing that smile, that gown, with that necklace dangling between your luscious . . ."

Fortunately, Drew didn't have to listen to the rest of Jared's sugary cooing because the man had buried his words against his wife's ear. Though Kate's sultry giggle left little to the imagination.

He turned away from the pair and Ross moved in to stand beside him as they overlooked the swirl of the dance floor. "Gad, Ross, how the mighty have fallen."

"And damned if he doesn't look happier than a bloody clam at high tide, lucky bastard." Ross lifted two glasses off a nearby serving table and handed one to Drew. "And you assigned to princess duty."

"My favorite kind of assignment, as you know." Putting his life on the line for another arrogant, ill-tempered royal. "But it's my fault this time. Stumbling into a hornet's nest."

"Punishment for doing your job too well, Drew."

"On time and under budget." It's what he did, without questioning. "I couldn't really refuse to finish what I began, could I? After all, the princess is a cousin to the queen."

Ross laughed and clapped him on the shoulder. "Ah, but who among them isn't, Drew?"

Indeed. Drew only grunted, deciding to reveal nothing more on the subject of the princess's family ties, at least for the moment.

"If the woman is any kind of a princess, Drew, she won't arrive until well after midnight."

And it was one minute till. Hours yet to go.

Time didn't seem to matter a whit to a royal. Keeping as many people waiting as long as possible seemed a heady pastime for most of them.

He should expect no less from Princess Caroline of Boratania.

Impatient to begin, he scanned the perimeter of the dancing below, assessing every move and gesture. He was on duty now, fully absorbed, carefully reading the room as he waited for this princess, who was indeed keeping everyone cooling their heels while she took her own sweet ti—

"Is that . . . ?" Drew heard from the crowd below as the music faded.

"It is!"

"So beautiful . . . !"

"So regal . . ."

The idling crowd that had formed on the landing above the dance floor suddenly closed ranks around the great arching doorway.

"Well, I'll be damned," Drew heard himself say to

no one in particular. Could it possibly be? A punctual royal?

Rumblings of "Look! She's here!" and "Oooo, let me see" tumbled off the landing.

The crowd parted and poured down the stairs to form a gawking, gossiping gauntlet, everyone wanting to get a closer look at the pomp that was billowing above like a glittering cloud.

"Midnight on the dot, Drew."

"I'll believe it when I see her, old man."

If this was indeed Princess Caroline making her grand entrance, she was taking her time progressing through her sea of admirers, still masked from Drew's vantage point.

Not that he cared. Palmerston would officially present him to her soon enough.

And the game would begin in earnest.

Drew had just put the rim of his glass to his lips when an awestruck silence rolled across the room toward him.

And then came the booming announcement from the top of the stairs, "The Princess Caroline Marguerite Marie Isabella of Boratania."

Good Christ!

The crowd had parted like a bank of sun-setting clouds, revealing from their midst the most astoundingly beautiful woman he'd ever seen.

A curling, shimmering crown of golden hair, eclipsing the marvel of the gleaming tiara, keenly bright eyes and a dazzling smile that knocked around inside his chest and kept him waiting eagerly for more.

"You've got the luck of the devil, Drew!"

Ross's voice popped through Drew's soddened

brain, a stunning reminder that he wasn't alone with the woman. He swallowed past a dry throat. "What's that?"

"I said you pulled this one out of your hat, man." Ross nudged him in the arm, once again bringing him back to the present. "She's . . . amazing."

"Which makes her all the more dangerous, Ross." The woman wasn't going to be easy to protect, not if she was forever surrounded by a swarm of courtiers like those who now followed her down the grand staircase.

The portly Prince of Fontmere stopped her on the third step, redcheeked and groveling, nearly drooling over her gloved hand.

The King of the Belgian's bastard son blocked her progress on the next step, and then another princeling and another. Each of them gathering her hand and her easy, elegant smile, vying for the favors of Boratania.

Playing bodyguard to a spoiled princess, no matter how stunning, was bound to be one massive headache after another. But at least the assignment would only last three weeks, a month at the most.

Then Her Highness would become Her Empressness and his job would be over and done with. Thank God.

Drew watched the princess's progress among the guests, dismissing the coiling knot of heat in the center of his chest, the driving, dizzying change in his own pulse. He kept a professional distance as he observed her in detail. The grace in her finest gesture, in the nod of her head, her regal bearing. The brilliance of her smile, her indulgence toward the lowliest baroness as well as the highest and the mightiest, always unruffled, aloof.

And yet, if he wasn't mistaken, slightly distracted.

The music began with a flourish, louder than before and more sweeping as the Duke of Bradford himself whisked the princess onto the dance floor.

Next came the stocky, floridly exuberant Prince Rudolph, then his self-conscious younger brother.

Followed by the architect Henry Cole, who seemed to engage the princess's interest completely with his wild gestures and whispered jests.

And then Sir Hugh de Ferrier, dandy and gambler; and the Earl of Stratton, who seemed to have lost his sense of balance.

"Gad, Drew, the woman's dance card must read like a page from *Burke's Peerage*."

Ironic, that. A secret he must keep even from Ross and Jared. Because a job was a job. It wasn't his mission to judge or make comment.

"The lot of a princess, I suppose," he said. No matter who they were.

"You'll let me know if you need me to fill in for you, Drew. Any time, any place: I'll be there. In fact, I'll take the case if you don't want to bother with it. With her."

"I'll keep that in mind, Ross, old man." Feeling a bit smug, because the princess was indeed an indulgence to look upon, Drew watched her more intently from the gallery, easily following her progress across the dance floor. Those dazzling, milky white shoulders that would surely taste of honey, the softly gilded upsweep of her hair, the delicately sparkling tiara crowning her head.

He found himself leaning his elbows against the railing, following the billowing sway of her gem-studded skirts, fascinated by the random glimpse of a dainty slipper that would peek out from the flounce of her hem and then disappear in the next measure of music.

"There's Palmerston, Drew." Ross pointed toward the undercroft directly across from them. "Looking for you, I wager."

"I'm not ready to be found." Drew looked from Palmerston back to the teeming dance floor, expecting to see the princess still in the arms of Count Bressington, but finding the man standing by himself among the dancers, scratching at his moth-eaten, painfully outdated wig.

And Drew feeling nearly as confused as he cast about for the woman.

Blast it all, he'd only just glanced away for a moment.

"I don't see her anymore, Drew."

"She's here somewhere." She must be. He scanned the swelling sea of dancers, searching for the telltale crown of golden hair. But Princess Caroline wasn't among them.

Wasn't holding court with her slavering admirers. Or changing partners. Or gossiping with the ladies.

The normal, highly steady beat of his heart rattled off center, leaving him with that familiar tic of danger ringing low in his left ear. An old injury with a long, dark memory that always sharpened his senses and set his muscles on edge.

"You've really gone and lost her now, Drew."

She'd vanished from the dance floor entirely.

Damnation! If she wasn't on the dance floor then . . . Ah, there she was, beneath the gallery, skirting the dancers, making a beeline for a small door at the base of the gallery stairs.

"Don't wait up for me, Ross."

Drew wound his way through the clots of people in the gallery, glad that he'd attended many balls at Bradford's home before tonight.

With any luck, the princess's trajectory would lead her through the service doors below and directly into his path as he slipped through a gallery door and down the back stairs.

But the blasted woman must have taken another corridor. He hurried along the service hallway, listening for her telling footsteps.

Ah, there they were. Soft, but *shooshing* along the passage that connected the grand ballroom with the service buildings.

A curious route for an innocent princess. Surely a secret rendezvous with an unsuitable suitor. Well, he'd been assigned to protect her from anything, and that was his plan.

So he followed her into a dimly lit corridor that turned sharply to the left and became a landing, and then a half staircase down to another flagged corridor. Not only her padding footstep, he was following her scent. Floral and soft, rosewood and orange blossoms.

On she led him with her fragrance, across the uneven tiles of a wet laundry and into a room stacked with terra-cotta pots, musty damp with planting compost.

Through another door into a glass conservatory and then she seemed to burst out into the garden as though she had been holding her breath.

She flitted quietly along the cobbled pathway, her willowy shadow merging for a moment with those of a neatly trimmed row of boxwood pillars that lined either side, then breaking into the moonlight, her gown a glittering cloud of silvery stars.

With admirable determination, she made a sharp left and hurried along the tall laurel hedge and its picket of Grecian statues. Drew followed, but held back against the trunk of a tree as the woman stopped in front of a dark, arching opening in the hedge and stared up at one of the pale marble figures flanking the entrance as though assessing its size and composition.

She brushed her palm along the top of the fat urn cradled in the crook of its arm, then straightened her skirts and darted into the darkness on her suspicious errand.

A rendezvous with a lover, an assignation?

Bloody hell, he hadn't even considered the very worst scenario. That the little fool was heading for a carefully set trap?

Damnation! His heart suddenly taking off like a rabbit, Drew ducked into the same opening. He had just made the first turn into the darkness when he heard a snap to his left and then felt the jab of something pointy right in the middle of his back.

"Hands up where I can see them!"

Drew held back a laugh at the false gravel in the voice, but dutifully raised his hands to his shoulders. "Anything you say, miss."

That got him a poke. "I don't know who you are, sir, or why you've been following me, but unless you leave this garden immediately, you'll find yourself in more trouble than you can possibly imagine."

Easy, Princess. "Oh, my dear, I can imagine a great deal of trouble."

"Sir, I know how to use this thing." She shifted to a more expert stance, doubtless learned in a fencing class with an epee.

"I'm sure you do, madam. But if you're seeking to frighten me into obeying you, I'm afraid you're going to have to use a more lethal weapon than that stick you're holding at my back."

She gave an inelegant snort. "Do not mock me, sir! I—"

Drew used her momentary chagrin to turn swiftly and grab her hand. He pulled the stick from between her fingers and leveled it at her nose. "Never threaten anyone with a weapon which can't possibly subdue them."

"I don't need advice from a . . . a . . ." She blustered at him, her eyes lovely glints of lavender moonlight, her fists jammed against her perfectly shaped hips. "Do you know who you're talking to, sir?"

"God, yes, madam!" Drew laughed, delighted by the low, lilting melody of her voice, at the shards of moonlight filtering through the leafy alley, playing softly down the column of her long neck. "You are a very dangerous woman who claims to know how to use a stick."

She tossed back her shoulders and lifted her chin. "I am Princess Caroline, the Duke of Bradford's guest of honor, and I command you to return to the ball and stop following me."

"Hmmm . . . Princess . . ."—he really shouldn't be toying with her—"whom did you say?"

He heard her stamp her slippered foot into the gravel pathway. "You heard me, sir. Now, go back where you came from and stop following me." She stuck out her arm and pointed toward the entrance.

Odd that the little princess wouldn't just turn tail and leave him standing there. Not that he would allow her to do that while he was in charge. She was his now to watch over.

"Why, Princess? So you can meet with your lover in the middle of this maze?"

She gasped and then sputtered. "How dare you speak to me that way?"

"I'm only looking out for your best interest, Your Highness." Drew shrugged and yanked a leaf off the hedge. "What if you're caught out here with your paramour? What will people say? With you a princess and all."

"I'm not meeting a lover, sir, not that it's any business of yours. Now go back to the ball before I—"

"I can't do that, Princess. Not without you. After all, if you're Princess Caroline, as you say you are—"

"I am!"

"Then you're the guest of honor tonight, and ought to be inside dancing with your many admirers, not out here unchaperoned."

"I don't need a chaperone. I'm perfectly capable of taking care of myself. Now, I'll thank you to excuse me—"

She tried to brush past him, but he heard a pair of voices just on the other side of the hedge coming their way. Hell, the last thing he needed was to be discovered in the bushes with the princess he was supposed to be protecting. Tongues would do far more than just wag.

He caught her arm and bent down to her ear. "You'll be quiet now, Princess!"

"Move, you big lout." She gave his chest a two-handed shove but he only brought her closer to him.

"Too late, Princess. We've got company." Hoping the prickly woman would take his lead, Drew pressed her backward into the laurel hedge.

"What are you doing?"

"Saving us both, madam," he hissed as he turned away from her. "Now, quiet yourself."

Hoping the large, shiny leaves would mask her completely from whoever was coming through the maze, Drew then leaned back against her, as though idling there against the hedge, not at all pleased at her curving softness he met there, at the plushness of her breasts, or her hot little fingers spread across his back.

"Are you mad, sir?" She shoved at him with a grunt, causing Drew to press harder.

"Keep still, madam!" he whispered over his shoulder. *Else this whole enterprise might perish before its birth.*

And Princess Caroline along with it.

Chapter 2

Caro was so startled by the huge man's shockingly rude behavior, she couldn't find her tongue, or her breath.

Couldn't hear a thing over the roaring rush of her own heart, couldn't think for the spicy bay scent of the rogue's coat, the wall of exotic heat and the thunderous power of him keeping her against the hedge.

She tried to wriggle around him but he only became broader, more immovable.

She found her voice at the very same moment she heard the giggling chatter coming toward them from around the next bend.

"Ooo, Hammy, dear, kiss me again! Your moustache tickles me so!"

"Oh, my delicious little Adelaide, I just want to eat you up."

Gad! It was Lord Hamilton and that silly daughter of Lord Melborough's. A pair of incurable gossips, who were sure to spread word of her misadventures in the maze, if they found her here with the great brute.

Which meant that she had no choice but to keep absolutely quiet and suffer the pointed branches grabbing her from behind as well as the sultry, unsubtle pressure of the huge man in front of her.

"I think the path goes this way. . . . Eeeeek! Oh, what is that, Hammy? A ghost?"

The brigand shifted his weight against her, broadened his shoulders, but said nothing.

"Here, here, sir!" good old Hammy said with a blustery roar and a lot of scuffling and brush quaking. "I say, who goes there?"

Her abductor scoffed with an actor's ease. "You injure me to the quick, Hamilton."

"Lord Wexford, as I live and breathe!" Hamilton must know the man, must now be shaking his hand. "Nothing to fear, Adelaide, this is Andrew Chase, the Earl of Wexford. My lord, this is Lady Adelaide Melborough."

An earl? This presumptuous man with the shoulders of an ox and the disposition of a bear and muscles of molten granite, was a peer?

"My deepest apologies if I startled you, Lady Adelaide," he said, settling his weight on his right foot. "I was just taking a bit of cool air."

Caro felt the man bend a slight bow toward the lady, a motion that brought her belly in direct contact with the hard flexing muscles of his backside for a short, wildly thrilling moment that made her breath catch in her throat and her heart rattle in her chest.

"I do understand, my lord Wexford. Hammy and I were just taking the air ourselves."

"We're engaged to be married, don't you know." Hamilton gave a belly-laugh.

"Then my best wishes to you both." Wexford's impatience for them to be gone rumbled across the bare expanse of her bosom, sifting like a breath through her gown and the silk of her camisole.

Caro wanted them gone just as surely, but Adelaide went on merrily. "Such an exciting ball, don't you think, Lord Wexford? With the princess arriving in all her glory. Looking just like a queen. Such an exquisite young woman. Regal to her fingertips! Don't you think so, my lord?"

Caro waited breathless for Wexford's response to Adelaide's question, though wondering why she cared. But his pause was every bit as prickly as his, "Mmmmmm . . . I didn't really notice."

"You didn't see her?"

Those huge shoulders rose and fell in a shrug. "One princess is more or less like another."

Adelaide gasped and then giggled.

Caro reached down and pinched the back of his knee, but he didn't even flinch.

"You'll think differently, my lord, when you take a good look at her. Right, Hammy dear?"

"Decidedly, Wexford! Come now, Adelaide, my love, let's us back to the ball before we're missed and tongues start to waggle."

"Good-bye, my lord! Do enjoy the night air!"

The moment Adelaide's trilling voice trailed off into the larger part of the garden, Caro gave the huge man a shove. "Get off me, you big lout!"

The beastly earl let up just far enough to turn before bearing down on her again in the darkness, so that all she could see of him was the pearly reflection of his white teeth.

"You have a very large temper for such a little princess."

"The size of my temper, sir, is in direct proportion to the size of my outrage. And you, Wexford, are completely outrageous. Now, let me go immediately, else you'll find my knee making direct contact with your precious family jewels."

The horrible man threw back his head and laughed. A full bellowing roar that filled the tight spaces between them and stole her breath away.

"Then, by all means, Your Highness, don't let me detain you." He then took a long step backward, swept his thickly muscled arm in front of him as he bowed his head and dropped to a very proper and elegant half-knee in front of her.

Quite elegant for such a huge beast of a man.

Chiding herself for once again yielding a moment to his exotic scent, Caro harrumphed and wrenched herself forward out of the brush.

"Ouch!" She went exactly nowhere.

The pointy hedge held fast to her puffy sleeve and to somewhere near her right hip.

Wexford kept his laughter close as he gestured through the moonlight toward the exit. "That direction, Princess. A quick right and then a left."

"I know the way out, sir!" More to the point, she knew the way in. So she threw herself forward again, but only caught herself more firmly, now at her left hip and her skirt and the other sleeve. "Blast it all, Wexford, you've caught my gown with your manhandling!"

"You're caught, Princess?" The man's dark amusement was as palpable as his towering height. "A pity. I'd begun to hope you'd changed your mind about deserting me."

"Get me out of here!" Time was running out and here she was arguing with a lunatic.

He cocked his head and leaned closer to her, all that stunning nearness a threat to her usual self-control, his whisper thoroughly unbalancing. "Is that a royal command, Your Highness, or would that be a request for me to help you?"

Fiendish man, he didn't understand a thing. "This is a very old and expensive gown—" And she had work to do tonight.

He chuckled low and took a deep breath. "I doubt you'd ever be caught dead in anything less."

The bloody rogue! If she could only get a good look at the man, but the hedge shaded his face and the moonlight had disappeared again. "If you will just unhook my skirts for me, then I could—"

"Well, now there's a proposition I don't often get from a princess. Unhooking your skirts . . ."

She heard herself sputter, felt her heart rise up in her throat. "How dare you presume—!"

"Oh, my dear princess, you'd be shocked to the tip of your succulent little toes at just how much I've dared to presume about you."

Succulent? Her toes! Of all the . . . Oh, my!

She should have felt fear as he moved closer with his enveloping heat.

Should have objected loudly when he wrapped his amazingly strong arms completely around her, wrapped her shoulders and her back and her hips in the hottest, most dazzling embrace of her life.

She certainly should have done much more than

gasp and turn her head toward his mouth when he exhaled along her bare shoulder, more than merely whisper a breathy little "Whatever are you doing, sir?" against his temple.

He paused for a long, motionless moment as though pondering something, then grumbled low and cleared his throat. "I'm unhooking your skirts, Princess, just as you commanded."

Oh, but he seemed to be doing more than that. Much more. His hands were huge, the heat of them playing in the heavy satin folds against her hip and then along her waist, sliding down the back of her thigh until she was holding her breath, a hundred curses, a thousand sighs trapped in her chest.

"Tell me, Your Highness, are these merely bits of glass bedecking your . . . *bunting* back here, or are they the crown jewels of Boratania?"

Caro could hardly think for the sound of her heart in her ears, for the stunning sensation of the ever so slight whisper of his masculine chin brushing across her very bare shoulder as he worked behind her.

"Are they, Princess?"

"What?" she finally managed, still not sure of his meaning, still reveling in the scent of him. Beads? The crown jewels? "Why, sir?"

He blew out another torrid breath of exasperation. It broke against her shoulder and danced across her bosom to lodge between her breasts like a delicious, stealthy caress.

"Because, Your Highness, I damn well don't want to be accused of being careless of your treasure."

He was too late for that. She was nearly out of time tonight and out of breath. Possibly out of her mind for coming out to the maze in the first place.

"The beads are glass, Wexford."

"Good, then I can . . ." He grunted, shifted his weight closer against her, thrusting her hip into his thigh, balancing her there.

"Then you can what, sir?"

He seemed to be gritting his teeth, growling under his breath as he started to tug on her skirt. "I can simply force the issue."

"Force? No! Wait!" She had been studiously not touching him anywhere—there was too much of him, too much power leashed inside him. Now she grabbed hold of his waist, the only part of him within reach. "Stop right there! What do you mean, force the issue?"

He stepped back to stare at her, his eyes glittering from his great height, the stars at his back, the moon painting his shoulders with silver. "You're stuck, Princess. I've freed your sleeves and your lovely hips, but from what I can tell, the beadwork at the back of your skirt has become permanently entwined in a couple of stubborn twigs."

She heard the flick of metal, caught the flash of steel in the moonlight. "That's a knife!"

"I won't be long." He started to reach behind her back, but Caro flattened her palm against his chest and he stopped.

"Don't you dare, Wexford! I'm not going to let you cut my skirts. The beads may be merely glass, sir, but this gown belonged to my dear mother. She wore it when she married my father, which makes it very precious to me, and part of the heritage of Boratania."

"I promise to do as little damage as possible." Then the lout ducked to the side, put his huge, hot hand right in the middle of her back, then bent her over his thigh as though to paddle her.

"Are you purposely trying to mortify me?" She tried to wriggle out of his impossible embrace, but he only clamped his hand down on her bottom and pressed her more firmly over his thigh.

"My dear princess, if you want me to save your precious gown then you'll hold still until I'm finished." He kept his hand there, his fingers spread across her backside as though he had free reign.

"Finished doing what, sir?" If she could only see. She could feel him sawing at something, muttering blue curses beneath his breath.

"There." He stopped suddenly and straightened. "That should do it, Your Highness. But come away gently."

Furious with the man and his methods, and with herself for landing in his path in the first place, Caro flung herself out of her prison into the laurel lane, suffering a pin prick to her arm and a yank at her scalp.

She was free, her dignity scratched but definitely intact.

Caro brushed at her palms, hoping there might still be time for her errand. "That will be all, Wexford. Please take your leave."

She heard the shadowy branches shifting as he stepped back into the moonlight, as tall as a bear and just as threatening. "Not even a thank-you, Princess?"

"For what? For pushing me into the bushes in the first place?"

"For saving your silky hide from ruin amongst your loyal subjects."

She hadn't any subjects, loyal or otherwise. Not that the man needed to know this. "Good-bye, Wexford."

"Aren't you forgetting something, Your Worshipfullness?" He was holding out something to her.

A circle of glittering bits of light.

"My tiara!"

"Yes, and what's a princess without her crown?" He sketched a bow toward her.

"Or a libertine without his conceit." Caro grabbed her tiara out of his hand and pressed it against her chest. Imagine if she'd lost it out here in the bushes while she was dallying with this phantom bandit who smelled of danger and the whispers of night.

Feeling suddenly horribly exposed to those darkly glittering eyes, she turned away and replaced the circlet, but when she looked back, the man was gone. Vanished without a sound.

Her wish had come true. Though he'd left his heat and his scent to linger on the misty moonlight, a memory which she planned to forget in the next five minutes.

"Blast it all." She'd been away from the ball too long by now. Too late to work her way through the maze for a look at the statue in the center.

A statue which, according to her exhaustive research had been stolen from her. From her family. From her dear Boratania, when it had been at its lowest ebb.

Not that she was accusing the Duke of Bradford of looting her kingdom himself, he wasn't old enough. However, if the statue was the one she believed it to be—from the rotunda of the Villa Rosa—then he had at least accepted stolen goods—knowingly or not—and she would have every right to reclaim it in the name of Boratania.

If the statue was here at all.

Well, then, she'd just have to see that the duke invited her back for another garden party. A party that would hopefully exclude the brutish Earl of Wexford.

Caro hurried back toward the conservatory, certain that she was being watched by someone, so distracted that she nearly jumped out of her skin when she pulled the door open.

"What have you been doing out there, Princess Caroline?"

"Lucinda! Sylvia!" Her two very best friends in the world stood blocking her way. "What are you doing *here*?"

"You invited us to the ball, remember," Lucie said, hooking Caro by the arm and pulling her inside the conservatory.

"Yes, I know! But how did you know where I was?"

Sylvia brushed at Caro's sleeve. "He said we'd find you here looking a mess, and you certainly do!"

"He who?" Caro's heart took a guilty leap, though she was perfectly innocent of any wrongdoing and knew exactly which man Syl was talking about.

"A tall, handsome fellow," Sylvia said, her eyes sparkling bright in the pale light. "Handsome actually doesn't begin to explain the way he—"

"Sylvia McCallvern!" Lucie giggled like they all had done when they were girls at school. "Don't tease! Oh, but Princess, he was soooooo lovely."

"What man exactly, Sylvia?" Caro hadn't really seen Wexford's face, beyond the steely planes of moonlight.

"He found us at the dessert table and asked if we were your friends, Lucinda de Taitville and Sylvia McCallvern. We said we were. Then he said that you would be needing our help before you came back to the ball. And indeed you do."

"I'm fine, Syl." Except for the unsettling question of how and why Wexford knew the names of her best friends.

"You don't look very fine, Princess," Lucie said, tucking a strand of hair behind Caro's ear.

"You look like you just had a fight with a cat. And lost." Sylvia took her by the elbow and led her back through the conservatory and into the well-lighted sewing room.

Caro shocked herself as she looked into the cheval glass. "Oh, dear."

"We told you so." Lucie picked a hairpin from Caro's hair and then stopped to stare into her eyes. "He didn't do this to you, did he? The handsome messenger?"

Caro opened her mouth to say yes, of course he did. With his boldness and his broad-shouldered heat, his large hot hands traveling where they shouldn't.

But that wasn't really the truth. Wexford hadn't hurt anything more than her pride. And she had been the one to accost *him*. Albeit with a stick.

And besides, Lucie and Syl would just be shocked to their socks. Though she'd known them forever, through joy and sickness and school and everything, she was beginning to feel an ever-widening distance from them. No longer a schoolgirl, too busy with her royal duties.

She missed them dreadfully, but it seemed that was the lot of a princess.

"Don't worry, Lucie. It was a hedge that got the best of me." Not the Earl of Wexford.

Not ever.

"We didn't think so, Princess Caroline," Syl said, picking the last of the hairpins out of her curls. "Something in those deep, dark eyes told us he was a man of honor."

"Is that so?" Caro hadn't seen Wexford clearly enough to tell much about the color of his eyes, let alone the rest of his face.

And a good thing, too. Once she was out on the dance floor again, if she accidentally locked eyes with him, she wouldn't blush or react at all, because she would never know it was him.

Though she might recognize the unusual breadth of his shoulders.

And the square-edged strength of his chin.

And the sound of his laughter.

Those blatantly sensuous hands.

The luscious scent of him . . .

His profile.

His power.

Yes, it was a bloody good thing that she wouldn't be able to recognize the man at all.

She would spend another few hours dancing, suffering the ravaging of her feet by dozens of pairs of ungainly boots, the dreary courting, and then return home to the loads of work she had left to do.

Restoring her father's old kingdom to its former glory was a devilishly difficult labor.

Even after Lucie and Syl put her hair back to rights and brushed her gown free of debris, Caro wasn't quite ready to return to the pressures of the ball. So she gossiped and giggled with her friends like in the old days, laughing and joking until she thought she would burst.

Then she steeled herself for the battle, thanked them for their friendship and their discretion, kissed them both on the cheek, and hurried off to the ballroom.

"Ah, there you are, Princess Caroline!" Lord Peverel drawled as he and his two associates met her en masse beneath the ballroom gallery.

"My lords, how delightful to see you all here!" Caro offered her hand to each of her acting ministers, more than grateful for all the advice they had given her about setting up her new government.

"A ball in your honor, Your Highness!" Lord Innes grinned at her with his round cheeks. "We wouldn't miss it for the world."

"And, begging your pardon, Princess Caroline, but if you check your dance card, you'll find me in line with all the others."

"I'm already looking forward to it, Sir Wellstetter." She tried to sidle past them, but they were as eager as ever to see to her every need.

"Just some final papers for you to read and sign, Your Highness," Innes said, beaming at her, "and you'll be ready for your triumphant return to Boratania."

Except that she'd never been there.

"So, how is your delightful collection of Boratanian treasures coming along, Your Highness?" Lord Peverel asked, absently straightening the stickpin on his neck cloth.

"It's expanding very nicely, my lord." Though she'd missed an opportunity just now in the maze, thanks to a certain prowling beast.

"That's good to hear, my dear Princess," Lord Peverel said, with a nod to his fellows. "Do let us know if we can be of assistance. Any time, for any purpose."

"Thank you, Lord Peverel. I'm very grateful to all of you." She turned to Sir Wellstetter. "And I'll see you, my lord, on the dance floor."

She left the delightfully eccentric little trio speaking overtop each other, wondering what had prompted Queen Victoria to choose these three men as her ministers.

Not that she'd had any complaints about them. It's just that they were a bit advanced in age and full of differing opinions.

And speaking of dance cards, she could only hope she wouldn't be accosted again on the dance floor by the bloody "Lord of the Maze."

He had a good kick in the nether parts coming, if he tried.

Chapter 3

"Drew, old man! There you are!" Ross was leaning smugly against the terrace doorway, detached as always, as always on edge. "Did you find your princess?"

"The woman is well and duly accounted for." Safely under the care of her friends. Because he'd made damn sure she'd gotten there. And then had skulked the situation long enough to hear them gossiping in the sewing room.

Which had been a good thirty minutes ago. Long enough for the daft woman to have decided to run off on another fool venture.

"You actually met the woman?"

Drew nodded and snagged two glasses of champagne from a passing footman and offered one to Ross. "We had a nice, long chat out in the garden."

At very close quarters. Very.

Ross took the glass with a skeptical brow. "You didn't do anything to offend her, did you?"

How could he not? The woman was a princess, with delicately cultivated sensibilities.

"When have I ever given offense?"

"That little incident with Grand Duke William Charles springs to mind."

"The bastard was drunk and brutal and deserved that dunking in the Seine." Drew ignored Ross's snort of derision and scanned the roomful of dancers for his troublesome charge, knowing that the woman had yet to return to the ballroom.

"Are you sure you merely chatted with your princess, Wexford?" Ross smiled crookedly as he reached across Drew's shoulder, then produced a branching twig with two small, shiny leaves attached.

Drew slashed Ross a frown, then grabbed the evidence and stuck it into his coat pocket. "I told you, Ross, we were walking in the garden, chatting."

Ross snorted. "God help you if she returns bearing a matching leaf. You'll be the talk of the town."

"And Palmerston would have my head. Credit me with some sense, Ross."

Only where the devil had the woman gotten to?

Drew was about to return to the service building to find the princess when he noticed a commotion in one corner of the ballroom. The crowd parted and there she was, entering the dance floor.

Perfectly coifed.

Perfectly gowned.

Perfectly calm.

Perfect, indeed.

A wake formed behind her graceful step, rapt lords, reluctantly dazzled ladies.

Bloody blazes, the woman was magnificent, radiant and distantly regal. And yet her soft scent still clung to his lapels and his neck cloth, the implacable memory of her silky shoulder against his chin. Her nape just a breath away, the smooth shell of her ear.

A temptation like no other he'd faced.

As he watched her progress through her admirers, he felt an overwhelmingly possessive pride in her bearing. A sense that they now shared secrets between them, and shadows and private hijinks.

Hell, they'd tussled in the bushes, played hide-and-seek, had dashed off an impromptu subterfuge. She'd boldly pinched the back of his leg!

A touch that had caught him off guard, had roused him, and left him aching.

"She looks bloody dangerous to me, Drew."

"Who is that?"

Ross snorted and gave him a wry look. "Your fairy princess."

"She's not mine, Ross."

"Yours to protect with your life." Drew could feel his friend eyeing him closely. "So how did the princess react when you told her about your mission to protect her? She must have been wildly grateful to you. Relieved, at the very least. Did she immediately honor you with a Boratanian knighthood? The Royal Order of the Shimmering Blade?"

"Stuff it, Carrington." The man never missed a bloody nuance, understood both Drew and Jared as intimately as he knew himself.

"Ah, then the mission didn't begin as well as you planned?"

"Frankly, Ross, I didn't bring up the matter. Not the right time or place."

Not with the princess as angry as a wasp, and used to getting her own way in everything.

Except, it seemed, in dance partners. To his experienced eye, she didn't look at all happy at the moment, though she was putting up an excellent front. Graciously laughing at every jest, changing partners endlessly, chatting politely as she was waltzed and flung around the room by every prince and peer at the party.

Occasionally her gaze left the dance floor and scanned the edge of the massive ballroom as though looking for someone or something.

The lover she'd stood up in the garden because of his following her?

A clock?

Another quick exit?

Her gaze landed on him for the briefest moment. She quirked her eyebrows with a question, but then glanced away from him without a hint of recognition.

Not an angry frown or even a snub.

Which could very well be the case—that she didn't recognize him at this distance. She might not have seen him well enough in the shadowy garden to remember him in the glaring light of the ballroom.

A pleasant advantage which kept him on the sidelines and out of the general disorder until the wee hours, when people began to leave the ball.

Ross had left at two, and Jared had taken his lovely Kate back to their town house for an early morning return to their refuge in the country.

"The trout are rising, Drew," Kate had said, with a gentle kiss against his cheek as the pair were leaving. "And you know how my Jared loves to fish!"

Jared had only smiled that new cat smile of his and swept his incredible wife into the night.

Lucky bastard.

"Ah, here you are, Wexford." Lord Palmerston steamed his way up the short flight of stairs toward Drew. "Behaving yourself, I see."

"While you were out on the dance floor romancing the ladies, you old fox."

Palmerston stopped on the step below Drew and put a finger to his lips as though revealing a great state secret. "Don't tell a soul, Wexford, but this is by far my favorite duty as foreign minister—dancing with the ladies."

"Your secret's safe with me, Palmerston." Daft or not, Drew had always liked the eccentric Palmerston—admired the man's quicksilver sense of outrage and his willingness to throw himself into the fray, no matter the cost.

"Which is the very reason I chose you for this assignment, Wexford." Palmerston joined him on the landing.

"Because I'm a fool?"

"Because you and your operatives will keep the entire investigation a secret." The man leaned sideways, speaking out of the corner of his mouth. "And you'll protect the princess with your life."

"That's my intention." Which meant that the sooner the reckless woman was off his hands the better.

Palmerston turned and narrowed his eyes at Drew. "She's not ever to know the rest of it, Wexford."

Drew stilled the sudden tic of irritation in his jaw. "By 'the rest of it,' Palmerston, you mean the truth about her." As though he had ever spilled a secret or failed to deliver as promised.

"Not *ever*, Wexford." Palmerston shook his head

fiercely, frowning deeply, his gray brows twitching. "It wouldn't serve the princess and there's far, far too much at stake."

Merely the fate and future of the great families of Europe. Drew understood only too well.

"Yes, I know, Palmerston." He clapped the man on the shoulder, hoping to alter his mood. "As I also know the princess is going to be spitting mad when she learns that you've turned her over to me, lock, stock and bloody barrel."

"Spitting mad, you say?" Palmerston drew back. "What the devil makes you think that?"

Drew decided not to explain his recent encounter in the garden with the nettlesome princess. It would only worry the man.

"Intuition," he said instead.

"Balderdash! Princess Caroline hasn't a quarrelsome bone in her body. She's quite the finest young woman you'll ever have the pleasure to meet."

Certainly the most beautiful. The most brazen.

"We'll see, Palmerston, I'll be waiting for your delivery. Shall we say a half hour. If you can drag the princess away from her admirers."

"A half hour then, Wexford!"

Drew made his way through the unsettling gauntlet of the Duchess of Bradford and her three immodestly marriageable daughters and out into the courtyard.

"To the Huntsman, Henry," Drew said to his coachman as he climbed into the cab.

"A bit of late-night gaming for you, sir?" Henry asked from the open door.

"A bit of late-night work, I'm afraid."

Henry's eyes glittered beneath the brim of his cap. "Ah, more of the usual?"

"That's my hope, Henry." The usual assignment, the usual royal. With such marvelously unusual eyes.

Henry nodded and smiled. "To the Huntsman then."

The Huntsman. His refuge.

Hell, lately the bloody club had become his home. As if he were some lonely old childless bachelor.

Scratch off *old* and that's just what he had become.

No, not lonely. He always had Ross to run with. And his operatives. The Factory.

And yet in the nearly two years since Jared had married Kate, he'd begun to notice an emptiness in his life, especially when he was alone, a great gaping hole that seemed to be opening ever wider in his chest, leaving a deepening need for something.

Someone.

I'm not meeting a lover, sir, not that it's any business of yours.

Not this particular someone.

Yet, for the moment, the princess was his business. Her every waking moment would be his business and his focus.

"I said, we're here, sir." Henry was holding open the carriage door and staring at him.

Doddering. Add *doddering* to *childless old bachelor*, and he was the exact image of old Biffy Tuckerton, who'd moved into the Huntsman five years ago and to anyone's knowledge hadn't stepped foot outside since.

"Thanks, Henry. Get yourself a catnap; I'll be needing you around the back in about an hour."

The club was nearly empty as Drew made his way up the wide front stairs and into the main lobby, across the marble inlaid floor, to the club room, then into the map room. He was just lighting a second lamp when he heard Palmerston's carriage enter the private alley at the back of the club.

The knock on the outside door came before Drew reached it. He opened it to Palmerston's footman and Palmerston himself standing at the base of the carriage steps.

"Please come out of the carriage, Your Highness." Palmerston seemed his most cajoling.

"For Heaven's sake, Palmy, why?" came the familiar voice from the darkness of the carriage, a little weary now, tinged with a yawn and more than a little annoyed.

Palmerston cast Drew a pleading frown and then peered back into the carriage. "Believe me, Your Highness, I'm only acting in your best interest."

"Going home and getting a good night's sleep is in my best interest," the woman said, still deep within the carriage. "Please, let's go. It's the dead of night. I'm exhausted and I think Fontmere broke my little toe with his enormous boots."

"I'm sorry for your toe, but you know I wouldn't have brought you here, Your Highness, if I didn't believe this a most important meeting."

A hugely impatient sigh rattled the carriage on its springs. "And what kind of meeting begins at three o'clock in the morning?"

Palmerston shot another glance at Drew, who was beginning to regret agreeing to the assignment. "The kind of meeting you can't afford to miss."

Drew heard the distinct sound of fingertips drumming on the interior wall of the carriage, and then, "If you really think it's that important . . ."

"It's about the future of Boratania."

Silence and then a little moan of distress. "Why didn't you say so immediately?"

Palmerston gave a little bow as he reached into the carriage and drew out the long, slender, gloved arm and then, inch by inch, the magnificent princess attached to it.

First, her satin slippered foot against the step, then her pale, trim ankle.

Then one flounce after the next, a foamy froth of beads and lace and chiffon.

And without a doubt, if one looked with a forensic eye, random bits of twiggy leaf entangled in the beading.

Her face was lit by the lanterns glowing from either side of the Huntsman's backdoor, her tiara removed, her golden hair, more enchanting for the slightly disheveled curls as she glided lightly down the steps and onto the cobbles. Her mouth was moist and imperial, her brow lightly fretting in her impatience as she touched Palmerston's arm.

"Then let's get this meeting over with, Palmy." She hiked a velvety dark cloak over her shoulders.

"My thought exactly, Princess," Drew said, a little bit in awe of all that beauty in motion, and a whole lot roused by the rosy sweet scent of her curling up the stairs.

Instead of waiting to be met by those dangerously blue eyes, Drew turned and slipped into the dimness of the Huntsman.

But not before catching the stubborn woman's very satisfying gasp of horror from the steps.

Yes, we all have our secrets, Princess, he thought with a jangling breath and the distinct feeling that he was already in more deeply than he'd planned.

I won't tell yours, if you don't tell mine.

Chapter 4

Princess!

That voice! The earl's. Wexford's! She'd know it anywhere!

Deeply coursing and dark. As invasive in this back alley as it had been in the garden maze.

And now he was here?

With Palmerston?

She glanced toward the doorway to confirm her suspicions, but the large shape had vanished once again into the swirling darkness beyond.

"Just what sort of place have you brought me to, my lord Palmerston?"

The man cleared his throat. "We're at the Huntsman."

"Oh, and what, pray tell, is the Huntsman? A shooting club?" Because she knew exactly who she'd like to shoot at the moment.

"It's a gentleman's club, Your Highness. We're just a few blocks from Saint James Square."

"Good lord, Palmy! This *must* be important if you've brought me to the back alley of a gentleman's club, in the middle of the night, without a thought to what the gossip sheets might say if I'm discovered here."

"Since when have you worried about such things, Your Highness?"

"You're the one who's always chiding me about my independent streak." She usually didn't have time for proprieties and the like. One of the benefits of being a royal was that she could be as eccentric as she liked and few dared to challenge her.

Except for the occasional situation that got completely out of control. Like in the maze tonight.

"I can assure you, Princess Caroline, that the Huntsman is a most upstanding organization. Prince Albert belongs, and the queen herself has been here many times."

"And I suppose Queen Victoria approves of that . . . that ogre who just greeted us?"

"Ogre, my dear? You can't mean Lord Wexford?"

She meant far more than that as she glared up at Palmerston's genuine incredulity. But she fought off her indelicate opinion of the man who had besieged her in the maze.

Not worth the energy to explain. She'd wasted enough time tonight.

"Never mind, Palmy. The man just seems . . . rude." Overbearing. Overwhelming. "And it's late. And what the devil does he have to do with Boratania?"

"You'll want to hear him out, Your Highness."

Palmerston had seemed unusually attentive tonight, had been so ever since he'd picked her up at Grandauer Hall. "I'm trusting you, my lord."

Caro lifted the hem of her skirt and hurried up the

steps into the dimness of the small anteroom. Though the earl was nowhere to be seen, his familiar scent lingered there amidst the leather and limestone, the stark memory of laurel and moonlight leading her down a short hallway.

"This way, Princess." That rumbling voice again, rolling toward her from a dimly lit doorway.

And then he was gone again, like a shadow, appearing again only as she reached the doorway herself.

He was standing inside, beside a table as she entered, bending to light a globe lamp, the flicker of the flame dancing with the deep shadows across his features.

"Welcome to the Huntsman, Princess Caroline," he said without a glance at her. "I hope you'll pardon the inconvenience of this late hour."

"You seem to be bent upon inconveniencing me this evening. Have you kidnapped me again?"

"He kidnapped you, Your Highness? When?" Palmerston had come through the door behind her and now bustled himself between them. "Wexford, explain yourself. I didn't know you two had met."

But the earl didn't seem inclined to explain a thing to the foreign minister. He only stood there at the table, staring down at Caro from beneath that shadowy dark brow, his face still more of a mystery to her than anything substantial.

And obviously challenging her to tattle on him like a spoiled child.

Not that she was about to give him the satisfaction of hearing her whine about their little encounter. They were both adults. She knew the risks of venturing out alone. Sometimes it was the only way to get anything done. Chaperones gossiped, men were too slow and careful of her every move, and most of her friends were too timid to follow her into the breach.

Except, of course, Lucie and Sylvia, who always seemed ready for an adventure.

"The earl and I met briefly at tonight's ball, Lord Palmerston. Merely in passing."

"But you said he kidnapped you. . . ."

Caro felt the tall man's gaze gliding over her face, his challenge deepening. "A simple jest between the earl and me, my lord. Nothing more."

Palmerston suddenly grinned broadly. "Very good news, then. Couldn't ask for a more auspicious beginning."

Beginning to what? Caro wondered, a hollowness gathering in her chest. But Palmerston was already setting his hat on the edge of the table.

"Now, Wexford, what say we get started."

"Indeed," Wexford said with a slow nod as he turned away to the very masculine fireplace with its elegantly carved heraldic crest.

"And since you've both been introduced . . ."

"Not formally, Palmy." Who was this mysterious man who held such sway over Britain's influential foreign minister?

"Oh, well, then, Princess Caroline, if you please." Palmerston smiled. "I'd very much like to present to you Lord Andrew Chase, Earl of Wexford."

"Very pleased to meet you, Princess." The man nodded haphazardly in her direction as he shrugged his broad shoulders out of his greatcoat.

"You needn't bother, Palmy. I already know who Lord Wexford is. But what I can't imagine is why he would have any interest at all in the kingdom of Boratania."

"I have no interest in your kingdom at all, Princess." Wexford turned back to her, tall and overwhelming. "My interest is solely in *you*."

Me? Caro swallowed, wondering if she'd whispered the little question, or had she only thought it?

Difficult to think at all with the earl staring down at her, completely derailing her train of thought.

"Why would you be interested in me, Wexford?"

"Because, Princess," he said, his dark gaze lingering on her mouth, "someone wants to kill you."

Caro blinked up at the man, annoyed by the sudden ringing deep in her ears. "Would you please repeat that, my lord, I don't believe I heard you correctly because"—she let out a silly little laugh—"I thought you said that someone wants to kill me."

That dark gaze then deepened. "Someone does, Princess."

"What are you trying to say?" Her heart added its clattering racket to the ringing in her ears. "Palmy, what is going on here?"

"I'm afraid it's true, my dear princess," Palmerston said, looking at her with pleading worry in his eyes, "he's telling you the truth. Your life has been threatened."

The words still made no sense, but now she found herself blinking between Palmerston and Wexford, her heart racing. "By whom? Surely this must be a joke."

Wexford dropped a scowl on her. "Believe me, Princess, death threats and assassins are nothing to jest about."

"Do listen to him, my dear. He's only trying to keep you alive."

"An assassin? But the idea is preposterous! If my life was in danger, surely I'd be the first to know."

Wexford laughed low in his chest and narrowed his gaze at her. "On the contrary, Princess, I can assure you that you would be the very last to know."

An icy chill settled across her shoulders, the certainty that she was looking into the dark eyes of a man who would know about such things.

"This is utterly ridiculous!" Caro gave a very unprincessly snort and fixed her gaze on the wide-eyed Palmerston. "If you brought me here, my lord, to convince me of this foolishness, then you've wasted all of our time."

She took a step toward the door, but her momentum was cut short by what must have been an iron band caught around her upper arm.

"Stop right there, Princess."

Wexford! Manhandling her again, as though she were a common washerwoman. "Let go of me this instant. Lord Palmerston, do something!"

But instead of leaping to her defense with his usual protective flustering, Palmerston was shaking his head at the earl. "You were right after all, Wexford. I thought for certain that the princess would believe you. And me."

Wexford brought her closer to his chest, her back pressed against all that heat. "Mark me, Palmerston, she'll believe when I'm finished with her."

"You are finished with me now, sir!" Caro stomped down on his boot with her slipper, but only managed to bruise her instep. "And mark me, both of you, I plan to have a word with the queen about your hijinks."

"Best that you leave now, Palmerston," Wexford said from far above her head, and far too near. "I'll take care of the rest."

"The rest?" Insulted at being talked about as though she wasn't in the room, Caro shot a glance up at the man, but could only see the underside of his chiseled chin. "I'm not the leavings from your dinner, sir!"

Palmerston nodded as he clapped his hat onto his head. "Do be careful, Drew. That's a very expensive dress the princess is wearing."

"So I've been told."

"Don't you dare leave me with this monster, Lord Palmerston!"

But the traitorous minister only shook his head at her and then left with the decisive closing of the door.

"Palmerston!" Caro was still staring at the door when she found herself being carried deeper into the dimly lit room and then dropped into a huge, overstuffed chair in front of the marble fireplace.

"Settle yourself, Princess."

"And you keep your hands off me!" Caro pushed herself to her feet and followed him.

But Wexford had strode to the door and turned a key in the lock, the only possible exit she could see within the walls of books and barred windows and hanging maps.

The man turned back to her, larger than ever, his glower fixed on her, making her eyes water and her heart pound in her chest. Then he nodded to the chair behind her. "Sit yourself."

"And make it simple for you and Palmerston to abduct me without a fight. Don't count on it."

"If I had abducted you, you'd know it by now."

"Then what's the term for keeping a princess against her will?"

"Insurance, Your Highness. Drastic situations call

for drastic measures." He had lit another lamp near the table and now stood fully in the light.

Dear God, what a handsome man he was. And what a very stupid thought, but it had struck her like a blow.

All those shadowed angles that had planed his jaw and his cheeks, now brought into perfect focus.

Though his eyes were still as dark as ever, unreadable, dangerous.

"Kidnapping a princess of the blood is about as drastic a measure as I can imagine."

"Then I suggest you begin by imagining yourself shot dead, Princess, an assassin's bullet lodged inside your pretty little head. Makes a terrible mess, I assure you."

Caro took a breath, fighting against the very raw image. "If you're looking to impress me with high drama and histrionics, sir, you've abducted the wrong princess."

Drew knew for a fact that the woman was the right princess. Right in every possible way.

Royal and outraged and pampered, an all too familiar combination. He'd confronted a hundred such tempers, had developed a stratagem of diversion for all occasions.

Yet the brilliance of her eyes was utterly unfamiliar to him. As unfamiliar as the dangerous intelligence that challenged him as she stood glaring at him, while the toe of her slipper tapped steadily, defiantly, beneath the edge of her beaded hemline.

Perhaps he would have to step more softly than usual, swallow a forkful of humble pie.

"After our earlier encounter this evening, Princess,

I can perfectly understand how you might doubt my motives."

"I don't doubt them in the least, Wexford."

"Of course." He chewed on another forkful. "But if you'll just take a moment to listen to a few of the facts—"

"Facts, indeed?" She laughed and unhooked her cloak at the neck, swept it off her shoulders and onto the back of a chair, just as a pugelist prepares to face off with an opponent. "More likely this is Palmerston's overprotective imagination. He sees plots and rebellions shifting around every shadow. You know the story of the boy who cried wolf one too many times. . . ."

"I assure you, madam, Palmerston is not the source of this intelligence."

"I know I'm going to regret asking this, Wexford," she said, folding her arms across her small but perfect bosom, giving the entire, alabaster display a stunning lift in his direction, "but exactly who is your source, if not dear, demented Palmy?"

"My source, Princess, is *me*."

"You?" Her brow went lofty and wry, her mouth curved into a devilishly disbelieving smile as she walked toward him. "Wherever in the world would the Earl of Wexford come by information about an assassin? At a fancy-dress ball?"

Of all the bloody stubborn ingratitude!

"Or in your box at the opera? In a hedge maze? I'm sure you spend a lot of time skulking in dark places."

"Actually, Princess, I first became aware of the threat at a coronation fete."

"Whose coronation would that be?" She stuck her

fist against her hip as though he couldn't possibly know a coronation from a cribbage game.

"Prince Wilhelm Georg of Heimburg."

She laughed and sat down on the padded arm of the chair, casual and confident, utterly defiant. "Will's coronation was two weeks ago. I couldn't have been a target because I didn't attend."

"I know."

She frowned at him. "How do you know that?"

"There's not much I don't know about you, Princess. Suffice it to say that word of an impending assassination came to me from an unexpected source. And if it hadn't, you'd doubtless have been dead three times over by now."

She stilled and studied him for a long moment, as though he finally had her full attention. "So how did you come to catch an assassin at a coronation fete? And why didn't I read about it in the *Times*?"

"It didn't happen quite that way, Princess. Assassins rarely present themselves for capture so easily. And even if he had, the public would never have learned of it."

"But you did catch him. He's safely locked up in a prison cell."

"I'm afraid he didn't make it as far as prison." Drew unlocked the bottom drawer of the desk safe and pulled out a file box.

"He escaped?" That seemed to get her attention.

"No." Drew caught her eye and said as pointedly as possible, "Though he tried to."

"Tried? Then . . . do you mean . . . he's dead?" she whispered, her soft brow dipping.

"He is."

"Dear God, that's . . . horrible." She exhaled slowly, sobered considerably as she raised her eyes to his. "But, if the man who wanted to kill me is dead, then he's no longer a threat to me, is he?"

"That's not how the game is played, Princess." Drew sat on the edge of the table, leaned toward her, marveling at the sweeping length of her deep golden lashes. "Because as long as the target remains alive, so does the threat."

"And you're certain that I'm the target?"

"You were a threat to someone just a few weeks ago, and unless something in your life has changed radically in the meantime, you're an even bigger threat now than you were then. Because doubtless there's a clock ticking somewhere against you, counting out your days."

A bit melodramatic, but the truth, nonetheless.

"But, why?" She drew herself up. "Who can I possibly be a threat to?"

"Believe me, Princess, if I knew the answer to that, I would never have bothered you with the matter."

She frowned at that, at the blatant implication, then shook her head and rubbed her neck as though she had a headache. "But it makes no sense. I haven't any enemies."

"You obviously do. And you can help me and my investigation by trying to recall if you've ever overheard something that didn't sit well with you. An odd comment, by anyone—a staff member, a friend—a meaningless inquiry about your schedule, your activities. Anything that might have felt out of place."

"Believe me, Lord Wexford, if I suspected anyone

of wanting to harm me or anyone around me, I'd have reported my suspicions to Palmerston immediately."

"I'm sure you would have, Princess. However, no assassin worth his salt would let on his intentions."

"I suppose not." She gave him another very sober look, this time tinted with impatience. "You wanted me to listen to the facts, Wexford. I guess I'm ready now. How did this all come about?"

Hiding his satisfaction, Drew slipped the report in front of her on the table. "The threat first came to light three weeks ago when a man approached a tavern owner on the waterfront at Gdansk, asking for directions to the nearest assassin."

"Good heavens! As boldly as that?" She glanced down at the report, then back up at Drew with those wide, blue eyes on fire. "'Please sir, point me to the nearest assassin'?"

"Arrogance is a common mistake among the wicked. Fortunately, the tavern owner is a friend of . . . well, let's just say that he has connections to the British Foreign Office."

"A Prussian tavern owner on a Baltic wharf?" She lowered herself to the very edge of the chair, eagerly peering up at him. "Why would such a man have any connections to Whitehall?"

Why indeed? "The point is that our contact stalled the man while he judiciously sent word through channels to a British diplomat in Brussels."

"Why didn't the tavern owner just have the man arrested immediately?"

"Because that would have tipped off the original source of the assassination contract, and that's who we need to find as quickly as possible." Drew pulled a lamp closer to the papers on the table in front of her.

"Besides, at that point in time, we didn't even know who the target was to be."

"You mean this assassin person didn't name me as his intended victim."

"Not even a hint. The target could have been a ship's captain, a butcher, a king . . ."

"Instead, it turned out to be me." She frowned and drew the paper closer. "How did you learn the target was me, then?"

"That took some careful investigation."

"What did the diplomat do when the information reached him in Brussels?"

Drew dragged his favorite chair to the map table and sat down beside her, pleased that she had settled into the story, pleased that she smelled of roses. "He couldn't really do anything until he uncovered the identity of the target, so he went to Gdansk—"

"Himself? He didn't send an envoy?"

"Let's just say that he's the sort who prefers to conduct his investigations firsthand." Safer that way. "He met the conspirator, a man named Herr Bechel, in the tavern."

"Face to face with a criminal?" She looked up from the paper.

"That's how the job gets done, Princess; the operative leading the conspirator through a series of questions, trying to squeeze a few clues out of him. Acting as though he would cooperate."

"Wouldn't Herr Bechel have been suspicious—chatting over an ale with a well-dressed toff?"

Yes, his little princess seemed well into the suspense of the story now, following the logic, her questions far more intense than he'd have expected.

"Our diplomat wasn't well dressed at all. I suspect

that, indeed I would hope, that he appeared to be not only a filthy drunk, but a genuinely harmless dockside vagrant."

"Ah, then, he was in disguise?" Her fine, bright eyes lit up in the lamplight gilding the tips of her lashes.

"That's also how it's done."

She laughed in amazement. "You seem to know a lot about this diplomat's investigations. Wait just a moment there." She stood slowly, stared at him. Through him, lighting little sparks in his chest. "You're talking about yourself, aren't you? You're the British diplomat."

"As I said, Princess, I prefer to conduct my investigations firsthand."

Caro didn't know quite what to say to the man who was lounging back in his chair, too large for it, too large for the room, for his title.

This very extraordinary earl with his long, powerful legs and that unfathomable, smoky gaze.

He was no ordinary diplomat, either.

No ordinary man.

And yet everything he'd said so far was simply impossible to believe. Some of it so downright absurd that she needed to hear more, needed to put a bit of distance between them so that she could think.

She moved to the far side of the table, her bare shoulders warmed by the low-glowing fire in the hearth at her back. "So, my lord, the dastardly Herr Bechel never guessed that you were not as you seemed."

"He didn't." Wexford's smile spoke reams about him. Daring and proud. And very, very good at his work. "But he did get a little deep in his cups and hinted at the purpose of his search."

"That he was looking for an assassin?"

"Only that he was in the position to pay good money to a man who didn't mind getting his hands a bit bloody."

"With my blood." A sobering image if she'd ever heard one, immensely personal. "What did you do next, my lord?"

He shrugged. "I volunteered to do the job myself, of course."

Caro nearly choked on her gasp. "You volunteered to kill me?"

"I didn't know you were the target at the time, Princess. Not that that would have mattered. Not that I would have murdered an innocent person." He seemed to think this was funny, though he had the grace to try to hide his smile in that squared-off jaw. "It was the perfect opportunity to learn the target's identification."

"So did he actually hire you to kill me?"

"Unfortunately not." He leaned forward in the chair, elbows on his knees, his brows lifted, teasing. "I knew he wouldn't. As drunk as Bechel was, he could tell that he needed someone more reliable than me."

She swallowed through a completely dry throat. "What happened then? Did you arrest him for conspiring to murder and then coerce a confession out of him?"

He stood, towering above her as he ran his fingers through his dark hair. "I let him go, of course."

"Of course?"

"This man was my only lead, Princess. I needed him to be free to follow his master's instructions. And I needed to be just as free to follow him."

She balked at the absurdity of his logic, but that

only made it seem more reasonable. "But isn't that dangerous? Following a man like that?"

"It's far more dangerous than not keeping him close in my sights."

"I suppose it is." What a dauntless man this earl was turning out to be.

And how unsettling to think that he had already invested so much of his courage in her.

"After a few false starts, Bechel led me quickly through Silesia, and then deep into Saxony and finally to eavesdrop on his meeting in Altenburg with the contact who would eventually arrange for him to meet Josef Tor, the man who was hired to kill you."

"The assassin." Already dead, but all of this happened so unsettlingly close to her beloved Boratania. "What then?"

"And, Princess, three days ago, after spending one long night in a very small, stifling attic"—he sat down opposite her and leaned forward—"I finally learned the worst of it."

"Yes?" she said, breathless with the nearness of him, the leashed power in his muscles.

He studied her as though he hadn't really seen her before, his eyes dark and deeply searching. "A name whispered so low that I barely caught it: Princess Caroline Marguerite Marie Isabella of Boratania."

Like a death knell. "Dear God in heaven."

"Indeed." He leaned closer, as though telling her a deep secret. "But what I didn't find out, Princess, is the information that will keep you alive into your old age."

"Which is . . . ?"

"Who it is that wants to see you dead."

Chapter 5

Caro shook her head and gripped the back of the chair, holding on for dear life, still unable to sort completely through the pieces of Wexford's story.

"But why, my lord? I can't imagine anyone hating me so much that they want me dead."

"Hate probably has nothing to do with it, Princess." His voice had gentled considerably, his gaze softening, judging her every move. "Everyone has enemies of one sort or another."

"I'm sorry, Wexford, but you must have misheard my name in that hot old attic." Her nerves jangling, she picked up the report he'd set out for her to read. But the words just swam and dodged. "This Tor fellow couldn't have meant me. It was some other princess, some other royal. I couldn't possibly be the target."

"Believe me, Your Highness, anything is possible when the stakes are high enough."

"What stakes?" Frustrated, she dropped the report

and paced away from the man and his impossible intrigues. "I've been living in exile since my birth."

"Yes, I know, Princess." He rose and leaned against the edge of the table and crossed his arms over his chest, all the while studying her with those dark, probing eyes of his, as though watching her for some clue. "Someone wants you out of the way. I don't know who. I don't know why. But it's my job to find out. Until I do and you're completely out of danger you'll have to remain in seclusion—"

"What did you just say? In seclusion?"

Drew had expected that very reaction from the princess—her eyes flashing out a blue-flamed warning, her fine shoulders straight, her royal chin raised at him as though a finely crafted weapon.

A magnificent bundle of outrage.

"Yes, Princess," he said, trying to moderate the moment. "You'll be locked up safely behind impregnable doors until—"

The woman laughed, a broad, unexpected sound. "You can't be serious!"

"Deadly serious. Until the matter is settled you'll remain out of the public eye and under guard."

"That's impossible!" She jammed her fists against her hips. "I can't possibly spare the time. I'm right in the middle of preparing the Boratanian exhibit for display at the Great Exhibition."

"The exhibition in Hyde Park." He'd seen the note in her dossier and knew she wouldn't like his solution to that particular security problem.

"That's right. I've been collecting the lost and stolen and looted treasures and artifacts of my country since I was old enough to understand their meaning, and just a few weeks from now I must have a representative group ready to display for Prince Albert's Great Exhibition."

"Which is to be attended by hundreds of officials and foreign dignitaries and God knows how many of the general public who will come to gawk."

Along with the single assassin who will arrive with the rabble to pull off a shot at her pretty little head. Surely the woman could see the potential problem.

And yet her smile was quite proud. "If you know that much about the Great Exhibition, Lord Wexford, then you understand the enormous amount of work ahead of me, in public and in private. Not to mention all the pomp of getting ready for my investiture ceremony."

"As Empress Caroline of Boratania. Yes, I know that, too. The title comes to you, as the last member of your family, when you reach your twenty-first birthday."

Power and privilege and an enviable lineage, with a coronation ceremony attended by thousands. Motive enough to be rid of a royal who's in the way of someone's villainous design.

"Both events are very important to me and to the future of my kingdom, Wexford. All of which will require hours and hours of my time. So I can't possibly seclude myself behind—"

"But you will, Princess. Else you might as well be walking around with a target pinned to your back."

"Don't be—" she stopped mid-denial, then frowned at him as though she'd caught him deliberately trying to shock her. "Surely it can't be as bad as that?"

"I don't know yet whose great scheme you're threatening, but you've given plenty of people plenty of reasons to be rid of you. Starting with your impending title, my dear empress."

"Why would anyone care? It means little to anyone but me. Why, it's hardly more than an honorific to emboss on my stationery."

"Perhaps, but it's an impressive title, nonetheless." Feeling as though he'd snagged her cooperation for the moment, Drew packed up the file box with its paltry contents. "Then there's the matter of your increased income."

"It's an entailment. Available only to me. If I die without issue it disappears."

"But while you live, that money must come from someone's treasury. Someone who might resent being a bit poorer for your gain."

"That's ridiculous."

"And lastly, Princess, are your ten square miles of Boratania, which is due to be excised from the flesh of another kingdom."

"A bit from three kingdoms, actually. But it's no more than a tiny spit of land on the borders between Saxony, Thuringia and Bavaria. It was pledged to me long ago when Boratania was vanquished. I don't see how it could possibly matter."

"My dear princess, in 1806 the Great Elector of Saxony declared himself king and allied himself to Napoleon against the rest of Europe. And for that sin, in 1815, as a result of the Congress of Vienna, the upper half of his kingdom was given to Prussia. His son is still complaining about the insult. I've heard him myself."

"Believe me, I know my European history very well, Lord Wexford."

"Then tell me why on earth His Majesty would

stand aside and allow even another square inch of his kingdom to be gifted to you for your birthday?"

"Because he's my cousin."

Drew laughed, then regretted its scoffing sound. "I'm afraid that blood is a lot thinner than any of us would care to believe."

"My blood is plenty thick, sir. Royal to the last drop. The land belongs to me, to my people. It's the last vestige of my family's kingdom and my cousins will support me."

For the first time Drew felt the pinch of carrying the secret he held against her, that she had a lot more than a few cousins to worry about.

"We'll discuss that later, Princess." Drew picked up her cloak from the back of the chair. "Come, my carriage is just outside. I'll take you home."

"That won't be necessary, Lord Wexford," she said with a sniff and a regal toss of her bejeweled head as Drew reached out with her cloak in his hands. "Palmerston's carriage is waiting for me."

With a twinkle of triumph in her eyes, the princess turned her long, straight back to him and proffered her lovely, white shoulders for him to drape with her cloak.

Which he would have done but the perfect slope of her neck and nape struck the breath from him, itched at his fingers, tempted him to slide them along her skin, to taste the forbidden.

All night she had smelled of rosewater; though he'd thought at first it was merely the scent of the duke's prized gardens. But the scent had followed her and now lapped at his chin, found purchase in his nostrils.

And now threatened to addle his wits.

"Not to disappoint you, Princess, but Palmerston's

carriage is no longer here." He quickly draped the opulent black velvet cloak across her shoulders, inadvertently skiffing his fingers through the escaping curls above her ear, doing his best to ignore the bolt of lightning that leaped along his arm and roared down his breastbone, right into his groin.

She turned and glared at him, chewing on the inside of her cheek. "Why?"

"Because you'll be using my carriage from now on, wherever you go, whatever you do." Which will be exactly nowhere, if he had anything to say in the matter.

"I've got my own chauffeur, thank you." She dismissed him with a shake of her head and started toward the door.

"Yes, but yours isn't armed, is he?"

She turned. "Of course not!"

"Nor is your carriage built to withstand a barrage of bullets."

Her eyes went wide with horror. "You can't mean that someone might really take the trouble to shoot at me in my carriage?"

"Like a sitting duck, Princess. I don't mind taking a bullet for you, but I plan to make it as difficult for the assassin as possible."

"Good heavens!" She held his gaze from under a fretted brow, took hold of his linen shirt cuff. "You'd take a bullet for me? Why?"

"As I've tried to tell you for the last hour, madam. That's my job."

She caught her lower lip with her teeth. "I don't think I like the idea."

"Then do as you're told and we'll both live long enough to see you crowned empress. You're to speak to no one of the threat against you. No one, do you understand? Not unless you clear it with me first."

"But why?"

"My investigation must remain an absolute secret."

"What will I tell my friends? With you driving me around in your carriage?"

He would have said, *You're not going anywhere for the next three weeks, madam, so no one will see us together*, but she probably wasn't quite ready to hear that yet.

"You'll tell your friends nothing, Princess."

"What about Lord Peverel? Shouldn't he and my other ministers know something about your theory?"

"Not until I've had time to vet them all."

"But the queen herself appointed him and the others as my privy council—"

He took hold of her upper arms, trying to make her understand. "Tell them nothing, Your Highness. Nothing. Not until I give the word. Promise me, Princess. Your life and the lives of so many others may depend on it."

"Is this really—"

He raised her chin with his fingertip. "Promise me."

She danced her blue gaze across his brow as he held her fast, finally settling on his eyes with a stubborn, but utterly reliable, "I promise."

"Good." Drew nodded and then released her.

"I keep my promises, by the way." That lovely chin was in the air again.

"I wouldn't expect anything less, Princess. Now, whether you like it or not, you and I will be together day and night until I've caught the person or persons who want you dead." He picked up his own coat off the rack near the door. "Or until they succeed."

"Succeed at wha—? Oh!" Her eyes widened. "You mean until they kill me!"

Drew couldn't help his smile. "Now, wouldn't that be a terrible waste of a beautiful, young princess."

Little spots of pink bloomed on her cheeks. "You're certainly treating my life lightly after all that blustering."

"Not me, Princess." He reached across the front of her and opened the door to the dim hallway beyond. "You're the one who doesn't seem to care."

"Of course I care."

"Then you'll do as I say, whenever I say it." He stepped into the corridor ahead of her, a habit that caused him to look both directions. "As to this particular moment, I plan to put you safely into my carriage and take you to your home, with or without your permission."

The princess plainly bristled at his effrontery, then she set her teeth behind her lovely, lush mouth before pronouncing, "Then you'd best take me straight home, Lord Wexford."

Instead of replying, he tucked her gloved hand inside the crook of his elbow and started toward the alley door, where Henry would be waiting with his own carriage.

She'd have to learn that when he said they would be together day and night, he meant close together. Near enough for him to put himself between her and a bullet if need be.

Of course, the real danger lay ahead, inside the walls of her own home, Grandauer Hall.

He had the distinct feeling that she wasn't going to like the changes he'd made there.

Wouldn't like them at all.

Chapter 6

Caro had never been so glad to see the moonlit granite gates of Grandauer Hall. A full half hour of Wexford's unending staring at her from the shadows across the bench seat of his impregnable carriage had nearly jangled her nerves to tatters.

Not to mention his bay-spiced scent, his power, his occasional query into her past, her future, rumbling out of the dimness, all at such close quarters.

"Here we are!" she said, perching herself on the edge of the bench and holding onto the door grip, hoping to leap out of the carriage as soon as it stopped in the portecochere.

Maybe a few hours of sleep would wash the confounding dread from her veins and clear her head of the terrible images and thoughts that Wexford had lodged there.

Especially the very troubling idea that the arrogant man seemed perfectly willing to put himself between her and an assassin.

Which made her entirely responsible for him, when she'd never really been responsible for anyone but herself in her entire life.

As the carriage drew up to the very dear and ordinary sight of her home, she felt his large, hot hand slipping around her elbow.

"You'll wait here inside the carriage, Princess, until I say it's safe to leave."

Then Wexford stepped easily through the small door, his weight against the outside step jolting her forward and then backward into the seat.

"Is this truly necessary, Wexford?" Caro righted herself and reached for the open door just in time for the man to slam it in her face.

"I said stay inside, Princess." He was standing just beyond the little window, leaning the brunt of his weight against the door while he talked briskly to two brawny men she'd never seen before.

She didn't mind him lending her a bit of support, or looking out for her, but keeping her prisoner in his carriage in front of her own house was just plain absurd!

"Open this door, Wexford!" She pounded on the jamb, then gave another shove with the flat of both hands, just as Wexford dismissed the two men and released the door.

Caro flew headfirst out of the carriage, her arms outstretched. She would have landed flat on the gravel drive in an ungainly slide but for Wexford, who turned to easily catch her in his arms like a sack of barley.

"You're safe now, Princess." He dropped her hips and then stood her on her feet as though he caught flying royalty on a daily basis, his grin as crooked as his brow.

"Of course I'm safe; this is my own home." She righted her skirts and her cloak then pointed into the darkness. "And who were those men?"

He smiled at some secret thing. "My operatives. They were just reporting that they have secured the grounds and the house and the perimeter."

"Oh, have they?" Caro was about to object to Wexford's high-handed intrusion, but she was weary, and after all, the man had brought her safely to her door, had now secured her property, however overbearing his methods.

"Well, then, good night, my lord. Thank you for escorting me home in such style and safety." She lifted her hems and started up the stairs, trying to dismiss the man who was doubtlessly staring after her.

She was just beginning to wonder why Sebring hadn't met her carriage with his usual butler's efficiency when the large, hammered-brass doors opened wide to a complete stranger.

He was dressed like a butler and looked like one as well, but for the burly girth of his shoulders and the thick scar running from just above his left eyebrow nearly to his jaw.

"Welcome home, Princess Caroline."

The voice hadn't come from the odd butler, but from the step just behind her.

"Who is this man, Wexford?"

"My operative."

"Where's Sebring?"

"On holiday in Brighton." Wexford walked past her up the steps and right into her house as though he owned it. He was waiting for her beside the incongruous man as she stomped into the foyer. "Princess Caroline Marguerite Marie Isabella of the kingdom of Boratania, this is Mister Harold Runson, your new butler."

"I don't need a new butler, Wexford." Caro's jaw ached from grinding her teeth. "I am perfectly happy with the one I have."

"But I wasn't."

"I'm pleased and deeply honored to meet you, Princess Caroline. Your wish be my dearest command." Runson bowed deeply.

"Then I wish you to leave Grandauer Hall immediately."

He cast a rolling eye at her and then at her surly escort. " 'Cept for that particular wish, I'm afraid." He bowed again and Wexford cleared his throat.

"That will be all for the moment, Runson," he said. "The princess and I have other business to attend to."

"Aye, sir." Runson tipped a finger at the earl, dipped another bow toward Caro and then disappeared into the darkness of the hall with a surprisingly nimble stride.

Caro swung on Wexford. "You put one of your spies in my house? Without asking my leave?"

He grunted and then stepped more deeply into her house. "Come."

"No, Wexford. This whole thing is getting out of hand. I'll ride in your carriage, but I want you and your butler out of here. Now!" Though he'd given her no choice but to follow his long strides around the corner into the main entry hall.

"And another thing, Wexford—"

She came to an abrupt halt as she entered the candlelit room. The man was standing between the grand twin staircases, holding court with a long line of uniformed servants—cooks and housekeepers, chambermaids and gardeners—none of whom she'd ever seen before.

"Ah, then, here she is, staff," Wexford said as he spread his arm in her direction. "May I present Princess Caroline of Boratania. Your mistress for the duration."

The duration?

They smiled at her as a group and offered that same bow, murmuring variations on "Pleased to meet you, Princess Caroline" and "Your wish is our command."

Fighting back a scream of utter frustration, Caro managed a simple, "Who are they, Wexford?"

He was hiding a smile of triumph inside that stony expression, an unraised eyebrow, his fine lips drawn into a careful line.

"Your new staff, Princess." The blighter had the gall to offer the slightest bow of his own before he turned his full attention to his wide-eyed conspirators. "It's four thirty in the morning, people. Nearly dawn. You know what needs doing."

Which seemed to mean silently vanishing into the shadowy reaches of her home like an invading army of fantastical creatures.

"What did you do with my household staff, Wexford, send them all to the Tower?" She'd had a full staff mere hours ago, when she left for the ball.

"To Brighton for a holiday, actually. With the compliments of the Foreign Office."

This whole thing was beginning to smell very badly. "Palmerston again?"

"At my request, Princess. If I'm going to protect you from assassination, I need to have my own people close at hand, not a group of untrained amateurs to get in my way. Secrets, Princess. Now, if you'll follow me, I'll see you to your chamber."

"I know the way to my chamber, Wexford." Caro tried to form a coherent thought, but the man turned on his heel and started up the stairs.

"And I've a couple of rules to address with you," he said with his easy stride.

"Have you now?"

Well, if the blackguard thought he could just waltz into her home and start tossing rules around, expecting her to obey just because he thought that someone was trying to kill her, he'd better think again, because he was sadly mistaken.

"I know you'd rather I leave, Princess." He'd stopped midway up the curving staircase and was now looking down on her with that arched brow. "Believe me, I'd rather not be here either. But at the moment, we're stuck with each other, whether we like it or not."

"Stuck with each other how, Wexford?" If she didn't know better, she would swear that the man had just moved himself into her house.

He had continued up the stairs without her and by the time she reached the wide landing he was halfway down the corridor, heading toward the Tudor wing.

And her bedchamber, where an unfamiliar chambermaid was waiting at attention outside the door.

"Morning, my lord," the woman said to Wexford as she efficiently opened the door for him.

"Morning, Tweeg," he said as he strode past her into the room.

"If you want anything, Princess Caroline . . ." Tweeg gave her a confidently steady gaze, one that lacked the usual chambermaid's shrinking shyness that had always grated on Caro's nerves.

On duty and ready to take a bullet for her too, Caro wondered.

She shook off the feeling and entered her room ready to throw him out, completely unprepared for the sight of him lighting a lamp beside her bed. His broad shoulders bent, his hands bronze and steady with the match flame.

Intensely inviting.

Looking just like he had moved in to stay.

"My rules are simple to follow and quite basic, Princess. You'll go nowhere without me or one of my operatives at your side. Period."

Caro blinked and cleared her head of the man's powerful influence. "Is that why you've just barged into my private chamber, Lord Wexford? Do you plan to spend the night beside me in my bed?"

Oh, wonderful, Drew thought, wrestling suddenly with a crystal-clear image of the fiery woman, smiling up at him from the bank of pillows, draped across the bed in lace and linen and moonlight.

Her scent bedeviling him as it was now.

All that lovely golden hair, teasing him, inviting him to thread his fingers through it.

Christ, this was a perilous business. He took a breath of fresher, less-dangerous air.

"I don't think that will be necessary, Princess. As long as you follow a few simple rules." He went to one of the tall windows. "Such as keeping these drapes and shutters closed at all times."

She was standing like a sentry in the middle of the room, her glare fixed on him. "But I like to sleep in the breeze and wake up to the sunlight."

Another image to wrestle to the ground. The morning sun entering through the window, slipping across rumpled bedclothes, limbs tangled—

"I'm afraid you won't have time to miss either if a sniper gets to you from one of your hedges out in your garden."

"Of course, and will you be nailing my door shut and shoving my meals under the door?"

A tempting idea which would solve just about everything.

"As long as you clear your intentions with me, Princess, you can go anywhere in the house, at any time."

"Anywhere in the house, Wexford?" She stared at him for a long moment before draping her cape across the back of a chair. "And when I need to go into London, must I file a request with you?"

"In triplicate, madam." *Not that you'll be going to London or anywhere else.*

He could tell by the irritated tilt of the woman's hip and her little sniff that she still didn't comprehend the gravity of the situation.

"As you please, my lord. Now I'll say good night."

He didn't believe an ounce of the woman's sudden cooperation. But she should at least be well protected from her own opinions until the morning.

"Good night, Princess."

And besides, he would be lodged in the next room, just in case.

He closed the woman's door behind him, a bit surprised that she hadn't hurled her slipper at the back of his head.

Mrs. Tweeg was still posted in the corridor outside the door, as alert as a mother badger. "Everything all right in there, sir?"

Drew grunted. "Don't let her out of this chamber for any reason, Tweeg. No matter what kind of wild story she tries to tell you."

Tweeg winked as she crossed her arms over her ample bosom. "The princess won't get past me, sir. Not even if her hair's on fire."

Drew laughed. Tweeg wasn't a woman to cross, as many an undisciplined prince had discovered the hard way.

He checked with a few of his operatives in the kitchen and along the perimeter of the house, and then caught himself yawning broadly as he went back upstairs and into the darkened chamber beside the princess's.

Too exhausted to even light a lamp, Drew shrugged out of his waistcoat and was just removing the studs from his shirt when he heard a scraping against the wall that his chamber shared with the princess's.

He listened carefully for a moment, then leaned his ear against the green, silk-covered panel and smiled.

The little minx.

As the thought settled against his brain, a mechanism clicked deep inside the wall.

Then a crack of flickering candlelight appeared behind the gilded molding, and the panel began to swing open.

Drew planted his foot in its path and the door stopped halfway open.

"Oh, blast," came the skulking whisper.

Then a shapely, alabaster hand appeared at the edge of the panel, and then her head with its mad crop of hair let down for the night.

And then her heart-shaped face, those gleaming blue eyes and her perfect mouth opened in shock as she saw him.

Drew removed his foot from the panel and it popped open. "Can I help you, Princess?"

"Oh!" She gasped as she stumbled into the room with the candlestick, startled and growling in royal outrage. "What are you doing in here, Wexford, spying on me?"

His yawn was genuine and noisy. "I thought I'd grab a few hours of sleep."

"In the chamber connected to mine?"

"Exactly, Princess. Now you can tell me what you're doing sneaking through the walls? Afraid of meeting Mrs. Tweeg in the hallway?"

"This is my house, I can go where I please." She made a point of surveying the room carefully, her satin-slippered foot poking out from beneath her nightgown and a lightweight, form shaping, linen robe.

"Then I warn you not to try to climb down the wisteria trellis outside your chamber window. You'll find a sharpshooter at the base who'll only carry you back up again."

"Just what did you mean that you were going to sleep in this room? Every night?"

"Until the matter of your safety has been settled, one way or the other."

She narrowed her eyes at him, stubborn as ever. "You mean dead or alive?"

"Please, madam, no more escape attempts."

She pursed her lips and shook her head. "I wasn't planning to escape, Wexford. I was . . . looking for something." She sauntered toward the hearth, her candle leading the way, reminding him of how she'd traipsed along the duke's garden path earlier in the evening.

She had been looking for something, then . . .

For someone.

"What exactly were you doing tonight at the ball, Princess, prowling alone through a pitch-dark garden?"

Caro hadn't yet been able to still the thrashing of her heart since finding the huge man waiting for her just on the other side of her chamber wall, and now the low rumble of his voice curling toward her out of the darkness only made the thrashing worse.

Made her face flame and her fingers tremble.

Turning back to look at him as he emerged from the shadows into the pool of her candlelight hadn't helped either.

"What I was doing, Lord Wexford, is of no interest to you," she said, trying to regain her composure because she had been testing her boundaries. "And I wasn't prowling."

"You were flitting through the shadows between the topiary sculptures and the fountains, keeping a close eye on the windows and doors of the ballroom." Wexford had come into the fullness of the candle flame, looking more devilish than human. "Whatever you call it, Princess, you didn't want anyone to see you."

"You're right, I didn't. But not for any reason you might expect."

He reached out and took the candlestick from her, his smile never reaching his eyes. "Meeting a lover?"

Caro held back a gasp but not a burst of laughter. "I'm afraid not, Lord Wexford." That's the last thing she needed to juggle at the moment.

But her answer only seemed to make him frown more deeply at her. "Had anyone contacted you prior to the ball, requesting to meet you in the maze?"

"I'm not a fool, sir."

He exhaled hard and frowned at her as he set the candlestick on the mantel. "Then someone else? Someone you might even believe that you can trust?"

"Are all diplomats this suspicious?"

He straightened, focusing all that towering interest on her mouth. "If not an assignation with a lover, who were you going to meet in the maze?"

"Who was I meeting?" Caro laughed at his confusion and sat down on the hearth stool. All right, if he really wanted to know. . . . "Nicholai Gora."

"Well, well, well, so there *was* a man. I thought as much." The earl grunted and leaned down to her. "How well do you know this Nicholai Gora?"

She laughed, because now she held all the secrets for a change. She flicked her fingers in the air, trying to look as careless of her reputation as he must believe of her.

"Actually I don't know him at all. Though I've read enough about him to find him immensely admirable. Yet I assure you that he has nothing to do with your investigation."

"You're not in the position to judge. Admirable or not, he could very well be a danger to you."

"I doubt that very much." Unless he fell on her.

"Don't be a fool, Princess." He knelt and leveled a

finger at her nose, shook it at her. "There's nothing more dangerous than an unarmed woman, royal or not, agreeing to meet a man, a complete stranger, in a garden maze in the middle of the night, without a bit of protection."

"You were there," she said slowly, certain that she'd remember that encounter for the rest of her days.

"You thought you were alone!"

"I was hoping I was."

"Are you completely mad?" He stood and stalked away to the desk on the opposite wall. "Anything could have happened to you."

"But that's not how it turned out, is it? Thanks to your interference, I never got a chance to see him."

A match flared and Wexford's deeply planed features flickered to life. "Because I stopped you before you could run headlong into the maze and spring Gora's nefarious trap. You have to stop trusting so blindly."

Great heavens, she was enjoying this too much! "I'm sure he wasn't planning any kind of trap."

"How the bloody hell did he contact you?" Wexford set the match to the lamp then stalked back to her, never taking his eyes from her. "Was it through one of your servants?"

"Nobody contacted me." Perhaps she'd let this go on too long, too far. "I'd heard a rumor where I'd find him, so when the opportunity presented itself at the ball tonight, I took advantage and went out to the garden to see him for myself."

"Without telling anyone what you were doing?"

"I didn't want anyone to know, because they usually don't understand." Secrecy was her greatest ally.

"And I wasn't even sure he was the right one. He's very old, very fragile."

"Old?" Wexford eyed her sharply.

"Very old. He was last seen in the chapel of my father's chateau in Boratania more than twenty years ago."

The earl shook his head as though trying to clear it of cobwebs. "Are you saying that Nicholas Gora was a friend of your father's?"

"Not a friend." It was long past time to confess. "Gora died nearly twelve hundred years ago."

"Twelve hundred years?" His jaw squared off, became stony. "What the hell are you trying to tell me?"

Feeling just a little guilty for leading him along, Caro stood up. "Simply that I was in the garden tonight, hoping to find the marble statue of Nicholai Gora."

He blinked at her from beneath a dark brow. "You were looking for a statue?"

"Saint Nicholai Gora. He was a Benedictine martyr killed in the year 632 in a battle with barbarians from the north. He's mine, Wexford. Boratania's. He was our greatest hero and I want him back where he belongs."

He hadn't moved a muscle. "A *statue*, Princess?"

Perhaps she had taken this ruse a bit far, too much like taunting a bear with a very short stick. Twice in one night. "It's not just any statue, after all."

"Bloody hell, madam!"

Drew stopped himself from launching into a longer, darker curse, wanting nothing more than to turn the foolish woman over his knee and . . . damnation! Not that he'd ever lay a hand on her or anyone weaker than himself. Violence only begat more violence.

No, but he did want to make her understand, to make her see the danger, the precariousness of her situation.

And, by God, to find out if those luscious, rosy lips that glistened so sweetly in the lamplight really tasted like pink sugar.

God knew his hands had already tasted the perfect roundness of her hips, was bewitched by the know-it-all shape of her pose near the fireplace. Her head tilted, her hip slung against the flat of her hand.

"Is this your plan to thwart me, Princess?" He started toward her, unsure of his own intentions, not sure he cared.

"I don't know what you mean, Wexford. Nicholai Gora is the patron saint of Boratania. And stay right where you are." She pointed into the narrowing breach between them.

"Riddles and rhymes, Your Highness? Is that what I'm to expect from you?" And still he advanced on her, ever so slowly, so that he could watch her squirm as he had. "Dancing around the truth, spinning wildly dangerous tales and wasting precious time when your life is hanging in the balance?"

"I did nothing of the sort. I only meant to impress upon you my concern for the past and the future of my lost kingdom. I can't allow it to fade into history and be forgotten."

"How can you help to insure Boratania's future if you're dead?"

She opened her mouth to speak but chewed on

her lower lip. "You don't understand what I'm trying to do."

"And you still don't believe that nothing stands between you and a bullet but me."

She had sobered in the last few moments. "I do believe you, Wexford. It's just . . . difficult to take in all at once. I've never been stalked by an assassin before."

Hell, now he felt like a loutish barbarian. "Yes, well, then I suppose we can defer this until the morning."

"Till the morning, then." She hooked the candlestick off the mantel, then brushed past him.

"One more question, Princess."

"Yes?" She stopped at the opened panel and turned.

"Do you always use secret passages for your errands?"

She smiled sideways. "Sometimes I even use the hallway. Good night, Wexford."

Drew held the panel open for his royal charge as she slipped past him into her chamber.

"Sleep well, Princess," he said, stealing a breath of her warm, trailing scent as he shut the door between them.

Drew leaned against the panel for a long time and listened for suspicious sounds from beyond: heard the padding of her footsteps from her bedside to just on the other side of the wall, and then the thump of her fist. Then across the room to the wardrobe and finally back to the bed.

Until he was hearing—possibly merely imagining—the dip of her weight against the mattress, the shuffle of silk and linen as she slipped between the sheets, a muffled sigh as she lay back against the . . .

Bloody hell, the woman had a damnably distracting effect on him. Sent his thoughts wandering where they shouldn't, filled him with a longing for the kind of contented bliss he had never imagined possible until Jared had wed Kate.

Now he'd found himself judging every woman he met against his hopes. Clear eyes, a willing soul, softly ringing laughter, delight and determination.

Not Jared's life, but his own, with all the trappings. Children and noise and someone to share it all with.

He hadn't meant to notice the clarity of the princess's eyes, or the willingness of her soul, but he had. Not that it mattered in the least.

She was someone else's happily ever after.

And it was his responsibility to see that she survived, whether she approved or not.

Expecting more of her tomfoolery at any moment, he changed out of his formal clothes into a shirt and a suitable pair of trousers, then pulled up an upholstered chair in front of the panel, sat down and propped his feet onto a stool.

He slept with one ear open to the sounds from the next room and woke to the banging of a fist on the secret door at his back.

"My lord! She's missing, my lord!"

The princess! Damnation!

Drew was already pulling on his boots when he opened the panel to Mrs. Tweeg's frenetic pounding and her head poking through.

"She's vanished, my lord! Into thin air."

"I doubt that, Tweeg." Drew shrugged into his coat and buttoned it as he followed the woman back through the passage into the princess's chamber.

"See for yourself, sir. Gone like a vapor."

"She's an ordinary flesh-and-blood woman." Ruled by a mind rife with royal mischief.

"She didn't pass by me, sir, and Gerald saw no one come down the trellis, or over the top of the roof." Mrs. Tweeg must have already drawn open the shutters and drapes and she was now gesturing out into the blazing sunlight.

Drew walked along the opposite wall. "And I checked when we were here last evening after she left for the ball: There's no secret door in the east wall as there is in the west. She escaped some other way."

The little fool. Drew scrubbed his fingers through his hair, the action causing him to study the pale green panels in the ceiling.

"Look there, Mrs. Tweeg." Each of the gilt-framed panels was identical to the others but for one, just to the left above the wardrobe, where a fine-lined shadow sharpened one edge.

"I'll be jigged, sir. So your princess disappeared through a trap door in the ceiling. Just like a regular mountebank!"

An exit he hadn't discovered among the many others on his earlier inspection.

"Doubtless a bloody drop-down stairs from the room above." Damn the woman and her antics. "You stay here and look for more, Tweeg. I'm going after her."

Hoping the woman hadn't gone gallivanting across the countryside just to thwart him, Drew grabbed his jacket, then left the chamber and found his first clue to her whereabouts with Mackenzie and his kitchen staff.

"Breakfast for you, my lord?" The tall man was bent over a large iron pot, humming.

"Maybe later, Mackenzie. Right now, I'm looking for our peripatetic princess."

"A lovely young woman, she is, sir."

"Except that she's not where I left her in her chamber last night."

"She's an early riser, this one. Not like some royals we've tended."

"You've seen Princess Caroline this morning?"

Mackenzie squinted at the case clock on the window sill. "Fifty-three minutes ago, my lord. Wearing the plainest rag of a gown and an apron that she surely must have stolen from the scullery."

To play peasant girl out in the lane? Without an ounce of protection? "Why, Mackenzie? Where is she now?"

"She left here with Wheeler close on her heels. She said something about the orangery."

"Blast it all."

Chapter 7

"The bloody orangery," Drew muttered as he stalked into the new investigation room that he had hastily arranged in the east-facing parlor. "Where the devil is the orangery?"

His most efficient intelligence clerks from the Factory popped up out of their chairs and dashed to the wall where a tapestry had been removed and stored and an overlarge map of the estate now hung in its place.

"Here it is, sir!" the men said as one voice, a pair of fingers flanking a building on the map, a good six hundred yards from the main house.

"You'll find it perched on the pinnacle of a south-facing berm. . . ."

"Thank you, Mr. Helston!" Drew left the house in the middle of Helston's description and was striding toward the blasted orangery less than five minutes later.

He hadn't had a spare moment to study the map of

the grounds. Hell, he'd only learned three days ago that Princess Caroline was the target and the last thing he had expected when he arrived back in London yesterday morning with the report on the assassination plot was that Palmerston would assign the blasted project to him.

He should have insisted that Ross take it from—

Hell and damnation! That was the orangery! Could the building have been more exposed, more vulnerable to an assault? It was a huge, hexagonal structure of glass and brick and iron, the inside visible from four sides. And one of the myriad doors was gaping open and unattended.

He edged up to the building and peered through the doorway, expecting to find it lush with palms and ferns. Instead, it was stacked high with islands of crates and barrels.

But nothing moved.

Nothing. Not a sound.

And the silence clenched at his gut.

His nerves on edge, his ears alert for any movement, he walked the outside perimeter of the enclosure, looking for breaks in the glass and jimmied latches, the telltale marks of an attempt to gain entry.

He caught a movement at the far edge of the woods, but relaxed almost immediately as he recognized Blackburn patrolling the grounds, knowing that Shepherd would be close behind.

And still he found no sign of scraped iron or distressed glass, no footprints along the massive glass walls, no suspiciously matted grass that might indicate that someone had lain in wait for a perfect shot at the princess.

Nothing but a hauntingly familiar voice coming from around the brick-end of the building.

"If we give that crate a shove, Mr. Wheeler, I think it'll fit right back here."

And Wheeler's groaning reply. "What've you got in here, Princess, lead shot?"

Drew exhaled a blue curse and a grunt of relief as he strode toward the open doors of the wagon shed.

The princess and Wheeler were just hoisting a small crate up onto the tailgate of a wagon, both of them straining at the task until the crate dropped into place, causing the bed to sag slightly.

He should have been blazing with outrage at the woman's antics. Instead, he found himself pausing at the door like a besotted swain, watching her in silence, his heart beating more steadily now that he'd found the blasted woman, though his pulse took a profound turn toward the hotly carnal when she looked up and into his eyes.

Golden tendrils of curling hair cascaded off her shoulders. A rag-plain dress, just as Mackenzie had described, complete with cobwebs and bits of grass. But she wore it like a dewy fairy queen.

"Good morning, Wexford," she said with a cocky tilt of her head and a slow, sweeping glance that raked upward from his boots to the top of his head, finally resting softly on his face.

"Princess," he was all he managed through a throat that had dried up along with his anger.

"Ah, g'd morning, sir." Wheeler gave him a rueful nod as he touched the brim of his cap. "Thought it best to give Princess Caroline a hand with her chores."

The man had the instincts of a fox. "Indeed, Wheeler."

"And you've been the greatest help to me, Mr. Wheeler. I thank you." She grinned at the man, whose eyes went a little moony while she efficiently brushed a stripe of dust off his jacket sleeve. "However, I think this is about the last of it for today."

"If you're certain, Your Highness." Wheeler shot a glance at Drew, obviously looking to do right by the situation.

"If she needs anything else moved, Wheeler, I'm sure I can handle it."

The princess sighed and teased a wink at Wheeler. "I suppose his lordship can manage, Mr. Wheeler."

He'd never seen the hard-nosed Wheeler blush before, or stammer, but there it was. "Ah, good then, Your Highness, I'll be off for a quick breakfast."

The princess took a startled breath. "You haven't eaten, Mr. Wheeler? Great heavens! Why didn't you say something earlier?"

"Well, I—" Wheeler cast Drew another "help me please" smile.

"Because you needed him, Princess," Drew said. "That's his job." And she couldn't have chosen better. Wheeler was a crack shot. The shed was well protected from snipers and yet had excellent sightlines against a sneak attempt.

She flexed her brow at Drew, then softened it for Wheeler. "Next time, Mr. Wheeler, just tell me. I'll not have my staff thinking I'm an ogre."

So they were *her* staff now. Good.

Wheeler turned a goofy grin at her. "Oh, we'd never think that of you, Your Highness. Never." He dipped the princess a courtly bow and left them at a jog.

She watched the man for a moment then scrubbed her palms together, and turned all that bewitching charm on him, stunning him for a moment. "I hope you slept well, Wexford. You'll need your strength if you're to keep up with me today. Even here in my own home."

He knew that she was waiting for him to take the bait, to demand to know what the devil she was doing out here in the open and how she had escaped him out of her chamber.

Let her wait. Keeping a royal off balance kept the control in his court.

"I slept like the dead, Princess," he said, stifling the sudden yawn that would give him away.

She dipped him the tiniest frown and then blinded him with a smile. "I'm pleased to hear it, Lord Wexford. I hope you don't mind my borrowing one of your operatives, since you've sent off all my assistants on an expense paid holiday."

"I'm actually pleased to see you abiding by at least one of my rules, Princess: taking an escort with you wherever you go. However you seemed to have forgotten that you weren't supposed to leave the house."

"I never promised that I would abide by your rules, my lord." She flashed him a challenging smile as she climbed nimbly up onto the wagon's running board. "Only that I would ride in your carriage and keep your investigation a secret. And I will."

Drew scrubbed at his raspy chin, finding his jaw tightly clenched beneath. "Madam, your safety is the paramount concern in any policy that I establish—"

"I'm glad you brought that up, Wexford," she said, leaning easily against the side of the wagon, her elbow resting between the horizontal slats, "because I've had time to think about the threat to my life and though I absolutely believe everything you've told me—that someone out there"—she gestured to the wide, random world—"is determined to kill me, I just can't allow a cowardly enemy to keep me from my official duties."

"What the devil does that mean, madam?" Fearing the worst of the woman's stubbornness, Drew caught the top slat with his hand, purposely towering over her. "Your official duty is to stay alive."

"Which I plan to do, Wexford, by allowing you to conduct your investigation as you see fit." She reached into the wagon bed and struggled for a moment to shift one of the crates, before Drew gave it a simple shove and it clunked into place.

"You're *allowing* me, madam?"

She nodded blithely. "*And* I'm accepting your protection—"

"Accepting it?"

She looked up at him with honesty blazing in her blue eyes. "With my heartfelt gratitude for risking your life, but with one condition."

Drew caught her upper arm and eyed her closely, knowing that he'd regret asking the question because he couldn't possibly go along with any of her harebrained suggestions. "What condition is that?"

"You can follow me as closely as you like, bundle me up in your bulletproof carriage, install your operatives in my house, surround me with a battalion of sharpshooters, whatever you need to do"—she blinked up at him, then touched the center of his chest with the tip of her hot little finger—"as long as you stay out of my way so that I can go about my business."

"Stay out of your way?" He laughed out loud—couldn't help it. "Madam, your safety is not a matter presented to you for your approval."

"Who else then, if not me?" She snorted lightly, bent down behind her, then lifted a small keg onto the tailgate. "It's my life. My kingdom. My future. I'd like to think I have some say in it."

He still had time to foist off the case on Ross. The man had certainly seemed willing to take his place last night.

More than willing.

"Well, have I, Wexford?" She had hoisted herself into the wagon bed, where she now stood glaring down at him with blue-tinged determination in her eyes, her hands braced against her lithely perfect hips. "A moderate say in my own life?"

He doubted she had a moderate bone in her body. "That depends, madam, on what you mean by *moderate*."

"What I mean, Wexford, is that I won't be put into a hatbox for safekeeping. But neither will I fight your efforts to protect me, if . . . you don't try to stop me from coming and going as I need to."

He tamped down his urge to bellow at her. "Princess—"

She knelt down to him from the wagon bed, her eyes narrowed and only inches from his. "Believe me, Wexford, if I could spend the next three weeks locked in my library reading or having tea with my much neglected friends, I would do so gladly. I would love to live the life of an ordinary royal. But I can't."

An ordinary royal? Bloody hell, the woman wasn't ordinary in the least.

"I'm a princess, soon to be the empress of my father's long-lost kingdom. My duties and obligations are legion and they must come first, yesterday, today and always. Otherwise, I might as well not be a princess at all. So you'll have to work around me, sir, or work with me. If you want my cooperation, you're going to have to employ an ounce or two of your own. Do you understand?"

He understood only too well: that his princess would be uncompromising in her demands, that he was in for a rocky journey.

And that Ross had been far too willing to take on the case. Let him find his own princess.

"Work around you, madam?" he asked, grasping at any straw that might mitigate the situation. "What exactly do you plan to be doing for the next three weeks?" He knew her schedule, but not the details.

Her eyes brightened as though she knew she'd beaten him, then her smile returned with the flick of a fawn-colored brow.

"This, my lord," she said, standing as she spread her arms to encompass the wagon and the shed and the many containers stacked around it. "The Great Exhibition is only two weeks away."

Excellent. Good. Grand. He chewed on the side of his tongue and then asked as calmly as he knew how. "And this is part of your display?"

Reluctant to give the inch that might become half a league, Drew picked up two kegs off the ground and set them into the wagon bed for her.

An offering of sorts. An unsettled contract.

"This is but a small part of the treasure." She

rammed the two kegs against the others then sat down on the tailgate, tucking a loose strand of hair over her ear, her legs dangling amongst the folds of her skirts.

"What treasure?" He didn't like the sound of that. A storehouse of riches to tempt a hundred thieves, a thousand assassins.

"Come, let me show you."

Before he could offer to help her down from the tailgate, she scooted forward, only to snag her skirt on something behind her. His endlessly tempting, pink-cheeked princess trapped and fully at his mercy.

"Well, blast, I'm stuck." Again. Just like last night in the maze. She twisted around to free herself, but Drew caught her left wrist with her first awkward tug.

"Allow me, Princess." Drew leaned around her, suddenly overwhelmed by the nearness of her warmth, by the golden hair tumbling over her shoulder, by her enchanting scent of morning glories and sunlight.

By the rousing closeness of her as she whispered so near his temple. "It's good to know, my lord, that you're not only prepared to protect me from hedge mazes, but also from dangerous splinter attacks."

Caro couldn't remember ever having a man take such liberties with her person as Wexford had done repeatedly in the last ten hours. Certainly never a man with such broad shoulders, with such an encompassing presence.

And now he was nearly wrapped around her once again, in the full light of day, his hot chest pressed against her thigh, sending little vibrations rippling through her like a pebble tossed into a warm summer pool.

"I'm bound to protect you from anything at all, Princess." One of his powerful arms was working at her skirts and the wagon bed, the other was gripping his own knee as though it would, on its own power, attempt to grip hers. "However, you need to lean away from me so that I can—"

He stopped abruptly as she leaned away from him, then took a deep breath, cleared his throat, gave a tug and then her skirt came free of the thick, daggerlike splinter.

His gaze was fierce and fixed on hers as he lifted her off the tailgate and set her onto her feet before backing away from her. "Don't do that again, Princess."

As though she'd had any choice. "I'll do my best to stay clear of all splinters, nails and button hooks."

"See that you do." Then the man stalked past her and into the orangery, stopping abruptly a dozen feet inside the door, his fists stuffed against his hips as he surveyed her carefully arranged stacks of crates and barrels.

"Why, Princess, are you keeping all the treasures of Boratania in an unguarded glass building?"

"I'm not that foolish, Wexford." But appeasing him somewhat might aid in her negotiations with the hardheaded man. "The orangery was built on top of the undercroft of a twelfth-century abbey. Which makes for a very secure treasure vault beneath."

Still he eyed the contents of the room, his right hand flat against his thigh, as though he had a knife hidden nearby, ready to use on an assassin who might be lurking behind every corner.

"Then what are all these crates doing here?"

She walked past him and patted the top of one, just for good measure. "This is only the staging area. It's where I pack up everything as it comes in before storing the items safely downstairs."

"What sorts of things do you have here, madam?" He rattled the lock on a leather-strapped crate, disdainful and impatient.

"Well, statuary, pottery, wood carvings . . . for example"—she drew a key from the ring in her pocket and popped open the lock on one of the iron-bound chests—"this contains some very old, very important Boratanian weapons that were looted from my family's castles during and after the war."

"If they were looted from your country years ago, Princess, how did they end up in your possession?" He lifted the rounded lid off the nest of excelsior and rested it carefully against the chest.

"I bought a few and some were given to me as gifts. Guilt works very well. But the most effective of all has been just plain stealing them back."

Wexford narrowed his gaze at her. "What did you say?"

Perhaps she had just confessed a sin he hadn't found in her dossier. No going back now; he would learn of her exploits sooner or later. He was bound to be suspicious of everything she did or said. Especially after she'd played such a childish game with him that morning, sneaking out of her chamber merely because she could, and because she knew it would gall him.

"You heard me right." Feeling a bit like a thief unloading ill-gotten goods at the pawnshop, she folded back the wad of packing material and removed the long canvas bag. "Whenever I see an item that I recognize as having been stolen from Boratania in her hour of dire need, I simply confiscate it on the spot."

He stared bluntly at her. "You must be mad, Princess."

"Furious, if you must know." Though she had learned long ago to curb her anger and to just do what she knew was right. "You'd be furious, too, if your fellow peers thought nothing of walking off with your family's treasures."

That seemed to catch him by surprise. He laughed without an ounce of humor. "I suppose I would, Princess. But—"

"Whether they realized it or not, Wexford, the looters not only made off with items of incalculable value, but in the process they seized the history of my kingdom. As though they had erased its past from all memory."

"That's called the spoils of war."

"I call it stealing, my lord."

"Indeed." He gingerly pulled the sword from the canvas sleeve, then gripped the weapon firmly, raised it masterfully in his large, bronze hand.

Her warrior protector.

The ancient blade was long and broad and made of black iron. And he wore it magnificently well. The handle had once been highly filigreed, though now it was well worn, its gems smoothed and bright.

"You're holding Boratania's ceremonial sword of state." She found herself smiling up at him as she traced her fingertip down the length of the blade toward the hilt, startled at the thrill it sent through her arm, as though it had somehow come alive in Wexford's hand.

He lowered his dark gaze to her, his breathing steady though suddenly deeper. "It's quite remarkable, Princess."

"It's very old." Caro swallowed hard and pulled her hand away, easing the heady jangling only slightly. "According to my records it dates back to at least 583, when the house of Grostov was established. Though the rubies weren't set into the handle until about 1182. To commemorate the king's impending crusade into the Holy Land."

Wexford lowered the blade from its angled, upward thrust at the ceiling. "Joining King Richard, I assume?"

"Unfortunately, the king died of a fever and never quite made it out of Boratania. His son and heir was only an infant at the time, which set off a seventeen-year regency, so nothing came of the crusade but the rubies in the sword. And a crown and scepter."

"Do you intend to put the crown jewels of Boratania on display at this exhibition?" The amazing man then flicked his wrist and caught the sword by the hilt, the blade tip pointing toward the flagstone floor.

Show-off, she wanted to say as he extended his arm. The lout didn't deserve the satisfaction.

"The Boratanian crown jewels will remain safely locked in the undercroft until the day of my investiture. After that, I'll be taking them home with me to Boratania."

For some reason, that seemed to catch the man off guard. "You're planning to leave?"

"That's the point of all this, Wexford. After my investiture, I'll be returning to my homeland."

"Ah, yes. Your ten square miles of Boratania."

And how close she was to going home after all these years.

"My very own ten square miles, Wexford. With two castles, three old castle towns, a half dozen manor houses and numerous farms." She held out the canvas sleeve for Wexford, watched as he tilted the tip of the blade into the opening and sheathed the sword with a flourish.

Aware of his gaze on her, she replaced the sword and then the packing in the crate, which she locked with a resounding *snap*.

"Are you sure all your treasures will fit when you get there?" He circled a bank of crates, thumping them as if they were melons.

"I know exactly where everything came from and where everything will go. Every candlestick and tapestry. I've been planning this for years and years. I've recorded it all in a master log." Always delighted when anyone showed the slightest interest in her collection, Caro pointed to the pair of granite corbels sitting atop her worktable. "These belong on the facade of the opera house in the town of Ebeling."

He eyed her like a wolf as he continued his circling. "You mean to put them back?"

"I mean to completely restore every inch of Boratania after I become empress. At least my ten square miles of it."

He picked up one of the granite corbels as though it were made of papier-mâché, not solid stone. "Have you rescued all of the crown jewels?"

"Half of them. The scepter and the ancient ceremonial sword I just showed you. I'm still missing the orb and the crown itself."

"Rescued from whom?" He upended the corbel and studied the base.

"From whom, indeed?" The whole matter still rankled when she thought of it, still brought a blot of anger to her cheeks. "The scepter was hanging in the throne room of my Danish cousin, King Frederick III."

He set the corbel beside the other, frowning at her as he walked toward her. "You broke into the king's palace and stole the scepter?"

"I didn't have to break in. I was attending a royal birthday party and I recognized it amongst a display of other weapons. I exclaimed loudly enough for all to hear how grateful and delighted I was that my dear cousin had been keeping my family's precious ceremonial sword safe for me for all this time. Then I had one of my footmen immediately remove it from the wall. It was on its way to England the next morning."

He had been peering down at her, as serious as a judge, when he suddenly broke into a huge bellow of laughter that rang on and on, until he was wiping at his eyes with his sleeve.

"You're quite the thief, aren't you, Princess? A brazen daylight robbery in front of a hundred witnesses! And poor old Frederick, without a boot to stand in."

"Whatever it takes, Lord Wexford," she said, not knowing what to make of his expansive amusement. "Besides, it was just a scepter. Brass, not gold, studded with a few barely precious gems. Not that it matters. Frederick had known all along that the scepter was mine. And that I was right to reclaim it."

His humor had cooled, though his gaze hadn't, nor the tip of his finger that he touched to her chin. " 'Being right,' Princess, will make you enemies quicker than anything else."

"Not Frederick. And I can't possibly take the time to care, Wexford." Or to wonder at the growing flush that seemed to emanate from their point of contact, that seemed to be gathering between her breasts and spreading out from there. Utterly undone and thoroughly overexposed by the man's nearness, Caro dashed around him to her main work area. "Um . . . well, and back here . . . I haven't cataloged any of this yet, though I've had some of the items for months. I'm falling more behind every day."

And bloody hell, Princess, I seem to be following you like a lamb to slaughter.

Drew had always prided himself on keeping a cool, professional distance from the objects of his assignments, no matter how beautiful or seductive, no matter the temptation or the willingness of the woman.

Yet, here he was, less than a half day into the job and he was near slavering after this one, sniffing at her fragrance, his eyes forever wandering over her curves and angles.

"Are you all right, Wexford?" Her voice slipped through him from around a tall stack of crates.

"Just . . . yes, Princess. Looking at this"—he picked up a brass object, then set it down again with a clunk—"this bowl . . . thing."

Or whatever.

Drew had been surprised to see that the work area looked more like a jumble shop than her tidy storage space, with pottery and tools and rolled-up lengths of fabric. A worktable stood in the center, a thick loose-leaf book lay open in the center, flanked by two lamps and an inkwell.

"As you see, Wexford, it's a bit of everything, all of it waiting for me to enter into my logbook." She reached into an open barrel and pulled a rectangle of muslin, unwrapping what appeared to be an old book. "This is a late seventeenth-century book of Boratanian game birds. It was illustrated by Jan Romigliov, published by Kuehn and Company of Tinlincken—"

"And stolen from whom?" Drew hid his amusement by leafing through the fine engravings, unable to ignore the soft, rosy scent of her morning bath rising off her nape.

"Actually, Wexford," she said with a glittering, sideways glance as she whirled away from him, lavender on blue, "I found the book on a junk wagon in Edinburgh."

"A lucky find." Though he doubted that she would have stopped at grabbing the book off the queen's own lap, if she'd come across Her Royal Majesty reading it.

"I'm always on the lookout for . . . ughhh." He turned to see her hoisting a great iron piece from the bottom of another crate.

"Bloody hell, Princess!" Drew wrestled the iron weight out of her hands and clunked it onto the floor beside the worktable. "Good lord, madam, it's an andiron."

"Which once resided on the hearth of the banner hall at Croff castle."

He swiped a stray rag around the head of the andiron. "It's dusty and full of soot, madam. How do you know where it came from?"

"Believe me, I know exactly." She muttered as she flipped through the pages in her logbook, found her place and pointed to a carefully printed line. "Here's the description from Count Croff's last will and testament dated 1829: 'iron with brass fittings, eighteen inches tall, of a Boratanian beehive and bee design.'

He died alongside my father. So we know it belonged to him at the time of the siege. Since he died without heirs, his goods would have come to the crown, therefore anything in this document is fair game."

"Princess, you'd have made a fine lawyer."

"Too many rules to follow." She turned up her nose and tossed him a grin as she went back to her rummaging.

He studied the pages of the madwoman's hefty logbook: her neatly printed hand, precise and strong, minute details and historical descriptions, each carefully scribed into the long columns.

Item.
Item last seen.
Item located.
Item rescued.

Dates and times of her various crimes of passion. The logbook was tabulated into categories.

Would that the clerks at the Factory kept their intelligence records with as much organization and detail.

"Can I give you a hand here today, madam?"

She frowned as she clunked a brass pot on the table. "You must have better things to do, my lord."

Anything to keep you safely indoors, Princess, and out of range of an assassin.

And closer to me.

"If you're going to be here, madam, so am I. You might as well put me to work."

All the better to keep his thoughts in check. She was fast becoming an impossible distraction, and though the place looked a hodgepodge, there actually might be clues to the threat against her.

"Well, then," she said, as she poured a shilling-sized pool of beeswax-scented oil into the center of a flannel rag, then started shining the bowl, "would you mind setting the andiron right here next to the pot?"

He didn't mind at all, not even carrying this bloody chunk of cast iron for the second time. Ross had been right to envy him, and this particular mission, at least at this particular moment.

Most of their assignments didn't smell a tenth as good as Caro, or sound as sweet as her laughter.

She set a primitive wooden coffer on the table beside the logbook. A beehive adorned one corner of the flat lid, a trail of bees danced along the edge.

"You won't believe where I found this one, Wexford."

"If I said the pope's sideboard, Princess, would I be far off the mark?"

She laughed again. "It's an ancient relic coffer. It belonged to the church of Saint Hildebrandt. As far as I can tell, it's been empty for centuries." She lifted the brass latch and carefully propped the lid backward against the inkwell. "See . . . empty. And interesting only to me. Which is why I can't believe that Lord Peverel, my very own acting chancellor, was harboring it in his library."

"Old Peverel?" Another innocent victim of the lunatic princess. "What did he say when he saw it marching out the door? Or did you simply put him to shame as well?"

"I doubt he's even noticed. I'd come to drop off some papers at the time, but he wasn't home." She had turned to rustle inside a nearby crate and now returned to the table with a tarnished silver candlestick, a small ruby red glass cruet, and another book. "I found these in his library, too. I guess no one is immune to a little looting."

Even you, Princess.

"Peverel might have been saving them for your collection." He picked up the battered silver candlestick, its value obviously nothing more than sentimental.

Which doubtless gave it nearly magical powers, in the princess's eyes.

"Lord Peverel is a helpful-enough man, but he's never shown a moment's interest in anything Boratanian, save the structure of my government. He's a legal scholar, he's elderly, he's an Englishman, for goodness sake; I doubt he'll miss a single item, and wouldn't care a whit, even if he did."

"You're probably ri—Get down, Princess!" Reacting out of habit to the sudden scrape of a man's boot entering the orangery from the west, Drew shoved the princess to the ground and stood in front of her.

She grabbed hold of his calf with both hands. "What are you do—"

He managed to reach backward, clamped his hand over her mouth, and whispered, "Quiet."

"You in here, my lord?"

"Here, Runson." The danger dissipated like a vapor. He should have recognized the man's long stride.

"There you are, sir!" Runson came lumbering around a stack of boxes, his natty butler's disguise just barely believable.

Then Runson stopped to stare at the princess still clinging to Drew's thigh—very high up on his thigh, her fingers warm and close and kneading where they shouldn't be. "We're holdin' a rather overdressed man and his two assistants in the cloakroom. Says his name is Vincent."

"Vincent!" The princess rocketed to her feet, using Drew's coattail as still another startling handhold. "Heavens above, I completely forgot!"

"Forgot what, Princess?"

"An appointment!" She grabbed up her big logbook and took off at a run.

"Wait, Princess! Oh, damn and hell!"

The woman was as arrogant and stubborn and unpredictable as any royal he'd ever met.

She'd obviously learned from the best. A complete surprise to him, because, despite her beauty and her fine bones and her command of everything around her, she wasn't a princess at all.

A scandalous secret.

One that he would take with him to his death, if need be.

Chapter 8

Drew caught up with her and her flying skirts a dozen yards from the orangery, this woman who could sprint like a deer. "Don't ever bolt from me like that again, madam!"

"Sorry, Wexford. But Vincent is going to be absolutely furious with me." She kept striding forward as though she hadn't heard him. "He doesn't like to be kept waiting. Heaven knows how badly he'll react, with Runson locking him in the coat closet."

"Just who the devil is this Vincent fellow?" And why does he matter so much? He shook off the twinge of jealousy, her sudden angst over this man.

Not that he would allow her to see him until he was cleared of any entangling cobwebs.

"Vincent is the preeminent costumier among the fashionable."

He couldn't have heard her rightly. "He's the what?"

"You must have heard of him. He designs and

makes costumes for all the best fancy-dress occasions. He's a very busy man. And now I'm late for a fitting."

"Fitting for what?" Drew hooked her elbow with his hand and stopped her, not remembering any fancy-dress occasions in her official schedule.

"My gown . . ." She frowned up at him, her eyes snapping with impatience. "For the tournament at Lord Swanbrook's, two days from now."

Oh, that debacle! Swanbrook had been touting the event for the last year.

"You know the kind of thing, Wexford. Medieval tents and banners and horses, feasting and jousting, archery demonstrations—"

A bloody shooting gallery. "You're not going."

"Don't be absurd. I have to attend." She harrumphed at him and started toward the house again, brushing aside the limb of a densely laden lilac bush and launching its powerful fragrance into the air. "It's another event connected to the Great Exhibition, hosted by Viscount Swanbrook at his estate in Hampstead. I'm representing Boratania."

"I know what it is. You are *still* not going."

"The festivities start at noon. I'm one of the Damsels of the Dell, attending Lady Phyllis, Countess of Swanbrook, the Queen of the May. I've promised Swanbrook and Prince Albert that I would—"

"I'll send word to Swanbrook and the prince that you're under the weather. I'm sure they'll forgive you."

"I can't do that." She had stomped up the stairs into the side entrance of the house and now pulled open the door with a good bit of pointed force. "Not only am I a Damsel, Wexford, but Queen Victoria has arranged for me to be formally introduced to Prince Malcomb of Tragovny."

"Why the devil would she do that to you?" He followed her through the door and down the polished walnut hallway.

She rolled her eyes at him. "I'm a princess of the blood, my lord. Like it or not, I have no choice but to make a royal match with a royal prince."

With Tragovny? "God, no." Drew felt a hot stone drop from his chest and groaned under his breath as it landed with a sizzling thud in the pit of his stomach.

"I can't help that the queen is always on the lookout for a potential bridegroom for me. It's inconvenient and annoying, but she is the queen, and I—"

Drew stopped her just before they entered the foyer, trapping her with his arm against the walnut-paneled wall, keeping his voice low and his mouth near enough to kiss her. "And the queen is considering Malcomb of Tragovny for the job?"

The most violent, profligate, drunkardly prince he'd ever had the displeasure to meet?

She shrugged one shoulder, her breath warm and billowing against the underside of his chin. "I have to marry someone, someday."

"Well, you're bloody well not going to marry Prince Malcomb."

"Is that so?" She set her ponderous logbook on the side table and folded her arms across her chest.

"Not while I still have a breath in my body."

"And just who suddenly appointed you my matchmaker?" He could feel her foot tapping against her skirts, causing the slightest pressure and release against his knee. He found himself staring at her lips, imagining their plumpness tasting of lilac and lavender.

"Lord Palmerston did, the moment he assigned me to protect you."

"From an assassin, not from a husband."

"From anyone who might try to do you harm. Including . . . no, madam, *especially,* that puling, vicious Prince Malcomb. I won't allow it."

Her eyes softened suddenly to the blue of cornflower. "*You* won't?"

"And that's another reason you're not attending Swanbrook's little tournament the day after tomorrow or any other day."

Her voice broke into a harsh whisper. "I'm fully aware of the prince's behavior, sir. He's my third cousin and his transgressions have been an embarrassment to the family since before I can remember."

"Which makes him eternally ineligible for you."

"I agree with you completely, my lord." She tapped his chest with her finger, throwing his heart into a spin, shooting sizzling ripples of heat deeper into his groin with every tap. "But Malcomb is family, as is the queen, and I've never met him and it's not as though he's planning to clout me over the head in the Grand Pavilion, or in the middle of the lists with thousands of people looking on, and then drag me off to his cave."

Drew realized too late that the woman had lulled him and slipped out from beneath his arm and was heading for the foyer. "We're not finished here."

"No time, my lord. Vincent is waiting!"

"Damn this Vincent!" Drew followed her into the cloak closet vestibule.

"I'm coming, Vincent! Please let me in, Mrs. Tweeg."

Good old Tweeg was standing guard in front of the closet door with a chiding brow. "You'll not fool me again, Princess Caroline."

"I'm sorry, Mrs. Tweeg. I was unpardonably rude to pull such a prank this morning. It won't ever happen again."

"Indeed it won't."

"So, Princess, you intend to completely ignore my professional advice and attend the tournament anyway?"

"This is a perfect instance of your having to work around me, Wexford. But don't worry, with all those royals roving around the grounds, I'm sure there will be bodyguards aplenty on the scene."

"Including me, Princess." And another two dozen of his finest.

"Of course." She smiled up at him. "I wouldn't have it any other way."

Nor would I, he thought, but wisely didn't say.

"Besides," she said, "I mean to rescue a set of golden wall sconces at the tournament."

"Good God."

"Is that you, my Princess?" The door thumped, one rousing fist against solid walnut. "Your people have been horribly rude!"

"Yes, I know they are, Vincent." The princess scowled hard at Drew. "But we're having a bit of mechanical trouble with the lock."

Suddenly certain that this man was no threat to anything but the princess's sense of fashion, Drew nodded at Tweeg and the woman clicked the key in the latch.

"Come with me to my dressing room, Vincent!" the princess announced as the door flew open to a chaos of complaints and lush velvet and deep satins which followed her up the stairs like a cloud bank of exotic chattering birds.

She stopped at the top of the stairs. "Will you come too, Mrs. Tweeg?"

"Me?"

"After all, you are my chambermaid."

Tweeg cast Drew a rueful look, but then plodded obediently up the winding stairs.

"Will I see you at supper tonight, Wexford?"

It was a challenge, plain and simple. A test of wills.

"Till then, Princess."

He stood there admiring the fine turn of that ankle in those sturdy little boots as she started up the stairs, amazed that something so ordinary could provoke him to stare.

And stammer.

And wish for a different ending to this story than the one he was duty bound to play out.

Determined to keep the woman alive despite her bullheaded recklessness, Drew made a detour to the investigation room where he jotted a few notes about the morning's findings, then took a fast horse to the Factory to dig more deeply into the princess's past.

"Farewell, Princess!" Vincent was still waving madly from the carriage window as it sped down the drive into the twilight. "You'll be the highlight of the tournament!"

"That you will be, Your Highness!" Mrs. Tweeg

was positively preening now as they stood together on the portico, Caro's earlier indiscretion forgiven. "And won't his lordship be surprised."

"Deep green is definitely his color." And doubtless his calves are marvelously muscular.

"But you really must mind his word and take care of yourself, Princess Caroline."

"I'll do my very best, Mrs. Tweeg." Feeling that she might be exposing her erstwhile chambermaid to an unknown danger out on the portico, with the woods growing deeper shadows in the distance, Caro stepped back inside and Tweeg followed.

"I'll just go back upstairs to see to the chaos that Vincent made of your dressing room."

"You're a dear, Mrs. Tweeg." More than that, the woman had the patience of Job and a keen eye for color. And seemed utterly delighted that she, too, would be wearing her own rust red medieval gown and whimple.

She watched the woman hurry up the stairs, wondering, as she had done all through Vincent's visit, what sort of roguery Wexford had been up to in the meanwhile.

He wasn't with his operatives in his bustling investigation room.

"His lordship said he was going into the City for the rest of the afternoon, Your Highness. Then to his gentleman's club, I believe."

"Ah, the Huntsman." For some reason she'd rather not explore, she felt a bit deserted by the lout, exposed to preposterous dangers she didn't even believe in. "Did he say when he'd be back, Mr. Helston?"

"In time for supper," said the short man who was

standing in front of a huge map of Grandauer. "He told us to be sure to tell you that."

The parlor looked nothing like it had. . . . Great heavens, was that only yesterday morning? Her delicate tables and lace coverings gone, replaced by worktables and filing drawers. An entire armory in place of the fern stands.

And these men who seemed to be taking the threat against her life as seriously as Wexford. Which was fast becoming as much a comfort as it was a bother. She was trying her best to cooperate, but the timing was simply awful.

"Have you any daguerreotypes of your kingdom, Princess?"

"What's that, Mr. Helston?"

"Photographs of landscapes or landmarks, etchings of towns or bridges?"

"Well, yes! Would you like to see them?"

"The more information we have on the case, Your Highness, the better chance we have of seating you safely on your throne."

"Good, then. I'll see what I can find."

The lights in her library had already been lit and her boxes of daguerreotypes were right where she'd left them on the hearth table.

She had recently begun sorting through the elegantly posed photographs of her royal aunts and uncles, cousins and second cousins. Dozens and dozens and dozens of them, sent to her every Christmas over the last few years. Not only daguerreotypes of people, but of crown jewels and tea sets and carriages, whatever could hold still long enough for the camera to capture their image.

Her dear Boratania. The home she had never seen, but that she loved just the same.

She started putting aside those that she thought Helston might find useful. But the sun had set into a softly glowing orange, and now a chilly breeze from an open window was fluttering the stack of papers on the desk.

She went to a window to close it, but found it already shut tight.

Wondering where the odd breeze was coming from, she started toward the next window, and suddenly stepped in a pile of broken glass.

"What the devil?" Startled by the unsettling feeling, she backed away from the crackling sound, the odd coldness settling in her stomach.

"What is it, Princess?"

Wexford! He was back from the City, and already there at her side, agile and alert.

And her heart must be beating from sudden fear and not because his voice had a way of heating her veins as though it were her pulse.

"Be careful, Wexford. It's broken glass." She pointed to the mess on the floor, looked more closely at the window, and found the empty pane.

"Bloody hell, be careful!" Wexford shoved her behind him and yanked the drape closed. "Please, Princess Caroline. You must keep the curtains closed! Halladay!"

Three men had followed him into the library at a run, and now swarmed around her, walling her off from whatever danger they thought she was in.

"Stay back, Princess," Wexford said, standing firmly between her and the glass, as though she would somehow slip and accidentally cut herself to death.

"A break-in, sir?" one man asked.

"Has all the earmarks, Halladay."

"How long ago, do you think?"

"Since yesterday at noon," Caro said, distracted suddenly by a prickly feeling that something was out of place. "I was in here just before lunch and all the windows were intact, the glass doors closed." And the drapes drawn.

The four men had stopped their careful inspection and were now looking at her, four pairs of eyes that seemed surprised to see her.

"Noted, Princess," Wexford said finally, as though she were his clerk. And then they all went back to examining the glass and exclaiming over the door latch and hinges.

"Broken from the outside, sir, making the glass fall inward, giving immediate access to the latch."

"And to all these boxes," Caro muttered to herself, finally realizing what had been making the hair on the back of her neck stand up, and now her heart start to pound with dread.

The library had become the repository of all the Boratanian documents and books and manuscripts that she'd managed to collect over the years.

Neat cardboard boxes, labeled and arranged on the bookshelves and in the glass-fronted cabinets below, each according to their value and importance, ready to be installed in the library in Tovaranche castle.

Merely a lot of paper and ink and words. Hardly of a moment's value to anyone but herself and some future Boratania historian.

And yet someone had found them dear enough to

rifle the boxes, scattering loose pages below the shelves.

"I think I might know what the burglars were looking for, Wexford," Caro said, swallowing hard against a rising sense of fear and outrage. "Look here. These boxes."

"What's that, Princess?" He was still across the room with his operatives, studying the windows and the floor and the drapes in his professional and efficient way.

"Please," she said as she stooped to pick up the pages and right a box that had been knocked to the floor.

She felt Wexford kneeling beside her a moment later, watched as he took the page out of her hand and looked at it. "What's happened here, Princess?"

"I didn't leave this mess here yesterday afternoon. I would never."

"I'm quite sure of that." He picked up more of the loose papers that had fallen under the table.

"I don't like this, Wexford." She gathered up a handful of paper, feeling violated to the core.

"Nor do I." He turned to his agents. "Halladay, go take a detail outside and secure the rest of the doors and windows."

Caro watched them leave, hoping they would be safe out there in the twilight. "I don't understand, Wexford. What could a burglar possibly be looking for in these boxes?"

"Indeed." Wexford was frowning as he skimmed through each page, scrubbing at his chin with a knuckle.

"You're very thorough, Lord Wexford." Exhaustively intense.

And so . . . mysterious.

"A habit, Princess." He looked up at her with those serious, dark eyes, a hint of a smile tucked into their corners.

And if Wexford was right about this threat to her life, if the assassin was as real as the broken glass and the papers scattered under the shelves, then that could only mean that everyone around her was in danger.

Especially Andrew Chase, the Earl of Wexford, who had promised to take a bullet for her.

A bullet that suddenly seemed so possible.

"Whoever did this, Princess, could just as easily be searching for some kind of document as the crown jewels or an ancient bronze mortar and pestle."

"What sort of documents? What could they possibly have been looking for in the library that's of any value to anyone?" She rattled the pages in her hand, suddenly terrified for Wexford. And Wheeler and Mrs. Tweeg.

"It could be anything and nothing at all."

She held up one of the discarded pages. "Certainly not this ancient court decision over the ownership of a milk cow? Or a seventeenth-century license to brew brown ale on Sundays?"

Or possibly, Princess, they're looking for solid proof that you're not really the Princess Caroline.

Drew had been wrestling with the possibility ever since Palmerston had assigned him the case. That the source of the danger was the woman herself.

In the wrong hands, that information could be explosive—to every royal house in Europe as well as devastating to the princess herself.

His princess.

The wild-eyed woman who was staring defiantly at the scattered papers and then directly at him.

"We've got to stop them, Wexford." Her eyes brightened with a kind of crazy courage. "And it's time I started helping with my own investigation."

Chapter 9

Good Christ, no! "Helping how?" Drew asked, fearing the woman's reckless determination.

"Sorting through the library and all these papers for clues would be a good place to start."

Better yet, a safe place to start. "A fine idea."

"It's such an eclectic collection. Town charters and personal letters and declarations of war." She started laying out papers on the desktop. "Here's a letter from my father to one of his generals permitting him to buy a hundred horses from the king of Prussia."

A stack of paper ought to keep her busy and out of trouble for a while. He pointed to the gilded and embossed emblem at the top center of the page.

"This must be your family crest?"

"The bee and the beehive. That's right." She brought it closer. "And here you can still see the hive resting in a field of clover, all of it wrapped in a band of iron."

"The meaning?"

"The Latin motto translates to something like 'due diligence, common wisdom and fruitfulness.' "

"I don't see anything there that might be a threat to . . ." He stopped because she was staring at the middle of his chest, lighting a deep fire with her gaze.

"Is this *your* family crest?" She took one of his coat buttons between her fingers and studied it closely.

"My family crest?" He'd never been asked that before. And wasn't sure how to answer, because the crest had always meant so much more than that.

More than family. More than his life.

"I noticed it on the fireplace mantel at the Huntsman." She held it still, her fingers slipping along the linen folds of his neck cloth. "And on the ceiling bosses, the tea cups."

"You're very observant, madam."

"I can't help myself." She shook her head ruefully. "I've been looking for looted objects for such a long time that scouting a room and making careful assessments has become a dreadful habit."

"Then I guess I'm lucky you didn't steal the brass door hinges."

"You're lucky they hadn't been looted from one of my castles. But they weren't. I know. I looked. They too were crested with your sailing ship, and the rampant lion and these three swords overlaid by a rose. It's very lovely." She patted the button and his chest, altering the beat of his heart. "Is the emblem very old?"

"Quite recent, actually." Bought with blood and secrets and unspeakable tales, and struck with a solemn, sacred pledge.

"Interesting." She peered more closely, fretting her

brow. "There are four arrows behind the shield. What does it mean, my lord?"

"The ship indicates progress through commerce, and the lion, loyalty—"

"To your sovereign, Queen Victoria."

At times like this it felt like blind, stumbling loyalty. Testing his covenant as well as his intentions. "To my queen and my country. To friends."

To Jared and Ross, and to Thomas, who couldn't come with them.

"And the three crossed swords?"

"The courage to endure." His heart ached suddenly with the sharpness of the hollow memory. The anger as bitter as ever, the helplessness as stark as midnight. "And a debt that's yet to be paid in full."

"A debt to whom?"

If only we hadn't waited that one day longer. If we'd left when we'd had the chance. If Craddock's heart hadn't been quite so black and tattered.

"It's an old debt, Princess. One that can't ever be truly canceled or satisfied."

"Is it a family obligation?"

"I don't have a family."

She caught her lower lip with her teeth. "I'm so sorry. Have they all passed on?"

"They must have by now. I don't remember much of anything about them." Only frightening shadows and a whisper and someone gently squeezing his hand an instant before he was dumped onto the bone-snapping chill of the workhouse's stone floor.

"Not anything?" She brushed the back of his hand with her fingers. "Then we have that in common: orphaned early and raised by relatives."

"If I have relatives, madam, they've never made themselves known to me."

"But you're an earl. Didn't you inherit from your father or your uncle? Your grandfather, certainly?"

She was going to nag the truth out of him, not that it mattered to him in the least.

"If I recall, the only thing I inherited from my father was my height. At least he seemed a giant to me. But he wasn't an earl. He was a Thames ferryman and he died of stab wounds received in a struggle with a drunk who chose to pay his fare with the point of a blade instead of the coin of the realm."

She shook her head. "Your father was . . . but then how did you become an earl?"

"Hard work, madam."

"You were a soldier?"

"Not in regular service." Far more dangerous than that. "Though I have earned my titles by taking a bullet or two for queen and country."

"You've been shot?" She touched her lips with her fingertips.

"A few times. The last was in the process of heading off a war with Sweden. Quite recently, in fact."

"What war with Sweden?"

Indeed. "And it earned me the earldom. So did negotiating the Treaty of Eltz-Marienlange and a trade agreement between the warring Ceylonese tea barons and the last of the East India Company."

And helping to loot the grain warehouses of the privy council to save the lives of starving children in Ireland. Though the queen would have his head if she knew, and Jared and Kate didn't want the conspiracy generally known.

"So after all your exploits, you've chosen your own family crest."

"We did. Jared and Ross and I." In an act of grand larceny, and in memory of young Thomas. "We share the crest."

"That's an odd arrangement. Who are these men?"

"The finest in the world." She smiled at that, as though she highly approved of him having fine friends. "We met as boys in the workhouse."

"Doing what?" Though Caro knew in the deepest part of her what he was going to say before he answered, her heart dreaded the possibility, her stomach ached like fire.

"Working, madam." He seemed so nonchalant.

"In the workhouse?"

"Slaving, really. Growing up there together."

"How horrible!" Caro swallowed the tears that were gathering in her throat—he wouldn't want to see them. "To have to spend a single day of your childhood in such a terrible place! Where are these men now?"

He lifted his chin at her, this very proud man. "Jared is the Earl of Hawkesly."

"I believe I've met his wife briefly. Lady Kathryn. Lots of children."

Wexford smiled as fondly as a dear uncle. "Lots and lots . . . and lots of them. They stopped at fifteen adopted. God knows where they'll stop with their own."

"And Ross?"

"Carrington. The Viscount Battencourt. He's the real soldier among us. Though also not in the regular army."

How easy it was to admire a man with such a large, generous heart.

She caught up the button on his chest again, startled this time at the heat of him against her fingers. She'd wanted to ask about the tiny words she could see inscribed across the crest, but now had to steady her breathing first.

"What does it say here on the ribbons? The letters are very small."

"On the left is *Exitus acta probat, fiat.*"

" 'The end justifies the means'?"

"And 'let it be done.' The left says, 'with loyalty, courage and enterprise.' We were perhaps a bit overly poetic when we created the design. But it was heartfelt. Still is."

"It's very fine." *You're very fine, Andrew Chase.* "I'd like to meet them both sometime. After I've rid myself of random assassins. I wouldn't want to endanger them as well."

"The possibility of danger would only entice them, madam. They both enjoy a challenge. In fact, I've had to beat them away from this assignment with a stick."

"Your pardon, Princess." Runson was standing in the doorway, his knuckles poised near the doorjamb. "You've three visitors. The Lords Peverel, Wellstetter and Innes."

"Heavens, Runson, you didn't lock them in the cloak closet, did you?"

"Tempted to, Your Highness"—he nodded toward the foyer—"but they looked harmless enough, so I put them in the east parlor, with Wallace on guard at the door."

"Thanks, I'll be right there." Although she hadn't been expecting them. And wondered what they would make of her "entertaining" the Earl of Wexford.

"Your privy council, madam?"

"Truly harmless, Wexford. But what will they think of you being here?"

"Tell them that the Foreign Office has engaged me to consult on your transfer to Boratania."

"You mean like a removal concern? You're packing up my pots and pans and moving me out?"

"Hardly, madam. Tell them I'm negotiating your borders and waterway treaties."

Not a very convincing explanation, but Wexford seemed satisfied and was already at the door, leading the way for her through her own house.

The three men rose from their individual chairs and dropped into courtly bows as Caro entered.

"Welcome to Grandauer, gentlemen." She could feel Wexford standing close behind her as Wellstetter and Innes hurried toward her, smiling broadly.

"You're looking lovely, Princess."

"Thank you, Lord Innes."

Innes scowled at Wellstetter. "Our princess always looks lovely."

"And I would like to introduce Andrew Chase, the Earl of Wexford. Palmerston has been kind enough to arrange for Wexford to use his diplomatic skills to help me with the border surveys and those impossible waterway treaties. As he's pointed out so clearly, one can hardly run a country without water and proper borders."

"Indeed," Peverel said, nodding. "I'll admit that I hadn't given such a thing any thought at all."

"You three have been marvelous, Lord Peverel. Now what can I do for you tonight?"

"You have a fine home in Grandauer Hall, your highness." Peverel studied the room with his usual attention to detail, then beamed at her. "But as you have company, we'll stay only long enough for you to sign a few papers."

Caro felt Wexford shift behind her and wondered how a man could live his life suspecting everyone he met of nefarious motives.

"What kind of papers this time?" They seemed endless.

"Setting up your own personal treasury, Princess Caroline." Wellstetter pulled a portfolio from beneath his half-cape and spread it open on the table. "Transfers to the Bank of Boratania from your accounts at the Bank of England."

Innes added his finger to Wellstetter's pointing. "Right here are your considerable town rents and your farm and faire revenues."

"Your taxes, Princess," Peverel added without even looking down at the document, his hat in his hand, his attention still wandering the room as though he were bored and wishing he were at his club.

One detail heaped upon another, coming faster as the time grew closer. Time when she would be an Empress and her family would be restored to the great names of Europe.

Caro signed countless pages, with Wexford sprawled in a chair, pretending disinterest as he read a copy of the *Times*, when she knew that he'd rather be reading every line from over her shoulder.

Making her feel much better because he was watching over her—this man who had taken bullets for other people and survived. Which wasn't soothing in the least.

Even a cat has just so many lives.

"You'll be at the Swanbrook tournament, Your Highness?" Peverel was already standing by the door, crooking his finger at his compatriots.

"I wouldn't miss it for the world, Lord Peverel." *Assassin or no.* She couldn't allow her enemies to keep her from carrying out her duties.

The men nearly backed into Runson with their duckish bowing. But her "butler" cleared his throat, averting a collision and steering her privy council out into the foyer and finally through the door.

"Will these three be your permanent counselors, Princess?" Wexford asked as he led her back to the library and shut the door behind them.

"Only until I can hold a parliamentary election. Then, just as with the English Parliament, the prime minister will select his ministers and I will live by his choice of council." Though it all still seemed a far-off possibility. "At least that's how it's supposed to work."

"Just curious as to how a new empress goes about starting a kingdom from scratch."

"Frankly, I hadn't thought that far until Palmerston explained the process to me and then the—"

A knock sounded at the library door.

"Come in!" Caro said without thinking.

"Who is it?" Wexford was already at the door, listening vigilantly, as he flashed a frown at her.

"Mackenzie, sir. I thought you might be takin' a workin' dinner in here with the princess."

"Mackenzie is a renowned chef, Princess Caroline." Wexford threw open the door to the man and two of his burly kitchen staff. "I'm pleased to say that I stole him from the Compte de Ferrat about seven years ago—"

"Been the best seven years of my life, Princess." Mackenzie tossed her a huge wink as his male, very out-of-place-looking staff of cook's assistants carried in a pair of trays, and made room for the luscious smelling food on the low table by the cold fireplace.

"Why exactly do you like working for the earl, Mr. Mackenzie?" A full-blooded, red-bearded Scotsman who was also a reknowned chef?

"Where else, Your Highness, can an ordinary man risk his life for queen and country at the same time he's preparing a pheasant under glass?" Mackenzie poured the wine into two of her finest stemmed glasses.

"He likes the danger, Princess." Drew winked at her that time, setting her heart to fluttering.

"Never know where we'll be from one assignment to the next. Exotic spices, flying bullets and wild game." He threw back his head and laughed. "Ahhhh, cheffin' doesn't get any better than that, Your Highness."

"Welcome to Grandauer, Mr. Mackenzie. May you find your assignment here long on exotic spices and short on bullets." She lifted the covered dish and found a succulent game hen steaming on a bed of rosemary. "Though if you're not careful, Wexford, I just might loot Mr. Mackenzie from you and take him back with me to Boratania."

"Have a care with your hide, Mackenzie; the princess is a master thief. And as you know, I'm a jealous employer."

"I'm takin' no sides, your lordship, but may the prettiest of you win." Mackenzie's eyes flashed a grin as he pulled the door closed, leaving them alone with the most fragrant meal Caro had ever smelled.

"Master thief, am I?"

"Unbelievably good, Princess. The best I've met in a long while."

Caro, please. For some purely pathetic reason, she wanted him to be that intimate with her name, as intimate as he was with her eyes.

And her chin, the tips of her ears.

And her mouth. Just the way he was gazing there at the moment as he took a sip from his wine, leaving traces of himself, memories that she would cherish long after this was all done up and written down in the history books.

"Are you married, Lord Wexford?"

Drew nearly choked on his mouthful of wine. Now *there* was a royal change of subjects, with a royal tilt of her perfect nose and a gaze so direct it wasn't fit for polite company.

He swallowed hard and steadied his breathing as he tried to decide her game, and if he wanted to play.

"Is that important?"

She shrugged as she carried a lamp from the desk to the low table. "You're a guest in my house, following me everywhere I go, as though you were my shadow. I think I ought to at least know your marital state."

"Why? Have you designs on me?"

She laughed lightly and turned up the flame. "Don't be absurd."

"Because if you do fancy me, Princess—"

She flicked an imperious brow at him. "I don't. I couldn't possibly."

"Good, because if you did, much as I'd regret it, I'd have to decline your advances."

"Ease your mind, Wexford." She left him a teasing smile as she retrieved her own wineglass. "I have no intention of making improper advances to you, and you know it. I was merely curious about your life when you're not plaguing me."

"I'm not married." Doubted he'd ever find the right kind of wife.

She eyed him, making a half circuit around him. "I didn't think you were."

He was feeling quite thoroughly inspected, her gaze as warm as a brandy. "What gave me away?"

She sat her glass beside the tray. "Your hair."

"My what?"

"You wear your hair longer than the fashion. Most wives wouldn't allow you to venture far from the house without an everyday trim."

Drew frowned and made a show of raking his fingers through his hair. "Am I that unkempt, Princess? I'll have to speak with my valet."

"That's not what I mean. Your hair is quite nice. It's just that a wife looks after her husband's appearance to the last nuance. Puts her mark on him."

"What, like a tattoo? Her name? A monogram?"

She was standing very close, looking up at him with a keen eye. "A style, my lord. A distinctive look that she appreciates in a man."

He'd never heard this before. Though he'd never stand to be groomed to a woman's plan, he could imagine his princess giving it a good try. He might even submit to her attempt.

But she was spoken for in that royal way.

"I know it's a bit out of order, Wexford, but I'd like to make a request of you."

Drew found himself too often just staring at the woman, unable to look away from all that beauty, from the intriguing way her lips moved when she spoke, from the glittering blue of her eyes.

A deplorable habit that he would have to break before it broke him.

"What is it, Princess?"

"It's *that*, Wexford. What you're doing. I would appreciate very much if you stop calling me 'Princess.' "

"Stop . . . What?"

"Please stop using my title. It seems very formal when you say it."

"I'm sorry. I can't do that, Princess."

"It's simple enough. I know you can do it. You've proved to me that you can see through solid brick, and read minds. Surely you can call me Caroline."

"I . . . can't."

"I insist. A royal command."

"That's hardly fair. . . ."

"Just wait till I'm an empress then."

"Madam, you're . . ." Stubborn. Compelling. Damn. "Very well, if you insist. Here goes—"

He cleared his throat to attempt this feat of impropriety, shaped his mouth into the start of her name but couldn't quite manage. "I don't think I can do it, Your Highness. You are the Princess Caroline. 'Princess' is your office, a tradition. And I'm bound to protect everything about you."

Especially her title.

Especially that.

She huffed and put a stubborn hand against her

hip. "But the way you say 'Princess' makes it sound as though you don't like me, as though I'm a bad taste in your mouth."

God knows she'd be a very sweet taste in his mouth, sultry and salty and warm.

"I'm sure I don't know what you mean."

"'Anything you say, *Princess*,'" she said, spitting the last with a curling lip, a deliciously piratical growl and a sideways thrust of her hip.

Now Drew was laughing. A princess with a sense of humor—utterly beyond his experience. "I didn't mean to offend, Princess."

"See what I mean?" She frowned dramatically and dropped the pitch of her voice an octave. "'I didn't mean to offend, *Princess*.'"

Another explosive impersonation that suddenly felt and sounded too familiar.

"That bad, am I?"

"Much worse when you're angry at me."

"Impatient."

"What?" Her voice had softened to silk.

"I get impatient, not angry. You're stubborn, Princess."

"I'm Caroline. Caro."

"Caroline Marguerite Marie Isabella, empress-elect of Boratania. I know."

"No one ever calls me just Caroline anymore. Not even my best friends, at least not since we were children. Not even at tea or when we're just shopping or playing whist." She fixed her soft gaze on him, heating his blood, giving him far too many ideas. "Won't you please try? As a favor to me."

Such an intimate request, ripe with trust and honesty and the truth. But she seemed so keenly eager, and her name felt like honey on his tongue.

"In private only, Princess?"

Her eyes brightened, within a breath of her triumph. "Of course."

"And only when I feel the moment is proper."

"Proper?"

"Outside of this dangerous business between us? I know my place in your life." Professional. Distant.

A furrow flickered across her brow and then she nodded. "All right."

"All right then"—she stood there looking up at him, eyes wide and waiting, until he said, ". . . Caroline."

Then she smiled at him and his heart lurched and swelled, as though he'd just performed a trick of magic.

"Then that's settled, my lord," she said, turning away from him with a flick of her hem and heading to the table and its tray of food.

"Andrew."

She turned and cocked her head at him, narrowing her eyes. "What do you mean?"

"A fair exchange, Princess. If you insist that I call you Caroline, then I'll feel much more comfortable if you refer to me as Andrew."

"Andrew." She seemed to linger over it, smiled when she finished.

"Drew, actually. My friends call me that. After all, Wexford is merely my title, the name of my estate grounds. Frankly I've always felt odd about it. Like being called the Great Northern Railway or Cheese Wheel."

She burst into peels of laughter, a sprightly, joyful

sound. "Cheese Wheel? You . . . ? Oh, my lord, you . . ." And still she laughed. And laughed.

He liked the bright sound of it. Shiny silver, the small, unexpected ringing of a bell.

"You know what I mean, Caroline."

She pointed at him, including him, still laughing, but sagging now against the desk. "You . . . you surprise me, sir! The Great Northern . . ." Her laughter gave way to giggles and wiping at her eyes. "I've never thought about a title in that way before, but you're right."

"Naming a person after a place? Yes, well, I've always thought that titles were more than a little absurd."

"You wear yours well, Wexford."

"Drew. Please."

She'd recovered, leaving her cheeks blushed and her eyes sparkling as she studied him. Leaving him with a hope that she would laugh again soon.

"Very well . . . Drew." She smiled with a silent and cunning challenge. "Shall we have supper, then? I wouldn't want to disappoint Mackenzie by letting his superb meal grow cold and inedible."

"As you please . . . Caroline."

Still, he found this informality between them highly uncomfortable. Not because of their disparate titles—that had always seemed a false economy of privilege. Randomly bestowed, not earned.

It was the intimacy. The growing familiarity with a woman he was supposed to be protecting.

The guilt over being able to talk so easily to her about the truth, when every moment of every day he harbored a secret that belonged to her, that could alter her life forever—her image of herself if she ever learned of it. All he could do was to keep her safely out of trouble until her coronation, until she left England for her beloved Boratania.

And hope to hell she didn't learn the devastating truth in the meantime. Or ever.

Dinner became a chaotic work session, with the woman popping up from the small table a half dozen times to fetch another pile of documents.

The stacks grew taller and more numerous. Letters to her mother from the far-flung members of her family. To her father from his generals and other kings. Bills of sale and menus for state dinners.

Stories cut from newspapers. Opera programs.

Hundreds of invitations. Calling cards.

Each of them safely unremarkable.

"These are all so amazing to me, Drew." Her eyes often glistened as she examined the papers. "I've been so busy collecting these boxes of paper, I've never really taken the time to study any of it. But it's like taking a journey backward into a time I can only imagine. When Boratania was a rich and influential kingdom, when my family name was respected, and my parents were alive."

Her parents. Bloody hell, this was the worst kind of torture.

Knowing too much.

Beginning to care too much.

The night ended in the same way that the next day began: with the princess spending the morning poring over the boxes of papers, and then the next afternoon and the next safely cataloging more of her precious treasures. Until three full days had passed with Drew no closer to understanding who was trying to kill her.

He had turned Grandauer Hall and its extensive grounds into a fortress where she was well-shielded from any possible assassin, where every square foot was doubly secured.

He'd set his specialists at the Factory to work on investigating the few leads he'd collected.

Though no one was to know of it but Palmerston, he would saturate tomorrow's tournament at Swanbrook's estate with his operatives. The princess wouldn't be able to breathe without running into one of his most trusted men.

Certainly not without running into himself.

A very pleasant prospect.

Chapter 10

"Oh, you look magnificent, Princess Caroline!" Mrs. Tweeg was standing to one side of the cheval glass, beaming, her hands clasped against her bosom.

Caro studied her own reflection and had to agree. "Vincent has truly outdone himself this time."

Yards and yards of rich, royal blue velvet. Long, pointed, medieval-styled sleeves trimmed in stark white pearls and gilded braiding, girdled low at her hips with a Boratanian belt of gem-studded golden medallions.

Along with an equally delicious blue velvet cap with a long, silky white veil trailing down her back to cover her hair.

And for some perfectly ridiculous reason, she had been wondering all morning what Drew would think of her gown. Not that she could let that matter at all.

"You look quite smashing yourself, Mrs. Tweeg." Caro looked on in delight as the woman checked her own image in the mirror for the tenth time.

"I'll just go downstairs and see that all your bags get into the carriage. Highly trained operatives they may be, Your Highness, but they are men, after all."

Tweeg left Caro looking at the other costume hanging from her bedpost.

His costume.

Drew's.

Vincent had put together a marvelous one, complete with sword, hat, and cape.

Though Andrew Chase, the Earl of Wexford, didn't exactly seem the fancy-dress type. Actually getting him to wear it might prove to be a little difficult.

She'd heard him stirring about his chamber before dawn, had listened to him stalk down the corridor shortly afterward, but hadn't seen him all morning.

Hadn't had time to mention the costume to him.

Perhaps if she sneaked into his chamber through the secret panel and laid out the cape and tunic casually on the bed so they were there when he returned, he might not object so vehemently to wearing them. Because he would definitely object.

Picking up the outfit, Caro moved the delftware vase on the bookshelf and activated the latch behind it.

She pulled open her side of the bookcase, passed through the narrow passage in the wall, then shoved open the panel on his side, hoping to be in and out in a moment.

But, oh, dear sweet Lord!

The chamber wasn't empty after all.

He was there.

And the sight of him stopped her in her tracks, struck her speechless.

No, not just speechless. She was . . . utterly dumbfounded.

And he was . . . naked.

Naked, and just standing there. Handsome. Fresh out of his bath and glistening and staring right back at her.

"You were saying, madam?" That was a smile she heard but didn't see.

Because she wasn't looking anywhere near his face. Couldn't look there. It was safer to look . . .

Heavens, she couldn't look *there*.

Even though she *was* looking *there*.

She gulped and expelled a hot breath. "Well, then, Drew, I can see that you're . . ." *Large.* ". . . busy."

Great heavens! She just couldn't stop seeing him. Everywhere. All of him!

His very broad, very sleekly bronze chest that tapered to a tightly muscled belly and powerful hips.

And densely muscled thighs.

And the darkly shadowed root of him, thick and alive and mysterious.

"I *was* busy, Princess."

And now, thank God, he was turning his back to her, striding away.

Though the delicious sight of his buttocks and his broad, strongly corded back, and those long, powerful legs, wasn't helpful in the least to regaining control of her breathing or her thought process.

"What can I help you with, Princess?"

Let me touch you.

"Great heavens, did I say that aloud?"

Everywhere, Andrew. I'd like to touch you everywhere.

"Did you say *what* aloud, Princess?" he asked, still turned away from her.

Oh, good. Then she hadn't been babbling to him.

Good also that the folds of his silken robe now swirled around him, breaking off her vision.

"Oh, well, nothing." She cleared her throat of the tension there. "I'd been thinking that I should really have knocked first."

"Indeed, Princess, you should have." He seemed to be purposely calling her Princess again. Raising her business title between them. Though this particular moment seemed as far removed from any kind of business as the moon.

"I certainly will next time, Lord Wexford," she said, watching his every move as he finished tying off his robe and turned toward her.

"An excellent precaution, Princess, if I'm to remain safely on my side of that wall." She didn't know what to make of the darkness of his eyes, or the tempting danger she could sense behind them.

"What do you mean by that, Wexford?"

He sighed heavily. "My job is to protect you, Princess. From everyone, including myself."

"Yourself?" Caro laughed and sat down in a very comfortable, overlarge wing chair, his costume in her lap. "I have no reason to be afraid of you, Andrew. After all, you've insisted that I trust you with my life."

"It's not your life that I'd be afraid of taking, my dear Princess. It's . . ."

"Then, what?" His smile was crooked, but his eyes were fixed intensely on hers. Oh, dear. He'd meant her . . . honor. "Oh, my."

"Yes, my dear Princess. Oh, my."

Her heart started pounding again, twice as quickly and twice as hotly as it had when she'd come upon him stark naked in the candlelight. "Because you find me attractive."

"Indeed."

"And so this can be a problem between us."

He arched a roguish brow. "Because, my dear, I find you more attractive than any woman I've ever met, and I refuse to let that become a problem between us."

Dismissed as a problem. Declined, before she'd had a chance to savor the feeling of being wanted by a man who thought she was attractive.

A man that she might want right back—given the appropriate circumstances.

Mired to her nose in a predicament of her own making, Caro stood up and started back toward her room before she remembered why she'd ventured into his chamber in the first place.

"Oh, dear." She didn't really want to turn back and look at him, but she couldn't very well toss the costume over her shoulder at him and just bolt. "I've brought you this to wear today."

He was scowling at her when she turned back to him, one dark brow raised in an ominous slant. "Thank you, but I have my own clothes to wear."

"But I had Vincent assemble a knight's costume for you."

"No."

"Swanbrook has insisted that everyone wear a costume, Drew."

"Not me. Besides, I'll be on duty, Princess."

"I'm afraid a full costume is required of anyone who sits in the Grand Pavilion." His scowl deepened and he seemed to grow taller the longer she spoke.

"So if you're planning to post yourself anywhere near me, Drew, you'll have to wear this. Or something."

He didn't say anything for a very long time, only glared at her and then at the costume she was holding up and then at her, and then he finally growled out a "bloody hell!"

Relieved to her bones, she hooked the costume over the back of a chair and sidled toward the open panel.

"Thank you, Drew."

"Don't thank me, madam."

"I'll leave you to get dressed. I . . . um . . . hope you accept my apology for staring at you earlier. It's just that I've . . . well, I've never seen a naked man before, and I didn't quite know what to do, or, um . . . where to look, actually."

His brows shot up into his forehead, disappearing under the dark tangle of his finger rumpled hairline. "Leave, madam. Please."

"At least I've never seen a naked man made of actual flesh." Her cheeks were already aflame—why not set them on fire. "I must say that you're far more inspiring than any statue in my collection."

That only made him frown deeply. He strode to where she was standing beside the panel and held it open for her. "Be ready in twenty minutes, Princess."

"Right." Her knees wobbly and her cheeks tingling, Caro ducked back into her own room, jumping out of her skin when Drew closed his side of the door firmly behind her.

Her skin still tingling with his delicious heat, Caro shut the bookcase with a resounding *clunk*, then went back to the mirror to straighten her cap.

And to see if she could possibly have changed in the last few minutes.

Her cheeks were still blooming crimson, would probably remain so until she was an old woman. Her heart was still slamming against her chest, her pulse thundering in her ears.

And that was a kind of smile she'd never seen before.

Elusive, wiser, profound, tucked like a secret into the corner of her mouth.

And why not? She'd just seen her first man without his clothes. And not just any man, but the most amazing man she'd ever met.

An earl, because he'd worked hard for the honor.

A champion to his friends.

A man who had repeatedly pledged himself to protect her with his life.

Naked.

"Bloody wonderful!" How the devil would she rid herself of that distracting image?

Just don't think about it.

She hurried down the stairs in her amazing blue gown, not thinking about the man in the room upstairs.

Not, not, not.

"Was his lordship surprised, Your Highness?" Mrs. Tweeg asked, from the base of the stairs.

"Surprised?" *Not half as much as I was.* "Let's just say that he'll wear the costume, though not happily."

Caro went to the library and gathered up her traveling journal—she was certain that Swanbrook was harboring a Vermeer portrait that once hung in her mother's sitting room, made sure that she had a silken favor to bestow upon the knight who would be representing Boratania in the lists.

And by the time she returned to the foyer, Tweeg was standing at the bottom of the stairs, preening in her whimple, with Runson and Mr. Mackenzie, looking up at something on the landing.

Caro knew exactly whom she would find at the top of the stairs, and in what mood.

Thunderous.

But he was splendid!

Breathtaking!

Her very own Green Knight, clad in his fine tunic and very, very well fitted britches, the hem of his long cape trailing behind on the marble stairs.

And, oh, the afterimage of his nakedness:

Bronze and glistening.

The corded muscles of his thighs shifting as powerfully as they were now as he continued down the stairs, glaring daggers at her.

And at his operatives, who stood red-cheeked and wide-eyed as though on the brink of breaking into laughter.

"Don't even think it," he said to the entire group as he strode past them toward the door. "Come, Princess. Let's get this damned thing over with."

Chapter 11

"Were you aware, Lord Wexford, that this is the first tilting tournament since the one at Eglinton in 1839?"

"That's because, Your Highness," Drew muttered through clenched teeth from his post just behind his eager princess in the grossly gothic grandstand pavilion, "it turned out to be the biggest disaster ever conceived. Three days of rain, a hundred thousand people in attendance. It's no wonder why it's taken so long to mount another."

"Don't be such a spoilsport, my lord." The woman smiled broadly and sat forward as she looked out over the colorful field of tents and banners, the well-groomed lists. "The sky is as big and blue as the sea, the breeze is cool, and I've never seen so many people having so much fun in my life."

A sinister detail that had caused him to post two rings of his operatives around her today, costumed quickly from the wardrobes of the Factory and not.

Nearly thirty men, alert to any possible threat to the princess.

"Call me unduly cautious, Princess, but Swanbrook and your cousin Prince Albert are tempting fate. Look at them out there: two dozen wild-eyed, undertrained men armed with deadly lances, thundering down the lists on massive horses, charging headlong toward each other with bloodlust in their eyes and sawdust in their brains—"

"Oooooohhhhhh . . . !" The princess jumped to her feet with the rest of the spectators as Bucky Bledsoe was launched backward from his armored horse by Ollie Pierpont's lucky lance.

"Ohhhhh . . . no!" Everyone in the grandstands held their collective breath as Pierpont reeled wildly in the saddle and finally lost his seat as well, crashing to the dusty ground on the opposite side of the list fence.

"Yaaaayyyyyyy!" The crowd whooped and bellowed as both men were hauled to their feet like a pair of metallic crabs and held upright by their erstwhile squires.

"That being the third lance between these two brave knights," the announcer shouted, "the match goes to Sir Pierpont . . . the Steady."

The crowd erupted again as "Steady" Pierpont waved his arm before being led, wobble-legged, off the field.

Pomposity heaped upon pomposity, danger upon needless danger.

At least the Grand Procession had begun and ended without an international incident: his endangered princess resplendent in her medieval finery, riding in the open, atop a greenery garnished wagon, while he and his men walked alongside. She had waved and smiled at the cheering crowd that had lined the meandering path from Swanbrook's enormous house, through the garden, and finally around the inside perimeter of the tournament grounds.

He had only just breathed a sigh of relief when the archers began their demonstrations of skill directly in front of the heavily festooned court of the Queen of the May, not fifty feet from where Caro was sitting with the other Damsels of the Dell.

The absurd tilting tournament had finally begun in earnest in mid-afternoon. And now, two hours later, another pair of knights approached the ladies in the pavilion, both dressed in shiny, undented armor, with gilded helmets, and crowned by feathers.

Alert for trouble, Drew stood up and surveyed the two men and their entourage, though he knew that they had already been vetted at their individual dressing tents by his operatives. Any change in personnel meant a possible new threat.

The herald looked harmless enough in his bumbling with the leather-cuffed pedigree scroll.

"My lady Countess of Swanbrook, Queen of the May, and her beauteous Damsels of the Dell, please allow me the honor of introducing my liege, Sir Ranulf the Fierce, of Upper Wigmoor Street, Mayfair."

"My ladies!" Sir Fierce waved his gaudy helmet in the air and then bowed from atop his steed to the Queen of the May.

But the feathers on his topknot swept across the horse's ears and the huge beast snorted, bucked at the idiot on his back, then stomped around in a small, annoyed circle until one of the squires caught its bridle.

The princess stood up as the next young knight approached the pavilion. But before Drew could stop her, she stepped forward to the railing.

"Princess, stop."

But the hardheaded woman ignored him as he moved in behind her, taking up his post just in front of her chair, pleased to see his protective perimeter of men also adjusting to her foolish movements.

"My dear ladies of the Queen's court," bellowed a second herald, "with utmost pride and all due humility, I announce His Splendidness, Lord Broadsword of Swanbrook, riding today at the pleasure of Princess Caroline Marguerite Marie Isabella of Boratania."

A roar of approval rose up along the grandstand, and then another when she waved expansively at the crowd with a blue-and-gold square of silk.

"It would please me greatly, Lord Broadsword of Swanbrook, if you would carry my token into battle." She leaned deeply over the railing, startling Drew.

Bloody hell! He nearly dove after her before realizing that she was merely beckoning to the young knight on the dancing palfrey.

The apple-cheeked young man trotted forward on his horse and bowed with a flourish, grinning like a loon at all that beauty focused on him.

"With every fiber of my being, Princess Caroline." He reached out and took the silk token from her, put it to his nose and sniffed, before he tucked it into his sleeve. "And in the name of your beloved Boratania!"

The rascal boy. Swanbrook had obviously schooled his son in the art of the tournament, and the countess was beaming at her son from her ornate throne.

The three lances were run blessedly quickly. Two misses by both charging knights, and then the young Swanbrook's deft clout to the middle of Ranulf the "Farce's" chest, which sent the man pitching off his horse and the crowd roaring to its feet.

"Bravo, Sir Knight! Bravo!" Caroline shouted over her own applause as Swanbrook took his bows. "Wasn't he wonderful, Lord Wexford!"

"The boy's alive, Princess," Drew murmured, out of the countess's hearing, "I'll give him that."

She raised that brow and then a smile. "Aren't you glad I insisted that you wear a costume? You'd look completely out of place if you hadn't."

So would his operatives, he realized now. They had complained bitterly at having to wear doublets and hose and choking little capes, but they would have stood out in their mid-century caps and coats and neck cloths.

"I'll remember you endlessly, for this little caper alone, madam."

That only made her smile grow brighter. "Then my work is done, my lord."

"Ah, there you are again, Princess!" He knew that grating voice as he knew an alley full of battling tomcats.

"And you, Prince Malcomb!" Drew caught Caro's eye-rolling glance as the densely dressed royal shoved his way up the stairs and into the pavilion, three bright red ostrich feathers bobbing from his slouching Elizabethan cap, an open bottle of wine in one hand, a wide-eyed young woman on his arm.

"How goes the tilting, madam?" Malcomb bellowed forth as he dropped into the chair beside hers, ignoring Drew, letting his bewildered female companion find a place to stand on her own at the back of the box.

"A win for Boratania. Lady Swanbrook kindly lent me her son as my champion."

"A pleasure, my dear princess." The Queen of the May was still beaming. "I'm so proud of my boy."

Malcomb waved a royal hand. "Mark me, Your Highness, I would have joined in the tilting contest myself," he declared for all to hear, "but that would have taken me from your side here in the pavilion, and I could not have abided that."

"I appreciate your thoughtfulness, Prince Malcomb," Caro said as the slithery man bent over and gave her a loud, drunken, smooch on the back of her hand—which nearly brought Drew to his feet. "But I really couldn't have asked for a better champion than Lord Broadsword of Swanbrook."

"Perhaps next time, Your Highness." The oaf looked up from her hand and wriggled his kohl-darkened brows at her. "At our marriage celebration, eh?"

Drew readied his fists for the prince's jaw, but kept them to himself as Caro pulled her hand expertly out of the man's grip and stood up.

"Now, Malcomb, that would be leaping a bit ahead of ourselves, wouldn't it?" She looked up at Drew over the top of the prince's feathered hat and nodded almost imperceptibly toward the stairs.

Well. Could Her Highness, the self-reliant princess, actually be asking for his aid?

"Your pardon, Princess Caroline," Drew said, keeping his smile to himself as he wedged his body squarely between Caro and the prince. "But haven't you promised to meet Lord Peverel about Boratania's new library?"

She put her fingers to her lips in surprise. "Dear me, is it that late, Lord Wexford? Then if you'll please excuse me, Lady Swanbrook, Prince Malcomb . . ."

Caro couldn't stand another moment of Malcomb's boorish blathering. She sped down the stairs into the main aisle, with Drew thankfully on her heels and at least three of his men filling in around and ahead of her. Mrs. Tweeg hadn't yet returned from the food vendors, but would doubtless deal with Malcomb's vulgarities with her usual efficiency.

The poor man, if he tried.

"Great heavens, Wexford, have you command of an entire army?" She slowed when he placed his broad hand on the small of her back, collecting its astonishing warmth, the simple pressure making her feel far more protected than the sight of his wall of sharpshooters ever could.

"*Better* than an army, Princess," he whispered close to her ear as their progress slowed in the crowd, "my own specially trained force. But they're only as capable as their ability to keep you and your enemies in their sights."

Caro heard most of his words, something about his army and her enemies, but he had such an overwhelming presence that all she could really think about was how fine he looked in green brocade, and how broad his shoulders were.

And how natural it seemed that he would be her unwavering protector.

That he was so willing to give his life for her. She

remembered that only too well, and it had begun to worry her, because his chest was such a broad, warm target.

And she'd felt the strong beating of his pulse in his hand.

"I do try to behave myself, my lord."

"Then where are you off to now, Princess? The appointment with Peverel was just a ruse to extricate you from the prince's clutches."

"For which I shall be forever grateful to you, my lord Wexford." She stopped and turned to him, not wishing to shout. "But I'm off to the ladies' comfort pavilion. You see, I really *did* need to take a break. An . . . um . . . a private break, if you please, and I haven't time to wait for Mrs. Tweeg."

He caught her arm before she could hurry away. "If you should need help, just shout for it. I'll be waiting just outside the door when you're . . . um, well, finished."

"Yes, yes." Feeling as closely watched over as a three-minute egg, Caro wound her way through the crowd toward the ladies' comfort pavilion surrounded by Wexford and his agents.

She smiled at the two chambermaids as they pulled aside the canvas drape and then she slipped through the doorway into the warren of masking curtains, needing all the privacy she could find.

The pavilion hadn't any roof, was open to the bright blue sky, and had been built in the midst of the garden with the huge swan fountain at its center. There were umbrellas and chairs, settees to rest upon, maids to touch up one's hair, cups of wine and cool water.

She found a cubicle, finished quickly and was just

accepting a hand towel from a maid when she heard her name called and a familiar giggle.

"Don't you look just magnificent, Princess Caroline!" Lucie crooned and took Caro's hand, giving her gown a quick scan. "You're the absolute sensation of the tournament, isn't she, Sylvia?"

"You are that, Princess!" Sylvia grinned and grabbed Caro's other hand. "You've stolen the eye of every man, on the field and off."

Lucie giggled again. "Especially that big, handsome Earl of Wexford, who's never more than two strides behind you. The same one from the ball!"

Oh, dear. If Lucie noticed, then surely others might have . . . and wouldn't that be quite the scandal! But better a scandal than the truth about Drew's real purpose. And a perfect bit of cover for them.

Caro rolled her eyes in a great drama. "He's really been a pest, ladies. He's advising me on my waterway treaties and border surveys, and oh, what a bore he is on the subject!"

Sylvia clucked her tongue and winked. "But you certainly can't fault the view, Princess."

"No you can't, Sylvia." *But oh, my, if you only knew the view I had of the luscious man this morning.*

It was still with her, bronze and shimmering.

Her face began to flame with the memory, her fingers tingling at the thought of touching him.

"Well, yes, ladies, I must be going"—she gave each a hug and a kiss on the cheek—"else the man will surely launch into another of his endless theories on canal traffic versus railways."

Their good-byes took a few minutes, and then the pair went flying off toward the comfort cubicles themselves.

Caroline turned to leave, but in the labyrinth of canvas she suddenly found she had no idea which opening she'd arrived through.

But she wasn't about to shout for Wexford to come rescue her. She was a grown woman and could find her way out on her own, thank you very much.

Besides which, what an everlasting scandal to have Wexford come racing through the ladies' pavilion like a desert sheik come to add women to his harem.

Simply impossible to imagine.

So she went west. Always a lucky direction for her.

And great heavens, it couldn't possibly have been more lucky.

The St. Timmin's Cloister bell! As well as its great brass yoke. Stolen from the abbey in Boratania within a week of her father's death. Here it was, in the far corner of the garden, standing as an ornament in a patch of Swanbrook's yellow pansies.

She ran to it, took out a pencil from her belt purse, unfolded her ever-ready sheet of vellum and began to draw the details, noting its measurements, its hallmarks, taking a rubbing of the delicate filagree on the yoke.

Wanting to be sure that she'd gotten enough of the details to make a positive identification once she checked her resources, she raised up the drawing in front of her face and adjusted it side to side with both hands and moved backward down the cobbled path until the proportions of the drawing matched the actual size of the bell.

"Good enough, I think." She gave the design one last blinking scan, then lowered the drawing.

But instead of finding the St. Timmin's bell and the

bed of pansies and the boxwood hedge in front of her, she found a sea of men's faces.

Elderly faces, mostly. A half dozen pairs of eyes staring back at her in wide-mouthed surprise.

"Your Highness!"

"Princess Caroline!"

"Boratania's own!"

And then these same six men clapped their hands to their hearts, fell to their knees and began singing,

"Hail, hail Boratania!
Guided from above.
Mist-strewn hills
Rocky rills,
Dear kingdom that I love—"

"Wait, wait, stop!" Stunned nearly speechless, Caro waved her hands at the three men kneeling directly in front of her. "Please, stop!"

The anthem faded and the bearded man in front of her stood tentatively.

"As you wish, Your Highness. Sorry if we offended, we were just overcome by—"

"May I ask . . . Who are you, please?"

The group shared a few shy glances at one another, then a second man stood with a groan and bowed.

"My name is Karl Brendel, and these other men, Caroline Marguerite Marie Isabella, Princess and Empress-elect of Boratania, are your loyal subjects."

Subjects? But she didn't have subjects.

A third man stood on shaky legs and revealed a very plain-looking sword, his eyes worried as he spoke, "Wilhelm Belvedere, Your Highness. We have come to pledge to you our steadfast hearts, our hallowed honor and our strongest swords."

Come from where? she wanted to ask, but they all seemed so intent.

The men smiled broadly at her and nodded eagerly as Wilhelm raised the old, well-used sword into the air in what might have been a highly charming salute, but just as he was tilting t he handle in her direction, she heard her name bellowed from behind her.

"Head down, Princess!"

And then a scrambling scuffle to her right, and poor Wilhelm went flying along the cobbles, landing in the bed of pansies with a man straddling his chest.

"No!"

But before Caro could rescue Wilhelm, she was scooped up, enfolded and was being carried away from the melee in a very familiar pair of arms.

"What the devil are you doing, Wexford!" Caro kicked at him with her feet, but found nothing but air.

"Now are you satisfied, Princess?" He jounced her as he stalked along the cobbles.

"Satisfied that you are a lunatic! Release me!" Caro smacked at his shoulder, but he just kept walking.

"See what happens, Princess? I leave you alone for a moment and—Owww! Damnation!"

"Are you mad, Wexford?" Caro gave another twist to the lean muscle at his waist and the beast finally set her on her feet against the back of a hat vendor's wagon.

"In case you hadn't realized it, Princess Caroline, that old man was about to ceremonially separate your pretty little head from your shoulders."

"No, he wasn't, Wexford, you big lout! That nice

man had just pledged his undying fealty to me and was offering me his sword."

"I know what I saw." Wexford was hunkering over her like a branching oak.

"And I know what I heard." Caro stabbed her finger toward the group of men cowering near the bell, surrounded by Wexford's agents. "Those people are my loyal subjects!"

"Your subjects?" He straightened.

"And you just struck one of them to the ground. An elderly one at that. I ought to have you clapped in irons. However, if you'll excuse me, I need to go make amends." Caro ducked under his arm but the man caught her again and spun her.

"You're not going anywhere, Princess, until I tell you it's safe."

"My subjects are waiting, Wexford." She pulled away from him, but he followed and stopped her with the towering bulk of his body.

"When did you meet these so-called subjects?"

"About three minutes ago. They seemed very nice. And since they happen to be my only subjects, I'd better do something to prove to them that I will protect them from tyrants and bullies like you and your agents, or they might find someone else to honor."

"Three minutes ago?" He was still blocking her way like a mountain range. "You let a half dozen men approach you all at one time without a thought to their motive?"

"I didn't have a choice, Wexford. They just appeared before me out of thin air."

"And that seemed perfectly reasonable to you, madam? Utter strangers appearing out of nowhere to pay homage to you?"

"They're not strangers—"

"Princess Caroline!" Wilhelm was waving at her, straining against the agent's hand clamped down on his shoulder. "Are you all right?"

"I'm fine, Wilhelm. Now, let me go, Wexford." She managed to finally drag her warden back to her worried-looking subjects and went to Wilhelm's side. "How about you? Have you broken anything?"

"Not even a scratch, Princess Caroline." Though the man had just been rubbing his shoulder.

"I'm so sorry, Wilhelm." She checked the same shoulder, but found nothing broken. "These men are here to protect me, and they didn't understand what—"

Another man joined Wilhelm. "But we understand completely, Your Highness. They were only doing their jobs, as they just told us. And very well, I might add. Any one of us would give our life to protect you from harm."

Too many people seemed willing to throw themselves in front of the nearest train for her.

She glanced up at Wexford and his glowering frown. "I'm sure that won't be necessary." She took the man's thin leathery hand. "Your name, sir?"

He shuffled and shied like an old plow horse. "My name is Erasmus Uechersbach, Your Highness."

"Well, Mr. Uechersbach, I'm most grateful and honored by your pledge."

"We would have contacted you sooner," Erasmus said, swallowing hard, "but . . . well, it wouldn't have made any difference until now."

"And you surely didn't need to be burdened with the lot of us," added Wilhelm.

"Believe me, you're no burden to me." So this was

what it was like to have her own people. "But if you are my subjects, where have you been all this time?"

She heard Wexford muttering behind her, doubtless scowling at the men like a thunderstorm.

Another man stepped forward, older, but of thick-muscled peasant stock. "Johannes Halstedt, Princess. I was your father's equerry, as my father was before me."

"How truly wonderful!" Caro swallowed back a lump in her throat. "I have so many things to ask you."

"Ask anything you wish of me, Your Highness." He bowed again. "Though I've been living away from Boratania for a very long time."

Wilhelm patted the man on the back. "It was best that Johannes leave the kingdom after it fell. He was wounded while defending Tovaranche castle alongside your father, and he wasn't welcomed by the new regime."

Her father. Her family! "Then you're a true hero, Johannes, and you're very welcome by me. A most loyal subject, to be sure."

"Come, come, I wasn't the only man among us to help your family, Princess Caroline. Each of us here has a similar tale. Wilhelm was one of your father's generals, Erasmus was the master of the hounds—"

"I've kept his favorite lines intact, Your Highness, wolfhounds and mastiffs."

Her father's hounds! She had all their papers!

"Karl was ambassador to Prussia—"

"Though a lot of good that did us in the end, Your Highness."

"Marcus was your mother's favorite gardener, and Gunnar here was the court composer—"

"Your music, sir!" she said, as thrilled as though she'd found her family, "I have much of it catalogued at Grandauer Hall! You must come look through it."

"You found my music?" The old man's eyes glistened with tears beneath his shaggy eyebrows. "Oh, my dear Princess Caroline, I . . . well, we've been waiting more than twenty years for you. Waiting and hoping."

Karl clasped Gunnar around the shoulder. "And now that you're about to regain some of Boratania, Your Highness, we thought—"

"Just a small piece of it," she said, never realizing before just how small ten square miles would be. How would she feed these few people? And what about their families? And the people who already live there?

"In any case, Your Highness," Johannes said, "that's why we've come all the way to London. To share in the great, historical celebration."

Wilhelm had been looking up at Wexford, his old eyes wary and shy. "So we'd best be going now. You've got this fine tournament to attend, and we had promised each other not to be a bother to you."

She grabbed Wilhelm's bone-thin hand. "But you're not a bother at all. You couldn't be!" They were like family! After all this time she'd spent alone. "In fact, you've come at the perfect time to help me get ready for the exhibition. Imagine that, Wexford!"

But Drew was still frowning, his arms crossed over his chest. "Indeed, Princess."

"Oh, pinch me for a fool, men!" Johannes said, slapping his thigh. "We've even brought something for you. Besides the sword, of course."

The men began to murmur in happy anticipation

among themselves. Wexford's agents had stepped back to the edge of the melee and now they moved forward again while Marcus laid a long, rectangular crate at her feet.

Wexford himself moved in beside her, as though he suspected the box might contain a ticking bomb.

"For you, Your Highness. In memory of Boratania, the way it used to be." Johannes unlocked the latch and opened the lid while Marcus lifted out the excelsior to reveal a shiny brass beehive-shaped object, about a foot in diameter. Attached to the top of the hive was a three-foot-long brass pole and on top of that, five swarming honeybees.

The two men lifted it carefully out of its nest and held it upright in front of Caro.

Caro blinked at it, at a memory of something she'd only seen in etchings. And then her eyes filled with tears that spilled over and onto her hands.

"Great heavens! It's the Tovaranche spire! Where did you find it?"

The men looked at one another knowingly and smiled as though she'd just passed an exacting test, and then Johannes said, with an even larger smile, "It was rescued by the late Lord Minorhoff from the looters the night your parents died. And kept by his good wife until just last month."

Caro traced her fingers along the polished ridges of the hive, amazed at the smoothness, trying not to weep. "I'm so grateful to you all. I thought it was gone for good."

"There isn't much left of the old world, Princess Caroline, but you have the time to start over again."

Starting over again suddenly seemed very important. For her family. For her subjects.

"I think you'll be pleasantly surprised at what all I've recovered, Wilhelm." She touched the spire again, wondering if she should include it in the exhibition. Or was it too precious to put on display?

"You've been most wonderful to receive us without notice, Your Highness."

Which gave her the best idea she'd had in a long while. "Where are you lodged, Johannes?"

The man began to stammer. "Well, we're at the Sip and Whistle tavern. That is to say, Your Highness, we've not really been in town long enough to arrange for suitable rooms as yet, but—"

"Then don't, Johannes."

"What do you mean, Princess Caroline?"

"I have the perfect solution to both our situations."

No, Princess, don't!

But hell and damnation, she did it anyway! And Drew realized the woman's unacceptable intentions too late to stop her, and could only listen in horror as she announced her invitation to her little group of potential assassins.

"You'll come stay at Grandauer Hall for as long as you need to. All of you. As my guests."

Drew bent to her and whispered into her ear. "That's not possible, Princess."

"Don't be absurd, Wexford." She jabbed a pointed elbow into his ribs. "There's room at Grandauer to sleep a hundred guests."

"I can't have them underfoot." Though to a man they looked harmless enough, elderly and dewy-eyed as they took in every movement the woman made.

"I promise you won't even see them. And they can help me enormously with the exhibition, relieving your own men and speeding up the process. How can you possibly object?"

Bloody hell, he could spend the next week objecting, but he doubted she'd listen to a word of it, unless and until one of them came at her with another ceremonial sword.

And there was something else that troubled him more deeply. These men, if they were truly from her father's scattered court, doubtless held vast secrets that she should never hear.

One of the clues had revealed itself moments ago, but she hadn't caught its meaning.

And now she was happily chattering with them, asking more questions, listening raptly, giving them directions to Grandauer Hall: "But only two hours out of London, gentlemen! You must come!"

"Sorry, Wexford, she got away from us." One of his operatives, Davidson, came to stand beside him, looking more than a little uncomfortable in his jester's costume.

"And me, Davidson. Which makes me even more suspicious of these faithful Boratanians. You heard their names and where they are staying. Stop off at the Factory and spare nothing. And do make it fast."

Davidson was studying the motley group of men. "Don't look much like assassins, do they?"

"I doubt that Guy Fawkes did either. Bring me any information you can find on the lot of them, how they got here, where they were this morning, where they've spent the last twenty years. Including any mention of Boratania itself. Anything from any source."

It took another fifteen minutes before the princess had sent off her new subjects in a proper carriage, and only after a promise from them that they would arrive at Grandauer Hall as soon as they could pack up their belongings.

"They won't be able to come to the Hall before tomorrow, Wexford."

"I can't say that I'm disappointed. But I can say that you are completely mad, madam!"

"It's a change in plans, that's all. You don't like change of any kind, do you?"

"You lied to me, Princess."

"When?"

"I let you go alone into the ladies' pavilion only after you promised to come right back out the same door—"

"I tried! Have you ever been in there?"

"As a matter of fact, I had to . . . Dammit, woman, someone hit me on the head with a teapot before I'd gotten three feet inside." His head still ached from it.

"You deserved a good clonking if you went barging in. And I didn't try to escape you. I merely couldn't find my original point of entry, so I picked an exit and left."

"And then what? Ten minutes later I find you gallivanting around the garden, unprotected, with a group of strangers who—"

"And look what I found," she said, throwing her arm toward the large bell on its stand, "merely by chance! It's from St. Timmin's abbey."

Of course it was. "At the risk of repeating myself, Princess, you're a bloody lunatic."

She lifted her bright eyes to him. "But at least now I'm a lunatic with loyal subjects."

"Well, then, shall we take it with us?" Drew made a show of trying to pull the bell post out of the ground.

"Don't be silly. I'll send someone for it."

"Under dark of night."

"That'll cause the least embarrassment for old Swanbrook." She grinned at him as she laughed, with the sun glistening on her lips and the tip of her nose. "Come, my lord. We'd best get back to the tournament."

"That eager to see the prince again?"

"Royal sacrifice in the name of my new subjects, Andrew." She started off along the cobbles in her ususal haste. "After all, I really ought to be there in time for the tilting awards to be announced."

She dodged vendors and barkers, and yet the small children seemed to know that she would dance a little jig with them and pull waxed-paper-wrapped candies from her purse.

It was like following a piper.

"Have a care, madam!" he said, finally catching up to her antics.

"I'm sorry, Drew, but the children are just too precious to ignore. And I doubt any of them are armed with a shiv. Oh, look, it's Lord Peverel, standing near the knight marshal's booth. He seems a bit pale for such a bright afternoon."

"Gad, and I thought *my* costume was overdone." The poor man was talking with one of the squires, his shoulders weighed down by a burgundy cape with heavy gold braiding.

"Good day, Lord Peverel!" Caroline said with a nod to the man as they passed him.

"What? Oh, Princess Caroline!" Peverel's face did seem paler than before, his eyes flitting from Drew to the princess and back again as the squire bowed and left them.

Caroline took Peverel's hand, her gaze taking in every inch of the man's face. "Are you feeling all right, my lord?"

"Oh, yes, yes, yes! I'll be fine. Just a long day for an old man, you know." He smiled wanly. "But you're looking more beautiful than ever, my dear princess. Always such a boon to my old eyes. Do enjoy yourself today, madam. And you, Lord Wexford."

The man dropped his gaze to the ground and hobbled off through the crowd.

"I don't like leaving him, Drew," she said as they started up the stairs into the queen's pavilion. "I hope he's not taken on too much as my acting chancellor."

"I'll ask around about his health. Palmerston might know if the man's in trouble."

"I do need him to help form my government, Drew, but not at the risk of his health."

Fortunately, Prince Malcomb had taken his obnoxious party elsewhere, lifting the tone of the rest of the contest.

The presence of the Princess Caroline seemed to be the highlight of the Grand Pavilion. Drew could only stand back and admire her endless energy and her kindness.

And hope to God that no one would ever take her dreams from her.

Chapter 12

After the tournament and the fancy-dress ball that followed, it had taken Drew a full hour to disentangle the princess from her devotees, load her and the exhausted Tweeg into his carriage and start it rolling down the road.

"See, Drew, it was a wonderful day, without a single incident."

"I'll leave my conclusions until after my operatives can report back to me about what they saw." He unhooked his damnable cape and laid it aside.

She leaned back against the seat beside the already snoozing Tweeg and eyed him across the darkness. "It must be awful to be constantly on the lookout for villains behind every bush and pillar."

"If only villains were that cooperative, madam." Then he wouldn't have this gnawing in the pit of his stomach. "By the way, I think you should know that I sent Davidson and Grant to check on the credentials of your so-called subjects."

"I would have thought you'd lost your edge if you hadn't, my lord. And if you hadn't assigned a carriage full of your agents to travel ahead of us right now as well as the one following behind us." She laughed lightly, and leaned back against the small window. "But you won't find anything untoward. I can tell a good and true man from a bad one just by looking closely enough."

"No, you can't."

"Take *you* for instance."

"Leave me out of your game, Princess." And yet he did want to know her opinion of him.

"You're a good and true man, Drew."

Well, then. Now that's a damn fine thing to know. Though he kept his smile inside his chest. "That's scant praise from a lunatic princess."

"With loyal subjects."

"I keep forgetting."

She beamed him a dazzling smile, which caught the edge of the moonlight on the window. "I know what I feel, and I can feel that you haven't a dishonest bone in your body, any more than my subjects do."

If only she knew all the truths that he knew about her. "Dangerous assumptions, my dear princess."

"Don't think you can hide it from me under all that stalking and blustering. You're just the sort who—"

"Shhh, Caro!" Drew leaned forward to listen. The carriage's gentle turn became a sideways jerk, and then it slowed to a halt.

"I don't like this, Princess." Drew shot to his feet and shoved her away from the door into Tweeg, who had snapped to attention. "Stay down. Both of you."

"Drew—"

"What is it, sir?" Tweeg asked, blocking Caro's body with her own.

"Shhh . . ." He felt one of his guards drop from the roof to the ground, heard the doors of the other carriages open just as the warning bell jangled above his head, a signal from the driver's seat.

"That's the driver." He twisted down to her, taking her chin between his fingers. "And this, Princess, isn't a practice drill. Stay with Tweeg."

A bad feeling roiling in his gut, Drew slowly opened the little window to the driver's cab, saw Casserly drop from the roof of the carriage in front of them.

"What is it, Henry?" Drew asked their driver.

Henry sat still in the seat, his eyes flicking over the dense understory. "Looks like someone's dropped a tree in the lane ahead of the front carriage, sir. Not a natural fall, it's been chopped. I saw Trevor head toward the—"

Before Henry could speak another word, a bullet smacked into the carriage wall just above the window.

"Down, Henry!"

Another blast, and then Henry's bellowed curse. "Damnation! My . . . arm."

"Stay put, Princess!" Knowing that Tweeg would keep her inside, Drew threw himself out the door, staying low as he dragged Henry out of the driver's seat, then began struggling to haul him to the carriage steps. "Hold on, man."

Another blast against the sidewall, and then Nicholas shouted from the roof of the carriage. "To the left, Casserly!"

In the next instant, Drew heard a half dozen shots fired into the brush from the two other carriages.

Stark silence followed the deafening roar. Drew could only hope for the best as he propped the struggling Henry against the steps.

"Lemme at 'em, sir!" the man said.

"Quiet, Henry."

"What's happening out there, Mrs. Tweeg?" The princess's timing was as regal as ever, but at least the sound of her voice meant that she hadn't taken a bullet.

"We got him, sir!" Trevor called from somewhere deep in the thicket. "Dead."

Henry was cursing a blue streak. "A bloody ambush, sir! Caught like rats, damn their eyes."

"And you'll live to curse again, Henry. But you're riding inside."

"I'm all right."

"You're not." Drew looked up to see Trevor stomping out of the woods with a few others, their medieval garb incongruous with the modern guns they carried.

"You'll have to get us out of here quickly, Trevor. Tell Nicholas to have the body taken back to the Factory. Halladay and Wyatt can stay and investigate the shooter's blind."

"Henry's been shot!" the princess said, her head popping up from over Tweeg's shoulder.

"We need to get Henry to Grandauer. Tweeg, you get up front to cover the driver. Quickly!" Drew and Trevor had to wrestle Henry into the carriage.

"Sorry, Princess Caroline." Henry flopped back against the seat and pulled off his hat. "I'm bleeding all over the upholstery."

"Dash the upholstery!" She wedged herself onto the seat beside him. "We'll do something about this, Mr. Henry."

"Ah, I don't need anything."

"Ballocks!"

"We're a mile from Grandauer Hall," Drew said, as the carriage bolted down the lane behind their escort.

He took a careful look at Henry's face for signs of shock. But the man was a tough old bird and the princess seemed in her element.

"You'll have to stop squirming, Mr. Henry, or you'll lose even more blood." Caro was already tearing at the hem of her petticoat, ripping a small gash in the silk with her teeth. "Was that a highwayman, Drew?"

"He was waiting for us."

"You mean waiting for *me*," she said, gazing up at him directly as she ripped the petticoat with a tug. "Just as you said: like a duck in a shooting gallery."

That was coldly sobering realization he saw glittering brightly in her eyes—that her own carriage wouldn't have held up under the assault. "Indeed, Princess."

"Can you hold up Mr. Henry's arm for me, Drew? Carefully." Though the carriage wheels jolted them along the rutted road, she gently moved the man's shoulder and positioned his arm.

"That's a hell of a princess you got there, boss." Henry twisted woozily in the seat and gazed with moon-eyes at the woman.

Indeed she was. Quite remarkable for a princess.

For anyone.

"Then sit still for her, Henry," Drew said, supporting the man's arm with both hands while the princess adjusted the bloody sleeve.

"This might hurt a bit, Mr. Henry."

But the man just kept grinning at her as she

wrapped the expensive silk ruffle around the wound.

She was a singular wonder, this royal, with her concern for Henry and her quick thinking and her uncharacteristic disregard for her wardrobe, after all that cooing about Vincent's fine designs.

Caro tried to still her heart from its racing. She'd never before felt death snapping at her heels.

Or been a terrifying threat to the people around her, to poor Mr. Henry, who'd merely been driving her home from a silly tournament.

And Drew, who stood fiercely over both of them, supporting himself with his arms and legs, watching for trouble through one window and then the other.

"We're here, Princess." A moment later they were pulling through Grandauer's portecochere, then around to the side entrance.

Wexford was out of the carriage and directing his staff in all directions.

"Henry's caught a bullet in his arm, Brunson," he said, easily hoisting Henry out of the carriage. "I'll take him downstairs. Go get Wheeler."

Feeling utterly helpless, Caro caught up with Drew as he supported Henry into the house and down the stairs to the butler's quarters.

"I've had no experience with bullet wounds," she said, holding open the door to the butler's pantry, "but I've got a good stock of—"

"Not to worry, Princess," Wexford said as he hefted Henry onto a daybed. "Wheeler was a battlefield surgeon; he knows all about bullet wounds. He's saved my hide a few times."

"Wheeler!" Henry shouted as he struggled to sit up. "Not that old barber!"

"Stop your thrashing, Henry," Drew said, easily pinning him back against the bed while he glanced up at Caro with serious eyes. "Shock, I think."

"All right, everyone out of here!" Wheeler had come through the doorway like a general, his tone and manner far different from the easy-natured man who'd helped her load the wagons a few days ago.

"He's lost some blood," Caro said, bending over the wound alongside Wheeler, "but not a dreadful amount."

"Good to hear, Princess Caroline. Now leave."

"If you need medicine or bandages, there's a cupboard full in the pantry."

"We'll be fine here."

"Come, Princess." Drew had her by the upper arm and was tugging her out into the corridor.

"I should stay and help." She tried to stop him, but he merely tucked her hand into the crook of his elbow.

"Wheeler does his best work alone and with cannonballs flying over his head."

"But, great heavens, it's all my fault." She hurried along, trying to match Drew's determined stride.

"What's your fault?"

"That! What happened to Henry! If it weren't for me, he wouldn't have been shot."

Drew laughed but kept walking toward the main stairs as though on a mission. "How do you figure that?"

"You warned me that I was in real danger."

"You can be a bit reckless, Princess. But you seemed to understand well enough."

"But I didn't, Drew. Not really, not deep down inside where it counts." She stopped him at the bottom of the stairs, held fast to his elbow, a little dizzy from the horror of it all. "Breaking into the library was nothing compared to this! Henry was nearly killed today, on my account!"

"My operatives know the risks."

Drew seemed so unconcerned about the danger.

"But it could have been you. Or Tweeg or any one of my subjects who happened to be standing near me. I can't just stand around and let that happen again."

He studied her with a half smile. "I don't know about you, Princess, but I'm going to bed."

"Just like that, Drew? After you've been shot at?" Her own blood was aboil and his seemed as cool as a deep mountain spring.

"It's well after midnight, and we both look as though we've fought the battle of Agincourt."

Caro looked down the front of her gown, which had been so grandly medieval that morning. She'd added streaks of dear Mr. Henry's blood to the lace, and had shredded her hem.

Drew didn't look much cleaner, with his knees muddied and his sleeve torn.

"But what about the investigation? The evidence?"

"It'll keep till morning. Now, if you'll excuse me, I want to check on something in the investigation room and then I plan to sleep for a few hours." He touched his forehead with the tip of his finger, then climbed the stairs.

"Drew?" she called to him, feeling a little set adrift by his departure, wanting to go with him but knowing that he was probably better off on his own just now.

He stopped and turned, his studied patience as clear as his weariness. "Yes?"

"I wanted to . . . well, to thank you. For putting up

with my . . . stubbornness. After all, you must have far better things to do in your work than to be playing nanny to me, watching my every move."

He took a long breath and then sighed. "You're not the worst royal I've ever had to watch, Princess. Not by any stretch."

She wondered what he meant by that. And if he could possibly hear her heart bounding around inside her chest. "Still . . . thank you for saving my life . . . again."

"My pleasure, Princess."

She was pretty sure the pleasure must be all hers. Especially as she watched him continue up the stairs. All shifting muscle and confidence.

And clearly ready to die for her, for his loyal agents, for his queen.

What a fine man. Such an easy heart to love.

Not that she did. Or could ever.

Gratitude would have to do.

But she couldn't go to bed without checking on Henry herself. She ducked back into the sickroom and was pleased to see his wound for herself, clean and already well stanched by Wheeler's skills.

"The bullet took a healthy chunk out of his arm," Wheeler said as he applied a poultice and began to wrap it with a strip of bandage.

"But he'll be all right?"

Henry stirred and laughed at something in his laudanum-induced sleep.

"Don't give him another thought, Princess Caroline. I've known Henry a long time. He's taken far worse than this and lived to tell the tale."

They were such an extraordinary group, Drew's

band of agents. Men and women, young and old, a family of sorts.

"From what I hear, Mr. Wheeler, you've extracted a bullet or two from the earl himself."

"Three, if I recall. From various parts of the man."

Which made her recall the dark scar she'd seen on Drew's bare shoulder that morning.

Which made her recall the rest of him.

All the rest of him.

"That's not very lucky of him, Mr. Wheeler."

"He's lucky as a dozen cats, Your Highness. Though when his lordship is focused on an assignment he doesn't give much thought to his own safety." Wheeler winked at her, then went back to his close work.

"I'll definitely keep that in mind, Mr. Wheeler. And in the meantime, please let me know how Henry is doing, or if he takes a turn."

Reassured by Wheeler's confidence in Drew's luck and his own healing skills, Caro started toward the back stairs and her chamber, but then changed her mind and hurried toward the library, past the low voices coming from the investigation room.

Because it was high time she started helping Drew investigate who might be trying to kill her.

Whoever they were, they couldn't hit the broad side of a barn.

And why not start at the very beginning of her life? The library, with all its stockpiles of Boratanian documents, was the perfect place to begin her search.

At the very beginning. With her parents. Her grandparents, if she could find out anything more of them.

Knowing just what to take, Caro grabbed the long

leather case that held the family tree and went up the stairs to her chamber.

But as she changed out of her much-abused velvet gown and into her linen nightgown and her favorite silk robe, something began to niggle at the back of her brain.

Something she'd heard recently.

Today at the tournament, in the Grand Pavilion.

Or in the garden.

The sky was so blue then.

And there was the abbey bell standing amongst the pansies.

And the spire, glistening gold in the sunlight.

Marcus had been holding it.

And Johannes.

Yes, it was something Johannes had said. An off-hand remark that she'd clearly heard, but since it hadn't made sense at the time, she'd dismissed it.

The late Lord Minorhoff. Something grand he'd done for her father.

No, that wasn't it. But so close.

Her parents?

Of course! Lord Minorhoff had rescued the spire from the looters!

The night your parents died.

"My parents?" A funny thing to say, because they hadn't died the same night. Or even in the same country.

But twenty years was a long time ago.

And Johannes was old, doubtless easily confused about things that had happened far in the past.

Facts easily fell out of sequence, became generalized, one legend eventually merging with another and becoming an altogether new tale.

She was making too much of Johannes's rambling.

No, it was time go back to the beginning, and before that.

She unbuckled the strap around the long, ornately embossed leather case that had protected her family tree for time out of mind.

The thick parchment had been folded centuries ago like an intricate puzzle by some monk with too much time on his hands, with this corner tucked behind that edge, leaving Caro to wrestle with each crease and pleat. The stubborn chart grew larger and larger until it reached its full four-foot-by-eight-foot size, revealing the beautifully illuminated emblems of heraldry, the finely scripted names and titles, important dates, and the web of lines and curves that intersected so many lives.

She unhooked two landscapes from the picture rail and hung her family tree by its integral iron grommets, then stood back and looked at it.

"There I am!" Her name boldly scribed near the bottom, just beneath the connected line of her parents. She'd been added by someone soon after she was born.

"I wonder who?"

Too much to think about tonight.

. . . rescued by the late Lord Minorhoff from the looters the night your parents died.

And there was that oddity.

In the morning. She'd tell Drew about it the moment she saw him. After she'd checked in on Henry.

And read the reports on the shooting that nearly took the man's life.

Becoming an empress was a lot more difficult than she'd ever imagined.

And a lot more dangerous.

She tried not to listen for sounds coming from the chamber next to hers, but couldn't help noticing the silence. She doused the lamps and snuggled into the downy comfort of her own bed.

Her last thought, as she slipped into her dreams, was that the man in the next room looked magnificent in any century.

And that he doubtless hadn't a nightshirt to his name.

The stuff that dreams were built upon.

Chapter 13

"You were there when it happened, your lordship," Trevor said, sliding the last of the report across the table into Drew's hand, "have I got it all down here?"

"I was there all right, Trevor, but I was inside the carriage at first and then didn't see much as I went after Henry." Drew kept his yawn behind his fist as he quickly scanned the page in the pool of lamplight, and then slipped it behind the other pages. "But your story seems to fit exactly with mine, so until you talk to Henry and the others in the morning, let's call this the official report."

The door burst open to Wyatt's never subtle entrance, a rolled bundle under his arm. "Here's our would-be assassin's clothes, your lordship, contents of his pockets intact."

"And I've made a chart of his blind, as well as the roadway and the approaches," Halladay said, dropping his carefully detailed pencil drawing onto the table. "At least as much as I could determine by lamplight. I'll add to it in the morning."

"And the body, Wyatt?" Drew asked as he unrolled the bundle of carefully folded clothes.

"On its nasty way back to the Factory. The bastard. Should have a full report by noon."

"And tomorrow will be soon enough for the rest of it, gentlemen. I don't know about you, but I want out of this miserable costume. And if I never have to see another tilting tournament, it'll still be too soon."

"I did like the fruit pasties, sir," Trevor said, patting his considerable chest. "And the ladies were fine to look at as well. Our princess most of all."

A dazzling iridescence of blue and white and gold.

"Thanks to all of your vigilance and quick thinking, we still have her with us."

An unthinkable loss if he'd failed her.

"Sleep well, gentlemen. I'll have breakfast brought in here at seven, and we can start then."

Unsettled by a growing sense that he was missing a crucial clue, Drew stayed behind to read over the "Princess Files" and to right his thoughts. But his thinking was sadly rattled tonight.

And his tunic had begun to itch.

He climbed the stairs and listened at Caro's chamber door. No sounds at all, no light under her door. She must have fallen asleep.

Doubtless priming herself for tomorrow's battle against her assassin. That's just what he needed right now, the potential victim mounting her own investigation.

This marvelous woman who never did anything halfway.

To ensure his privacy before he bathed, he made

sure that his door was locked and then wedged a chair against the connecting panel.

He slept badly. Chased that bloody Prince Malcomb through a garden fountain; tilted at teapots; took a bullet in his shoulder and a lance in the middle of his chest that sent him backward into a soft, soft place.

A warmth against his face.

The sweet lilt of Caro's voice inside his head, inside his dreams. Alongside his ear like a whisper.

"Just as I suspected," she said.

No, not in his dreams. In his room! Not more than a foot from him.

He kept his eyes closed, fearing the worst of her boldness. "Are you dressed, madam?"

"Of course I am." He felt her leaning closer. "But I don't think you are."

"Damnation!" Drew opened his eyes and reached for the counterpane. It was safely above his waist, though not for long if he didn't move quickly. She was far too close for comfort, and he'd been dreaming of her.

He sat up, knees bent to hide himself, and glared his best at the woman who had somehow found a way into his room despite his best efforts. Like a mountain mist, a ghost slipping through a crack in the molding. "What the devil are you doing in here?"

She hiked herself up onto the edge of the bed. "I knocked, Drew, but you didn't answer."

"I was asleep."

"I know. I could hear you snoring all the way from my room."

"I don't snore."

She laughed and ran her fingers through the hair at

his temple, brushing it back off his forehead. "Then you must have had a great lion in here with you, because I heard such a roaring—"

"What do you want?"

"I want to ask you something." She folded her hands in her lap.

"Couldn't this have waited until breakfast? What time is it?"

"A bit after six in the morning. I was wondering if you heard Johannes say the same thing I did yesterday?"

Christ. She *had* heard.

Drew scrubbed at his face with his palms, wishing it all away. Yet he had to ask. "What was that, Princess?"

"He said that Lord Minorhoff had saved the Tovaranche spire the night my parents died."

Playing dumb was his safest course. "And?"

"Is that what he said? 'The night your parents died.'"

Not knowing where she was going with her logic, he could only shake his head and hope for more information. "I don't know, Caro. Why?"

"Because . . ." She stood and ambled away to the cold hearth, tapping a fingertip against her upper lip. "It's absolutely nothing, really. But it's just an odd thing for him to say, because my parents didn't die on the same night."

"It's been a long time, Caro. Memories become jumbled together."

Or, bloody hell, Johannes was there when they died. The floor seemed to shift below the bed.

"That's what I was thinking, Drew. After all, Johannes must be well into his seventies."

Though the man had seemed sound of mind enough. They all did. And that was the trouble.

"And there's a chance you heard him wrong, Princess. With all the excitement of meeting your subjects and finding the spire."

She nodded. "It was quite a moment, wasn't it?"

"Just leave it be, Caro. You wouldn't want to embarrass Johannes by questioning his memory."

Or learning a truth that would eventually lead to so many others.

"No, no, I wouldn't want to press him. Yes, well, thank you. I guess I'll be leaving now."

"Leaving for where, madam?" Here he was, trapped beneath a counterpane without a stitch of clothing.

She measured her gaze down the length of him as though she had read his mind, and then went to the wide-open panel in the wall. "Oh, I thought I'd stroll on into London."

"Princess!"

"Or maybe just downstairs to check on Henry."

The minx. "Don't coddle the man."

"Henry deserves all the coddling I can give him, my lord. After all, he nearly died for me."

Drew waited for the sound of his wayward princess replacing the swinging bookcase on the other side of the wall before he threw off the bedclothes. He dressed quickly, and just as quickly made it to the investigation room.

The place swarmed with nearly a dozen agents, and smelled deliciously of the huge breakfast Mackenzie had laid out on the sideboard.

"Ah, there you are, sir!" Nicholas met Drew with a heaping plate and obviously an appetite to match.

"The bloody bastard wasn't in our file of local criminals."

"A name?" Drew grabbed a piece of buttered toast from a silver rack on the sideboard.

"Not even a hint."

That would have been too damned simple. "Where's Halladay?"

Nicholas had popped a rasher of thick, pink bacon into his mouth and now chewed through it while he talked. "Took a detail to the site of the ambush at first light. Should be back any min—"

Nicholas had stopped chomping on his bacon and was looking past Drew to the doorway. The whole room had come to a complete stop.

"Good morning, gentlemen," came the low, meadowy-warm voice that had become so fondly familiar.

"G'd morning, Princess . . . Your Highness . . . Majesty . . . madam . . . Well, hello . . . blast—" and every other possible greeting from a dozen different men. Along with stumbled bows and half salutes and a whole lot of stammering.

She was standing in the doorway, taking it all in with her usual studied grace. She'd added that same homespun smock over her skirts that she'd been wearing a few days ago in the orangery—her work outfit, with its modest shapelessness and big pockets and slightly raveled flounce.

And suddenly all he could think about was the slender turn of her ankle, her pale stockings and delicate slippers.

"I wanted to be sure that all of you know how much I appreciate the fine work you did for me yesterday and last night. And for all the other times you've devoted to my safety that I wasn't even aware of."

"Anything for our princess," Wyatt said with an unnecessary bow.

"I can't begin to tell you how grateful I am—" she touched the back of Wyatt's hand and the man's jaw went limp. "And I promise to be on my best behavior from this moment on. Tell me what to do and I'll do it."

Drew knew better than to hope she was going to spend the day simply catching up on her letter writing.

"Now, Lord Wexford," she said, turning those eager blue eyes directly on him, "if you'll catch me up on the investigation, I'll get right to work."

Bloody hell! Be careful what you wish for. An eagerly determined princess might be far more dangerous than a dismissive one.

Or a stunningly beautiful one.

With luminously blue eyes and long, gold-tipped lashes.

And a curling halo of sun-bright hair that he wanted to run his fingers through.

That smelled of her rosy lavender soap and—

"Ah, yes, Princess." Trying to reassemble his addled wits, Drew was about to ask if she would like to take a seat and listen to the field reports, but her brows suddenly came together. She gasped and made a beeline for the items spread across the top of the large table by the window.

"Great heavens! Where did all of these things come from?" She reached for a silver cigar tube, then seemed to think better of it and merely peered closely at it, clasping her hands safely behind her back.

Drew raised his brows to his cadre of agents so they would stand down, and then relaxed somewhat as he sat on the edge of the tabletop.

"They were found at the scene of the ambush."

"All of this?" She looked at the matchbox and then the metal hair comb. "Was it just strewn around randomly, or—"

"Most of it in the assassin's pockets."

"His pockets?" She glanced up at him, her forehead a puzzle of lines. "Then how did you get—oh. Of course." She stopped and then stared back at the array of the dead man's personal items, her luscious mouth set for a moment in a grim line. "I see."

"If I may, sir?" Trevor had been watching Caro's every move, and now reached across the desk, picked up the metal daguerreotype and handed it to her.

Drew moved in behind her, looking over her shoulder, trying to ignore the fresh scent of soap at her neck, the riotous curls at her nape, as she carefully studied the very formal portrait.

"Have you ever seen this man, Princess?" he asked, rather smoothly for a man on the brink of arousal.

"It's not the assassin, Your Highness," Trevor added quickly, as intent upon watching her run her fingertip over the surface as Drew was—as all of the other men were, as though her next words would solve the entire case.

"That's Antwerp behind him," she said.

"How's that?" Drew asked, thoroughly surprised at the confidence in her voice.

"Well, the backdrop is a large painting of the Grote Market and the guildhalls in the square. That's the cathedral tower in the background."

Of course. The painting was dark and Drew hadn't yet given it a good look. "Anything else?"

She narrowed her gaze at the photo. "Hmm . . . he probably has some association with the city of Bruges."

"Because . . . ?" Drew asked.

"Because the lace tablecloth was made in the Bruges double-swan pattern, a hallmark of the venerable Zwin-Lanchaise factory. And that stone bear statue standing upright beside the vase of roses is the town symbol."

Drew tried not to smile at his clever princess. No reason at all to feel pride in the woman's intelligence, but his agents were nodding at one another. "Anything else that strikes you as relevant?"

"The man is wearing finely tailored clothes, expensive linen, a silk cravat from Paris." She tapped at the neck cloth pin in the photo. "And if I'm not mistaken, my lord, he's a member of the Guildmen of Bruges."

"Who are the Guildmen of Bruges?" Wyatt asked from his perch on the window seat, his breakfast plate untouched.

"It's now an association, but it originated in the fourteenth century as a single officeholder who managed the guild activities outside the town wall."

"How the devil do you know all this?" Drew asked, leaning against the table again so that he could see her better.

"Because my grandfather, King Alonzo III, was an

honorary member and I have his pin—one just like this one—in my personal collection."

The group gave one of their collective mumbles of appreciation.

"Amazing work, Your Highness!" Allenby said, adding a long whistle.

Amazing indeed, because the pin connected her, however loosely, to the man who had taken a shot at her. Or not.

"But you don't know the name of the man in the portrait?" he asked.

"Sorry, I've never seen him before." She handed back the daguerreotype and went back to inspecting the items on the table. "Where did you find it?"

"In his coat pocket."

"Loose or protected?"

Drew had the distinct feeling he'd lost control of the interview. "In his wallet. Why? Should that make a difference?"

She shrugged. "I'm certainly no expert in logic, my lord, but it seems to me that the only reason the assassin would go to the trouble of carrying and protecting a tintype portrait is that the subject meant something very special to him, personally."

"Like a brother," Wyatt said, leaving the window. "Or a cousin. An uncle."

"Only if the uncle was the same age as our dead man," Nicholas said, taking another quick look at the portrait. "Because, of course, this daguerreotype couldn't possibly be more than about twelve years old, which makes the subject too young to be our assassin's father."

"However," Caro added, as she continued to inspect the other pieces of evidence, "he could be a hero to the man. Someone he admired or who inspired him? A patriotic leader?"

Drew's thought exactly. Though it didn't matter. Whether the tintype turned out to be an important lead or a sentimental souvenir, he couldn't take the chance of not investigating it.

"It may be only a wild goose chase, Wyatt," Drew said, handing the tintype to the agent, "but I need you and Nick to leave for Antwerp immediately, track down the photographer and identify the man in the photo."

"And the date it was taken," Wyatt said, tucking the daguerreotype into an envelope, then into his coat pocket with a pat.

"And the reason it was taken, if you can, Mr. Wyatt," Caro added, with a gracious smile to the two men, who were already gathering their belongings. "After all, there may have been a set of photos taken at the same time."

Wyatt gave her another gushing bow, with Nicholas adding, "With your safety uppermost in our hearts, Princess Caroline."

"Stay under cover, gentlemen." Drew spoke this last instruction as the two men went speeding off on their mission to save the princess.

The woman seemed to collect loyal subjects by the bushel, without lifting a finger.

"What else did you gentlemen learn at the scene of the ambush?" She turned to the three other men in the room, lighting their stern faces with her smile. "How long had the man been waiting?"

"Perhaps I can answer that, Princess Caroline," Halladay said as he strode through the doorway with Tucker and Knox on his heels. He handed his improved diagram to Drew. "Long enough to have eaten every crumb of the lunch he'd brought along in that tin box."

Knox joined her at the table and pointed to the small pouch of shredded tobacco. "He'd smoked at least four bowls of excellently rich tobacco."

"And, Your Highness," Casserly said, never to be outdone by one of his fellow agents, "our man had downed three pints of Guinness, bottled by Woodward, Nash and Ingersoll, brewers to the queen."

According to Halladay's diagram, he'd also spat tobacco like a camel and pissed a half dozen times, but Drew decided that the princess didn't need to hear that sort of detail.

She had already picked up the folded copy of the *Times*. "It's dated yesterday." Her brows were deeply winged when she looked up at him. "But if he had a newspaper with him, it means he was a literate man."

"Right."

"Educated, at least enough to read English."

"Exactly."

Hell, if she wasn't already a busy princess, he'd hire her on at the Factory. Though he had already gleaned all there was to learn from the evidence spread out in front of her, he was thoroughly enjoying listening to her logic.

"He was alone, wasn't he?" she asked, "otherwise he wouldn't have needed the newspaper."

"He was completely alone," Halladay said.

"Which is the mark of a professional assassin," Drew added. "As is carrying no papers or any other personal item that might identify him should he be captured."

"Then that must make the daguerreotype twice as significant, my lord. Because he took quite a chance carrying it in his pocket. It must have meant a great deal to him—or he was a complete amateur, after all."

Exactly the reason Drew had just sent two agents to Antwerp in such a blazing hurry.

"Suffice it to say, Princess," Drew said, "the man had been lying in wait for your carriage for a few hours."

"But how did he know we would take that road yesterday? It's not the main route to Grandauer Hall." She raised her startled gaze to him. "You don't think someone is watching the house?"

"More likely someone knows your schedule to the minute."

"Dear God, how? Oh, wait!" She pointed toward the door. "I keep my calendar on my desk in the library, which was broken into and—"

"You *kept* your calendar on your desk, Princess." He patted his coat pocket. "I've got it now. Which brings us to your new loyal subjects."

"Oh, and what about them?" she said with a snappish snort, as immediately defensive as he had anticipated.

"Davidson, please explain to the princess what you and Grant discovered in just an hour's investigation." Drew settled into a chair, wanting to get this over with as soon as possible.

The princess stood above him, her fists on her hips. "You couldn't have found anything, Wexford."

"Tell her what you discovered, Davidson."

The big man demurred, shrugged his beefy shoulders as he flipped through his notepad. "Well, there's not too much to tell, Your Highness."

She fixed her glare at Drew as she said, "I didn't think so."

"It's just that I followed the carriage to their lodgings in a disreputable tavern near Holborn Bridge, where I found them to be in possession of a great deal of money."

The princess looked between Drew and Davidson. "How do you know this about them?"

Davidson's brow dipped. "Because I saw for myself, Your Highness."

"Do you mean that these men walked into the tavern, opened up a strongbox and spread their money all over the table for everyone to see?"

"Well, no, Your Highness. I . . ." Davidson shifted his weight and cast a wary look at Drew. "The money was in the room they shared."

She turned the full force of her blue-eyed inquiry on poor Davidson. "So, they invited you to their room to show off their cache of gold?"

"Bank notes and coin, actually, Your Highness. But I was alone in their room at the time." The usually unyielding man was nearly quaking under the princess's quiet anger. "The owner of the inn was happy enough to let me in after I'd crossed his palm with a suitable reward."

"You bribed the innkeeper and then searched their room without their permission, without *mine*?"

"But he had *my* permission, Princess," Drew said, rising from the chair. "I'll take the blame for any sleight against your sovereignty. The point is that these relatively simple men are traveling with a huge amount of money."

"They're exiles, Wexford, about to return to their homeland! It's probably all the money they have in the world."

"But it's also enough money for them to fund a clever plan to assassinate you."

"Is it now?" She straightened to her most rigidly royal posture. "May I see you privately, Lord Wexford?" She turned on her heel and glided out of the room into the foyer, where she whirled on him and took him by the lapels to whisper at him.

"I won't have you persecuting my subjects, Drew. This is completely unnecessary."

"It might well be, Princess, but until I know the source and the intended use of those funds, your Mr. Brendel and his friends will remain under my scrutiny."

"You can scrutinize them all you want, but you'll keep in mind that, as my subjects, they are under *my* protection. I insist you bring your suspicions to me before you act upon them." She sniffed at him. "Now if you'll excuse me, I have my own investigation to begin."

Her *own* bloody investigation? "Where?"

"If you must know, I'm going upstairs to get my logbook and the chart of my family tree. After that, I'll be in the library. Unless you object. Do you?"

"As long as you stay within the house, Princess."

"Thank you," she said with a regal toss of her head.

Caro could feel Wexford's arrogant gaze following her all the way up the stairs.

Though his gaze was hardly an uncomfortable thing. It was sultry and seeking and always seemed to make her heart stutter in her chest.

But it did make it difficult for her to think.

And she really had to start thinking quickly if she was going to make it through this horrible mess without any more bloodshed.

Chapter 14

It took Caro a good fifteen minutes to refold her family tree and pack it into its leather case, even though she was only going to unfold it again as soon as she got it back down to the library.

She was met at the bottom of the foyer stairs by Mr. Runson, striding toward her from the front gallery. Though his formal butler's suit was perfectly pressed and fit to his hugeness, the poor man looked as uncomfortable as an impatient cat trapped inside a drainpipe.

"Good morning, Princess Caroline. Since his lordship left the house for a moment with his agents—"

"Left the house?" How silly to feel left alone. "Did he say why?"

"Something about inspecting the ambush site for himself. In any case, I thought you needed to know that there's a small caravan coming down the drive toward the house. Are you expecting anything like that today?"

A small caravan? "I don't recall arranging to meet with anyone here at the house today." But with all that had happened in the last few days, she could easily have forgotten.

"They must not have come through the main gate, else Lawson would have sent word. I'd best send them away, Your Highness." Runson took off for the front door.

Certain the mistake was hers, Caro ran past him and made it there first. "Let's look and see who it is, Runson. I'd hate to turn away someone who's come all this way to see me, just because I forgot."

Reminded suddenly of Drew's many warnings and the terrifying ambush and the bullet that hit poor Henry, Caro carefully pulled aside a corner of the lacy curtain at the side window and peered out at the drive-up.

The sky had clouded up in the last half hour and now a soft, misty rain was falling on the soggy hatted driver of the canvas-topped wagon making the curve, and the two carriages behind him.

Two carriages?

"Do they look familiar to you, Your Highness?" Runson asked from his perch at the other side window.

"Not offhand, Runson, but I wonder if the wagon is bringing items for the exhibition?" An absurd thought; she'd had to fight and steal and beg for the Boratanian items that she had stored away. Very little had been just handed to her on a silver platter.

"I'll go ask, Your Highness."

"No wait!" The driver of the wagon looked up toward the window as it came abreast of the wide steps. "Why, it's Karl Brendel!"

Her subjects! Caro threw open the door and shot outside into the drizzle to the sound of Runson bellowing after her, to him following her down the steps toward the wagons.

"Come back inside, Your Highness!"

"Dear Mr. Brendel! Hello and welcome!" She met the man as he lumbered down from the driver's seat. "I had so hoped you would come stay with us!"

"Your pardon, Princess Caroline." Brendel dipped into a deep bow, the rain pouring off his hat brim onto his boot. "It just took us a while longer to gather everyone together."

Caro took his hand and raised him. "But you're here and that's what counts. Along with all your worldly possessions, from the looks of this caravan."

"With your kindest permission, Your Highness." Brendel bowed again.

The two other vehicles had stopped and now the carriage door flew open, disgorging four children, who took off as a squealing pack, running out into the knot garden in the center of the circular drive-up.

"Who are they, Brendel?" Caro had never seen so much energy in one place. Two boys, two girls, skipping along the white gravel paths, leaping over the short boxwood hedges.

"The children belong to us, Your Highness." He looked fondly out onto the madness, then gestured behind her, back toward the other vehicles.

"Us?" Had the man been recruiting subjects for her off the streets of London?

"I hope you don't mind, Princess. We've a few extras among us. Children, grandchildren, my wife and Wilhelm's wife. Couldn't very well leave them behind at the tavern."

"Of course not!" More than just a few loyal subjects—whole families of them to take with her back to Boratania!

Brendel smiled as an older woman stepped out of the first carriage and started after the children. "And there's my wife, Dorothea, right now."

"Robert Frederick," the woman shouted with an amazingly loud voice, "you come back here right this minute! Get away from that fountain!"

"The boy in the gray cap is our grandson," Brendel continued, rolling his eyes as the lad slipped out of his grandmother's reach. "He's eight."

"Grandfather, look!" the boy shouted, standing on the edge of the pool. "Little orange-and-white fishes swimming around in here!"

"If you'll excuse me, Your Highness. Frederick, you heard your grandmother!" Brendel hurried off after the boy and the other children, who must have all been cooped up in the carriage for hours on end.

By now an amazing mob of people was emerging from the two carriages: at least six more than yesterday's delegation, and her drive-up was beginning to look like a train station.

Twelve, all totaled! More subjects than she could ever have hoped for!

Drew wasn't going to like this at all.

"Dear Princess Caroline!" Johannes was hobbling quickly toward her through the misting rain. "I do hope we haven't come at an inconvenient time for you!"

"On the contrary, Johannes." Caroline caught his hand as he tried to drop into a bow, wanting to ask him directly about his odd statement but knowing that Drew was right about not questioning the elderly man's memory. "I'm thoroughly delighted to see so many of you."

In fact, she was delighted to the marrow. And prayed that neither Johannes nor any of the others would ever learn that they'd caught her completely by surprise with the size of their group.

"The children will settle right down in a few minutes," he said, his eyes worried. "It's just that they haven't seen such wide-open spaces for a good many months."

"I'm so glad to have them. Now let's get everyone inside out of the rain."

She sent the wagon around the back to be unloaded into the conservatory, then led the rest of her drenched entourage into the foyer with their loose baggage.

"Please make yourself comfortable, everyone," she said over the din of whispering and shuffling footsteps.

Then she turned to Runson, who'd been shadowing her since she'd gone outside to meet the caravan. "Take my guests out to the conservatory for the moment. We'll need to open at least eight rooms in the east wing, and see that they have a midday meal in the dining room."

Runson raised a thick, suspicious eyebrow over the heads of the milling crowd and whispered, "If you don't mind me speaking my mind, Your Highness, his lordship isn't going to like this one little bit."

"I expect he'll raise the roof, Mr. Runson," Caro whispered back, "but as you can see, I don't have time to coddle the man's temper. You can tell him that—"

Runson was now looking past her toward the

doorway they'd just entered through. "You're just in time to be telling him yourself, Your Highness."

"Ah, there you are, Lord Wexford," she said, grabbing a stout breath of courage before turning toward the doorway. "Our guests have arrived."

"May I see you in the library, Princess?" He didn't look at her, didn't even stop long enough to wait for her reply; he just kept walking down the gallery toward the library.

She had half a mind not to follow him, but she didn't want him returning to the foyer and frightening her subjects. They were already enough on edge.

"Are you leading public tours of your home now, Princess?" Drew was standing in the center of the room, his boots planted hard against the thick carpet.

"You know very well who those people are: my subjects. You knew they were coming." She closed the library door to shield the guests from the argument that was doubtless about to explode between them.

"And they have conveniently multiplied like rabbits."

"They're called families."

"They can't stay." He came toward her, stopping just a few feet from her. "We haven't finished collecting information about them."

"How long would that take?"

"A week, two at the most."

"After the exhibition opens and after my coronation? What would be the point? It won't matter one way or the other. I suggest a compromise, sir."

Drew had never seen her eyes quite so brightly blue, sparkling with unfeigned resolve, her dangerous devotion to her providential subjects.

And now this even more dangerous talk of compromise.

And the sobering sight he'd caught, of Johannes standing in the foyer, exclaiming to Wilhelm over a caseclock with the Grostov family crest carved into the oak door.

An innocent enough act, except that they doubtless knew too much.

He'd left her alone for only a few minutes, trusting that he would receive word of their approach in time to turn them away. But the misfit group had apparently gotten lost and had picked their way through the woods. Blackburn had been about to warn them off with a shot when he'd seen Caro run out and greet them.

Yesterday it hadn't mattered that she'd opened her home to them, but this morning had changed all that.

He couldn't have her pressing Johannes for an answer until he knew for himself what the answer might be. Her curiosity would only lead her to heartache. And the only thing he could do to stop it was to deflect her interest.

"What sort of compromise, Caro?"

She had been watching him with a cocked hip and a rebellious eye. "I will give you leave to investigate my subjects as you please, sir."

"Will you, now?"

"Their entire families, as well." She tapped his chest with her fingertip. "Respectfully."

"I'm always respectful."

"And take extra care with little Robert Frederick. He looks dangerous to me."

They were safely back in the realm of dodge and parry. "And in the meantime, Princess?"

"They stay here."

"In the stables."

"They are not livestock!" She harrumphed at him and then started toward the library door. "They're staying in the hall, in the east wing, where they can have a bit of privacy and the children can play as they please. Surely you can work around them."

He knew she wasn't going to budge on this, not with the lot of them already taking root in the conservatory.

He followed the woman out the door toward the kitchen. "Princess—"

"You're a member of a gentleman's club, Drew. You must know how much one can learn of a man simply by sharing a meal with him."

"Supper?"

She went breezing through the kitchen door, stopping everyone in their stride. "Good afternoon, Mr. Mackenzie!"

Mackenzie grinned at her with his whole face. "Good afternoon, Princess. Runson just told me there'd be another twelve for supper."

"Exactly! You're a life saver, sir!"

The man beamed. "I'll be serving poulet sauté à la plombière, with a D'Artois of apricot for dessert."

"You'll love living in Boratania, Mr. Mackenzie!" she said, casting a smile at Drew when that big lout Mackenzie kept grinning at her. "And I know his lordship will miss you."

"And I him, ma'am!"

"You're not going anywhere, Mackenzie," Drew said, suddenly wanting to include Caro in that command.

Her fondest wish meant that she would be leaving

England to make a better life for herself, meant leaving him the lonely man he'd been before meeting her.

"And if you can make small cakes for each of the four children to take with them to a little party in the stable," she was saying to Mackenzie as she scooped her finger around the strawberry smears left on the inside of the morning's jam compote. She waggled her red fingertip at him. "With a cherry-cream topping. I'll be forever grateful."

Mackenzie nodded a bow at the princess. "It'll be a pleasure, Your Highness."

Sheesh!

She popped her finger into her mouth and was out of the kitchen a moment later, heading toward the foyer with Drew close behind.

"You're mighty free with my operatives, madam. They've got their own jobs to do."

"That's what comes of distrusting my staff enough to send them on holiday."

"Where are you off to now, madam?" Watching after her was like chasing thistledown.

"To the conservatory to meet the rest of my loyal subjects. You might come along, Drew. A good time to insert yourself among the suspects."

He damn well couldn't risk leaving her alone with any of her "subjects." He knew Caro would honor her promise with regard to Johannes's offhand remark. But her hospitality was already making the atmosphere like that of a family reunion, where people would be eager to share beloved tales of old with her—where facts would become entangled with lies.

"Thanks, madam, I think I will join you."

"I thought you might!" She flashed him a dazzling smile just as she stepped into the conservatory, leaving him no time to reply as the exuberant crowd surrounded her, habit forcing him to pull her back against him.

The two women dropped into deep curtsies and the men bowed again and again. The children were at her feet, looking up in awe.

"Are you really, truly a princess, miss?" asked a tiny girl in an even tinier voice.

"I am, indeed, sweetheart. Princess Caroline." She bent down to the girl and brushed a strand of damp hair off her forehead. "What's your name?"

The child's brown eyes brightened. "I'm Marguerite Belvedere."

"Ah, I have a Marguerite in the middle of my name." Caroline lifted the giggling girl into her arms.

"And that's Oscar, my brother." She was pointing at a boy of about five, gazing up at the princess with wide-mouthed adoration.

"I'm so glad to meet you, Oscar." She shook the boy's hand, and then Annora's, who seemed related in some way to Marcus. "Welcome all of you!"

"Who's that?" asked Marguerite, pointing over Caro's shoulder at Drew.

Caro turned and smiled up at him with a "Here's your chance, master spy" grin. "Ladies and gentlemen, I'd like you all to meet Andrew Chase, the Earl of Wexford. He and his staff are helping me prepare for my relocation to Boratania. *Our* relocation."

"C'n I help, too, Mr. Earl?" asked the little girl who had taken up residence in Caro's arms and now turned her big eyes on him.

Drew didn't quite know what to say, didn't need the pint-sized help but didn't want to hurt the child's feelings.

"I think, Marguerite," Caro said, clearly amused at Drew's distress, "that Mr. Earl has plenty of help. But I surely could use some."

"Then I'll help, too!" Robert Frederick said, tugging on her sleeve and gaining her smile.

"And me!"

"Me, too!"

"Excellent, children. But in the meantime . . ." She turned to the door and pointed at Runson. "Do you see that nice man over there?"

"Yeesssss!"

Runson's brows shot into his hairline, though he kept silent, obviously waiting for Caro to pronounce his fate.

"If you go with him, he'll take you off to the kitchen for an apple."

Runson's eyes grew large in alarm.

"Yaaaaayyyyyy!!!" The children left the conservatory in a noisy stream, running ahead of poor Runson, who cast Drew a baleful frown before he lumbered off after them.

Everyone in the conservatory exhaled as one. "Thank you, Your Highness," Karl said. "They get restless."

"I know how they feel, Karl. I'm restless, too. I want to go home to Boratania, as I'm sure all of you do. But first we need to settle all of you into your rooms here at Grandauer Hall. Then we can meet and make some plans over lunch."

She seemed to have worked out all the lodging arrangements in her head, and herded the adults up the stairs like a dancing piper.

"You'll have this entire wing to yourselves."

Trying to look helpful, Drew had relieved Wilhelm's wife of a basket of what must be rocks and now embedded himself inside the group, shadowing Johannes, watching Caro efficiently point the different families toward their individual rooms as though she were a hotelier and they were her paying guests.

Which meant that his staff would now be wasting more of their time changing linens and chasing after every little whimper.

"And here's the sunroom for the children to play in when they're not playing outside. I'll hire a tutor tomorrow for the two older ones—"

"A tutor?" The question sputtered out of Drew, but only earned him one of Caro's frowns.

"You've been so very generous to us, Princess Caroline," Johannes said, approaching Caro more hesitantly than before, setting off warning bells in Drew's head. "So I'm sorry to be asking another favor of you—"

"Just ask, Johannes."

"You see, we've brought with us most of our private wealth, coin and bank notes and a few gems that some of us have collected over the years—"

"And you'd like a safe place to store it all while you're here?" Caro turned to Drew for a quick flick of a brow, this woman who seemed to be able to unerringly read a person's motives. "Of course. His lordship will be able to help you whenever you like."

Johannes nodded eagerly at Drew, and then back to the princess. "You're such a blessing to us, Princess Caroline. Whatever we can do, you have our deepest loyalties."

"Be careful what you promise me, Johannes, because I have great plans for every one of you to help me finish up my preparations for the exhibition."

Not before Drew had a chance to find out what the man had meant by his comment about Caro's parents. Surely he could find the perfect opportunity.

"I don't know how we can be of help, Your Highness."

"You will, Marcus, when you see my collection. But that's for later. For now, please settle in, and I'll see you in the dining room in an hour. If you need anything, I'll be downstairs in the library."

In a very few minutes the corridor was empty and blessedly quiet, and Caro was walking with Drew toward the stairs.

"There, Drew. All safely settled in. You'll hardly know they're here."

"You must be joking, Caro. A house full of people, wandering around at all hours."

She slowed as they started down the stairs, studied him slightly from behind. "Where is your home, Drew?"

"What do you mean?"

"Where do you sleep when you're not on an assignment somewhere?"

Indeed, where did a man of the world call home? "I have rooms at my club."

"But you're an earl. You must have an estate somewhere. County Wexford? I don't think there is such a thing."

"I own a good deal of agricultural property around Shropshire and West Riding. But it's leased out, for the most part."

"Ah, a wicked absentee landlord. I should have guessed." She was smiling back at him as he caught the thick oak newel post at the landing and used it as pivot.

"I let others profit. I prefer to sit back and collect rents. I can't spare the time to do otherwise."

"So you live in a couple of rooms?"

"I do have a house in Cornwall. Only a cottage, really." He followed her through the library door, wondering what it was about this woman that made him babble like a Fleet Street gossip. "It's out on a spit of the coast, rocky as hell, completely surrounded by uncultivable ground."

"I love the sea, and a rocky coast best of all."

"At its finest with a storm pounding in off the ocean." *And a wife like Caro, a few children.* "But I don't get there very often."

"You really do need to take time for yourself now and then, Drew." She stood over the worktable, working at the buckle of a strap that wrapped a leather case.

"First, Princess, I need to see that you're happily coronated."

"It's been nearly a week and I'm still alive." The buckle came loose and she started wrestling to unfurl a thick parchment.

"Miraculously. What are you doing?" Drew grabbed the stubborn piece before it could flip itself off the table.

"Good, thank you," she said, still wrestling with her end. "It's my family tree. Obstinate as an old milkcow."

She began unfolding it before his eyes, one flap after the next until it had dwarfed her.

"It hangs right here." She reached up to slip the thong around the filagree hook at the base of a sconce and he did the same.

Then he stood back and took in the whole thing. The Grostov family, since long before Charlemagne.

Every sire and scion, down to his Princess Caroline.

"Another daring rescue, Caro?"

"Oh, not this. I've had it since before I can remember. Though I don't look at it very often."

"And what do you plan to do with it now?"

"I thought it might help me understand why someone would try to have me killed. And why me, Drew? Why not Queen Victoria?" She pointed to the line above and to the right of her own name. "Or my cousin the Grand Duke Leopold II?"

Because you're the threat, Caro. You, personally. He believed that now more than ever. "How exactly did your father lose his kingdom?"

"Betrayal and conniving, I'm afraid. But it can't be that. It was too long ago."

"A quick invasion?"

"A slow one, actually. Boratania had been under a state of siege by three of its neighbors for more than two years. Over an age-old dispute about who had won what war. From what I understand, people were starving in the streets, the army had been decimated by injuries and disease."

"I imagine the outcome must have looked quite bleak to your parents."

"They couldn't have known just how bleak things were going to get."

"Few of us can see into the future, Caro. Most people wouldn't *want* to know."

"I'm sure my father would have liked to have looked ahead, just a week or so, because when his most trusted friend offered to deploy his own troops into Boratania to strengthen the borders and break the siege, he eagerly agreed."

"That was the Grand Duke VanGroyen. Your father's third cousin, twice removed."

"In this case, blood counted for nothing at all. As it turned out, Stephan VanGroyen was the most treacherous man in the whole of Europe."

"That's saying a lot, madam, considering the cast of characters."

"Which is a great shame. Because my father welcomed VanGroyen's aid as a friend. I wish I'd gotten the chance to know my parents."

"Things would certainly have been different for you, Caro." Though she couldn't possibly know just how different. "So your father invited his worst enemy through his fortified gates?"

"Father was so relieved that he greeted the duke's advancing army into his own capital city of Tovaranche with a grand salute and a military band. It wasn't until the terrible man signaled his troops to turn and attack my father's soldiers that he realized the extent of the treachery."

"He didn't just invade Boratania, as I understand it. The duke then invaded one of the warring duchies and usurped that throne as well."

"With the blessings of the third duchy. But not before putting my father to the sword and causing my mother to flee for her life with the servants. She went into hiding, even though she must have been heavy with child at the time. With me."

Not with you, my dear. When the beleaguered queen was last seen trying to escape the attack, she was wearing a heavy ermine cloak and had a fortune in gems and jewelry sewn into her bodice, which would indeed have made her look pregnant. Though she never left Tovaranche.

So when she died in the attack, the rumors of her rounded shape provided the perfect piece of fiction to the powerful men all across Europe who needed to keep a Boratanian heir in reserve.

A simple ruse, with such long-lasting consequences.

A dangerous secret that too many important people needed to keep quiet.

Was that truly the answer, then? Was the secret of Caro's identity about to be exposed?

And was someone, or some agency, willing to kill her to keep it cloaked?

Christ! That was the only explanation that made sense.

"Everything went so badly for them, Drew, so quickly," Caro said. "A kingdom lost, a people. Two lives and a marriage, a family. It's very sad, isn't it? So unnecessary."

Except that I would never have met you, my dear. "Most wars are completely unnecessary."

"To think that my mother was in her mid thirties by that time, and yet I was her only child. One she never got to hold in her arms."

Oh, my dear, if you only knew.

"Can you imagine all those years of disappointment and sorrow? And then imagine my parents' joy when, in the midst of a horrible siege, they realized my mother was with child."

Imagine.

"Though they both must have been hoping for a son to inherit the kingdom of Boratania," she added in a tiny voice, so unlike her.

"No male heir could have bested you at caring for their legacy, Caro."

Her eyes were sparkling with unshed tears, this brave young woman who carried the world on her shoulders.

"You're very kind, Drew."

"I'm very lucky, madam." He tipped her chin up with his knuckle. "Instead of you, I could have drawn the task of protecting Malcomb from his gambling debts."

She smiled wanly and her tears slipped down her cheeks. "The lesser of two evils."

"The lesser of nothing in the world, Princess."

Then he did a foolish, foolish thing, forgetting himself and the distance he'd worked so fiercely to keep from her.

He kissed her.

On the cheek, but too near her mouth.

And he lingered there too long.

"Oh, my . . . Drew," she breathed against his eyelashes.

Nothing left to do but kiss her flat on the forehead, a smacking, platonic kiss that was supposed to mask his motives but only sealed his fate and left him reeling.

"Well, then," he said, his pulse raging and his head swimming as he raised up. "Till lunch then, Princess."

Drew wandered out of the library, dazzled and unfocused, and didn't find himself again until he noticed that he was standing in the investigation room, staring down at the items from the shooter's pockets.

"Ah, there you are, sir!" Runson said from the doorway. "Took the kids up to the east wing."

"Good to see that you lived through the ordeal."

"Ah, it were nothing. A good lot, they are. P's and q's and yessirs in all the right places."

"Let's hope we can say the same about the princess's so-called subjects, Runson. I want to know everything they do. Not only the men, but also the women. Where they go and who they talk to. Follow any of them who might leave the grounds."

"Right, sir. I'll let the rest of the staff know."

Just now Drew was heading off to find Johannes, hopefully to head the man off with a story about Caro being sensitive to anything that had to do with the deaths of her parents.

A blatant, unfair lie, but it would have to do for the moment.

Bloody hell, it was going to be a long, long day.

Chapter 15

"Why, this is a blessed miracle, Your Highness!"

Caro adored seeing the joy and wonder in Johannes's eyes as he picked up the silver salver, his growing smile as he lifted his spectacles and peered more closely at it. "Where did it all come from?"

She opened her logbook to the section on religious icons. "I've been collecting Boratanian artifacts for more than ten years."

Marcus was walking among the crates, reading the labels. "Do these all contain artifacts, Your Highness?"

"Every item examined against an historic reference, such as a vestment or a door knocker, or a painting, that sort of thing, and then catalogued in my logbook, packed away and stored safely in the vaults below for our return trip to Boratania."

"Simply amazing, Your Highness."

"It really is, Marcus." And until she met these fine

men, the artifacts had been her only contact with her country.

She noticed that Erasmus was peering at something partially hidden in a nest of excelsior.

"You're from Dubarre, Erasmus. You probably remember this." She retrieved the brass vessel.

"Yes, yes, indeed, Your Highness." The old man's hands shook as he took the chalice. "Dear Lord, I must have seen it at every Sunday mass for the first fifty years of my life. Drank from it at my wedding to my dear Greta. But I'd heard it had been stolen."

"Looted, Erasmus." She put her arm around his thin shoulders and tried to see the chalice as he did, as his beloved bride had, so many years ago.

"Then how did you come by it?"

"I looted it back, Erasmus." Though she couldn't recall from whom. There had been so many pieces, and she'd found the chalice such a long time ago.

She flipped through her book and found the entry. "Ah, yes! Nine years ago, from the vestry at York Minster."

"Great heavens!"

"If I recall, that's just what the archbishop said when I walked out with it."

Wilhelm came around to her side of the worktable. "What's this you have, Your Highness?"

"It's my current logbook. A catalogue of everything I've collected. I take it with me everywhere. I have a dozen of them in the library, a book for each of these categories. But this is the working book that I add to every day."

"Oh, I see." The old general pointed to the page with the listings of etchings. "I remember this one:

the Albrecht Dürer portrait of Alfonso-Gustav II. Didn't it used to hang in your father's great hall?"

"Exactly." Another confirmation that the portrait had once belonged to her family. "And here you can see that, until recently, my cousin Queen Victoria kept it in the breakfast room at Kensington. She was most gracious when I asked for it back."

Wilhelm laughed with his whole body. "Your Highness, if you're as courageous as an empress as you've been as a thief, then Boratania will be an international force to be reckoned with in just a few years."

"Just as I've been telling your princess, Wilhelm."

Drew! Caro turned toward his voice at the orangery door, her heart already thumping crazily in her chest.

He might have been answering Wilhelm, but he was looking straight at her, at her mouth where he had almost kissed her.

Almost, because he'd missed her mouth on purpose.

That was one thing she knew about her Lord Wexford: He didn't make mistakes.

A pity, that.

Perhaps he would try again.

"Good morning, my lord," she said, catching the edge of the table for balance. "I've been showing off the artifacts that we'll be returning to Boratania."

"An impressive collection, isn't it, gentlemen?" Drew said, still smiling at her as the men eagerly agreed.

"I never thought I'd see that statue of Gatkemeer the Destroyer again." Karl ran his gnarled hand over the lush marble figure.

Wilhelm shook his head in awe. "Or the Karenina tapestry. Last I saw, it was in the great hall of the Weavers Guild in Clarence."

"Let's hope that the items I've chosen for the Great Exhibition will impress the entire world."

"Are the wagons ready, Princess?" Drew asked abruptly.

"All three of them, thanks again to the remarkable Mr. Wheeler." She looked at the old mantel clock on the worktable and found the day wasting. "Good heavens, if I'm going have enough time to deliver all of them to the exhibition hall today, then we'll have to leave now."

"*We're* not driving into London, Princess. *I* am. My crew. I'll make the delivery. You're staying here."

Caro heard herself snort at the man; but nipping this one in the bud right away was her only hope. "Don't be absurd. You wouldn't know the first thing about who to see or what needs to be done there."

"You can draw it out for me."

"You cannot possibly talk me out of going with you, Wexford." She caught her finger in a buttonhole of his waistcoat and tugged at him. "But you *can* talk me into traveling in your amazing carriage. Which means we can haul even more things inside. An excellent work-around-my-duties, don't you think?"

To her great amazement Drew just stood there, apparently speechless. Then he leveled his finger at her. "We leave as soon as the horses are hitched, madam. Gentlemen."

Caro watched him stalk off toward the stables, wondering what would have happened if things could have been different between them. If only she weren't a princess-soon-to-be-empress, or if he were a prince . . .

"Pardon me, Your Highness"—Johannes came up beside her—"but you said we could help you in some way."

She turned to him. "In a very special way, Johannes, because you and the others know so much more about the history of all this than I do."

"Possibly a bit more, Your Highness. What is it you want us to do?"

"The items in these crates on this side of the room are listed in my catalog, but they haven't been entered into my logbook as being found." She picked up an oar from a longboat. "I would love for you and the others to examine what I've got here, and if you recognize anything at all, either here or down in the vaults, please add the information right onto the log page next to its number. Any story at all will be a treasure to me."

The men were all grinning from ear to ear, like children in a candy shop. It wasn't greed she saw in their eyes, not the prospect of the cool feel of gold in their hands.

It was the pure joy of coming home again.

"A million square feet of glass, Drew," Caro said, following his dark gaze as it once again traveled the soaring details of the huge Crystal Palace.

"An assassin's paradise, Princess."

"It's gloriously spectacular, though, isn't it? Designed and commissioned by Prince Albert and built in record time. More than eighteen hundred feet long and four hundred feet wide, over nineteen acres all under the same roof, which is one hundred thirty-five feet at its highest!"

"Truly a marvel of modern engineering, Princess." He stuck his thumbs into his belt as they walked down the transept. "But at the risk of repeating myself, it's also an assassin's fondest dream."

"How do you mean?"

He stood behind her and pointed into the galleries and along the railing of international banners and the vast expanse of glass and iron. "Pillars to hide behind during the bustle of the opening ceremonies, and railings and unobstructed lines of sight, not a single inside wall."

And his own men placed at crucial intervals, just as they were now. As they always were. She'd gotten so used to having them around, they'd become a sort of extended family.

"But the Crystal Palace will be so crowded, no one will be able to move, let alone aim a rifle anywhere."

"Assassins love crowds, my dear."

"Mine seem to love the woods, Drew. And the library. Much quieter places."

"Complacency will get you killed, Caro." His voice grew low and intimate. "And I wouldn't like that at all."

"Well, then . . ." She could feel her face growing warm, her thoughts tangling on themselves, on that kiss a few days ago, so she blathered on with her catalog of amazing facts.

"You can see how the entire hall is divided up into different courts." She'd been here so many times before in preparation for her own exhibit, had asked so many questions of the experts, she'd be excellent at leading in-depth tours, should the Royal Commission ask. "There's art and architecture from all the ages. Industry and commerce and raw materials . . . There! See that, Drew . . . that huge glass lantern? That's a lens for a lighthouse."

Drew seemed the stalking lion as he went ahead of her down the aisle, leading her around the huge stuffed elephant that was being muscled into its place in the Indian exhibit. "How many exhibits did you say?"

"Thirteen thousand."

"Bloody hell!"

"Including mine." Which was looking enormously impressive with everything unloaded from the packing boxes and now on display.

Looking suddenly, terribly vulnerable. "In your professional opinion, Drew, just how secure is the exhibition hall?"

"It isn't secure in the least, Princess."

"That's what I am suddenly realizing. That these irreplaceable treasures of Boratania are now fair game for anyone with light fingers." Wondering why she hadn't thought about the problem before this, Caro started off the platform. "Blazes! I'm going back to the exhibition office to find out what kind of—"

"I've already taken care of it."

"Taken care of what?"

"Security. The exhibit hall has a dozen guards on duty, posted around the clock, inside and out."

"But—"

"But because I knew it would ease your mind, Caro, I've already arranged to have two of my men guarding the Boratanian exhibit at all times. Starting right now, for as long as you need it."

Come home with me to Boratania, Drew.

"Thank you, Drew. You always think of everything."

Drew wasn't sure he could take much more of her smile. Too bright for his eyes, too large for his heart.

"It's my responsibility to prepare for every eventuality, before it comes to pass."

"I'm going to need someone just like you when I become empress."

"Just like me?" Drew stepped back and spoke without thinking. "Are you proposing marriage, madam?"

"To you?" Her eyes flew open, wide and blue, bolts of panic lighting them. "Oh, Drew, no! I didn't mean—"

"No, madam?"

"No, I just meant that . . . well, if you should ever find yourself in Boratania . . ."

He knew what she'd meant, felt it in his heart like an endless void. "You'll find me at your castle door, Princess, if I ever do."

"And if I ever need someone to watch over me again, Drew . . . well, I can't imagine anyone but you. So . . . thank you. Again."

"Come, then, Caro," he said, shoving his hands deep into his jacket pockets, not daring to do anything more than nod toward the aisle that was bristling with ancient agricultural implements. "I really should get you back home through the woods before dark."

She gave a long look at her elegant display, with its medieval tapestries and marble statues, portraits and baskets and all manner of brassworks. "It does look fine, doesn't it?"

"Less than a week and the rest of the world will have a chance to agree."

"I hope so." She picked up her leather folio and started down the aisle.

They passed by the Prussian textile exhibit, the woodcarvings of Württemberg, the Saxony china.

"The Steegman-Meyer porcelain factory used to be well within the borders of Bora—great heavens!" She stopped short in front of an unfinished display area. "Of all the nerve."

"What?"

"Do you see that silver goblet in that glass case in the corner." She pointed at a glass-fronted wardrobe and the array of glittering objects inside.

"Yes, why?"

"The goblet is mine."

"That may be, Princess, but at the moment, it's locked behind a glass door in the Hollen-Zwingen exhibit."

"Stolen from a pair of goblets that were given to my grandparents by King Frederick V on their wedding day."

"That may be, Caro, but you don't have your logbook with you, so you have no way of knowing for certain that this one is from the same set."

"The pair were struck just for them. There were only two and I already have the other."

Before he could react, the woman was standing in front of the case, picking at the lock with a hairpin from her now unwinding hair.

In the next moment, she had the goblet tucked under her arm, hidden by her cloak, and resumed ambling along the aisle.

"It'll serve them right."

"I never thought I'd get a chance to actually see you in action, Caro. My God, you're good. My very own royal thief."

"I'm not the thief in this drama, Drew," the madwoman said, as she stooped slightly to peer into another case. "I'm the relentless detective and, when necessary, I'm the ruthless liberator."

Of all the royals Drew had ever met, this one was the most brazenly fearless.

The most beautiful and the only one who had ever made him laugh from down deep in his gut.

He strolled leisurely beside her, playing her game, following her lead, feeling deeply involved in her mischief, which put him in mind of long ago intrigues with Jared and Ross.

"It's good to know that your conscience is utterly clear, Princess."

"Clear as the sky, Drew."

"You'd make a fine pickpocket, my dear. But some day you're going to be found out. And then what?"

"Then my Hollen-Zwingen cousins will just have to do without the goblet."

"They're sure to see it displayed in your exhibit."

"I hope they do. But there's nothing much they can say or do about it, is there? Keeping looted property when you know who the rightful owners are is shameful!"

"Tell that to the Egyptians."

"Exactly. My cousins know very well that I've been searching for looted items. I've even distributed lists of the most important pieces."

The woman was a walking, talking time bomb.

"Was that wise, Caro? Announcing to your potential victims your intention to rob them—"

"As I live and breathe, it's Princess Caroline!"

Drew recognized the voice to be Peverel's. It had come from behind the crystal fountain in the center of the transept.

"Lord Peverel!" Caro was already heading for the man, her hand outstretched and the goblet hidden. "How nice to see you here!"

"And you, Your Highness. You're looking very well these days." Though Peverel was smiling broadly, he looked as pale as he had at the tournament, as distracted. "How goes your exhibit? Have you finished installing it?"

"Nearly, my lord. There are still a few items left to bring. Then everything stays here until the end of the exhibition in August. By then I'll have been empress for a few months and will be living in Boratania"—she felt Drew's hand in the small of her back, a very gentle, intimate pressure that brought a lump to her throat—"and I'll . . . um, I'll be ready to return each item to its rightful place in my kingdom."

Peverel focused a rueful smile on Drew. "The princess is very organized. You must have discovered that about her, Lord Wexford."

"That and her skill at negotiations."

"Can I do anything for you, Lord Peverel? I mean toward my return to Boratania?"

"No, no, my dear Princess. All is in good order. Yes. A few loose ends that we can tie up at your coronation if . . . well, if need be." He gestured wanly back toward the Coalbrookdale Gates and shook his gray head. "As you know, I'm one of the assistants to the Royal Commission and I've a meeting this afternoon in the Exhibitors Dining Room. Last minute details and the like. So I'll wish you both a very good night."

"I hope he's all right, Drew," Caro said as the man hobbled away, past the mounted Victoria statue. "He still looks too pale."

"And far too busy for a man of his age. Come, Caro."

For the last few minutes, he'd been plagued by an odd feeling that something was out of place.

The scent of something. Or something that had brushed the edge of his vision.

He shifted his gaze from display to display, escorting the woman around the boxes and crates in the main aisle, the sundry industrial exhibits being assembled by a vast array of workman.

Probably just the din of the workmen and the sounds of hammers and shouted instructions around them on the ground floor and in the galleries. Besides, the place was crawling with his own men, each of them on high alert as he and Caro made their way toward the towering west exit.

He'd already sent the empty cargo wagons back to Grandauer Hall, but his own carriage was waiting outside in a line of others.

"This way, Princess," Drew said, taking her elbow and steering her outside through the stream of assorted people who were coming and going through the jumbled gauntlet of slate and stone and timber, waiting to be used inside.

"Less than a week before the Grand Opening, Drew," she said, stepping quickly to keep up with his pace, "I can only wonder if it'll all be finished in time.

"Not if someone doesn't free up this damned log jamb!"

"Oooh! Ouch!" Caught in the press of a passing group of construction workers, Caro stumbled and fell behind him a step.

"What happened, Princess?" Drew stopped and hoisted her upright and close to him. "Are you all right?"

"Fine!" She grunted as she reached down to the muddy path, picked up her fallen folio and that damn goblet, and came up frowning. "Impatient lout! Plowed right into me!"

"Let's get you to the carriage and then home." His heart pounding in relief, Drew pressed her arm more deeply into his elbow and increased his stride. He'd have carried her if there had been enough room on the plank walkway.

"A very good idea." Caro decided not to tell Drew that the clumsy oaf had smacked into her hard enough to bruise her ribs.

That would only send Drew flying after the poor man. And she really hadn't gotten a good enough look at him, or anyone else who'd been jostling her, to make an identification.

By the time they righted the carriage, she was completely winded by the effort to keep up with Drew's galloping stride. He had her bundled inside an instant later.

"To Grandauer Hall!" Drew bellowed to the driver. He threw himself onto the bench seat opposite her as the carriage leaped into the gravel lane. "The worst kind of situation, Caro. Suddenly, completely uncontrolled."

"It was really nothing out of the ordinary, Drew,"

she said, still catching her breath and rubbing at the stitch in her side. "A bit of mud on my cape, and on my folio. Other than that . . . well, that's odd."

"What's odd?" Drew leaned forward, elbows on his knees, his brow fretted as he looked into her eyes.

"The inside of my cloak is wet. Sort of sticky." She felt around the side of her dress. "So is my . . . oh!"

Caro had pulled her hand out of the shadows of her cloak and now found herself looking down at something dark and red all over her fingers.

"It's blood, Drew."

Chapter 16

"Christ!" He leaped across the carriage like a tiger, towering over her as he threw back her cloak. "They got to you, Caro! Right in front of my eyes! They got you!"

"It's nothing, Drew. I feel fine!"

He yanked up her bodice and cursed again. "Stabbed you right through your cloak, the bastards!"

"Stabbed me?" She unhooked her cloak at the neck and then tried to see for herself, but he was in the way. "Not badly, though."

"Damn it, Caro!" He flew to the little window in the driver's cab. "To the Factory, Davis! On the double!"

"If we can just get home to Grandauer Hall, Drew, then I can get out of these clothes and clean up the wound, and then—"

"Don't be absurd." He was already back on her side of the carriage, straddling her legs and bending over the wound as the carriage thrashed along the cobbled street.

A moment later the lout rolled her onto her face with a, "Sorry, madam. I have to see this."

"This?" The next thing Caro felt was him cutting at the ties at her back. "What are you doing?"

Her bodice popped open behind her and he quite expertly yanked the sleeve off her arm.

"Hold still, Caro."

"You cut off my camisole!" Completely bare! At least on one side.

"Shhhhh . . ." And now he was hunkering over her, gently pulling back the linen, staring, muttering curses. "Thank God for that. A surface wound. The blade must have been deflected by your ribs."

"I told you: I feel fine."

"Only because the bastard missed getting you with a solid, full-on thrust."

Full-on. "Oh." Her stomach gave a turn.

"A dozen bodyguards," he muttered as he probed around the wound with such gentle fingers, his breath so remarkably soft against her skin, she could just lie there forever. "And damnation, still they got through me to you."

"But not with a full-on thrust, Drew. Something must have worked." Caro closed her eyes, feeling suddenly, marvelously, sleepy.

"No, you don't, Caro." He pressed his palm and a square of something over the wound. "It's my handkerchief. Now, hold it here against your side and sit up. I don't need you going into shock."

"The only thing I'm shocked at, Drew, is you stripping off my clothes." Shocked and more than a little delighted.

"Couldn't be helped, madam. Now, hold tightly." He helped her sit up and tugged the bloodied, shredded camisole around her midriff to keep the kerchief in place, and then slipped her arm back into the sleeve of her shirtwaist.

"A few minutes, Princess, and we'll be there." He slid into the seat beside her and settled her back against his chest.

A very snug, safe place to be. "Where did you tell the driver to go?"

"Not far," he whispered against her ear as he pulled his cloak across the front of her, warm and scented with his spicy shaving soap.

A factory, he'd said. What kind of a factory? She could see that they were clearly heading toward Mayfair.

She turned slightly toward him and found herself supported by one of his arms and looking up into his face. Into that strong chin, those dark eyes.

"Thank you again, Drew."

He frowned down at her, obviously angry with himself. "Don't."

"But just imagine what would have happened if you hadn't been watching over me like a hawk. A full-on thrust, if you remember."

His eyes darkened further, his gaze trailing across her nose, her cheeks. "I damn well could have lost you just then, Caro. In the blink of an eye."

"I'm not that easy to lose, Drew." But, dear God, she could lose herself in his eyes.

"And so impossible to forget." His finger trembled as he brushed his knuckle along her jaw, then drew his fingertip slowly, softly between her lips, so slowly that she felt herself melting against him, hoping that he would kiss her this time. Full-on.

"Dear Drew . . . you, oh!"

But then the carriage rocked around a corner and he stopped, frowned at her and then said, "I'm terribly sorry, Princess."

She had been about to tell him that it was quite all right to kiss her, when, in the next instant, the lout covered her head in his cloak.

"What the . . . Drew!" She fought against this prison, more shocked than angry. "What are you doing?"

"My job, madam." Now he'd wrapped his powerful arms around her inside the cloak.

"Are you mad, Wexford?"

"I damn well hope I am." He dropped his words against her ear, a fiercely hot warning. "Keep still, Caro. It's for your own good."

"Is this your cure for a stab wound?" She kicked out, but met with the seat opposite. "Unhand me, sir!"

"Another three minutes, Princess, and we'll do something about this wound."

He was holding the kerchief against her side now, his hand covering hers, her arms trapped by his.

"You've kidnapped me again!"

"Only a precaution."

"Let me out of here." And yet she was wondering if she really wanted him to let her go. Except for the soft wool of his cloak that was loosening with every jostle of the carriage, she felt fine.

"You can take out your anger on me in just a moment, madam. Stop moving and all will be well."

Quite fine, indeed. And it was probably the shock, but she didn't care. Snuggled against the long length of him.

"I can't see a thing, Drew." She gave a good struggle, just for good measure. But he just held her more tightly, whispered against her ear more fiercely.

"That's the point. Now settle down. Or you'll break open your wound and start bleeding again."

The carriage turned sharply, then rolled to a stop.

"Here, sir!" came a voice from outside. And then at least three other voices.

"Hold still, Princess." She was suddenly completely in his arms and in the air, the cloak keeping her from seeing anything at all.

"Where have you taken me, Wexford?"

"She's been stabbed, Pembridge. Get the door, someone. Into the infirmary."

"Is this a hospital?" She felt a cool draft on her leg as he carried her down the carriage steps and then a few steps down into some damp-smelling place.

More muffled voices and shuffling and the odd feeling that Drew was taking her down into a dungeon.

"You actually *have* kidnapped me again, Wexford!"

"Shock," he said to the voices, who then laughed softly, knowingly.

And then the air was warm and stuffed with sounds and fragrances of all kinds.

"All clear, my lord."

Drew's cloak was whisked off her head as quickly as it had been put there. And she was still in Drew's arms, still on the move down a well-lighted but darkly paneled corridor. Still underground, she was sure, in a place that was oddly elegant and very, very masculine.

"Where are we, Drew?"

An older man opened a door ahead of them. "I'll get Fitzgerald. You've caught him in."

"Thanks, Pembridge," Drew said as he carried her

past the man into a room that could have been a parlor in any manor house, if it hadn't been underground.

"Are we in a cellar, Drew?"

He put her down on a settee. "Keep hold of that handkerchief."

"Who is Fitzgerald?"

"A doctor." He added a chunk of wood to the hearth fire, making it snap and pop.

"I don't need a doctor." Oh, but it did hurt a little to breathe.

"You're going to see one. A very good one."

"Is this a hospital?"

"No."

"You just happen to have a doctor handy."

"That's about it, Princess."

"Where have you brought me?"

He unfurled a plaid woollen blanket from the back of the settee and coaxed her like a child. "Now please lie down, Princess. Ah, here's the doctor now."

Drew met the man at the door without a preamble. "A stab wound, Martin. Fortunately it's not deep."

"Lucky young woman." The doctor peered at her from across the room, looking over the top of his spectacles as he shrugged out of his jacket.

"Of course, I need you to tell me everything you can about the wound." Drew shrugged out of his own coat, as though the pair of them were planning to operate. "The shape of the blade, the angle . . . you know what I need."

The doctor smiled at Caro as he approached, a man with a voice as smooth as cream. "My dear Princess Caroline, how I wish that we had met under better circumstances."

"I'm actually just fine, thank you." She tried to sit up straighter, but Drew had slipped behind the settee and put his hand on her shoulder.

"Just sit back and relax, Caro," Drew said softly into her ear. "We'll take good care . . ."

Of course, he would. And yet for some reason he was suddenly wearing a sickly sweet fragrance instead of his usual clear . . . clean . . . um . . .

"You won't feel anything, Princess, because . . .

The doctor's nice voice just kind of swam away from her, and Drew's did, too. The soft parlor lights dimmed and dimmed and dimmed . . .

To absolutely nothing.

"Bloody blazes, Drew, you look like hell!" Ross frowned up at Drew from his reading chair as he entered the otherwise deserted map room.

"Good, because I feel like hell. Where's Jared? Pembridge said he was here, too." A wonder these days; Jared spent most of his time playing squire to his wife in Lincolnshire.

"I'm right behind you, Drew." Jared had come into the room with two scones on a plate. "Hungry? I can get more."

"Angry, actually. The princess has been stabbed."

"What?" Jared put the plate down on the table.

"Christ, Drew!" Ross was already at his side. "Will she be all right?"

"By some bloody miracle. That's why I need you both to come downstairs." Drew didn't wait for them to follow because he knew they would.

He left the map room and took the backstairs down to the false door in the wine cellar, past the two security guards waiting on the other side, then led them through the Message Management Center of the Factory in the basement of the Huntsman, under the street, past the reception area and the chattering telegraph room, finally into the conference room where he'd collected the "Princess Files" and the initial reports on this most recent attempt on her life.

"Bloody hell, I was walking right beside her! And still they got to her." Drew couldn't help pacing the distance to the table and back to the hearth.

"Settle yourself, Drew," Jared said, catching his arm, stopping his progress. "You said she's going to be all right, and that's because you were there beside her."

Ballocks! "Next time she might not be so lucky."

"Can't you just keep her hidden away until the trouble passes?"

"Believe me, Ross, she's not that kind of princess. My carriage was ambushed and shot up on the way home from that bloody tournament she had to attend, because she was a Damsel of the Dell, whatever the hell that was. Today it was to tend her exhibit at the Crystal Palace, four days from now it'll be the opening ceremonies of the Great Exhibition with tens of thousands of people, and then three days later her own, very public, coronation."

"I see what you mean, Drew—the woman's every assassin's ideal."

"Ross telegraphed me about the ambush; that's why I came back to London. My Kate insisted."

"A very Kate thing to do, Jared. I don't know what you did to deserve that bride of yours."

"More's the point, Drew," Ross said as he leafed steadily through Caro's file, "what the devil has your princess done to make someone so angry at her? Why?"

Because she's not Princess Caroline, Ross.

She's not any kind of a princess.

A fictional life, fabricated out of bits and pieces by the great and powerful families of Europe strictly for the purpose of using her.

And Caro didn't know a thing about it.

Damnation, he'd love to be able to confess the truth to his friends. To have their insight.

But he'd made promises that he had no right to break, to Palmerston, to Queen Victoria and, though she might not know it, to Caro herself.

"I was hoping that you and Jared could investigate the stabbing. Go back to the Crystal Palace and ask around, in absolute secret, about the exhibitors, the workers, anything that was happening at the time."

"In secret, Drew? An exiled European princess has been stabbed, and you want it kept a secret?"

"From everyone, Ross. Fleet Street especially. Please don't ask me why. I've been sworn not to tell you, not anyone. It may even mean the princess's life."

Jared was sorting through the papers on the table. "Have you a description of the attacker? His clothes? Anything at all?"

"If you'll wait a few minutes, Jared, Princess Caroline will be here and you can ask questions yourself."

Ross snorted. "She's coming to the Factory?"

"She's already here, in the infirmary. Probably just waking up."

"You brought her here?"

"Didn't have much choice. Read through her file while I'm gone. I'll go check on her."

* * *

Caro blinked and blinked, trying to keep her eyes open and finally realized that she had nodded off for a moment.

"Good evening, Princess Caroline." Mr. Pembridge's voice paddled close and then swam away again.

Hmmmm . . . she must have nodded off again.

The bed was rolling. No, not the bed—the whole floor. She was walking. Trying to walk, but the path was so narrow, barely as wide as the soles of her shoes.

"She'll be coming around now, Drew."

And she was going to chide Drew for not kissing her fully on the mouth in the carriage, for whispering something into her ear that didn't make any sense at all.

Then it wasn't Drew at all, but a plainer man, shorter, carrying a bucket.

Stocky, like a bricklayer.

Sandy haired, with light eyes and snaggled teeth.

He wouldn't let her pass on the path, shoved her off balance with his elbow.

"Not too fast, Princess Caroline."

Caro felt as though she were blindly falling and falling. But when she finally was able to keep her eyes open, she found herself sitting upright on the settee staring into Mr. Pembridge's face with its craggy smile.

"Dizzy?" he asked, touching her forehead with the back of his fingers. "Sick at your stomach?"

"I'm fine, Mr. Pembridge." Except that she must have fallen to sleep right in the middle of a conversation with the doctor. "Where's Lord Wexford?"

"Ah, he's at a meeting."

"Can you take me to him?"

His gray brows dipped as he shook his well-groomed head. "Only if you can prove to me that you can stand and walk alone. I don't want you falling."

"I never fall." To prove she was capable of walking and talking, Caro stood and then staggered backward into the settee. She sat down hard, but in completely different clothes than she'd been wearing.

"Where's my dress?" It had been a pale lavender satin, and now this new one was not only yellow, but it was homespun and much too big for her.

"Sorry, Princess."

Drew! He was coming through the doorway, his smile huge and a bit lopsided.

"We had to remove your gown after we put you under."

Under? That didn't make any sense either. "I fell asleep. For no reason at all."

"Well, you're looking much better, Princess Caroline," Drew said easily, locking his dark gaze with hers as he approached her. "How are you feeling?"

He seemed even larger and more powerful than he had before, the master of this perplexing place.

"Surprised. And a little sore." She touched her side, finding a neatly flat bandage. "I seem to be fine."

Drew nodded at Pembridge. "Thank you, Pembridge. I'll take her from here."

"It's been a pleasure, Your Highness." Then the older man gave an elegant bow and left the room.

"You were given a gas called ether to put you to sleep, Princess." Drew sat down in the same chair that Pembridge had been sitting in. "And according to Fitzgerald, it's being used very successfully by an American dentist, and now here in England."

"For what?"

"As an anesthetic. The doctor put you into a deep sleep, which allowed him to examine your wound, then clean and dress it without your feeling pain."

Caro touched her side, the loose-fitting blouse. "So I was asleep?"

"With the after effects, for well over an hour."

She looked up at the mantel clock. "I don't remember a thing."

"You're not supposed to, Caro." He peered closely into her face in a very clinical way.

"Did you really need to take my clothes, Drew? I liked that gown."

He smiled and kissed the middle of her forehead. "It was in the way." And then her temple.

"I like that, Drew. I like that a lot." She closed her eyes—or maybe they were already closed—and offered her lips for another kiss.

But instead of kissing her, he took both her hands and helped her stand.

"Come with me." He offered his arm and then gently led her out the doorway through a warren of busy corridors, allowing her just a passing glimpse into rooms that were filled with a variety of incongruous activities.

A photography studio.

A tailor's shop, with a long rack of clothes against the back wall.

An enormous printing shop, clanking away.

A large room with at least a dozen chattering telegraph machines.

And finally a lushly appointed yet windowless

chamber dominated by a marble-faced fireplace, plush chairs and two men standing at a large oak conference table.

And they were staring at her.

She looked sideways at Drew and found him grinning at her. A very private smile, which he then shifted back to the other two men.

One of the men stepped forward. "Gad, Drew, you look much better with a princess on your arm."

"Princess Caroline, this rude fellow is Ross Carrington, Viscount Battencourt."

One of Drew's longtime friends. "I'm so very pleased to finally meet you, Lord Battencourt."

"The pleasure is all mine, Your Highness." He bowed elegantly and took her hand, every bit as dark-featured and handsome as Drew. And just as tall. "Though, I must say, Princess, you pulled the short stick on this bodyguard business. Wexford was obviously asleep at the switch. Now, had I been your bodyguard—"

"Bottle it, Ross." Drew poked an elbow into Lord Battencourt's ribs and gestured to the other man who had been smiling at their antics. "And this is Jared Westbrooke, the Earl of Hawkesly."

"A great honor, Princess Caroline." He too, bowed from a height equal to Drew's and Battencourt's, incredibly handsome, with a grand smile and a deep sense of contentment in his dark eyes.

"My Lord Hawkesly, I couldn't be happier to meet you. I've heard so much about the both of you. And I would know you both by your buttons."

Hawkesly had a thoroughly inviting laugh. "Our what, Princess?"

"The crest on your buttons." She tapped one of the

topmost buttons on his waistcoat, causing him to look down. "Lord Wexford told me about them."

Hawkesly arched a scandalized brow at Drew. "Telling tales again, Drew?"

If you only knew, Ross, Drew thought, still vastly uncomfortable keeping Caro's secret from his two friends, two men of great skill and even greater honor.

"Best that you stuff it, Jared," Drew said, because the man would be expecting a suitable comeback.

"And you, Lord Wexford," his princess said, with a furious cast to her soft brow, "can stuff it, too!"

Drew blinked at her and then at Ross and Jared. "What's that, Princess?"

"This isn't any kind of a factory, is it?" She looked back toward the closed door.

Damnation, she must have heard him bellow. He hadn't really been thinking beyond her safety at the time.

"What did you mean, 'factory?' " she repeated. "I heard you shout to the driver to take us to 'the factory.' " She gave the room a long stare, then walked forward to the table with all the reports strewn across its top. "This place is not a factory."

Drew glanced at Jared and Ross, but received only their haughty you're-on-your-own-chum smiles. "No, it isn't, Princess."

She harrumphed. "Police stations don't have printing shops or doctors on call, not to mention a room full of telegraph machines."

"She's very good, Drew," Ross said as he dropped into a chair, doubtless to watch how Drew would squirm out of this one.

"So, are we in the basement of Whitehall?"

An excellent assumption, however wrong. But it would serve to satisfy her curiosity and sound reasonable to anyone she might mention it to, including Palmerston, who knew all about the Factory. And he doubted that Caro could ever find the entrance to the Factory, should she ever decide to go looking.

Jared leaned against the mantel, wearing a very serious expression. "We can't answer that, Your Highness. National security and all."

She eyed them all, finally shaking her head. "I really didn't think you could."

She picked up one of the doctor's very clinical diagrams off the table. "And is this an outline of me?"

Hardly that. Curves and angles, but nothing at all like the real Caro. Which Drew had gotten an eyeful of as he'd help to change her out of her clothes.

"It's a drawing of your wound." Trying not to appear amused, Drew pointed to the V-shaped mark just below the sensuous line of her breast. "This angle shows where the blade entered. By the way, it was deflected by one of the whalebone stays in your bodice."

"Ah, that must be why I was wearing this"— she grabbed hold of her too-big skirts—"instead of my own clothes when I woke up from my little nap?"

"Sorry, Your Highness," Drew said. "I needed to tear your bodice apart to get to the stays." He showed her the page of calculations. "Your height, in your shoes, when compared to the angle of the nick that the blade made in the whalebone tells us that your assailant is left-handed and between five foot six inches and five eight."

"You can tell all that?"

"And much more," Drew said, leaning on the edge

of the table in order to better see her reactions. "Do you recall the face of anyone on the path who fits that description? Someone wearing a cap, disguised as a workman. Doubtless he would have made eye contact with you as he approached, just to be sure of your identity."

She looked at Drew with earnest eyes. "I don't think so, Wexford. I can't remember."

"His glance might only have been for the briefest moment. Take your time. Let your mind recall the path we took, the gravel, the mud, the jostling crowd . . ."

She sat down gingerly in one of the tall chairs, favoring her injured side. The gesture sent a chill of terror through Drew's shoulders. She'd been that close to death. The width of a blade, a longer stride.

"We were traveling so quickly." She seemed to be reaching carefully back into her memory of the afternoon. "Your agents seemed to be all around us. You had my arm, and—oh!"

"What?"

"Someone ran into me. Hard. Don't you remember? I almost fell. I dropped the goblet and my folio."

He had remembered all too well. But he hadn't wanted to cloud Caro's own recollection with his own.

"Sorry, Princess, but I didn't see anything about him. I was waving to the carriage driver."

"But I must have seen him."

"And you'll remember much of it if you just give it a bit of a—"

"He had light hair."

"Go on, Princess." Drew knelt in front of her and took her hand. "Light hair."

"Sandy and short. And he was carrying a bucket."

"Do you recall which hand, Princess?"

"Um, well it must have been in his right. He might be a bricklayer, with something, maybe a wooden handle, sticking out of his coat pocket."

"What kind of coat, Princess?" Ross was scribbling down her answers. "What color?"

She looked up at Ross without really seeing him. "It came only to his knees. Green canvas color, with leather or something brown, I think on the collar. Brown buttons."

"Good, Princess." Drew smoothed a strand of hair back behind her ear. "Anything else about his face? His age?"

"Your age. Pale eyes and an unremarkable moustache." She blinked hard at Drew as though she'd just noticed him, then she shrugged. "That's all, my lord. But it's definitely the man I remembered in my dreams."

"Your dreams?" Drew asked. "You've seen him before?"

"No. But his was the face I saw after you gave me that horrid gas to breathe. But I'm sure he's the man. I thought he had knocked me off balance with his elbow, or . . . with a trowel, because I thought he was a bricklayer. But that must have been when he stabbed me."

"Then he's left-handed," Jared said, looking down at Ross's notes. "Otherwise he'd have been carrying that bucket in his left hand. He needed his knife hand free for the attack."

Ross tapped his notebook. "And either he's actually a mason and would have fit right in with the workers at the Crystal Palace—in which case someone should know who he is—"

Drew stood. "Or he'd have been noticed for being a stranger who was trying to look like a mason."

"Come along, Jared." Ross stuck his notepad into his jacket pocket. "Looks like we've got work to do. Good day, Princess Caroline."

"You're leaving, my lords?" Caro wobbled to her feet, terrifying Drew as he caught her elbow.

"It's been a pleasure, Your Highness," Jared said, bowing before her hand.

Then they were gone. Carrying only half the truth.

And there was a dark danger in that.

"They're every bit as wonderful as you described, Drew." Caro was smiling after them. "I'm so sorry that you had to involve them."

"Like a pair of hounds on the scent of a hare." Drew collected all the papers off the table and shoved them back into the book file. "Now let's go see if we can jostle your memory even further."

Drew led her through the well-lit rooms and corridors, past areas that drew her rapt attention, trying to keep his overly curious princess from seeing too much.

"This is a very busy place, Drew."

"That it is, Princess," Drew said, suddenly sick to death of dealing in lies and shadows.

They passed under the Huntsman then under the alley to the basement of the building next door and into the active reports department.

"If you'll sit here at this table, Princess," Drew said, making sure that she was comfortable, "I'll bring you some photographs and drawings that might help you remember more clearly."

When he returned from the archive room, Caro

was napping on her crossed arms, sleeping off the effects of the ether and the shock.

"Caro?" he whispered into her ear.

"Ready." She raised her head, but was looking at him from under one droopy eyelid.

"I don't think you're ready for anything else tonight, madam." Searching the identity box would have to wait until later.

"Do you smell that, Drew?" She sat up straight and sniffed at the air like a hound.

"Smell what?" He sniffed twice but smelled nothing out of the ordinary.

"Roast beef with a morel mushroom and burgundy sauce."

"You must be hungry." And still a bit delirious.

"I can smell it here in the basement. I smelled it outside, and nearly two weeks ago in the alley outside the Huntsman. So you needn't put that damnable cloak over my head, Drew, because we're in the basement of the Huntsman Gentleman's Club." She waggled a finger at him. "And don't try to tell me otherwise."

"Caro—"

"Don't worry, Drew. I'm very good at keeping secrets."

So am I, my love. So am I.

"Then let's get you home to supper, Caro." Before she stumbled onto anything else that might give away her identity.

She yawned and nodded as she stood up. "Mackenzie will know just what to do."

Hopefully the man would know what to do with a slightly tipsy princess.

Chapter 17

"Wake up, Caro! Caro . . ." Drew's voice brushed past Caro's ear, soft and sultry. "Hey there, Princess, we're nearly back at Grandauer Hall. Time to wake up."

She didn't want to wake up, because that would mean Drew would no longer have his arms wrapped around her, that he wouldn't kiss her, that the carriage wouldn't just keep rocking down the road.

But it didn't. It stopped, the wheels crunching in the gravel.

"Thank you, Drew." Which was all she managed to say before Runson opened the carriage door.

"Hold on tightly, Princess." Drew scooped her out of the carriage and into the cool night air.

"Go on ahead, my lord," Runson said, "I'll bring in your things."

"And my folio please, Mr. Runson!" Caro said as Drew carried her up the front stairs, feeling slightly guilty for a little act of thievery she'd committed back at the Factory.

"Can you walk, Caro?" Drew asked, peering into her eyes as he entered the foyer, his manner still coolly clinical despite the warm thumping of his heart against hers.

"I'll be fine." Though she didn't want to leave his arms. Not ever.

"I'm sure of that," he said, setting her on her feet, then offering his elbow. "Let's get you to bed. Then I'll bring you up a tray of supper."

"I'm not hungry anymore. But I do want my folio!" Caro caught Runson as he was heading for the library.

"I'll take that, Caro," Drew said, startling her as he grabbed the handles before she could get to it. "I'm sure you won't be needing this tonight."

She laughed in relief. "No, but I think I'll stay in bed in the morning and catch up on some of my paperwork."

"You, madam?" His eyes flew open as he offered his steadfast arm again. "Linger in your bed? Somehow I can't imagine that."

"I couldn't have imagined being shot at or stabbed, until after I met you." Couldn't have imagined that she would ever have come to like the beastly Earl of Wexford.

Let alone admire him, or long to see his grin or feel the brush of his hand against hers.

"Touché." He smiled and led her with great care up the stairs and into her room. He lit a candle on her dressing table, then turned to her, seeming taller than before, the planes of his face deepening the mystery of him. "I'll call Mrs. Tweeg to help you undress."

"No, Drew. Please don't bother her. It's late." Caro

yawned as she wrestled with the clasp on her cloak. "I can do it."

"Here, Caro. I'll do that for you." His fingers were warm and so capable as he opened the clasp, made her gasp a little as they brushed across the base of her neck, leaving a trail of heat and yearning.

She looked up into his eyes, those glittering dark pools that she could so easily fall into and happily drown.

"Thank you, Drew."

"At your service, Princess." He smiled crookedly and draped her cloak across the back of the chair. He hadn't gone far, but he'd taken his heat with him, his strength. "Now into bed with you."

With you, Drew? Dear Lord, where did that come from? Inviting a man into her bed?

"Yes, Drew. Good night." She felt suddenly shy and wanton and altogether cheeky.

"Good night, then, Princess," he said from the door, closing it gently and disappearing into the night.

But certainly not from her thoughts.

Exhausted and aching and eager to be in bed, Caro unpinned her hair then reached too quickly around behind her to undo the buttons down her back and was reminded the hard way that she had been stabbed that afternoon.

"Ouch. Ooooo!"

"What is it, Caro? Are you all right?" Caro hadn't heard the door open, only knew that Drew had magically appeared in front of her in his shirtsleeves, his eyes fierce.

"Sorry, Drew, I forgot about my little accident. I can't quite reach the buttons of my blouse. Would you help me, please?"

He snorted as if she'd asked him to paint the barn with a toothbrush. "Then turn."

Caro turned, sweeping her hair up off her neck. "Thank you again, Drew."

She waited for the delicious feel of his fingers at her back. And waited. She knew he was still standing close behind her; she could hear him breathing, deeply, steadily.

"Is something wrong, Drew?"

"No." He dove into the buttons as though in a race, had them unfastened and the tails of her blouse hanging loose in an instant. "There."

"Thank you."

But he just stood there, tantalizingly close, his spicy heat pouring off his chest, seeping into the bare skin at her back.

"What's the matter, Drew?" She whirled around to face him, clutching at the front of her blouse, the back now gaping off her naked shoulders.

His gaze smoldered as he looked at her, his eyes darker than ever. "You're not wearing anything under there."

"You knew that. You dressed me yourself today, after ripping off my bodice, then drugging me and stealing my clothes."

"True, Caro. But at the time, I was terrified for you, hadn't given a thought to . . . well, to your state of undress."

She ought to be shocked to her soul, embarrassed by the intimacies he'd seen. Instead, something inside her seemed to be calling to him, her skin aching for his touch.

"But now you *are* giving it a thought?"

"More than a thought, Caro." He was standing close, towering over her, filling her field of vision.

"Are you really?" Every breath she took brought more of his wondrous scent inside her chest, swirled and eddied there.

"More than I dare." His face was deeply shadowed, devilish, his nostrils flaring as he suddenly slipped his huge, hot hands over her bare shoulders and drew her closer and closer until her nipples were brushing against the linen of her shirt and his shirt, making her gasp, wanting more of him. More of this.

"Your motives were irreproachable, Drew."

"*Were*, Caro." He was bending his head to hers, parting his lips as though he was planning to kiss her at last.

Please!

"What are your motives now, Drew?"

His eyes flickered, his mouth full and moist.

"Ohhhh, myyyyy!" And then she knew, because he was suddenly kissing her, thoroughly tasting her, holding her tightly, as if he would never let go.

"Ah, Caro!" His touch was mystical and everywhere, he possessed her mouth with his own, explored it with his marvelous tongue, calling her name and groaning long and low when she kissed him back. Her beastly earl turned generous lover, the delicious change in his body, the singular hardness pressing against her belly.

He was a powerful heat that seeped through her clothes and spread through her like a dizzying fever. The very same way he had spread so generously through her life and into her heart.

"Christ, what am I doing?" He set her from him

abruptly, his eyes wide with horror, his mouth glistening with the remains of her kiss.

"You were kissing me, Drew." Wondering why the man had stopped, she reached her arms up around his neck.

"No, Caro." He pulled her arms away and backed away from her.

Which made her blouse fall to the floor and left him staring at her bare breasts, his mouth working, little growling noises coming out of his throat.

She really ought to be at least a little embarrassed, but all his staring only made her want him to touch her there, to kiss her—

"Christ, Caro!"

Drew had never seen anything so beautiful in his life. Her soft, lush breasts, buoyant and pliable, candlelit and tipped in subtle rose. His palms ached to hold them, to cup them and taste them.

God, he wanted to claim her for himself!

To steal her away to some exotic island where no one had heard of princesses and spies and conspiracies. Where he could wed her and bed her and they could raise their children—

But that was impossible.

Moving a muscle was impossible, dangerous, because she was temptation made flesh.

"Enough!" His voice came out strangled as he stalked to her bed and grabbed up her wispy nightgown and tossed it toward her, not daring to look at her. "Put this on."

"Thank you, Drew."

He remained fully turned away, still quaking for her, listening to the rustle of her, dying of the scent of her, until he was sure she had donned the nightgown and stepped out of her skirts.

"Finished?"

"Yes." It was a confused little whisper that made him feel like a lout. Which was exactly right.

"Now, into that bed, madam." He pointed to the pillows and glared at her as she crossed in front of him.

But his glare only seemed to encourage her to smile back at him as though she knew exactly the extent of his problem.

Exactly the extent of his erection, still at full attention, still alive with the need for her.

She gingerly slipped under the thick counterpane. "Ohhhh, Drew, you're right. This feels wonderful! Thank you . . ."

Tempted beyond his ability to continue looking at her, he stalked away from her unfettered moans, her settling under the covers, and picked up the clothes she had dropped on the floor.

"Now then, Princess, I want you to stay in bed all morning and well into the afternoon. Do you understand me? As much as you believe that you're indestructible, and that you're feeling fine because you think that the bastard only pricked you, you need your rest. Is that clear?"

"Mmmmmm . . ." and then a soft yawn was her only comment, though he still couldn't risk looking her way.

He draped the clothes over his arm, trying not to notice that they still clung to the heat of her body. "I'll return these to the tailor shop at the Factory tomorrow. Mr. Matthews will clean them, then return them to his stock . . . Princess?"

She'd been very quiet. Too quiet.

"Caro?" But she was asleep, breathing deeply.

Her cheeks were a soft, healthy pink, her golden hair spread out on the pile of thick pillows. Her fine, slender body was resting, healing itself for the grueling days ahead.

And the long years of her life.

"How I'll miss you, love." He lightly brushed the backs of his fingers across her forehead.

Cool and dry. So very soft.

He leaned down and touched his mouth to her temple, lingered until she sighed and slipped deeper into the pillows.

"Sleep well, Princess." He tucked the edge of the counterpane under her chin. "It'll keep till morning."

"And ever after," she whispered in a voice that evaporated into her dreams and out of his reach.

Four days and he would be free of her.

And his heart could start beating again.

"Drew?" Caro came awake with her skin alive and her insides yearning for him, for his kiss.

But daylight had come and he wasn't still here in her chamber—though his scent lingered, along with that lovely memory of him.

As well as the guilty memory of her recent assault on his vaunted Factory.

Feeling like an unrepentant sneak thief, with the man she'd stolen from sleeping innocently in the room next door, she padded over to the desk for her folio, then back to her bed, where she dug herself into the covers.

She hadn't actually stolen anything. Merely a few

papers from a file that had just been lying there on the table in the Factory with her name on it. And one couldn't really steal something that belonged to oneself.

She'd lived by that rule for years now, and yet it seemed a bit shoddy now that she'd applied it to Drew.

But shoddy or not, it had to be done if she was going to launch her own investigation.

She opened the folio and pulled out the first document.

"From Palmerston." His note to Drew asking him to meet with him about taking the case of the Princess Caroline.

But scrawled across the bottom in Drew's bold handwriting were the words: "No. Not another foul-hearted, spoiled, despicable royal as long as I live."

"Well, thank you, Lord Wexford." No wonder the man had been so prickly and impatient with her at first.

And how surprising that he had kissed her so fiercely, so finely last night.

Well, this piece of paper obviously didn't belong to her, which made her feel even more like a fraud, like she was looking into Drew's private journal.

The next appeared to be a quickly sketched map of Grandauer Hall and its grounds, with red Xs at the gate and around the perimeter, with other notes and arrows.

"Security." He and his agents had certainly done a fine job with that.

And then a three-page report listing the same chronology of the initial investigation that Drew had explained to her. Before he knew that she was the target.

Before she was just another foul-hearted, spoiled, despicable royal.

Ah, but here was something that surely belonged to her.

An 1817 letter to the prince regent from her father, complimenting him on the fine greyhounds he'd received from the English king as a birthday gift.

"What an odd thing to keep in my file."

And here was an even more inconsequential note, dated 1823, from her own mother to Lady Minorhoff, inviting her to that afternoon's tea.

Both messages were plainer than plain. Hardly evidence in a conspiracy against her.

The same could be said for a household accounting page from a family clerk, or the Tovaranche cook's Candlemas menu and his list of ingredients.

Or this shaky scribbling from old Nanny Lambton . . .

"Caro?"

"Drew!"

His rap on her hallway door came a second later. "Are you decent, madam?"

Struck speechless, feeling like a lying, cheating swindler, she blinked down at the contraband documents strewn across her counterpane.

"Your breakfast and your bath, Princess."

"Yes, come, Drew," she called out as she stuffed the pages beneath the covers.

A whole parade happened next. Mrs. Tweeg and her minions, the tub and the steaming water, and then Drew himself entered from the corridor. After they all had left, Tweeg and Drew stayed behind, intently peering down at her, a breakfast tray in the maid's hands.

"His lordship tells me you've been wounded in battle, Your Highness."

Drew bent over her like a spreading oak. "You'll mind Tweeg while I'm in London, won't you, Princess?"

"You're going now?" She tried not to sound too hopeful, praying only for him to be away just long enough for her to finish reading the rest of the papers. "For how long?"

"That depends, madam." He leveled a finger at her, a softer note in his voice, a lower thunder. "And you'll behave. Tell none of your subjects about the incident yesterday."

"I promise, my lord." Caro nearly crossed her heart as a seal, but considering what she was hiding from him just under the counterpane, it seemed almost a blasphemy.

"Good luck, Tweeg." He tipped the woman a salute and then strode out of the room without another word to Caro.

"Are you ready for your bath? Or your breakfast?"

"Oh, breakfast, please, Mrs. Tweeg." Caro made room for the tray across her lap. "I didn't have dinner last night."

"Then eat up, Your Highness. The bath will keep warm for another half hour."

Then Caro was alone again, the pages at her thigh seeming to burn a hole there.

She retrieved them all from under the covers and read the next on top as she munched on a piece of toast.

A letter dated two days before she was born.

3 May 1830

My Dear Captain R,

Please deliver your precious cargo to her final destination with utmost dignity and meticulous caution. Yours is a mission of incalculable value to so many, and its clandestine nature cannot be overemphasized.

Gratefully,
GR IV

"Precious cargo? What the devil is this?" And why would such a letter be included among papers in a file compiled to investigate a threat to her life?

Who is this Captain R?

And what about GR IV?

"King George the Fourth?" He hadn't died until June 26 of that year, so he would have been king when her mother was spirited safely out of Boratania. Was this Captain R responsible for her mother's safe arrival in London, just in time to give birth to Caro herself?

Sobering indeed. After all, what if her mother hadn't made it here to England? If she'd been taken at sea with the unborn heir to Boratania.

A kingdom lost to the world.

And might soon be again if she didn't uncover the source of the conspiracy against her.

But the last page of the lot was a true joy, and she laughed out loud.

"I told you so, Andrew Chase, first Earl of Wexford."

Pleased as punch, Caro downed her breakfast as she soaked in her blissfully steaming bath, afterward suffering through Mrs. Tweeg's tending to her stab wound, listening to the woman's exclamations of outrage against her wicked attacker, as well as her pronouncement that the wound was healing quite nicely, thank you.

She dressed on her own in a lose-fitting skirt and button-front shirtwaist and then carried her folio downstairs.

As she approached the library, she heard Wilhelm and the rest of her subjects in a spirited discussion over the sale of a mule.

"All that trouble over a mule, gentlemen?"

"Your Highness! Good morning!" The men stumbled to their feet, greeting her randomly as she entered the room and dropped the folio into her chair at the desk.

"A very good morning, everyone." Very, very good!

But they were still bobbing and wavering, waiting for her to instruct them. She hadn't had much practice at being a ruling monarch, especially in such distinguished company.

"Please, do make yourselves comfortable." But they only stood looking at her, still poised at the ready. "I hope you've all settled in to your rooms."

"Oh, we have, Your Highness," Gunnar said, nodding, "and the children are very happy. Though we still cannot possibly thank you enough."

"You already have, Gunnar." And Drew's suspicions had been so wrong. "Why, imagine my delight to discover that your family is one of Boratania's most ancient."

Gunnar's eyes went wide. "The Hertenfels may be

nearly as old as the Grostovs, Your Highness, but they were scholars and scientists. We've no claim at all to nobility."

Which seemed suddenly nonsensical as she slipped the paper out of the folio and unfolded it to Drew's report on the indisputable pedigrees of her subjects. His diabolical Factory was good for investigating more than just mayhem and murder.

"I don't know why I didn't realize it sooner, gentlemen." She'd always concentrated on the *things* of Boratania, not its people. The artifacts, not the artisans. "Your house, too, Wilhelm. The Belvederes have been Boratanian for at least six hundred years."

"Proudly so, if you don't mind my saying, Your Highness." Wilhelm smiled and bowed grandly for her.

"You have every right to be proud, Wilhelm. All of you." She had nearly memorized the Factory report. "Karl, your Brendels were all ambassadors, just as you were."

"I've been more a gypsy these last twenty years, Princess Caroline." He sighed, his shoulders sagging as he nodded toward his compatriots. "We've all been."

And she was going to right that wrong as well. "Johannes comes from a long line of Halstedt generals, just as Marcus does through the Oderwald family."

"Well, Princess Caroline," Erasmus said as he folded his long limbs into a chair that was too low for him, "the Uechersbachs have always been just hound folk."

"Breeders of the three finest hunting hounds in all the world. And you still have them?"

"In direct line from your father's favorites."

"I am so grateful to you, Erasmus. To all of you." A watery lump rose in Caro's throat, years of not understanding the deeply personal connection she had to the kingdom she loved with all her heart.

And these men, their children and grandchildren, were the living symbols of Boratania's past, as well as its future. The treasures and artifacts belonged to them as much as they did to her.

Their roles every bit as important as her own.

"I have a huge request to make of you, gentlemen."

"Anything, Your Highness," Wilhelm said, and to a man their chests rose. They exchanged wide smiles and then turned them all on her.

"I know it's late notice"—she'd only just thought of it while in her bath—"with the coronation only a few days away; however, I would consider it a great honor if you would all take part in the ceremonies."

Caro didn't know what she had expected from her subjects, but it certainly wasn't the stunned, staring silence they were giving her.

"I know it's a surprise, gentlemen," she said, seriously concerned at the tears gathering in Johannes's gray eyes, "but I promise you that—"

"What is it you mean for us to do, Your Highness?" Gunnar asked, his voice quaking.

"Well, I'd like you to be my honor guard."

"Your what?" Karl had been quiet till then.

"It's simple, really. You'll walk down the aisle ahead of me in two lines—"

"Oh, no," he said, vigorously shaking his head, sharing his distress with the others.

Certain that she wasn't explaining correctly, Caro continued, cajoling. "One of you will carry my scepter and one will carry my crown—"

Marcus was now waving his hands in front of his chest. "Oh, no, no, that won't do, Your Highness."

The lot of them looked terrified.

"I don't understand, gentlemen."

"Your Highness, you humble us all," Johannes managed as he wiped his nose on his kerchief.

The other men stumbled to their feet again, Wilhelm wringing his hands. "No, but we really couldn't, shouldn't . . ." he stammered, shaking his head at the others.

"But why can't you?" Gracious! She hadn't insulted them, had she?

"Well, Your Highness, we . . . just . . ."

"I'd very much like all of you to be there with me when Boratania is reborn."

Marcus clapped his hand across his heart. "What if we fail, Your Highness?"

"Fail?" Was that all? "Well, I don't think you can fail, Marcus. You are all very good at walking in a straight line and holding things that are far more cumbersome than a scepter and a crown. Heavens, I've seen you with the children."

"But, but, this is your coronation, Princess Caroline," Johannes whispered as though someone would hear.

"And I can't imagine accepting my crown without all of you at my side."

They were staring at her again, still terrified of something. And then an idea came to her.

"I can show you what I mean, if that would help you feel better. We can practice right here in the library."

"Well . . . but . . ." Erasmus said in a very wobbly voice.

"The coronation takes place in St. George's Chapel

at Windsor Castle." Caro pulled her chair out of the way of the desk, flinching at the stitch of pain in her side. She ought to be more careful, but this was so important. "So we'll clear an aisle down the middle of the room, though the chapel is quite a bit longer."

Their eyes wide with doubt, the men quickly moved chairs and tables out of the way, making a path between the library door and the tall windows.

"Ah, we can use these." Caro grabbed the fireplace poker and a wreath of dried roses, then went to the door. "Now, form two lines on either side of the rug there."

They turned in a tight knot, then separated into two rows, facing Caro.

She handed the wreath to a surprised Johannes. "The crown of Boratania," she said with a smile. And the fire poker to Wilhelm. "The golden scepter."

"But Your Highness," Wilhelm said, looking up the shaft of the sooty poker.

Caro strode grandly between her subjects to the windows, grabbing a lap blanket off the back of a chair, stopped, and turned back to them as she tied the blanket around her neck with the fringe at the corners.

"Then you'll merely have to walk the distance of a hundred feet or so down the aisle."

They were standing stock still, silently looking back at her over their shoulders.

"You'll stop at the base of the altar." Afraid she was losing them entirely, Caro hurried on, the blanket trailing down her back to her hem. "I'll walk forward and stop just ahead of Johannes and Wilhelm. The archbishop will talk a bit and I'll pledge to serve Boratania and then the archbishop will take the crown from you, Johannes, and set it on my head."

Caro took the wreath from the man and crammed it onto her head. "Then he'll take the scepter from you, Wilhelm and hand it to me . . ."

Caro took the poker out of the stunned Wilhelm's hand and turned too quickly toward the open library door, dislodging the wreath and making it slip down over her eyes.

"See, gentlemen, it couldn't be simpler."

"But I must say, Princess," came a dear and familiar bass rumble, "I've seen more opulent."

"Drew!" Her heart stopped, then her pulse lifted and went sailing through her veins as she pushed the wreath up off her eyes.

Great heavens, could a man grow more handsome in the course of just a few hours? Taller, more devilish?

Because Drew certainly had.

"You're home early, my lord!"

Chapter 18

Drew found himself wanting to grin like a wild man at the bewitching sight before him. His exotically rustic princess surrounded by her wide-eyed tribe of loyal, benighted warriors.

She was homespun and otherworldly in that soft, loose-fitting shirtwaist, her hair hanging down her back, crowned in a spray of dried pink roses.

Charmed to the marrow and deeply roused by the crimson of her cheek, by the sinuous, sensual memory of last night's intimacies, Drew chewed on the end of his tongue to keep from laughing right out loud.

Because the blasted woman had stolen papers from her secret file right out from under his nose, from the impregnable, highly secure Factory.

"We were practicing, my lord," Johannes said, looking thoroughly scandalized.

Caro's grin was slanted and haughty as she dragged the wreath off her head. "For my coronation."

"I see." Though the spectacle of the real ceremony couldn't possibly hold a candle to the pomp playing out before him here in the library.

Caro turned back to her shell-shocked loyalists. "Please stand with me, gentlemen. I can't think of a more worthy group to share in my joy."

Whatever it was she wanted from them, now the men went sheepish and shy. Shuffling their feet, swaying from side to side.

"For Boratania?" Caro looked from face to face, her hands clasped together.

Drew was sure they would agree to her request, whatever she was asking; his agents had found nothing more threatening to Caro than old family loyalties and a quiet, admirable devotion to their princess and to their lost dreams.

Their hopes and love for Caro were plain in their faces, shown brightly through their eyes—as brightly as her love for them.

"You'd best give in to the princess, gentlemen, else she'll haunt you all your days."

As she'd begun to haunt his nights, his afternoons and his mornings.

The air he breathed and the rooms he entered.

"I *will* haunt you, gentlemen."

Wilhelm's worried frown lightened to a hopeful grin. "If you don't think we'll embarrass you . . ."

"You couldn't possibly, Wilhelm!" The woman paused then, suspended in her expectations as the men looked to each other for agreement.

And then in concert, they nodded at her, wanly and then eagerly.

"Oh, thank you all!" Caro clapped her hands.

"You're wonderful!" She fell on each man with a noisy kiss on the cheek, causing Erasmus to stagger backward into his chair in a happy daze. "And don't worry a moment about the ceremony. You're already perfect, but we'll practice again and again, if you'd like."

Drew watched the woman as she continued courting their resolution, riding out their courage until Gunnar was volunteering to play a traditional Boratanian folk tune on his concertina and Marcus was dancing hooked armed circles with Johannes.

"May I see you in the parlor, Princess? Alone."

"Oh . . ." She smiled at Drew, her cheeks pink and blooming with health. "Oh, yes, of course, my lord!"

"And bring your folio."

She stopped still for a moment, looked at him from under the dip of her eyebrows. Then she exhaled sharply, thanked her delighted subjects, grabbed her folio from the chair and beat him to the investigation room.

Drew shut the door behind them. "You stole papers out of my file."

"*My* file." She hefted the folio onto a table. "It had my name all over it."

"Did you hope I wouldn't notice a few missing documents? Or did you think I wouldn't care?"

"I wanted to see what was inside."

"So instead of asking my permission, you merely took it upon yourself to steal what you want?"

She gave an unconvincing shrug and then a long sigh which made her sound nearly contrite. "Sorry, Drew. It's become a habit with me. It was so easy. I just slipped them into my cloak pocket."

"How comforting." He'd been utterly bewitched by her at the time, still terrified for her safety, and angry, his confounded senses tied in knots.

"If I had asked to read through my own file, would you have allowed it?"

"No. I can't, Caro. I've got sources and methods to protect. Agents in the field, with covers to safeguard."

Your own identity to protect, Princess. From you and from those who would use the truth against you. Though he was certain she hadn't taken anything that would singularly give her away.

"Then here's everything back, Drew." She frowned at the papers that sprung out of the folio when she unlatched it. "I certainly don't want to cause any more bloodshed."

"Nor do I."

"But I do want to know why you've got such commonplace letters in here." She eyed him as she thumbed through the stack of purloined pages. "From each of my parents, a cook, my long-dead nanny—"

"Handwriting samples," he said, hoping that would be enough explanation for her. But she was looking at him askance.

"Why?"

"Because in the course of my investigation, I might need to verify the source of a document. Having signature samples on file makes my job simpler and the process faster."

She nodded. "That's very clever, Drew."

"A standard investigating technique," he said as he reached out to collect the stray pages of the file. But she plucked back one of them.

"What about this very cryptic letter to a sea captain. It's dated two days before I was born and signed by King George the IV, just weeks before he died. I can only imagine that he's talking about seeing to the safety of my mother."

The safe transport of her body in this grand ruse, my love. The last measure of her devotion to her husband and her lost kingdom.

And you hadn't yet been chosen from the orphanage, Princess.

"That's . . . um, yes, Caro," Drew said, putting the page back into the stack as he tried to form an answer that wouldn't feel so much like a lie, "you're probably right."

"Where did you get the letter?"

"Like the others, they came from Palmerston, from the Foreign Office files when I took on your case."

She snorted and eased back into a chair, narrowing her eyes at him as the sunlight streamed into the room and caught up like bits of gold in her hair.

"Ah, yes: the Case of the Foul-hearted, Spoiled, Despicable Royal."

He caught the smile crinkling up the corners of her mouth, his own words, his hasty judgment come back to chide him. "The very case."

She lowered her lashes and then raised her gaze to him with her blue, blue eyes. "I'm sorry."

Bloody hell, *he* wasn't. "No, you're not sorry at all, Caro. I know you too well."

"I am sorry for making you work that much harder for me. Sometimes I don't think before I act." She caught at the edge of her full, sultry lips with her teeth. "You've been my champion all this time—my hero—and I've been a lunatic princess."

A lunatic that he wanted to kiss again.

A princess he'd claim for his own if he could.

"But my favorite lunatic princess, Caro."

"Your favorite? Truly?"

"My favorite in all the world."

With whom I've fallen desperately, foolishly, in love.

Her smile fell with the tip of her chin. "Just a few more days, Drew."

"Until what?"

She sat forward on the edge of the chair as though to fling herself from it. "Until my life is safely out of your hands and I am crowned empress."

His stomach tightened, lurched at the thought of losing her, of not being able to look into those soft blue eyes every morning and every night.

Or hear her laughter.

Not that he could ever have taken a step in that direction. Their lives were as impossibly divergent as the sun and the moon. And he had a job to complete.

"I think we've got company, Drew!" She stood and hurried toward the front window.

"Two horses." He'd heard the hooves on the gravel at the same time she had. "It's probably Jared and Ross."

He had left word at the Factory that he'd be at Grandauer Hall, hoping they would have uncovered a bit of good news and come find him.

Drew reached the foyer in time to see Jared and Ross nearly knock Runson over as they came bursting through the door. Ross stopped and clapped the man on the shoulder. "That butler suit fits you fine, Runson."

Runson only grunted and went out the door to stable the horses.

"Tell me you found the bastard," Drew said in a

whisper, wanting to learn whatever they had to report without Caro overhearing anything that would cause her to start up another investigation of her own.

"Your man was a mason, all right," Jared said, leaning back against the paneled wall, folding his arms across his chest.

"Excellent!" Drew caught back the bellow of joy.

Ross handed Drew a notepad. "And he was employed by the Flannery Brothers, one of the contractors who were installing the fountains at the Crystal Palace."

"Then you must have gotten his bloody name."

"It was Cowling," Jared said, as though Drew would understand the significance. "John Cowling."

"Was?" Drew finally heard their deliberate reference to the past tense.

"Cowling's dead."

"What? How, dammit?"

"Stabbed."

"You're joking, Ross."

"I wish I were. I'd like to have led that particular interrogation myself. But his body was found around midnight, in an alley near the Dove pub in Hammersmith."

"Selfish bastard! Is that all Cowling left of himself? Did you talk to his—"

"Good afternoon, my lords." Caro came gliding toward them in her silent-heeled slippers and now offered a hand to Ross and Jared. "Welcome to Grandauer Hall."

Jared stood away and gave Caro a clinical scrutiny. "It's good to see you looking so well, Your Highness, after yesterday's close call."

She pivoted, obviously showing off her apparent

recovery. "If I were a cat, my lord, I'd still have seven lives left. And as long as I have Lord Wexford watching over me—"

"I told you she was mad," Drew shot to his friends as he headed back toward the investigation room.

"Who is John Cowling?" she asked brightly as they arrived in the room, casually glancing from one man to another.

Drew took her question, not sure how far he was going to go with his answers. "He's the man who stabbed you, Princess."

She said nothing as she went to the table where her folio was opened wide and now lacking the "borrowed" papers. Her eyes were darkly serious when she turned back to him. "And where is he now? In jail?"

Drew felt Ross and Jared shift their gazes toward him, felt Caro's settle on his.

"He's . . . he was killed last night, Princess," Drew said. "Stabbed. His body left lying in an alley."

"Dear God!" Her eyes grew wide and deeply blue. "Murdered, because he missed me by an inch."

"He wouldn't have lived long, Your Highness," Ross said, obviously surprised at Caro's plainspoken observation. "Whoever hired him would have made sure he wasn't around today to talk about it."

"What a very bad business," she said, scrubbing at her forehead with her fingers.

"But you were right about Cowling, Princess." Drew paged through Ross's notepad, plagued by the feeling that he was missing something vital. "He was a mason, a bricklayer, contracted to work on the fountains."

"And the man in the tintype? Have you heard back from Wyatt and Halladay?"

"*That* assassin's name was Paul Lauder," Drew said, pleased that the conversation had shifted to more solid ground. He pulled the daguerreotype from a pocket in his own folio. "This is his younger brother. A law-abiding tanner named Arnold Lauder."

"His brother?" She took the photo from him and studied it while Drew looked on.

"Paul Lauder emigrated from Bruges seven years ago, to settle in England. He's been living in London since then, and was a waiter at Tavistock's, the gentleman's club."

"Before he decided to become an assassin?" She lifted her eyes to him.

"So it seems."

"A Belgian waiter and a bricklayer?" She shook her head and peered out the window toward the orangery. "But that doesn't quite ring true."

Jared sat on the edge of the window seat. "Surely not the typical assassin."

She looked at Jared. "Then neither is the person who's hiring them to kill me."

"What do you mean, Princess?" Ross was studying her intently from across the room.

"I may be wrong, but wouldn't a typical conspirator hire an expert assassin, instead of sending someone to Gdansk to ask a taverner to ask someone to ask someone else if he knows any assassins who need a little work?"

"I see," Jared stood, his jaw squared as he worked through Caro's insight. "An amateur."

"An excellent observation, Princess." Drew had come to the same conclusion. "Because when that doesn't work, when the amateur assassin fails, the conspirator then hires the nearest waiter. And when that fails, the nearest bricklayer . . ."

A flash of wisdom went off inside Drew's head.

The nearest.

There was a commonality here between the assassins that he didn't want to share with Caro just now. Not before he and Jared and Ross could check it out without her.

And if he was right, he had no time to lose.

"Oh, bloody hell," Drew bellowed, making a show of yanking his watch from his waistcoat pocket and groaning at it. "It's nearly one o'clock! I've a meeting with Palmerston."

"Right now?" she asked.

"Sorry, Princess." He grabbed Caro's pile of stolen papers and stuck them into his own folio. "Can't be helped. You know how flighty he can be."

"Do give him my best," Caro said, with a raised eyebrow, "and my compliments on the fascinating operations in his basement at Whitehall."

Drew gave Jared and Ross a don't-ask look and started for the door. "You'll share my carriage, gentlemen?"

Drew gave them a look that insisted. He needed to talk in private with them.

He'd trusted these two men with his life for as long as he could remember, trusting them with the life of his princess had just become imperative.

Palmerston's warning notwithstanding.

He caught Caro's hand as they reached the door and gave it a squeeze before he put her fingers to his lips. "Behave, madam! Trust no one that I haven't introduced to you."

"I promise." She put her hand to her heart as though in pledge. "That goes for you, my lord."

"I'll do my best." He felt her watching him as he hurried down the stairs away from her.

"Will you be back for supper, Drew?"

The woman who had wrapped her soft fingers around his heart was standing at the door in her homey skirts, shielding her eyes with her hand and beckoning him home for dinner.

Tempting him.

Rousing him.

"I'll do my best, Princess."

"Good, then I'll see you at supper, my lord." She grinned at him, waved, then slipped back inside, leaving a dark hole in the sky above him.

"Never saw a man look quite so cozy as you did right then," Ross said to Drew as they tied the horses to the back of the carriage. "Except for you, Jared. Whenever you're with your Kate. Gad, it's a plague."

Drew climbed into the carriage, his bones suddenly as weary as his soul. "You know me, Ross, I keep myself as far removed from royals as I can."

Especially the warmhearted, generous, honorable ones.

God help me, I love you, Caro.

Chapter 19

Caro dashed through the rest of the day, her heart soaring every time she thought of Drew, and spiraling downward whenever she reminded herself that she had only a few more days in his company. Then he would be gone from her life.

Unless I steal you for myself, Drew.

It was only fair; he'd stolen her heart when she wasn't looking.

She would have insisted on going to London with him, but he seemed determined to leave her here, even concocting a meeting with Palmerston so that he and Ross and Jared could take off without her. Besides, she still had plenty to do, getting the most precious of the Boratanian artifacts packed and ready in time for the opening ceremonies.

Wary of stray assassins who might be lurking around the next corner, she engaged three bodyguards to help her in the orangery; Runson, Mr. Wheeler and Henry, whose arm was healing very nicely and who had been as difficult to keep in a resting mode as she was.

Within the hour the orangery was bustling with more help than Caro actually needed. Karl's wife, Dorothea, and then Wilhelm's wife, Gloriana, tended to the textiles, regaling her with their memories of Boratania.

And then the children came to join the fun, once they were finished riding their ponies across the estate.

And, of course, two by two, the men came to help and to chuckle about their part in the coronation ceremony, until the orangery rang with the sounds of celebration.

Eventually, the last few crates were carefully packed and the wagon loaded and the ties secured around the canvas to be taken to the Crystal Palace in the morning.

When supper arrived in the dining room, Caro watched the door as the soup came, listened for Drew's footfall in the foyer all during the meal. But he didn't come then, and didn't come as she settled with her subjects into the cluttered comfort of her library to try to make sense of her dozen logbooks.

She'd gotten used to worrying about him, so she tucked it away in the front of her heart and bent over her logbook, soothed by the sounds of the children running about and the men playing chess.

"What's this date here, Wilhelm?" Caro looked up from a line of Wilhelm's carefully added script.

"Let me see, your highness." Wilhelm hurried toward her from his bending over the chess game at the hearth table. "Now, where do you mean?"

"Here, where I wrote, 'carved wooden figure of a

dun cow,' you've added in green ink, 'Old Delsee, tavern sign, Rumdorf,' and is that date 1768 or 1763?"

"Ah, it's 1763, Your Highness. The date my great-grandsire opened the tavern doors."

"Isn't it amazing, Wilhelm, to learn that the Old Delsee in Rumdorf belonged to your mother's family. I'm just so grateful for all your help."

"That's checkmate again, Johannes!" Marcus bounced up from the settee and stuck out his palm. "And you owe me another shilling!"

Johannes shook his finger at Marcus. "One more game, Marcus. Double or nothing!"

She'd gotten so used to having her library look and sound like a market square on a midsummer holiday that she didn't know what she was going to do without them all living with her every day.

"You'd better go break that up, Wilhelm," Caro said, laughing at the lot of them, "before they start tussling on the floor."

"My pencil broke, Princess Caroline." Annora produced the broken point.

"You must be working very hard, Annora."

"Teaching Oscar to write his name."

Caro gave the girl another pencil from a drawer, and she went back to the pile of children in the corner.

Caro clarified Wilhelm's date and then flipped to the next category in the logbook, leafing slowly through the pages, looking for telltale green ink.

And wondering how Drew was doing. If he was safely out of the range of bullets that were meant for her.

" 'A sculpture relief of Aphrodite—overlooked the tulip garden in Velkert Castle.' Oh, my!" Someone had added, "One of a pair."

So one was still missing! Good to know.

Caro paged through to the next section in the book and found more green ink beneath her own catalogue listing for the old coffer from St. Hildebrandt's that she'd rescued from Lord Peverel.

Added after her own, "flat lid, trail of bees dancing along the edge," were the words, "rumored to have held King Varik I's crown, after 537; compartment hidden in bottom."

"A hidden compartment?" Caro looked up from this very interesting development to the intense chess game across the room. "Pardon me, gentlemen. Which of you found the secret compartment in that old coffer?"

"I didn't actually find the compartment, Your Highness," Karl said, looking over the top of the game, "because I didn't see the coffer. Must already be packed away."

"How did you learn about the compartment?"

"Way back when I was a boy." Karl squinted one eye toward the memory. "I remember the dotty old priest at St. Hildebrandt's whispering something about the secret slot holding a lock of St. Mary's hair. I only saw the coffer itself once, when it was paraded in front of us during the feast of St. Hildebrandt's. And I never saw it open."

A secret compartment, eh? Possibly not opened for centuries.

A tantalizing mystery that nagged at her for the next half hour until she couldn't stand it any longer.

She left the library, still abuzz, lit a lantern and hurried out to the orangery to dig King Varik's coffer out of its storage.

She unlocked the orangery and made her way into the undercroft to the crate marked MISC. WOODEN WARE. Moments later she was carrying the uninspiring coffer back upstairs to her worktable. She set it down beside the lantern.

Plain, unadorned but for a beehive in the corner and those Boratanian dancing bees.

"In the bottom." She lifted the brass latch and opened the lid wide. "Still empty."

"Princess!" Annora's voice pierced the walls of the orangery just as the children came streaming around the crates and into the work area.

Robert Frederick reached Caro first and clapped his palms together. "We just saw lotsa bats coming out of the barn!"

Marguerite's chin barely reached the tabletop. "What are you doing, Princess Caroline?"

"Is that a real treasure chest?" Oscar put his arms up for Caro to pick him up.

Resigned to her little crowd, Caro lifted the boy into her arms and sat him on the edge of the table. "It just might be, Oscar."

The bottom of the wooden box did seem proportionately thicker than it needed to be, and lighter.

Frederick stuck his nose into the box. "But it's empty, Princess, how can it have a treasure inside?"

"Not all treasure is the kind we can see, Frederick." Caro closed the lid and turned the coffer over to examine the underside. "The box is supposed to have a secret compartment."

Nothing out of place, no apparent levers or latches.

"Where do you think the secret's hiding, Princess?" Marguerite tapped on the side of the box.

"I don't know, but we'll find it here somewhere." Caro relatched the box, held it close to her ear, then shook it gently.

And heard the tiniest of sounds, a sluicing *click* that made her think of sea shells.

More determined than ever to solve the puzzle, Caro kept the latch closed and brought the lamp closer.

Which brought four little faces closer, four eager smiles, four pairs of bright eyes.

Suddenly thrilled by the mystery, by the everyday miracles that came in such small packages and in such dear company, Caro turned the coffer in her hands and studied every joint, knocked on every side, pressed every corner, until she was beginning to doubt the veracity of the priest at St. Hildebrandt's.

Finally she held the sides of the box with both hands and used her thumbs to slide the lid backward about a half inch, causing a chorus of *Oooooh*s from her audience.

"It moved, Princess!"

"It did." Caro's heart was pounding as she pressed up on the bottom of the front panel and it miraculously slid upward two inches, revealing an eight inch wide by half-inch high slot that seemed to run six to eight inches into the box.

"What's inside, Your Highness?" Oscar leaned over to look into the opening.

"Is it gold?" Annora tried to see inside.

"Candy?"

Not a treasure at all. "It's paper, children."

"Ahhhhh, phooey!"

"Paper?"

"Is it story time yet?"

"Soon, Oscar." All this while Caro was trying to fish the thickly folded pages out of the slot with fingers that were starting to shake with excitement.

With a little gentle coaxing and a handy hairpin, she finally hooked the creased edge and started tugging gently against whatever was still catching it up.

Great heavens, it could be anything! And very old. Scripted in the distant past, hidden to share with the future. Possibly in a language that she couldn't read.

"Here it is, children!" The packet popped out into her hands, and became four pieces of paper of different sizes and type, each folded singly, then the group folded together into a packet.

"Some goofy treasure, that is!" Robert Frederick said. "Let's go back to the barn and look at the bats."

"Tell us a story, Princess!"

The best kind of treasure. Caro couldn't stop her fingers from fumbling as she unfolded the first page.

His Majesty
Windsor Castle
2 May 1830

Per instructions, alterations to the Grostov family trees shall, from this time forward, read thusly:

Father: King Alexander Ferdinand Grostov III, born 11 November 1792, killed in last day of siege, 28 April 1830, Boratania.

Mother: Queen Genevieve Adelaide Teodora of Hosig-Trepp, born 8 March 1801, died 4 May 1830, Windsor.

Child: Princess Caroline Marguerite Marie Isabella, born 4 May 1830, Windsor.

Your Obedient Servant,
Earl Marshal
College of Arms
London

"King George, again?" Caro muttered.

"Did a king write a letter to you, Princess Caroline?"

"In a way, Annora." But a very long time ago.

There were the other papers in the bundle that she desperately wanted to look at. But the lantern light was horrid here in the orangery and there were all the little fingers getting bored and looking for more coffers to open.

"Come children! It is story time, after all."

"Yaaaaayyyyyy!"

Delighted with this new mystery, Caro quickly closed up the secret panel, reset the coffer lid, then opened it to the main compartment and shoved the bundle of papers inside.

Tucking the coffer under her arm, she led the children back to the house. Her hopes that Drew had returned from London were dashed when Runson met her with a message as they came through the side door. "His lordship won't be back until later tonight, Your Highness."

Caro's heart sank. "Did he say how late?"

"No, but, don't you worry about him, Princess Caroline. He'll be back as soon as he can, and sound as a bell."

"Is it story time yet, Princess Caroline?" Oscar was

standing at the library door, holding a large book by the Grimms, and surrounded by the other children.

Johannes came up behind them. "Now, children, you've plagued the princess long enough tonight—"

"Actually, Johannes," Caro said with a smile, "it's two minutes past story time!"

They followed her into the library and gathered around her on the settee like little rabbits.

"*The Six Swans*!" Oscar said, starting to climb into Caro's lap. Caro cringed, expecting a flash of pain at her side, surprised that she could so easily take the boy's weight, even with all his scrunching and wriggling.

"*Brother Lustig*!" the two girls shouted. "No! *The Wolf and the Fox*!" They settled on *Iron Henry* and then easily talked her into four more.

She'd convinced the adults that she would be fine with the children, so they had all gone upstairs. Oscar had fallen asleep during the first story and the others were yawning by the time clever Gretel shoved the ugly old witch into the oven and rescued Hansel from certain death.

"Gretel's as brave as you are, Princess Caroline!" Robert Frederick said, groaning as he yawned and stretched.

"Princess Caroline is lots braver, Frederick!" Annora closed the big book and clutched it against her chest. "She's been saving Boratania for us, all by herself, for a long, long time. Haven't you, Princess Caroline?"

"I've had a lot of help, Annora. You've helped me, and your papa has, and Oscar and Marguerite."

"And Oscar's grandpapa!" Marguerite said. "And 'Rasmus and Lord Wexford."

"And me!" Robert Frederick jumped to his feet and saluted. "When I grow up, Princess Caroline, I want to be your best soldier ever! I won't let anyone hurt you. Ever!"

Tears pooled in Caro's eyes. This dear little boy, so willing to defend her.

"I want to be the minister of the horses!" Annora leaped up and pranced around the settee.

Oscar yawned loudly and stretched out on Caro's lap. "Can I be your pudding minister, Princess?"

Caro leaned down and kissed him on his sleepy forehead. "You can be anything you want, Oscar. Especially my pudding minister."

"What about you, Lord Wexford?" Annora had stopped her galloping behind the settee and was looking toward the library door. "What do you want to be?"

Drew! Home and whole!

Her heart pounded madly at the sight of him standing in the doorway, so towering and fierce that she lost herself for a moment in the burning darkness of his eyes.

"Do you suppose there's any job in the cabinet for me, Annora?" Drew smiled at the children as he entered and lowered himself into the chair directly across from Caro.

"Ummmm," Annora said, coming around the settee to seriously study Drew. "Minister of . . . of . . . hedgehogs!"

"Hedgehogs?" Caro said, adding a laugh.

Drew nodded. "Of course, hedgehogs, Princess. After all, they're quite small, prickly . . ."

"And sooo cute," Marguerite added, leaping over

Annora to plunk down on Drew's knee. "And they need someone to look after them!"

"There, you see, Your Highness," Drew said, wincing slightly as Marguerite dug one of her sharp elbows into his ribs. "I pledge myself to you as your minister of hedgehogs."

"You do me great honor, Lord Wexford." Caro would have stood up, but Oscar had fallen fast asleep across her lap again. "But I do think it's time for all good ministers to be safely in their beds."

"Let me give you a hand, Princess." Drew stood up with Marguerite in his arms, shuffling her comfortably over his shoulder, not seeming to mind that the girl had a stranglehold on his neck cloth.

"Bedtime, children." Caro slipped the sleeping Oscar over her shoulder then took hold of Drew's outstretched hand and pulled herself to her feet.

They trouped up the stairs to the east wing and into the sitting room, where Karl's wife was embroidering the edge of one of the traditional Boratanian neck cloths for the ceremony.

"Ah, Princess Caroline!" The woman stood up smiling, setting aside her needle as she reached out for Oscar and Marguerite. "You and Lord Wexford have been awfully good to the children."

"They're a pleasure, Mistress Brendel." Caro gave Robert Frederick's dark hair a tousle. "I see a bright future for Boratania."

"We're gonna be ministers to the princess," Robert Frederick said, puffing up his chest.

"Yes, and my ministers need their sleep." Caro bent down for her kisses. "Good night, children."

Drew followed her silently out of the sitting room

but caught her elbow as they started down the corridor.

"I think the princess needs her sleep as well," he said softly, stopping her at the top of the stairs.

"Where have you been, Drew? I was worried to death." She leveled a finger at him, still so glad to see him safely home that she wanted to throw her arms around him and not ever let go. "And don't give me that spurious tale about Palmerston. You went off to investigate something with Jared and Ross, and you didn't want me to get in the way."

He shook his head, looking far from innocent. "You caught me, Caro."

"And was it worth the trip? Did you learn anything from your breakneck junket into London?"

"You gave me the idea, Caro."

"I thought so!"

He folded his stubborn arms across his chest and frowned at her with one eyebrow. "I was looking for a connection between the waiter and the bricklayer—"

"Did you find one?"

"Possibly."

"Then, sir, if you'll come down to the library with me and tell me everything you know, I'll show you what I found today among my treasures."

"What do you mean?"

Drew wasn't sure he liked the slyness of her smile as she hurried past him down the stairs, didn't like ambushes or dangerous surprises.

"It's probably nothing, Drew." She stopped at the base of the stairs and waited for him with a smile, only to speed ahead the moment he reached her side. "But I do like the mystery of it all."

"Mystery?"

"Do you recall that very old coffer I showed you in the orangery that first day? The one with the carved bees along the edge."

"Not particularly, Caro." What in all of Boratania wasn't decorated with bees? "I'm afraid that one of your artifacts runs together with the next."

"It was from the lot I rescued from Lord Peverel." She was waiting for him at the library door, and he couldn't help thinking that she was leading him down some rosy path.

"What about the box?"

"It was empty when you and I looked inside." She smiled again and flounced off to her desk. "So I logged it as an ordinary reliquary and packed it away."

"And then what?" He stood in the doorway, not sure that he wanted anything to do with this particular mystery.

"Then yesterday, Karl saw the listing in the logbook and remembered a rumor that the coffer had a hidden compartment." She turned back to him, holding the old coffer in her hands.

He remembered the box for its primitive simplicity. "And did it?"

Her eyes took on a smoky blue, her smile like a cat with a canary. In two moves with her thumbs, the front of the box opened to reveal a dark slot.

"Just as Karl remembered it, Drew!"

Yes, but thankfully empty. Barren of any dreadful secrets. His heart thumped to life again.

"A neat trick, Caro." Relieved to his bones, Drew started toward her as she closed the compartment and returned the box to its original shape. He was about to reach for it when she flipped open the lid of the main chamber to a pack of folded papers.

"But the neatest trick of all, Drew, is that I found these tucked inside the secret compartment."

He had no idea of the content of the papers, but a wintery breeze seemed to wash through the room, flickering the lamps and riling the ends of Caro's hair.

"What are they, Caro?"

"I don't know." Grinning at him, she put the coffer on the desk. "The children were helping me when I opened the compartment out in the orangery. It was too dark and too crowded to read more than one page at the time."

His heart stopped again. "But you did read one of them?"

"I somehow expected that an old reliquary coffer with a secret compartment would be hiding something at least a few centuries old." She handed the paper to him with a sigh, then peered at its florid script overtop his elbow while he tried to keep his hand still. "But as you see, it's a letter from the Earl Marshal's office at the College of Arms to King George the Fourth. A confirmation of the way my family tree should officially read after my birth in 1830."

A fabrication, my love. A letter between two men who thought nothing of playing with your life for their own purposes.

And yet a harmless-enough record in itself, a set of facts that have been taken as common knowledge through the years, fortifying her identity as the heir to Boratania.

"You can add this to your collection, madam." He handed the letter back to her, wondering how long Peverel had been in possession of the coffer. Moreover, who had stuffed these pages into it, and when? Certainly some time after 1830, after the royal conspirators had decided on the story they were going to tell the rest of the world about the fictional newborn Boratanian princess.

"With pride, Drew. After all, a king doesn't usually put himself out to memorialize a fellow king." She looked up at him with hopeful mischief in her eyes as she carefully laid aside the letter. "Exciting, isn't it?"

"Indeed." Though exciting wasn't the word he would use. He wanted to grab the folded sheets out of her hand and vet them alone, without the woman looking on. The rest could be anything from prattle to a cannonball.

"Well, this is a grand-looking thing, Drew." She had unfolded a much larger piece of parchment: formal, highly ornamented, illuminated in gold and bright colors. "And it's dated the day of my birth!"

Drew read as quickly as he could, searching ahead for traps and pitfalls.

By Royal Writ and Universal Decree,
We, the Undersigned, For Our Mutual Protection,
Do Hereby Defend the Right of
and Grant to the Legal Issue of
King Alexander Ferdinand III of Boratania
and his Queen Genevieve Adelaide Teodora,
the Title of Empress
and Land enough to Include 10 Square Miles
to be Occupied in Perpetuity
Upon the Twenty-First Birthday of Said Issue.

"Interesting, Caro," he said, exhaling in relief. Just another legitimizing document. With any luck, the others were as innocent.

"Look at all those signatures and ribbons and royal

seals!" she said with a joyful little laugh, running her fingertip across the very bottom of the page. "The heads of every royal family in Europe at the time! Which is amazing in itself, considering what a quarrelsome lot they were. Never agreed on anything!"

Except the creation of you, Caro.

"Except, Drew, they did seem to all agree that Boratania needed to be preserved." She looked up at him, her brow furrowed in thought.

"So they did."

"Guilt, do you suppose, for not coming to my father's aid?"

"It's hard to say." Impossible, actually. May she never guess the truth.

"Whatever the reason, this is the legal deed to my kingdom." She heaved a sigh and set the writ beside the Earl Marshal's letter, then unfolded the next.

He knew the source without even looking at the signature. Two pages of vellum on Queen Victoria's personal stationery, the crown of state with the highly ornate VR below that.

"Look, Drew. It's a letter from the queen to Lord Peverel." She gasped and looked up at Drew. "Which could only mean that he knew about the hidden compartment in the coffer. Because look. It's dated 24 July 1850, last year. 'My Dear Lord Peverel . . .'"

We are pleased that you have agreed to guide our dear cousin, Princess Caroline, in creating a Working Government for the impending restoration of her beloved kingdom of Boratania.

At the same time, Lord Peverel, we cannot stress Too Strongly the importance of keeping the Princess's State Secret, especially from the Princess, Herself.

"My what? State Secret?" Caro looked up at Drew, shock and confusion alive in her face. "What secret could she possibly mean, Drew?"

But Drew could hardly breathe for the sudden, stifling tightness in his chest, for his blood sloshing through his veins like ice water.

Stop now, my love. Please, don't ask a question of me that you're not prepared to hear the answer to.

"I'm . . . not sure, Caro." He wanted to read on ahead to try to protect her, but she had crimped the page and dropped her hand. "Come, let's read on."

Get it over with.

"I can assure you, Drew, that I don't know any state secrets, Boratanian or otherwise." In a defensive huff, she snapped the paper flat and Drew caught her hand to steady it, reading quickly.

> *Our European Cousins are also trusting your Complete Discretion on the matter, sir. As a point of fact, they insist upon it as I do.*

"Dear Lord, Drew, is my entire family keeping some enormous secret from me?"

Christ, the evidence was as plain as day, as plain as the bewilderment in Caro's beautiful eyes. And had the hearth been lit in the library, he'd have been tempted to toss it all into the hottest part of the flame and let it burn.

He could say nothing to her that wouldn't be a dishonorable lie, and he just couldn't bring himself to sully the trust between them.

So he said nothing at all, only read on, his stomach churning hot, his fingers cold as he clutched the queen's letter.

Failure to guard this State Secret shall be considered an Act of Treason and will result in Swift Justice.
Our Best Hopes for a Successful Enterprise.

It was signed with the queen's distinctive *Victoria, R.*

"Treason, Drew?" She was shaking her head, still scanning the letter as she raked her fingers through the curls escaping their bonds at her forehead. "The queen has threatened Peverel with treason if he reveals whatever it is that I've done, or am, or might do, that has made me a state secret."

"So it seems." His jaw ached like fire.

"What secret? And how could it be so utterly treasonable, so capable of causing—what? A war? A plague? A scandal?—should it ever come to be known to the public. Or to me? Because, blast it all, I don't know what it is."

"The queen has certainly set forth serious consequences, Caro," Drew said, measuring his every word for its truth.

"But why?"

He purposely ignored the question. "Is this all of the documents?"

"One more." She shook herself from wherever her thoughts were heading, set down the queen's letter and looked at her empty hand. "It was just here. A little piece of paper . . ."

She rustled between the three documents on the desk and then something else on the desk must have caught her eye.

"That's very odd." She picked up the Earl Marshal's letter to King George and squinted as she scanned it. "See right here at the top: *This* letter is dated two days before my birth and my mother's death. The same date as the letter from the king to Captain R about my mother."

Bloody hell, he'd been so distracted and defensive he hadn't caught the glaring contradiction.

"Obviously an error, Princess." And yet the starkness of winter had settled inside Drew's chest, making it hard to swallow and nearly impossible to breathe.

"I know that's it, of course. But still, that's very sloppy work for the man in charge of the entire College of Arms and all its heraldry."

Not if Queen Genevieve was already dead and you hadn't yet been born and left by your real mother in the orphanage for King George's most trusted minister to discover.

"Human failings, my dear. The College of Arms misspelled my own name repeatedly on my first letters of patent. Took three times to get it right."

"Oh, here's the other document; I must have dropped it." Caro knelt down and picked up a smaller piece of paper, yellowed with age. A farthing sheet of pale green stationery that made the hair on the back of Drew's neck stand on end.

Her name is Madeleine. A good gurl, nevr crys. Wood shurly keep her if I coud. Bles you.

"Oh, my Lord, Drew!" She looked up at him with horror in her eyes and then back at the page. "It's from someone giving up a child!"

Delivered with you to the orphanage. "Yes, it is, Caro."

And all he could do was wait helplessly for his love to make the devastating connections, wait and watch her heart break in two.

"But why is it here among the other papers?"

Caro swallowed the shuddering sob that suddenly formed in her throat, that made her want to weep as she looked down again at the watery ink and the faltering hand.

"It's so sad, Drew." Now she could hardly see for the hot tears swamping her eyes, spilling down her cheeks. "I can feel the love right here in my hands."

"She must have been a very brave woman, Caro." The steadfast energy of Drew's voice soothed her as he stood there beside her, his hand at the small of her back. He'd become her shelter, her gracious guide.

"Dear little Madeleine," she said, snuffling back her fanciful tears for this incongruous letter, "she probably never knew how much the sad young woman must have cared."

Drew was now looking down at the documents laid out on the desk, touching each in its turn, not looking at her, though his jaw was working beneath his bronze skin. Doubtless thinking that she was a simpleton for blubbering on about such a trivial thing as an old, discarded note.

Trivial? But then what was it doing hidden in the old coffer with the other documents?

"My family tree, the deed to my kingdom, an unknown state secret that involves me deeply . . . These three are about me, Drew." Her heart took a stark dive as she picked up the green stationery with its yellowing edges and its faded ink. "Drew?"

He turned his head and looked down at her, his jaw clenched, his eyes on fire. "Yes, Caro?"

"If those three documents are related directly and indisputably to me . . . why is this woeful little note among them?" Feeling suddenly lost, she went to stand beside Drew, her knees loose and watery as she once again looked down at the odd collection of papers.

Drew just stood there, unmoving and silent, his fingers tented against the shiny mahogany desktop, his chest rising and falling steadily.

She swallowed hard and looked down at the forlorn words, whispering them aloud.

" 'Her name is Madeleine. A good girl, never cries. Would surely keep her if I could. Bless you.' "

Breathless and catching back a sob, Caro looked up and into Drew's eyes, finally understanding his uncommon silence, his waiting for something.

"You already know what this is all about, don't you?"

His sigh was unsteady and long as he fixed his feverish gaze on her. "Just leave it be, Caro."

Her heart was thrumming madly inside her chest. "I can't."

Dear Lord! All the documents were about her.

The pedigree with the incorrect date.

The royal writ.

The bloody state secret.

Little Madeleine.

"Please, Caro, don't take this any farther." Drew reached out and threaded his strong fingers through her hair, cupped the back of her head, holding her gaze firmly, speaking slowly, as though her very life, and his, depended upon it. "Stop here, my love. Stop now."

"Oh, God, Drew, it's too late now. I know. I can't stop now!" The powerful, unalterable truth had slammed into her chest like a bolt of lightning, tearing another sob out of her.

"Please, Caro, don't!"

"But I'm *her*, Drew. I'm that little girl who never cries. I'm Madeleine!"

Chapter 20

"Caro, please, don't do this. Let's put these away for good."

"No." She looked down at the little note, and felt her tears falling all over it, onto her cold fingers. "Dear God, this poor woman is my mother."

"No one need know any—"

"And if that's true, who am I, Drew?" She sobbed uncontrollably, trying to swab the tears from her eyes so that she could see, so she could think, but they kept coming back, full force.

"Christ, Caro, don't!" He cradled her face in his warm hands, forcing her to look into his dark eyes, wiping her wet cheeks with his thumbs.

"Am I Madeleine?"

"You're the Princess Caroline," he said fiercely, his eyes dark and glistening, "the future empress of Boratania."

"But I'm not anything of the sort, am I?" She

pulled away from him and shook her head. "I never have been."

He looked at her for a very long time, deeply into her eyes. "You weren't ever meant to know, Caro."

"But you did know. And you didn't tell me." She couldn't seem to light anywhere, needed to walk and touch things, feel the cool of the marble on the fireplace.

"I took an oath not to, Caro. As the queen said"—he smiled wryly from across the room—"you, my dear, are one of the greatest state secrets of all time."

"Because I'm a complete lie? I'm not a princess of the blood, and you knew it. I'm the child of a woman so wretchedly poor she couldn't keep me."

"And so fond that she put you in the care of a foundling home." She could feel his gaze on her as she paced, following her every move, as though keeping her in check from a safe distance.

"So the real Princess Caroline died along with Queen Genevieve the day she was born, and I'm the replacement?"

He was silent for a moment and then sighed. "There was no Princess Caroline."

"What do you mean?" Caro stopped short, breathless and trembling as she watched Drew pick up the letter from the Earl Marshal, his fine mouth firm and angry at something.

"The king and queen of Boratania were barren."

"You mean that my mother wasn't . . . I mean, that the queen wasn't with child when she arrived in England?" How could that be?

"She wasn't."

"She didn't lose the baby on her journey?" Caro clutched at the furniture as she made her way toward him on legs that didn't seem able to hold her. "It wasn't stillborn?"

Drew caught her hands and held her up, looking deeply into her eyes. "Queen Genevieve was already dead and resting in her coffin when her body was sent across the Channel to her cousin King George."

"No, Drew! She couldn't possibly have been dead." Caro had memorized all of the stories a long time ago. *Her* story, her parents' story. The life that she had lived inside her heart. "Queen Genevieve was delivered of a daughter in Windsor Castle."

Drew was shaking his head as he lifted her chin with his fingertip. "They made you up, Caro."

"What do you mean they 'made me up?'" Tears welled in her eyes again, a shiver of unease tumbled down her back. Images of greasepaint and straw, thistledown and rainy alleyways.

"They needed a princess in a hurry," he said in a dark whisper, "and you were in the right place at the right moment."

They? "Who?"

"These men." Drew turned back to the table and held the royal writ in front of her, pointing to the line of signatures and seals. "Our own King George IV, Ludwig of Bavaria, Dom Miguel of Portugal, Francis of Naples, Tsar Nicholas . . . the list goes on."

"Why would these . . . these powerful men, who couldn't even agree on the shape of the full moon, make up a princess out of whole cloth and keep such a thing a secret for more than two decades?" She pressed her palm against the writ, wanting desperately to understand. "More's the point, Drew, why? What could they possibly gain out of such a bizarre conspiracy?"

"They needed a marker, Caro. A political wild card for them to play sometime in the future."

"A princess on ice." She couldn't stop trembling, felt her heart emptying.

"An empress to exploit, madam, if they ever needed one. The fall of Boratania had pitted the royal houses of Europe against one another. You were created as a compromise, and because of that, your true identity must remain a secret between them all."

A pitiful creature stitched together from a ragbag. Caro's knees gave out and she dropped into the desk chair.

"So, to be brutally honest, Drew, I am now, and always have been nothing but a fictional character, created for a royal pantomime. With no true identity, no family, no country, no past. No future."

Drew had never known a more real woman in his life. Her spirit sang inside his body, made his heart race and his pulse jangle. He'd spent every moment of their unorthodox acquaintance admiring her courage, her compassion. His loins in full rut, wanting her under him, sniffing after her, falling head-over-heels in love with a woman who could only remain a figment of his imagination.

But she wasn't fictional.

"My dear Caro, whatever their royal intentions, you have eclipsed them on every count. Shown them over."

"What a fool I've been." She stood in her teary courage and started her deliberate pacing again, making him ache to follow her, to take away the pain. "For over twenty years I've believed that I am a high-born princess. When in truth I am nothing at all."

He didn't like the sound of that. "You are still a

princess. In three days from now you'll be empress and on your way to your kingdom."

But she was shaking her head at him, her eyes fierce and red-rimmed. "You knew all along, didn't you, Drew? From the beginning of your investigation."

"Palmerston briefed me—"

"Palmerston! Damn the man! He's been lying to me all these years. Treating me like royalty when I was no better than the scullery girl in his town house. Who else?"

It wouldn't serve to tell her about Ross and Jared. Or remind her that Peverel certainly knew, and her favorite cousin Albert. "A select few, on a need-to-know basis. You are, after all, a state secret."

"Am I now?"

His heart stopped. "What do you mean?"

"I'm not Princess Caroline Marguerite Marie Isabella of Boratania, Empress-elect. Boratania will be much better off without me."

Hell and damnation! He was going to need another pair of kid gloves. "Without you, Princess?"

"Stop calling me 'Princess,' Drew. I'm Madeleine." Her cheeks were flushed as crimson as he'd ever seen them. She dropped into a high back chair and crossed her arms. The picture of a pouting princess.

"Oh, stop it, Caro." He stood above her, trying to catch her eye but failing. "Nothing has changed. Nothing *can* change. Boratania has no other princess but you."

"That's not my problem, Drew." She drummed her fingers on the arm of the chair, crossed an ankle over her knee as though trying to wall him off. "I'm not descended from the ancient, honorable house of Grostov. I'm not any degree of cousin to the royal houses of Europe, and God only knows who my parents were."

"But you are the Princess Caroline, no matter whose blood flows in your veins." He knelt down in front of her, and captured her hand and her watery gaze in one move. "By royal decree, you have inherited Boratania and all its histories."

"That would make me the biggest liar of them all. And I can't do that!" She hiccoughed and a huge sob exploded from her, followed immediately by another flood of tears and a lot of snuffling.

Drew pulled out his handkerchief and started dabbing at her face.

"If you don't think there are any royal liars out there warming their regal backsides on the thrones of Europe, then you're fooling yourself, Caro."

"Call me a fool, Drew"—she grabbed the kerchief and loudly blew her nose, wiping vigorously—"but I don't measure my ethics by the actions of others."

"But you were raised a princess, Caro, learned the burdens and blessings of being a monarch. Above all things, you understand your duty to your country."

"But I'm English. Not Boratanian."

"And Queen Victoria is German, not English. However questionable your lineage, you are, Caro, because you bear the title, the leader of your country, responsible for the welfare of thousands of people. For Wilhelm and Marguerite and Mrs. Brendel. All of them."

"But that would mean living out a wicked lie for the rest of my life." She dropped her head against the back of the chair and looked up at the ceiling, her cheeks glistening with her tears. "Swearing an oath before God and my subjects and the queen and all the other liars, and denying the truth in the same breath. I can't."

Oh, how he wanted to take away all her troubles. To tell Palmerston and the queen and all the others to go to hell. His heart ached to see her in such soul-wrenching pain.

And yet he had to go on fighting for her.

Against her.

"You can, Caro, and you must. Imagine the wrath of your royal cousins should you deliberately subject them to a scandal of this magnitude. If you expose your own identity as a fraud, then you put the legitimacy of every other monarch in jeopardy. Because, like it or not, my dear princess, you are still a closely kept state secret."

She sniffled twice more as she glared at him, her eyes intense and plotting, a dry sob giving a last rattle to her chest and shoulders. "That's it, then!" She thunked her palms against the arms of the chair and started to rise. "I'm going to go talk to the queen."

Drew caught her slender shoulders and held her in place. "Then you'll be talking to a wall. You saw her letter to Lord Peverel."

Her brow dipped in a weary frown. "Yes."

He brushed his palm across her teary cheek, such a soft place, vulnerable and warm. "She won't let you go, Caro."

She chewed on her lip, sniffled again. "I know. I'm a princess. I know how these royals think."

"So you'll stay?"

Another dry sob shook her deeply before she heaved a great sigh. "I haven't much choice, have I?"

"None at all, Caro. And God knows I'm not on their side in this matter."

"Then you think I'm right, Drew? Will you stand up for me then?" Her eyes brightened and she took his hand inside both of hers. "Convince them that my coronation would be wrong for everyone."

"I can't, Caro. It's got nothing to do with that." He sifted his fingers through her hair, felt its silkiness curling around his heart. "Believe me, I don't want you to be empress of anywhere."

"You don't?" He'd never seen her eyes so wide and wet, so deeply blue.

He took her face between his hands and kissed her salty cheek. "I want you to stay here"—kissed her sweet mouth—"and be my wife."

She was sighing, her eyes unfocused, her voice dreamy. "Mmmm, what's that, Drew? Your wife?"

"My love, if I thought it was the right and proper thing to do, I would take you into my arms right now, right here, and I would ask you to marry me."

"You would?" Such a hopeful, heart-shredding sound.

"Christ, Caro, you're the finest woman I've ever met."

"I am?" She looked stunned, her mouth pouty and moist from the chaste kiss he'd just put there.

"Kind and intelligent, and I love your smile. I love you. I want children with you."

"Oh, Drew!" She was weeping softly again, sharing his kiss, seeping into his soul.

"I want to climb into bed beside you every night of my life, feel your heart beating with mine, share your dreams and your hopes—"

"Oh, damn you, Drew!" She shoved at his chest,

launching herself backward into her chair. "How dare you say that to me?"

"Well, then." A good slap on the face would have been less shocking. He'd obviously been wrong about her feelings for him, hadn't expected her to reject him so emphatically.

"Damn you, damn you, *damn* you!" She stamped her foot with the final curse, threw herself out of the chair and crossed the room, putting the settee safely between them.

"My deepest apologies, Princess Caroline," he said, staggering to his feet, his heart shattered. "I've obviously overstepped my—"

"Dammit, Drew, first you convince me to accept my fate as empress, to spend the rest of my days as a lying, cheating usurper of kingdoms and then you . . . you stab me right in the heart."

"That wasn't my intention, sweet." He didn't know what to do here. The intricacies of love were more than a bit beyond his experience.

"Please, Drew!" She put up her hand like a wall, then sighed, her shoulders sagged. "Please, don't make it hurt any more than it already does. I've spent the last three weeks wondering how I could possibly live without you. Without your advice and your smile, your enchanting bluster, your delicious voice, the marvelous scent of you—"

"Good God, Caro!" His heart had begun to bang around inside his chest, lost and wild with the need to hold her, wanting a life with her as he wanted his next breath!

"And I've just dashed any hope of any future with you! So . . ." Her tears began streaming down her cheeks again, her voice silky soft, lilting. "So the very last thing I need to hear is a quite impossible proposal of marriage from the man I've come to love more than my life."

Drew wanted to cross the carpet and sweep her into his arms, to lose himself in her sweetness. Instead, he stood rooted there by his honor, by what he knew was right, by the bleakness of a future with her. "I'm sorry, Caro."

She sniffled and wiped her eyes with her sleeve. "I am, too."

"You're all right?"

She raised her sorrowful gaze to him, pools of blue fire and a fiercely defiant determination. "I have to be, don't I? After all, I have a kingdom to rule."

And I, my dear, have an assassin to ferret out.

"No, Caro, you can't go to the Crystal Palace with me today," Drew said for the third time to the most breathtakingly stubborn woman he had ever met. "Nothing has changed. There's still an assassin out there, doubtless more desperate than ever because you're still alive."

"What about the opening ceremonies tomorrow?" she tugged once more in obvious irritation on the rope that tied the canvas to the tailgate of the wagon. "After all, Drew, I'm the princess of Boratania! I'll be missed if I'm not there, won't I?"

Best not to oblige her sarcasm. "Tomorrow you'll be safely ensconced among many other royals and dozens of my agents. With me at your back."

"You could be there today, Drew."

"Princess . . ."

"But, Drew, these are the most important items for my exhibit." She patted the taut canvas. "I want them to be in place the moment the Great Exhibition opens."

"If you want this lot displayed, Princess, then you'll draw out a diagram for me, because you cannot talk me out of this. Not this time. I'll lock you in the wine cellar first."

"But, Drew, you—" She closed her mouth abruptly before saying, "I was going to exclaim that you wouldn't dare lock up a *princess* against her will, but of course you would. You've done it regularly since the first moment we met."

"And I'll do it again."

She frowned deeply at him. "Ohhhhhhh, all right!"

She stomped back through the orangery to her worktable, yanked a diagram out of the front of her logbook and showed him the list on the reverse.

She spent ten minutes explaining it all to him, drawing arrows and making boxes, time that he spent hoping that he'd understood her instructions, yearning for her.

"You're sure you have it, Drew?"

"I'm a quick study, Princess."

When he finally climbed into the wagon, his nostrils filled with her lilac fragrance, it seemed the most natural thing to do to lean down and kiss her good-bye.

But he couldn't. She wasn't his to kiss.

"Come right home, Drew." She put her hand on top of his, the gentle squeeze as telling as the worry in her eyes. "What I mean is, don't do anything foolish."

"Have I ever, my dear?" He left a smile with her as Wheeler climbed onto the bench beside him. Then he snapped the reins and the wagon rolled out of the shed on one of his last errands for his princess.

Two hours later Drew and Wheeler had made their way through the traffic in Kensington and had managed to park the wagon at the east entrance of the Crystal Palace.

Between he and Wheeler and three eager policemen who had recognized Drew and offered their help, the wagon was unloaded into the exhibit space in a few minutes.

The time-consuming part was comparing the bloody diagram to the exhibit and then placing each item exactly the way his persnickety princess had indicated.

"My lord, doesn't that round brass thing go on top of the cabinet instead of inside it?" Wheeler was staring down at the diagram and then up at the display, then flipping the page to its reverse.

"That's it exactly, Wheeler." Drew stalked up to the cabinet and made the change. "By God, I'd rather be posted fifty feet up a banyan tree in hundred degree humidity than to try to make sense of this. I think a pint at the Exhibitors Dining Room is the only cure."

"I'll not argue with you, sir." Wheeler was leading the way down the aisle in the next instant.

Drew followed more slowly, still appalled by the amount of glass and open spaces, noticing the Flannery Brothers themselves, patching up one of the fountains in the transept.

"Oh, damn." Realizing that he'd left his jacket draped across a statue in the exhibit, Drew started back down the less-crowded side aisle only to find someone standing on the Boratanian platform, peering inside the cabinet.

And if he wasn't mistaken that was Peverel.

"Good afternoon, Lord Peverel."

"God in heaven!" The man stumbled backward and then whirled around, wide-eyed. "Wexford! Ah. You startled me out of my skin."

Touchy old fool. He must have been lost in whatever he was looking at.

No, that wasn't exactly right. The man had been looking for something.

"Sorry, Peverel, I didn't mean to startle you."

Peverel laughed and fanned his face with his hat. "That's me, Wexford. Head in the clouds. I was just admiring Princess Caroline's fine exhibit."

"I understand she's been collecting Boratanian artifacts for years and years."

Including an old coffer from you with a few odd documents hidden away inside.

"Yes, yes, remarkable determination, hasn't she, Wexford?"

"Downright foolhardy at times."

Peverel only nodded and continued his indiscreet search.

It was on Drew's tongue to mention the coffer, but something stopped him, that jangled warning in his left ear that made him continue. "By that I mean the woman seems to have no compunction about just walking off with anything she thinks was looted from her family's castles at the fall of the kingdom."

She even got to you, Peverel, didn't she? Confiscated that box, right out from under your nose.

"Yes, a foolish, foolish girl, I'm afraid." Peverel was almost muttering as he stepped down from the platform and glanced up at Drew, his face as pale as usual, his eyes skittish. "And how fares the princess? All right, I assume."

Still alive.

"Very well, Peverel. Anticipating her coronation with great joy."

"Water treaties settling down, I suppose? Boundary surveys in place."

"Everything according to plan, Peverel."

"Good, good. Well, there's nothing left to do then, is there?" Peverel shook his head as though asking the question of himself, and then realized he wasn't alone. A man on the brink. "Will you be attending tomorrow's opening, my lord?"

"I wouldn't miss it. And you?"

He nodded and nodded. "It seems I must, sir. Duties and the like. We all have our duties, don't we?"

"Indeed." Drew watched Peverel wander off down the main aisle toward the transept. He seemed a husk of a man, distracted by something dark inside him.

And he'd been looking for something in Caro's exhibit. Something quite specific that he didn't find.

Curious, wanting to soothe the all-too-familiar unbalancing feeling in his gut, the ringing in his ear, Drew paralleled Peverel's route and kept an eye on the man as they both reached the transept.

That same feeling surged inside him again as Peverel stopped in front of the Flannery Brothers' brick cart and studied the fountain from its base to the stone dish twenty feet above him. He shook his head, started toward the south exit.

Drew dashed into the dining room and found Wheeler.

"I want to follow someone, Wheeler. You stay here at the Palace and keep watch over the exhibit. If I don't return in an hour, take the wagon back to Grandauer and tell the princess that I'll be home as soon as I can."

"Who is it you're tailing?" Wheeler rushed with him out of the crowded dining hall.

"Let's just say I have one of those feelings. You know what I mean. A snake in my gut."

"Then run, my lord!"

Drew made it to the exit just as Peverel climbed into a hansom cab, which moved immediately into the jostling traffic feeding out into the cobbled streets.

"Bloody hell!" Drew found one of the policemen who had helped him earlier and wrangled a horse out of him.

"With the queen's blessing, Lord Wexford!" the man said with a wave as Drew trotted off after Peverel's cab.

Drew followed well behind the vehicle, heading east along Piccadilly, trying to dismiss his suspicions as ridiculous.

Lord Peverel? Christ, the man had been retained by the queen herself to guide Caro toward an easy transition, to build a set of policies to help her through her first years.

Why would he want to hurt her? And yet the man had stashed away a most damning set of documents.

Which Caro had stolen back from him.

Still, Peverel didn't seem the type. And what would have been his motive? The man had obviously known all about Caro's identity. No, this was a wild goose chase. It had to be.

Still that snaky feeling churned up bile, and his heart thudded against his ribs like a sledgehammer.

He nearly stopped breathing when the cab turned away from the crowds in Piccadilly onto St. James and then rolled to a stop in front of Tavistock's.

The liveried valet opened the door of the hansom cab, greeted Peverel as he would a member in good standing, then escorted him through the door of the gentleman's club.

Not just any gentleman's club. Tavistock's was the place where Paul Lauder had worked as a waiter.

And Peverel was an assistant to the Royal Commission for the Great Exhibition. How many times had he walked down the main aisle of the Crystal Palace and seen the masons who worked for the Flannery Brothers?

Christ, not Peverel.

Because it made no sense at all.

Chapter 21

"The gown fits you to perfection, Princess Caroline." Mrs. Tweeg was standing beside Caro, beaming into the cheval glass at her.

Princess Caroline.

Caro was getting better at not flinching at the sound of her name. Whoever's name. It just didn't seem like hers anymore.

"The gown is certainly beautiful, Mrs. Tweeg. Certainly fit for a coronation." Brilliant white, and lush with satin, the bodice trimmed in real diamonds that were destined to grace the crown jewels of Boratania.

Because Drew had been right, nothing had changed. Nothing could change. Too many people were depending on her to be strong, to be a capable leader.

I love you, Caro. Such a simple declaration for such a grand-hearted man.

I want children with you. Dear Lord, they would have been fine children, and so well loved.

Everything had been said that could be said.

But the coronation was still a few days away.

The Great Exhibition was tomorrow.

It was nearly five o'clock, and Drew still hadn't returned home to Grandauer. Telling herself not to worry about him simply didn't work, only set her skin to aching and filled her eyes with tears.

"Well, I certainly can't wear this to supper, Mrs. Tweeg."

"That you can't, Your Highness. We don't want anyone to see it before your big day. Might bring you bad luck—like when a groom sees the bride before the wedding."

"Just like that, Mrs. Tweeg." Caro managed a smile instead of the sob that lurked just inside her chest, and suffered the dear woman's happy chatter as she helped her out of her stunning coronation gown.

Caro went downstairs a half hour later and nearly collided with Mr. Wheeler as she started through the doorway to the investigation room.

"Ah, there you are, Princess!"

"Oh, good, Mr. Wheeler, you're back!" Her heart leaped in relief, and she went speeding past him into the room, expecting to find Drew. But he wasn't there. "Did Wexford come back from the exhibition with you?"

"That's what I've come to tell you, Your Highness. We had just finished up the exhibit, which looks just as you wished it, by the way, when his lordship realized that he had some work he had to do."

"What kind of work?" Perhaps he'd found a piece of evidence that needed investigating at the Factory.

"He was going to tail someone."

That terrified her. "Who?"

"He couldn't say who at the time. It all happened very quickly. But he did say to tell you that he'd be here as soon as possible."

Frightened for Drew and weary to the bone, Caro wanted to sag into the nearest chair, but that might alarm the poor man. "Then good, Mr. Wheeler. Thank you for bringing the news, and for helping with the exhibit."

"It's been a great pleasure, Your Highness." He put his hand to his heart and then hurried off toward the kitchen.

Drew didn't come home in time for supper, or for the children's story time.

Caro lingered in the library until she was nodding off in a chair, then fell asleep in her chamber listening for the sound of him in the next room, praying that he would arrive safely.

But Drew wasn't back at dawn, wasn't there to take breakfast, either. And still hadn't returned as everyone began to gather in the foyer for their caravan to the Crystal Palace.

"Look at my new dress, Princess Caroline!"

Caro turned toward Annora's huge smile. "Why, it's lovely, Annora! And yours too, Marguerite. Mrs. Brendel, you're a very fine seamstress."

Both girls stretched out their hems and pivoted in little circles.

Karl's wife blushed with pride. "Thank you, Your Highness."

Runson appeared at Caro's side. "It's getting late, Your Highness. Time to load into the carriages."

"No word from Lord Wexford?"

"Just what we heard last night. Perhaps he'll meet you there."

Dear God, she hoped so. Otherwise . . . no, she wasn't going to think about him tailing an assassin through the dark alleys of London. Couldn't think about that bullet . . .

The three carriages rolled out of Grandauer Hall into a drizzling rain at noon, each of them bristling with Drew's agents. They managed to work their way along the muddy roads, then through the impossible traffic around Kensington, reaching the sunlit drive along the south transept of the Crystal Palace by four o'clock.

But so had the crowd of a half million people who were thronging the park, doubtless hoping for a glimpse of the queen's procession.

Caro stepped out of the carriage in front of the palace, her heart in her mouth as she scanned the entrance for Drew and his towering height.

But there was no sign of him anywhere.

She led her group toward the entrance, still looking for Drew around every corner, his agents pressing in closer to her, more obvious than usual. She flashed her season pass and her motley entourage was able to avoid the long lines of people because, of course, she was Princess Caroline of Boratania.

They shuffled into the great barrel-vaulted transept, past the huge grandstand that had been erected beneath one of the galleries. A raised dais with the queen's magnificently draped throne was roped off beneath the central arch, ready for the ceremony.

"I never expected anything half so grand, Your

Highness." Karl and his wife were standing behind her, their eyes wide with wonder.

Wilhelm only muttered to the others.

The children *oohed* and *aahed* at everything.

"There's a big stone lady on a big stone horse!" Marguerite shouted, tugging on Caro's skirts.

"They've grown a whole forest in here, Princess Caroline!" Robert Frederick was pointing at the huge old trees that had dictated part of the design and the exact location of the building.

"Those are elms, Frederick."

And that's when she finally saw Drew.

The blackguard!

Safe and sound and staring directly at her, his smile slanted and easy, his tall, shiny boot resting on the base of the enormous crystal fountain, his arms crossed over his broad chest as though he had been waiting for her.

"Look! There's Lord Wexford!" Annora said, taking off toward the man, the three other children racing along behind her.

Caro wanted to run to him, too. To throw her arms around him as Marguerite just did.

But this was the last place in all of London where she might have the liberty to do such a highly improper thing. She was a royal princess, after all, almost an empress.

And just now the Crystal Palace was mobbed with members of Parliament, orators, foreign dignitaries and statesmen, nobles and lions of industry, all of them awaiting the arrival of the queen.

But Caro had found Drew, and was feeling remarkably better already.

"Ah, Lord Wexford," she said, offering her gloved hand as he finally reached her side in front of the queen's dais. "I was afraid you wouldn't be joining us."

"A slight change of plans," he said, fixing his dark gaze on her and then lifting it to scan the galleries.

He seemed even more the caged wolf today. Nodding to his agents in some code she'd never noticed before, his muscles shifting beneath the fine cloth of his crisp linen coat.

He was freshly shaved, his hair trimmed, and his fine clothes clean and pressed to perfection. Which made her wonder, incongruously and with a stunning jolt of jealousy, where he'd slept last night after he finished tailing whoever it was he tailed.

What if he had found himself a comfortable private life, after all?

A woman to endow with his attentions.

Which he had every right to do, of course. She had no claim to him at all.

Except that he had stolen her heart.

And that he loved her.

"Did you sleep well last night, my lord?" Gad! What a prying thing to ask!

But his sardonic smile only deepened. "Hardly at all, Your Highness."

There! He must have been restless, or he worked all night . . . or he was . . . no! She just couldn't follow that image. Her Drew in another woman's bed.

"Did you and Wheeler have any trouble finishing the display, Lord Wexford? My drawing wasn't the best." She'd almost forgotten the reason he'd set out without her yesterday.

"We finished easily, madam, with time to spare."

She was about to ask Drew about who he had been following last night, when a cannon went off in the distance like a clap of thunder, rattling the iron and sending the children squealing.

"Did someone start a war, Lord Wexford?" Oscar put up his arms to be carried.

"Nothing to worry about, Oscar," Drew said, lifting the boy into his arms with such fatherly grace. "That's just to announce the arrival of Queen Victoria."

"Is she a real queen, Lord Wexford?" Oscar asked. "As real as our Princess Caroline?"

"As real as our Princess Caroline." Drew's eyes glinted intensely as he turned and looked down at Caro. "But not nearly as enchanting."

"Lord Wexford, please!" He shouldn't be saying such things. And still her heart skipped madly as he moved to stand behind her as he had promised yesterday morning.

Her loyal warrior.

Her thoughts were cut off by the raucous blare of a trumpet from the gallery.

"Looka there!" Oscar shouted from where he was hanging off Drew's shoulder. "Is that the queen?"

Her Royal Majesty entered the Crystal Palace with great pomp. Caro couldn't help looking at her cousin in a more tightly focused light. A conspirator in Caro's life. An active participant in a royal falsehood that had global implications.

Prince Albert strode grandly beside the queen, clearly pleased with his magnificent success, twice turning back to the Prince of Wales and the Princess Royal to keep them from wandering off toward all the wonders.

The queen took her seat on her richly draped

throne, to the applause of all. Next came Prince Albert's dry report from the Royal Commission and a short speech from the queen. Then a prayer from the archbishop of Canterbury, and the "Hallelujah Chorus" sung by an enormous choir accompanied by no fewer than five pipe organs.

There came another trumpet fanfare and the Great Exhibition was declared officially open.

A kind of disorderly madness happened next, as everyone shoved and jostled their way toward the exhibits.

Drew handed off Oscar to Karl, then kept Caro close to him near the dais, while the others floated out into the sea of attendees.

Caro tugged at Drew's elbow and he bent to listen to her. "Now, my lord Wexford, you'll tell me everything! Where were you last night? Did you find him?"

He was frowning deeply at something over the top of her head, his gaze dancing between the galleries, sliding over the top of the crowd. "Possibly, Princess."

"Who then, Drew?" She tugged on his arm again, but his attention seemed fixed on something.

"Ah, cousin, there you are! Albert, look, here's our beautiful Princess Caroline, looking lovelier than ever." Queen Victoria and her family had finally made their way off the dais through the clot of nabobs who were doubtlessly hoping for a place of honor during the queen's Parade of the Exhibits.

But instead of her usual feelings of affection for the queen, a shocking bolt of raw anger shot through Caro, striking her nearly speechless.

And yet the queen was beaming at Caro. "I'm so glad you could be with us today."

I'll bet you are, Victoria dear! Caro swallowed hard, hoping that she hadn't spoken aloud.

"Your Majesty, I wouldn't have missed a moment." *Though I shouldn't be here at all.* Caro managed an elegant curtsey, princess to queen. "The exhibition is marvelous."

"And you, Lord Wexford," the queen said, looking up at the frowning earl, tapping the buttons on his waistcoat with the tip of her finger, "are looking quite well, as usual."

"Forever at your service, Your Majesty," he said, barely sparing the queen a glance, which didn't seem to bother the woman in the least. Her golden boy.

Albert bent to kiss Caro's hand and then smiled. "Her Majesty and I are looking forward to your coronation, my dear."

"Yes, thank you, Your Highness." She wanted to pinch him hard but restrained herself.

Then, like a school of fish, the lot of them followed after the prince to begin the hours-long parade around the building.

"I'm expected to join them like the other foreign dignitaries, Drew."

"Not a chance in hell, Princess."

Drew hated being trapped like this in the middle of a crowd, no room to react, poor visibility. He pulled her against him and then whispered into her ear, "Walk with me, Caro."

"To where?"

"Out of here. It's too dangerous." And he hadn't been able to locate Peverel since the man entered

Tavistock's last night, though he'd spent most of the night following leads that all seemed to wind closer and closer to the man.

Circles of people, lines of connections. Significance of places, objects.

Because he was now absolutely certain that the threat was all about Caro's identity.

Who she was, who she wasn't.

And Peverel was involved somehow.

"But I can't leave, my lord. I have duties and I haven't seen my exhibit."

"You'll have to visit next week, madam. When you're empress." *And hopefully still alive.*

He started forward into the press of people, giving a nod to Halladay and Casserly as they fell into place a few yards ahead of them.

"Who are we looking for, Drew?" she whispered over her shoulder.

"We?" No wonder she was suddenly so remarkably cooperative, his reckless, beautiful operative, shifting easily to the right and then the left as he guided her forward, his hands spanning that perfectly curved waist.

He'd been a fool to let her come today; the place was a chaos of thundering voices and rambunctious children and blaring music.

A colorful military band was carving a strident, sinuous path toward them, the conductor's baton bouncing high in the air, the horns swinging from side to side in rhythm.

Drew started to guide Caro around them, but the mob only packed in more tightly, stopping to stare, becoming a wedge as well as an ever-strengthening eddy as they approached an intersection.

"Lemonade! Gumdrops!" A vendor shoved through the crowd with a tray slung from his neck, causing a clot of thirsty people to stop right in front of them.

A rowdy column of boys called out to the man, pushing their way in front of Caro, knocking her forward and shouldering Drew backward.

And then he lost her, lost the heat of her against the palm of his hand.

"Caro!" Drew reached out for her, made a grab but missed, sending his heart racing in stark terror.

But she had recovered and was grinning when she looked back at him, separated from him no more than two arm lengths.

And then three.

"Drew?" She caught hold of her lower lip with her teeth, reached up to wave at him.

And then she disappeared into the crowd.

Vanished!

"Caro!" Suddenly frantic for her, Drew swam forward, shoving people aside one by one, gaining on her as she was hustled along by the mob just ahead of him.

Closer and closer until he need only push past one of the trumpet players and he would have hold of her arm.

But then the world slowed and he saw everything at once.

Caro pivoting toward something to her right.

The crowd parting for the briefest moment.

And Lord Peverel, small and ferretlike, saying something to her.

A movement of the man's hand at his pocket.

And then a small flash of silver, his arm raised toward Caro.

"Nooooo!" Drew sprang forward across the top of

the crowd, crashing into Peverel and knocking the small pistol out of his hand.

Drew regained his balance and turned at the same time to find Caro wide-eyed and horrified, miraculously alive but still blocked from him by the crush of people.

In that same moment Peverel wriggled out of Drew's grasp and dashed off toward an exit in the north end of the transept, slipping through the throng like the slithery weasel he was. Seeing that his operatives were quickly closing in on Caro, Drew took off after Peverel.

The bastard had broken out into the open air, bloody nimble for a man in his late sixties. Drew followed across the grass, his fury boundless, growing ever more treacherous as he quickly gained on the man.

He reached the western corner of the exhibition hall not ten yards behind Peverel. But the man's stride was beginning to falter as he approached the steam plant.

"Stop, Peverel!"

Still the old man trudged on, slowing, stumbling, until Drew merely grabbed him by the collar and dragged him up against the brick wall at the back of the steam plant.

"Please, no, Wexford!" Peverel covered his face with his thin arms, whining, gasping for every breath, his muscles hanging like a ragdoll. "Don't hurt me! Don't!"

"You bloody bastard, I ought to kill you right here!" Drew shook the man by the shoulders, wanting to pummel him to a pulp but pinning him against the wall, forcing his head up. "You betrayed her! The innocent princess you had promised to champion."

"No, but I—" His pale gray eyes widened, the whites of them spidered in red. "I didn't mean—"

"You didn't mean to have her murdered?" The man's gaze dropped and Drew gave him another shake. "Look at me, Peverel. You hired assassins to kill her! Why did you hate her so much? What the devil did she do to you? Tell me before I kill you myself!"

"Please, please, Wexford! I don't hate the princess. She's—" Peverel's lips were cracked and dry, his mouth working without a sound.

"She's what? In your way? Worth some kind of fortune to you? What?" Drew shook him again, telling himself that the bastard wasn't worth killing.

"I wasn't supposed to tell—"

"Tell what?"

Peverel licked his lips. "The queen . . . She threatened to charge me with treason if . . . if . . ."

Drew leaned closer to Peverel. "If you revealed the secret of the princess's birth? The truth?"

Peverel's eyelids fluttered as he stared up at Drew. "Oh, God! You know too, Wexford?"

"Of course, I know, damn it! Your assassins put me on the case."

Peverel was trembling uncontrollably, still breathless. "Does . . . does she know? The . . . the princess?"

"Yes, Lord Peverel, I know."

Caro! Drew's heart stopped at the soft sound of her voice behind him, and started again to know that she was alive and safe.

"Princess." He turned to her, not caring that he held the man with one hand, letting him slump against the wall. He wanted to enfold Caro in his arms, to kiss her senseless. To keep her always with him.

But Halladay and Casserly and two other agents had spaced themselves out a few yards behind her and she seemed fixed on Peverel, who was now leaning low against the wall, his head bowed, his gnarled hands covering his eyes as though Drew would strike him.

"Why, Lord Peverel?" she asked, quietly approaching him. "What did I do to you?"

"Nothing. Nothing." He shook his disheveled gray head, still hiding his eyes. "You were kind. I was a fool, Princess Caroline."

"You should have just asked me about the coffer, my lord."

The shivering coward raised his hands and looked up at her. "But I thought you knew . . . about the box. The compartment in the bottom. That you would open it and find out . . ."

"Not until two days ago."

"Oh, dear God." Sloppy tears began to stream from the man's eyes.

"You could have made up a story, my lord. Any story. I would have given it back, for as long as you needed it."

His eyes grew wide in horror, as though he just realized that he'd taken a needlessly violent path, with an unthinkable destination. "I . . . I just . . . I didn't think!"

Drew had had enough of the man's drivel, yanked him back onto his feet. "So you decided that the solution to your pitiful personal problem was a dead princess. Three men dead because of your incompetence! Your arrogance!"

"You see I . . . I had no choice, Wexford." Peverel looked from Drew to Caro, his eyes pleading, his voice quaking. "I'd committed high treason. Me! A Peverel! Oh, my God!"

The man broke down completely, sobbing, sinking to the ground in a pathetic ball, his knees around his ears.

Drew turned away from the sickening sight of him, felt every bit as drained as the wily old bastard, though his outrage kept him on the edge, ready to lash out.

But Caro was there beside him, lacing her gentle fingers between his, smiling up at him. "A rather underwhelming villain, isn't he, Drew?"

Drew couldn't help but smile, touching her chin with the tip of his finger. "Hardly the international criminal I'd first suspected."

"But you, my Lord Wexford, will always be the hero of my heart. Thank you."

Oh, if they were only alone here in their own fairy tale, if they were free. . . .

But reality was strewn about all around them. Peverel fallen into a heap at their feet, sobbing, a wall of agents standing guard not two dozen feet from them.

The rumble and hiss of the steam plant at their backs.

The exhibition.

Caro's coronation.

The end of all things.

"Halladay!" Drew shouted, "you and Casserly take Peverel out of here, to Whitehall. I'll follow you in a moment."

"Be careful with him," Caro said, as the two men lifted Peverel to his feet. He hung his head as he was hustled past her.

"Come, love, I'll take you back to your subjects before I leave," Drew said, hooking her hand around his elbow and starting off across the grassy expanse toward the so aptly named Crystal Palace.

"Then you're not staying, Drew?" He heard the melancholy in her voice, though she looked every inch the regal princess, fully in control.

"Palmerston is inside the hall somewhere; he'll want to be with me when we interrogate Peverel."

"And then you'll come home?"

Home. How in the world had *home* come to mean Caro? And how was he going to live without her?

"I'll see you as soon as I can, Princess." He stopped with her just inside the entrance, wishing he could hold her hand, wishing he could kiss her. "Now, go on inside and enjoy your triumph. There's Wilhelm now, waving at us. I'm sure your subjects are looking to celebrate with you."

"Thank you, Drew." Her eyes were a soft, clear blue, but teary and full of sorrow. "For everything."

"It's been the greatest honor of my life, Your Highness." He left her while he still could.

Chapter 22

Caro spent the rest of the evening with her subjects, exploring the Great Exhibition, from gallery to gallery and back again, delighted with the Boratanian display, impressed by the amazing steam-driven machines that seemed capable of doing and making anything imaginable, without human intervention.

"Isn't that the biggest elephant you've ever seen, Princess Caroline!" Oscar had been her constant companion during the tour, seeing the world from her arms.

"It is, Oscar, and I know just where to find the biggest bag of gumdrops! Come along, children!"

There were costumes from every country, a medieval court, raucous music, fine tapestries, timber from the dense Canadian forests, exotic smells, and the free-wheeling laughter of the children, all of it blending together to make an unforgettable event.

Caro did her best to keep Drew tucked quietly in

her heart, where she could take him out when she needed him. But he was such an insistent man, impossible to ignore, even when he was miles away and she was tucked up in her bed, listening for him to come home.

But the caseclock just kept ticking away the minutes, counting out the last of her days with him.

The last of her nights.

"I love you, Drew."

He was in her dreams, but distantly, a sea of people bobbing between them. She could never quite reach him, never got to feel the power and heat of his hands meeting hers.

I love you, Caro!

Drew?

Farewell, my princess . . . my love.

Drew!

She woke with a start, reaching for him, a sliver of brilliant daylight falling across her face from the window.

"Drew!" She left the bed with a leap, opened the bookcase then knocked properly on the secret door.

Princess to warrior.

Because it was the day before her coronation and, though she'd learned the worst about her past, Drew had been right about her destiny. Being born into a royal family was strictly a matter of chance and was no guarantee that the person would have the wisdom to rule.

When he didn't come to the door, she called his name and knocked again. "Drew, are you dressed?"

Feeling a rising panic, Caro opened the door and found nothing of Drew. His bed was made up. His clothes were gone as well as his shaving gear. Even the scent of him had disappeared, as though he'd never come through her life.

Less than a ghost.

Her heart breaking into bits, Caro bathed and dressed and went downstairs, hoping to find him in the investigation room.

But that, too, had been restored to its previous condition, the wall map gone, the files, the clerks. All the furniture back in place.

"Excuse me, your highness, but will you be taking breakfast here in the parlor?"

She turned toward the familiar voice, shocked to find her butler Sebring and not Mr. Runson.

"Oh . . . Sebring!" Her mouth went dry. "Welcome back! I hope you enjoyed your holiday."

Sebring grinned. "Oh, yes, Your Highness, we all did. You were most generous with us! An unexpected holiday in Brighton! How could we not enjoy ourselves?"

"So . . . everyone has come back?" And Wheeler was gone, and Tweeg and Mackenzie and all the others whose kindness and expertise she'd come to admire.

"To the last gardener, madam. And we're ready to serve you. Shall I bring your breakfast here?"

Another day of losses and change. "I'll have a tray in the library. And thank you, Sebring."

The house was too quiet, with the children at their morning classwork and the men doubtlessly somewhere practicing their part in tomorrow's processional.

And no sign of Drew.

She missed him everywhere, in her heart and in the library, his advice and his strength.

Tears clouded her vision as she stumbled to her desk. She wiped at her eyes and sat down, almost missing the tented note beside her inkstand.

Her hands shook as she opened it.

My Dearest Princess,

I assume that my name was inadvertently overlooked when the invitations for your coronation were sent out. I have taken the liberty of "rescuing" one for myself. I wouldn't miss it for the world.

Best wishes for a long and happy reign,
Andrew Chase, Earl of Wexford

Caro put her head in her arms and wept.

But the day sped by quickly, the coronation activity level increasing by the hour, until the early evening had her running between Queen Victoria's marshal-at-arms giving her instructions in the parlor, her subjects in the library, the children's drawings in the dining room, the seamstress in her bedchamber, the flamboyant Chef Soyer in her kitchen with his menus and assistant cooks.

Gracious!

It wasn't until she had tended to everyone and was heading upstairs toward her bedchamber for a restless night that she noticed a light in the east-wing sitting room. She found Wilhelm talking quietly there with Karl and Johannes.

"Good evening, gentlemen. Enjoying the quiet?"

"Ah, Princess," Wilhelm said, standing with the

others as she entered the room, "resting up for tomorrow."

"That's just what I was going to do." She suddenly remembered Lord Peverel, the loss of his guidance, her need for a familiar face or two. She sat down in a chair beside Johannes. "I was just thinking that I'm going to need all of you with me after the coronation."

"And we'll be there at the reception to do whatever you need us to do, Your Highness."

Wilhelm clapped his palms on his knees as he sat. "Soon to be Her Majesty, Empress of Boratania."

Empress. Could her lost mother ever have expected her to bear that title? Would she be amazed? Proud?

"It's not the reception I'm thinking of, gentlemen, though I do hope you'll take full advantage of the celebrations. It's afterward, when we return to Boratania that I'll be needing your wisdom and guidance."

"Ours?" they said as one.

"I'll be putting together a privy council, and I can't think of six more qualified men to appoint."

"Privy council?" Johannes sat hard. "Us? Are you sure, Your Highness?"

"Very sure." More certain now than when she entered the room. "I'll need a chancellor and someone to administer the treasury and the courts. The six of you embody the best of Boratania's past and a zeal for the future. You're fair minded and modern and loyal."

"We do love Boratania, Your Highness—"

"Please think it over, Karl." Caro stood and started for the door. "Talk it over with the others. I don't want to pressure any of you, but I do think I'm right. Good night, gentlemen."

She smiled to hear their stunned enthusiasm as she hurried down the hall toward her chamber.

After all, an empress had the right, the obligation, to choose a suitable council.

And she was quite sure that Drew would approve of her choice.

"You've been three times up the side aisle, Drew," Jared said from his leaning post just inside the unused west door of St. George's Chapel. "You'll wear out the queen's good stone floor with your pacing."

"I'm not pacing, Jared," Drew said under his breath. Though he stopped and jammed his fists into his coat pockets, not yet able to take a seat among the others who had been filling the nave for the last half hour. "I'm just ready to be finished with it all."

Anything to stop the empty aching in his chest.

He was a bloody coward for not staying behind to accompany Caro to her coronation today. Though he couldn't have ridden with her inside her carriage; ceremonial protocol would have kept him way in the rear of any caravan.

And yet he could have skipped out on Palmerston's meeting about his next mission and stayed around Grandauer Hall yesterday to give Caro a bit of moral support.

But there was danger there and temptation beyond his will to resist. His job was done. Best to move on.

"I'm proud of you, Drew!" Jared clapped him on the shoulder. "You caught the villain in the nick of time. Peverel will spend the rest of his miserable life in a cold Scottish prison. Your princess is still alive, and in just a few minutes she'll be crowned the empress of Boratania."

And she'll be lost to him forever.

"Yeah."

Jared was studying him with a raised brow. "Bloody hell, Drew. She's the one, isn't she?"

"The one?" Drew found himself standing in front of the Urswick Chantry, staring at nothing in particular, waiting for the sound of Caro's entourage on the stairs from the undercroft.

"Dangerous to fall in love with a princess, Drew."

"Ours is dangerous work, Jared." A bullet in his heart would have been kinder, quicker. "But then I knew that when I took Palmerston's assignment."

Though he hadn't known that Caro would become a part of him, that she would take hold of his soul.

"You don't have to stay for this, Drew. Kate and I can give your best to the new empress—"

"No, Jared. But thanks for trying. My assignment was to see Princess Caroline crowned empress, and I'm going to see it through." Even if it killed him.

"And after that?"

Oblivion.

"Your coastal report, Jared, remember?" Drew slanted his friend the most suspicious glare he could muster. "Conveniently in Cornwall, I might add."

"Near your much neglected home." Jared smiled. "It was Kate's idea. She thinks you need a rest. I think so, too."

"Bloody hell, you've got the most scheming, meddlesome wife!"

"That's just jealousy talking, my good man. You know as well as I do that Kate's schemes invariably work out for the best. I've learned to go along with them."

"Well, be sure to thank her for me." An attempt at

sarcasm, but a few days of quiet while he compiled Jared's bloody coastal reports for the Home Office sounded a bit too good to grouse about.

"You can tell her yourself, Drew, she's sitting in the third pew with Ross."

"Go join them, Jared. I won't be sitting." He planned to stay just long enough to see the crown placed on Caro's lovely head, and then he would leave.

Cowardly, but he couldn't bear more than that.

"As you wish, Drew." Jared offered his hand. "Do take care. And I'm sorry."

So am I.

Jared barely made it to his seat when the music began and Drew heard the fateful sound of footsteps coming up the stairs from the undercroft.

Caro! His princess.

Feeling like a bloody sneak thief, he moved halfway up the outside aisle of the nave, then stood beside one of the columns, a post that would give him a full view of the entire processional.

Close enough to hear for himself Caro swear the oath that would finally make her an empress.

A clean break. A slice through his heart.

Trumpets suddenly launched into a fanfare that arched through the fan vaulting, and Drew held his breath as the procession came into view at the back of the chapel.

Johannes and Wilhelm were at the lead of their two small columns of her loyal Boratanian subjects. Proud and determined, looking very capable, wise and ready.

His heart saw her before his eyes did, a brief glimpse as she moved into place behind them. Bits of her that raised his pulse and brought a lump to his throat.

The organ music rose with the trumpets, then the procession started down the aisle in earnest.

God, she was beautiful. Regal and ready to take her place in history.

His Caro. Brave and good, unwavering and honest.

His heart clenched as he saw her scanning the crowd for him, subtly, her chin high, her eyes glinting brilliantly as they traveled the width of the nave. Her golden hair was piled in curls atop her head, crowned with a small circlet of diamonds that would soon be replaced by a more elaborate crown.

Her gown was snow white and flowing, sashed across her left shoulder in a rich purple. She was draped in a lush, blue cape that was edged in white fur. Diamonds glinted from everywhere, as though shards of moonlight had attached themselves to her for a better view of the sky.

And then her eyes found him across the heads of the congregation.

"Caro," he heard himself whisper, a breathless prayer for her.

She smiled just for him, her eyes growing large and damp, glittering with unshed tears.

Then she passed him by, leaving him behind.

I love you, Caro.

Drew! Caro had prayed and prayed that he would come today. But she hadn't expected her heart to take off like a rabbit when she found him standing apart from everyone else. His jaw squared, his eyes haunted and fierce.

She had been perfectly fine when she left Grandauer Hall in the company of Queen Victoria's officials, had rationalized the facts, had sorted through and swallowed the falsehoods about her birth, fully determined to sacrifice the truth for the good of her people.

Who weren't her people at all.

But she had arrived in the undercroft at St. George's Chapel with a wicked dread churning in her chest, the stink of charred feathers, the metallic taste of lies.

Something was deeply wrong.

A lie was a lie. And such iniquity would only grow ever more evil over the years, more deeply woven into the fabric of Boratania.

And yet, here she was, artfully processing through a sea of dignitaries, kings and princes, dukes and margraves, moving inexorably toward the archbishop of Canterbury, in all his sacred and gleaming vestments, who would soon give his blessing to this travesty.

Then what?

Ahead of her, Johannes and Wilhelm reached the bottom of the dais steps and the procession came to a halt, just as they had practiced.

The music changed, and now she was supposed to walk between the two columns. Between these good men that she had come to love and respect. Men whom she could not lie to, who deserved better.

Men whose lives she was still responsible for, no matter that she wasn't truly their princess.

And shouldn't be their empress.

The archbishop was looking down the aisle at her over the top of his spectacles, nodding subtly at her to join him, when all she wanted to do was turn tail and run out of the chapel and into the street.

But she had given her word not to disturb the status quo. She certainly didn't want to be responsible for threatening the already shaky political landscape of Europe. Or the ancient and powerful families that ruled the world; Romanovs and Hanovers, Habsburgs and Saxe-Coburgs.

And yet it occurred to her that an empress could bloody well do anything, decree anything that she thought would benefit her kingdom.

Anything at all.

In fact, it was her duty to serve her people with the truest intentions of her heart.

The truest intentions.

Dear Lord in heaven! The answer had been staring her in the face for days.

Her heart in her throat, Caro straightened her shoulders and started down the aisle between her beaming subjects, certain that they would be ready for her announcement. Hoping so.

She knelt in front of the archbishop, who was smiling down on her in his divine benevolence.

He called the congregation to pray for the princess, for God to give her wisdom and long life, compassion and faith, justice and truth.

Yes, this was the right and good thing to do, she could feel it deep in her soul.

"Princess Caroline Marguerite Marie Isabella, empress-elect of Boratania . . ."

The archbishop chanted, celebrated communion and blessed all the days of her reign. He crowned her and draped her shoulders in her new royal cape, handed her the beautiful scepter, kissed her forehead—

And then he declared that she was now "Empress Caroline of Boratania."

There, Drew, I have claimed the title as was my duty, she thought, as she turned toward the congregation and her subjects, who were bursting with pride.

As she caught Drew's eye, he touched his fingers to his mouth, bowed slightly, gracious to the end, and then turned on his heel and strode out of the chapel and into the sunlight, taking her heart with him.

And now it was time to make her first decree as Empress of Boratania.

She turned to Queen Victoria and Albert who were sitting in the royal box, beaming at her. So kindly, so unsuspecting.

"Thank you, Your Majesty, for giving me aid and comfort for all these years. Boratania thanks you as well, and will remain your faithful friend."

She felt taller as she spoke, somehow grander for her new title, her voice filling the nave with the brief acceptance speech she had planned, her heart pounding in anticipation of the impromptu addition that was sure to send shock waves ricocheting through the halls of Europe.

She looked down at her once-exiled subjects. Tears of joy were streaming down their cheeks, matching her own.

I do this for you, gentlemen, my friends.

For your children and grandchildren.

For justice and liberty.

For your dear Boratania.

"As you all know, my dear ladies and gentlemen, Your Majesties, the kingdom of Boratania was abandoned in its time of greatest need, an evil time of great upheaval in the world. Ancient alliances torn asunder, iniquitous wars and revolutions, despots and sycophants."

Everyone exchanged sober nods, having heard the tales or remembering the evil for themselves.

"But these are brighter, more hopeful times, as our Prince Albert's Great Exhibition has shown us so splendidly."

A roar of approval and applause for the prince rose up into the vaulting. He whispered something to the queen, then they both nodded, clearly pleased.

Caro continued, her palms sweating, her heart beating so loudly she could barely hear herself speak. "Boratania has been reborn in an age of progress and industry, of educational reform and enlightenment." Her mouth dried up, but she wet her lips and filled up her resolve with the sight of her subjects' eager faces.

The new citizens of Boratania.

"An enlightenment that has exposed to the world an inalienable truth. As Thomas Jefferson declared in the document which severed the ties between Britain and her American colonies nearly a century ago, governments derive their powers by the consent of the governed."

The effect of these revolutionary words seemed to roll down the aisles like a shimmering wave. Murmurs of 'derive their powers' and 'the governed' and the polite clearing of throats.

"I, too, believe in the capacity of the people to govern themselves with wisdom and resolve. That when planted in fair and fertile soil, the seeds of self-determination will sprout and flourish."

Now the utter silence in the chapel was deafening. Faces of pale stone looked back at her from the pews.

"To that end, and by immutable royal decree, the government of Boratania will consist of a prime minister and a parliament, elected by a free and equal vote of all the people."

That seemed to relax the congregation somewhat; Europe was rife with parliaments and prime ministers.

"Until such elections can be realized and a constitution is lawfully established, the government of Boratania will be administered by a commission of six loyal citizens, whom I herewith name." Caro looked down at the good and wise men who had encouraged her, who loved Boratania with an unshakable faith in its future.

Whose claims to the land had endured for centuries and were as deeply rooted as the mountains.

"Wilhelm Belvedere," she began, and then, "Gunnar Hartenfels, Johannes Halstedt, Karl Brendel"—each man's eyes flew wide as she called his name—"Erasmus Uechersbach, Marcus Oderwald. Gentlemen, if you'll join me up here."

They stammered and stalled as she beckoned, but took the steps and clumped around her when she reached out her hand to them.

"My lords, my ladies," she said, tears swimming in her eyes, slipping down her cheeks, "you see here before you men of great wisdom and courage. They have sworn their abiding allegiance to me, and as such, to Boratania. I have, therefore, rendered myself unnecessary."

A rumble began to grow in the congregation and around her on the dais.

"Unnecessary? What do you mean, Empress Caroline?" Wilhelm whispered behind her.

"As empress of this magnificent kingdom, whose

legacy will thrive in their care, my first and final decree shall be . . . the abolishment of the Boratanian monarchy."

A huge gasp rose up from the crowd, spilled over into the aisles and rang against the stained-glass windows.

Shoring up her courage for the inescapable consequences, Caro took a deep breath, then reached up and grasped the rim of the crown so recently placed upon her head.

Another gasp, more cries of shock and scandal.

The gold was thick and warm, the precious stones cool against the pads of her fingers. A priceless, weighty thing that now belonged to the citizens of Boratania.

She tugged and the crown came off easily.

"It's done," she whispered to herself.

And nothing she had done in her life had ever felt so good, or so very right.

Chapter 23

"I've left a pot of hot water for your bath boiling on the stove, my lord. Will that be all for the evening?"

Drew looked up from his dry report, bleary-eyed and slightly surprised to find that his housekeeper hadn't yet left for her home in the village; she had five sons and a husband to feed, fishermen all.

"Ah, yes, of course, Mrs. Peterson." He stood up from the desk chair, his back stiff from inactivity. "Supper was excellent, as usual."

"And there's more on the hob if you should find yourself peckish come midnight." She tied a scarf around her head and hefted her netted satchel over her shoulder as he followed her to the door. "If you should need anything, sir, you know where to find me."

A quarter mile down the lane, on the edge of the village. "I do. Thank you. My best to your family."

Drew opened the cottage door for the woman and watched until she became a silhouette moving against the steely sea and the storm clouds that had been riding the horizon all day, waiting for something.

He stood in the doorway for a time, looking out on the empty cliffs, the empty sky.

He'd been hoping for a bit of peace in this lonely place. But he'd had no real peace at all in the last two days. And nights. She followed him everywhere.

The fairy-tale empress who had blithely drifted into his life, changed him utterly and then drifted out again.

The wind came up suddenly and blew a clatter of leaves past his boots and into the small entry.

He shut the door against the coming storm and poured himself a bath. He read the two-days-old *Times* while he soaked until the water grew cold.

He dressed in a loose-fitted work shirt and a pair of trousers, threw on a robe, then scooted his chair up to the blazing hearth and settled in for another night of trying to concentrate on Jared's coastal defense reports while being chased by the wily Empress who had ripped his heart out of his chest—

Rap, rap, rap!

"What the devil?" What sort of bloody fool would be out at night in weather like this?

Rap, rap, rap, rap!

He tied his robe at the waist and went to the door, bracing his shoulder against the panel as he opened it against the storm.

"What is it?" he shouted into the salty wet wind.

Something weighty hit the middle of the door, shoved and shuddered against him, and then let up while more leaves blew in past his legs.

"Damn ruffians!" Drew slammed the door shut,

locked it and then leaned back against the thick oak panel to survey the mess.

Leaves and bits of twigs had scattered themselves all over the damp floor. Mrs. Peterson wouldn't be happy.

He grabbed up a handful of leaves and took them back with him to the parlor and the hearth flames. Back to the—

"Good Christ!"

Someone . . . some *creature* had made itself at home in front of his fire. A figure small and quaking, and now hunched over to catch the heat inside its large cloak.

"Who the hell are you?" He was about to pounce on the bizarre figure when it made a sound that caught him in the middle of his heart.

"DREwwwwwww!"

"Caro?" He was on her in a breath, lifting the hood of her sodden cloak, his heart slamming inside his chest.

"C–c–cold." She looked up at him, her eyelashes starred with rain, her teeth rattling madly. "Sooo wwwet."

"Bloody hell, woman, what are you doing here?" Not waiting for an answer, he stripped off her cloak and wrapped her head to toe in the thick blanket from the back of his chair, then sat on a hearth stool and pulled her onto his lap, inside his embrace.

"W–w–warmer n–n–ow."

"You're not." She was shivering uncontrollably. And miles from where she ought to be. "What were you thinking, Caro?"

"Y–y–you."

"Christ, what have you done?" They must be looking for her everywhere. Had she changed her mind and run away from her duties? No, he'd seen the archbishop place the crown of Boratania on her head. She wouldn't run.

Not that it mattered at the moment, with her suffering so with the cold. Terrified that she might become ill, he wrapped her more tightly in the blanket and slid his fingers through her wet hair to warm her nape, tilted her chin to him.

"How did you get here; walk from London?"

She managed to shake her head. "T–t–train."

Good Lord! "You didn't walk here from the station at Exeter?"

More shaking of her head, less trembling. "C–c–c–carriage ride."

"You got yourself this wet, walking here from the village?"

"Lost." She sniffled and closed her eyes, tucking her head beneath his chin, snuggled more deeply into his arms, quieted with a long sigh. "Thank y–y–you."

"Bloody hell." Now what? He was holding an escaped empress in his arms. One who was doubtless being sought by every authority in the kingdom. For all he knew, the army might storm the cottage any moment.

"Why, love?" he whispered, gazing down at her. "What are you doing here?"

"Had to . . . find you."

Hell and damnation! He'd never been so happy to see anyone in his life, and never so bloody angry. He had finished his assignment with her, had set her aside for the next assignment. He would have forgotten her after a few months, if only . . .

Now there was a lie. She was completely unforgettable. Everything about her. But at least he'd begun to negotiate his way through the memories of her.

And yet here she was again, ambushing him in the closeness of his own cottage when she ought to be holding court in the great hall of Tovaranche Castle. Drenched and lovely and enfolded in his arms.

Bloody hell, and the sooner he returned her to London the sooner Palmerston would have his runaway empress back.

A hot bath would help warm her up for the return; water was still hot on the stove.

He stood and carried her to his chair, doing his best to keep a professional distance as he pulled the blanket around her shoulders.

"Stay here, Your Highness. I'll be right back." He moved the tub into the kitchen near the stove and poured a bath for her. But when he returned to the parlor, she was standing with her back to the fire, huddled under the blanket, looking at him with pleading eyes.

"I d–d–didn't mean to worry you, Drew."

"Worry me, madam? You're an empress now, an international figure. You can't just leave your duties and come here on a whim—"

"Not a whim, Drew. I came"—she shivered from her head to her knees—"looking for a suitable position."

"Suitable *what*?" Relieved that her wry humor had returned and that she was looking slightly more pink than blue, Drew lifted her into his arms and carried her toward the kitchen. "Very funny, Caro. But you have a position: lunatic empress. And as soon as you're warm, I'm returning you to Palmerston."

"He knows where I am."

"He knows? And he approves?" Shocked to the marrow, he stood her on her feet near the stove and peered into her blue-violet eyes.

"I don't believe he did, n–not really. Not in his heart. But he didn't have a ch–choice. I'd already decided I couldn't be . . . an empress."

Still stunned from her first declaration, he could only stammer. "What are you . . . What the hell does that mean, you decided you couldn't be an empress? People don't just decide these things."

She glanced down at the stone floor and then back up at him, clutching the blanket closer around her shivering shoulders. "Well, I . . . I did. Had to."

His heart had taken off on its own, thudding wildly in his chest, and he feared the worst. "You took the coronation oath. I heard you myself. So did hundreds of others."

She smiled flatly, and swiped a strand of wet hair off her cheek. "But you didn't stay, Drew."

He couldn't. "Christ, Caro, what have you done?"

"I . . . um . . ." She shivered again, a lingering shudder that ended with her teeth chattering for a moment. "I . . . abolished the monarchy."

He couldn't have heard her correctly. "Abolished?"

She nodded, sniffled. "It means I gave up my crown, my title."

"Christ on the cross! I know what *abolish* means!" God, the havoc she had set into motion. It would take years of negotiation for him to repair the damage. "Do you know the extent of what you've just done?"

"I didn't make the decision lightly, Drew." She frowned deeply at him. "I knew exactly what I was doing."

No, she didn't. She couldn't. Well, then, he would fix it as soon as he could make it back to London with her. But right now she was nothing but a trembling bag of sticks. "All right, Caro, into the bath with you."

"Now, *that* I won't argue about, Drew." She dropped the blanket from her shoulders.

He had no trouble keeping a clinical distance as he untied and unhooked and helped her out of everything but her camisole and drawers. He left her to do that chore herself, with an emphatic, "Stay in the water, madam. There's more heating on the stove."

He shut the kitchen door before she could answer, and while he still had his senses.

Because as cold as she was, with her skin goosed and pale, her hair hanging in straggling tendrils, she was still stunningly beautiful.

And wearing the skimpiest silk camisole, her nipples like fine little beacons for his hands, his mouth.

"Bloody hell." He leaned back against the closed kitchen door.

"Ohhhhhh, it's wonderful, Drew." She sighed, a sultry little mew. "You're wonderful."

"No, madam, I am disappointed. Now, soak!" Still stunned at the woman's foolishness, Drew went back to the parlor and hung her wet clothes on a drying rack in front of the hearth.

He tried to read his damn report, but soon found himself pacing in front of the fire, running through all the scenarios that might restore Caro to her rightful throne.

And Europe to its natural order.

He shouted, "Cover yourself, madam," before he burst into the kitchen to pour more warm water into the tub, leaving her a large towel and managing to avert his eyes.

Thirty minutes later, she stepped from the kitchen wrapped in the towel, from her knees to where she'd tucked it under her arms. She was a healthy pink again.

Too healthy.

Now, all he had to do was to remain unyielding and unsympathetic, rather than stand there stammering something about how bewitching she looked, how he wanted to explore his way through that golden curtain of hair, how all he really wanted to do was to forget who she was and claim her for his own.

To make endless love with her for the rest of their days.

"Now, into your clothes, Empress. Where's your bag?"

"I'm not an Empress, Drew, and I haven't any clothes." She scooted past him to the hearth, where she turned her back to the heat.

"You came all the way from London without a change of clothes?"

She nodded toward the window. "My satchel went over the edge of the cliff."

"Over the edge?" His stomach lurched. "How? What the devil were you doing out there?"

"I told you I got lost between the village and here. It was awfully windy and I couldn't see a thing in front of me. I kept getting blown toward the edge."

Bloody hell, the woman would never be safe.

"Then wait here, Caro." Drew returned to the parlor with one of his nightshirts, then slipped off his robe and handed it to her as well. "Get into these. I'll bring up some more firewood."

Before I lose myself in you, madam.

Drew stomped down the stairs into the cellar, muttering to himself as he loaded his arms with pieces of wood, then stomped back up the stairs to give warning that he was returning.

"Are you decent, madam?" he shouted from the stairwell.

"Yes, come, Drew." Her voice was a sweet melody, drawing him the rest of the way up the stairs.

He made the parlor in time to see her slipping into his robe. His nightshirt draped nearly to the floor, her feet poking out from under its hem. Her hair was already drying, shimmering waves of gold, a bit wild about the ends.

The Empress Caroline in all her royal finery.

"You left, dammit! After all we talked about."

She shrugged, making the robe slide off one of her shoulders. "It was the best thing, Drew."

"When did you do this?" He thunked a log onto the woodpile.

"At the ceremony, by decree. Oh, let me do that." She grabbed the next piece of wood out of his arms and added it to the stack beside the hearth.

"Bloody hell, you abolished the monarchy in front of the crowned heads of Europe?"

"In front of Queen Victoria and everyone." Off came another log; this time she placed it in the flames. "I had to do it that way."

"Dammit, Caro. How the devil am I going to fix this?"

"It doesn't need fixing, Drew. I hope it can't be." She finished stacking the wood and brushed off his sleeves. "I've taken care of everything. Tied up all the loose ends—"

"Leaving Boratania to swing in the wind! Without you as their empress, Caro, without an ordained leader, you've thrown your kingdom to the wolves."

"Boratania doesn't need me anymore, Drew." She found a broom leaning in the corner and started sweeping up the wood chips they had just scattered on the floor. "I made sure of that."

"Madam, Boratania needs you now, more than ever." He followed her, catching a bristle across his shoe as she swept toward the front door.

She stopped, her palm over the end of the broom. "I didn't leave Boratania without a leader, Drew, I left it to the people it belongs to."

"To the people?" What the devil was she talking about?

"It was really quite simple. I merely declared a parliamentary government, appointed Wilhelm and the others to create a constitution"—she took a breath, then smiled brightly at him—"and then, by royal decree, I abolished the monarchy."

"Just like that?"

"Exactly like that." She went back to her sweeping, collecting the leaves that had chased her into the house when she entered.

"And then what, madam?" He caught her by the shoulder, and the robe drooped. "The queen just sat there, said nothing?"

She seemed to cast back in time, her eyes wistful and content. "They all just sat there once I had made my royal decree. After that, well, then all hell broke loose."

"Christ, Caro!" But then a tickle came into his heart, a simple delight at the thought. A wish that he'd been there to see it for himself.

His princess, his love, stunning them speechless, showing them what true nobility was.

"I had to do it that way, Drew; in front of everyone at the ceremony, more than a thousand witnesses, and then in a meeting with the queen afterward, in which, well, I resorted to blackmail."

"You blackmailed Queen Victoria?"

"Along with Archduke Franz Karl of Austria, Tsar Nicholas of Russia and the king of Denmark, to name a few who were there."

Then he understood. "You keep quiet about their roles in your scandalous origins, and they leave Boratania alone." Not a woman to cross.

"Exactly." She set her mouth in a stubborn line, regal to the marrow, whether she liked it or not.

"You never said a thing to me of your grand plan, Caro." He thought they shared a deeper trust than that.

She laughed lightly. "I didn't know myself until I was in the midst of the procession. I was such a jumbled mess inside. I knew that accepting the title wasn't right. That *I* wasn't right. I'm not Boratanian. I'm English, to the soles of my feet."

"But would you have told me, Caro, if you had known your intentions beforehand?"

"I don't know." She cocked her head at him as she

put her hand on the latch. "It was a matter between me and my conscience, Drew, between me and the citizens of Boratania."

Not giving him a chance to react, she shouldered open the door, then swept madly against the wind and the rain.

Madwoman! He dragged her back inside and rammed the door closed with his shoulder, then leaned hard against the panel and stared at his windblown ex-royal, not sure exactly what the hell he ought to do next.

Because this particular assignment was obviously not finished.

"This is all very interesting, Caro," he said, as steadily as he could, "but why did you come here?"

"Why?" Caro's heart stopped and then dropped into her stomach. Of all the questions Drew could have asked when he found her on the doorstep of his cottage, that wasn't the one she wanted to hear.

Where else would she come but to the man she loved? The splendid man who had so fiercely declared his love for her only a few days ago.

But now his eyes had grown dark and unreadable, his jaw squared and set, as though she suddenly meant less than nothing to him.

"Um, well . . . Drew," she said, shifting her gaze to the floor, then sweeping lightly at the clean mortar between the flags so she didn't have to face his disappointment. "I just. . . . well, I thought I should tell you myself about what I did after you left the chapel. Instead of letting you read about it in the *Times*."

The scandal had been splashed all over every newspaper in the kingdom, not to mention Europe.

"Then you're fortunate, madam, the village news

shop runs a good half week behind the rest of the country." He reached for the door as though to open it and evict her, but only shot the bolt into the lock.

"Yes, I'm very fortunate, Drew." Because it seemed he wasn't going to toss her out into the storm! At least not yet. "And the last thing I want is to be a bother to you!"

In fact, she meant to be helpful. Indispensable to him. She had already swept the floor.

"A bother, madam?" That was definitely a sarcastic bellow.

Knowing just what to do next, she strode through the parlor into the kitchen at the back of the cottage, hoping Drew would follow her, hoping he would see how useful she could be.

"Have you a housekeeper, Drew?"

"Mrs. Peterson, when I'm in residence here. Why?"

Well, then, she couldn't be his housekeeper.

He stopped at the door and leaned against the jamb, watching as she started swabbing up the puddles she had created around her bath tub.

"Have you a cook?"

"Also Mrs. Peterson."

"How about a gardener?" She wrung out the towel into the sink drain then dropped to the floor again, feeling Drew's gaze following her every move.

"In case you didn't notice when you were out dancing along the cliffs, madam, the only thing that grows around the cottage is moss and heather." He was suddenly kneeling in front of her as she scrubbed at the floor, frowning as he trapped the sloppy towel beneath her hand with his own. "What are you doing, Caro?"

"I'm just cleaning up the mess I made here."

"Admirable, madam, but why?" He captured her hand between his own, not letting go when she pulled at it.

"Because it's my mess. And since I'm no longer a pampered royal, I'm going to have to learn to take care of myself."

He raised a wry brow, his eyes softening into the smile she loved so dearly. "You were never a pampered anything, Caro."

"But now I'm completely without resources," she said, standing up with the rag and wringing it out in the sink again, "So, I was thinking that if I can prove myself useful to you, perhaps you'll let me stay on here when you're not in residence."

He rose slowly, shaking his head as though he didn't understand or thought it was a completely unacceptable idea. "Stay on here, madam?"

"In exchange for doing your laundry or wood-chopping or—"

"You, Princess?" His eyes widened and then he laughed, long and low, as though he thought her incapable of a little hard work.

"Well! Then perhaps I can serve as your jester, Lord Wexford." She tried to drag the tub closer to the drain in the floor, but it wouldn't budge, so she grabbed the broom and started sweeping where she had just scrubbed. "Better yet, Drew, you can recommend me to the household of one of your colleagues."

He'd sobered completely. "You're serious?"

"I'm penniless."

He eyed her. "And you want me to give you references?"

"That would be very helpful." And a last resort, but

she was beginning to panic. "It's going to take Palmerston years to forgive me. And I'd rather not ask the queen."

He folded his arms across his chest, then studied her from beneath his dark brow. "Very well, Princess. I need a valet."

Not sure she'd heard him right over her nervous sweeping, she leaned the broom against the cupboard door.

"Did you say 'valet'?"

"I usually don't employ a valet when I'm here in the village. And Mrs. Peterson isn't really suitable."

"But I *am*?" Most valets were men. All of them, in fact.

"Come to think of it, I could use someone to set out my clothes every day, and keep them pressed and clean." He turned and wandered idly out of the kitchen, leading her into the parlor. "To tend to the fire—ah, you see it's getting a bit low, Caro."

"Oh, yes." Valet didn't seem a very good fit, but she ran past him to the stack of wood and quickly added a log to the flames.

"And to see that my breakfast tray arrives on the spot of eight, along with the latest issue of the *Times*, which you can pick up in the village the night before." He waved the folded newspaper at her as he sat down in the big chair. He slumped casually, then raised his foot onto the hearth stool. "After dinner, I prefer two fingers of brandy. You'll find a glass and a bottle of Napoleon's best behind the cabinet door."

"Here?" Caro followed the man's lazy point, opened the cabinet, poured the brandy, then handed the glass to him.

"And, of course, madam, I will also need my

shoes removed—" he wriggled his foot back and forth.

It wasn't until Caro had knelt and yanked off both of his shoes—

"And replaced by my slippers, which by the way, I keep on the floor of my wardrobe."

—that she finally heard the amusement in his voice.

That she finally looked up into his face and found a smile tucked badly into the corners of his fine mouth.

The lout was toying with her!

"Blackguard!" She slapped his foot off the stool and would have grabbed her clothes off the drying rack so that she could go stay the night in the village, but he caught her by the upper arms before she reached the hearth.

"Caro, wait!" He was smiling broadly again, though his eyes were entirely earnest. "I'm sorry."

"You don't believe I'm serious, do you?"

"About being my valet?"

"About being penniless, Drew. When I abolished the Boratanian monarchy I also abolished my income. Every penny of it! I need a job."

His eyes had been so intense, his mouth so fierce. And now a kind of peace came over him, a wistful, wonderful smile.

"Then be my wife, Caro."

"Your . . ." A howling wind must have come up just outside the cottage, because she suddenly couldn't hear for the wild ringing in her ears. "What did you say, Drew?"

But now he was threading his fingers through her hair, his eyes sparkling, his mouth moist and nuzzling at her temple, the warm, brandied sweetness of his breath sending shivers down her neck, through the thin linen of the nightshirt to the tips of her breasts.

"Will you, my love?" He nibbled and tasted and groaned as he came ever nearer to her mouth, touching his fingers to her lips, smiling down on her.

"Will I what?" And now she was shamelessly slipping her arms around his neck, tugging on a hank of hair at his nape, rising up on her toes to be closer to him, to his kiss, to the miraculous words he whispered against her lips, his gaze lighting on her eyes.

"Will you marry me, my love?"

Oh, she heard that! All of it. Saw the adoration in his eyes. "Oh, Drew . . . oh, yes!"

"Sweet Caro!" And then her magnificent warrior, her courageous protector, the man of her dreams, covered her mouth with his, completely, absolutely, dizzying her with a hungry, driving moan that rose out of his chest and filled her belly with brilliant sparks that sizzled along her ribs to the center of her.

Drew was sure he was dreaming a very erotic dream. Must be a dream because Caro was here in his cottage, wrapped in his arms.

No longer a royal, no longer forbidden.

And she'd just said yes.

Had just slipped the tip of her tongue between his lips to dance with his own.

She was lush and warm and clinging to him as though she couldn't get enough of him. Squirming her hips against him as though testing the shape of his rock-hard penis.

"It's lovely, Drew." As though she knew that she had caused it.

"Is it?"

"Oh, yesssssss."

Which only made him harder, only deepened his need for her. A need that he'd spent the last month denying, suppressing after it had become an undeniable truth, fighting to do right by her with every fibre of his soul.

Now she was his. His Caro. His miracle.

His breath and his blood.

"Are you sure, Drew?" She had somehow managed to climb up onto the hearth stool, which brought him closer to her delicious mouth, to her wanton, greedy kisses.

"Sure of what, love?" He was only slightly conscious of her question, yet fully aware that in a single roll of her shoulders she had shrugged out of his silk robe completely and was now standing in front of him, clad only in his linen nightshirt.

A very thin garment, never used so well.

Tempted beyond his will, Drew fit his hands against her lithe little waist, stilling his thumbs when they wanted to explore the flat of her belly, the curves and the valleys.

She suddenly caught his face between her hands, her eyes bright, her cheeks aglow with the firelight. "Are you sure of all this, Drew? Of me?"

His heart was thudding against hers. "Love, I've never been so sure of anything in my life."

"Nor have I!" Her smile was glorious, her kiss consuming, luxurious.

"Oh, Caro!" He heard himself groan again as she slid the tip of her tongue along the line of his jaw and caught his earlobe, tugging, sucking, turning his groan into a throaty gasp, and his need for her into a living thing.

He found that his aching hands had drifted upward on their own over the nightshirt and along her ribs, until they fit perfectly just beneath the gentle rise of her breasts. Perfect and sweet. Soft mounds that he wanted to touch, to kiss and taste.

"Your hands are so warm, Drew, and wonderful!" Her breath brushed against his ear in a long, melodious sigh. She writhed against the length of him, flushed with pleasure, her eyes half lidded.

He had been fiddling dangerously with the flat pearl buttons that ran down the front of the nightshirt. Flirting more dangerously with the irrational idea of undoing them one by one.

"Do you suppose, Drew . . ." Unable to resist another moment, Drew slid his thumbs over her nipples. "Oh, Drew, that's, ohhh . . ." Her eyes flew open, she grabbed his shoulders and she arched against him, then mewed and swayed and laughed low in her throat.

"You were asking, love?"

She smiled coyly, raking her fingers through his hair. "Only wondering, really. If I'll be as good a wife as I was a valet?"

He clutched her bottom, ripe and firm, pulled her closer against him to catch her squirming full on. "Better, I hope, madam."

"I was that bad?" She stepped back from him, a sly lift to her smile that made him want to tease right back.

"That inexperienced. As a valet."

"Then let me show you what a fine valet I would be, should you hire me on as your wife." Her warm fingers began unbuttoning the front of his shirt, one button, one succulent, exploring kiss beneath it, teeth and tongue. "I'll do your buttons every morning and every night, my lord."

And he damn well wasn't going to stop her from her exploration.

"Have you any references, madam?" Not that she needed any, not with the way she played her fingers against his chest, a button at a time until she had shoved his shirt off his shoulders.

"I was a princess once upon a time, my lord." She was working on his cuff now, nibbling at his wrists, trapping him in his shirt, still brushing her belly against him.

"Were you a good princess?" he asked, gasping as she reached for the buttons at the front of his trousers. "Christ, Caro! That's . . ."

Marvelous! The lightest brush of her fingers across the taut fabric where he bulged and throbbed and ached for her was an ecstasy.

"I tried to be a good princess, my lord." She nuzzled at his neck as she shaped her hand over the length of his erection, took his gasp and his groans into her kiss.

"You were good, Caro. You are, my love." So good, so lush, so unbridled with her fingers and her heart.

"And you are very sturdy here, Drew." She looked into his eyes as she fondled and caressed, measured and moaned along with him, until he was breathing like a horse and his head was light from lack of air. "Thick and soooooooo long."

"Oh, Caro, that's . . . too . . . enough!" He grabbed her hands and kissed her palms, the thrusting, grinding pleasure too great at the moment to give her free rein to unfasten the button at his waist.

"Enough, Drew? Oh, but I could touch you there

forever." She looked up at him, truly confused. She really didn't know. "And with your trousers off—"

"I would lose complete control, my love!" Would haul her to the thick carpet in front of the hearth and drive himself into her, into the sweet oblivion of her softness.

"You, lose control, Drew?" She still cooed and arched against him, gripping his bare shoulders, riding the length of him with her mons, her face golden in the light of the fire, this wanton woman who would always be his princess.

"Lose control completely, love." She had rid him of his shirt and now he was doing the same for her, his fingers quaking to be rid of her buttons, to be sliding his tongue across her nipples. "Do you know what a temptation you've been to me all these weeks?" The top button came easily open, her skin tasted of clear water and her lavender. "Sleeping just on the other side of a not-very-secret panel from you."

She gasped and moaned. "Only proving, my lord, that you would never lose control, would never . . . oh, Drew, I like your mouth there, and your hands. Right there . . . yesssss!"

He was cupping the undersides of her breasts through the linen of the nightshirt, rubbing their tightly erect tips with his thumbs, dazzled by the passion in her eyes, in her throaty whimpers.

"I love you, Caro!"

And they would marry the moment he could rouse his ravenous bride-to-be from the cottage. Which might just be a few amazing days from now.

"Oooooooooh, Drew!

Caro knew she needed something deep and mystical from her magnificent earl, was sure she would die of the pleasureful wanting of it long before he could give it to her.

Sex. Copulation. She knew that was it, the end product. That he would somehow manage to thrust his huge, glorious ramrod of a penis inside her, in the place where all this delicious yearning was coming from.

The technical *how* of it all was the question, the delicious anticipation that seemed to steal her breath away as if she'd been running alongside him at the edge of the sea cliff.

That made her knees weak, and keeping her balance on the hearth stool a bit precarious.

She held tightly to her extraordinary protector, the man who loved her for not being an empress.

His chest was broad and dark gold, lightly furred with silky dark hair that she loved to run her fingers through.

And now he was tantalizing her with his mouth, his fiery tongue, nipping along her collar bone, at the base of her throat, and across her shoulder, until the nightshirt drooped to her elbow and slipped below one breast, exposing it to his smiling, hungry gaze.

"My beautiful Caro." He ran his tongue across his lips as though he hadn't eaten in weeks. "May I taste you, love?"

"Taste? Oh, myyy yessss!" He was slow and taunting, the touch of his mouth dizzying her as he came ever closer to that point of sensation, until he was teasing at her nipple, licking softly, flicking his tongue, crimping with his astounding fingertips, lighting a fire so deep inside her she was sure it could never be quenched.

"I wonder, does the other taste as sweet, my love."

He gave a soft tug to the nightshirt, and it slid down her arms, catching at her wrists for a moment, and then at her hips. Then the linen slipped right on down to pool at her ankles, leaving her standing before him utterly naked and exposed to his wolfish ogling.

He wore a smile that said he'd just won a prize. Or learned a secret.

"If you'll allow me, Princess."

"Anything, Drew." Her heart, her soul. He caught her chin, kissed her deeply, brought her closer until her aching breasts were bobbing against his warm chest.

And then he started nibbling his way across her belly, his hands sliding down her back, to her bottom, kneading there as he made love to her breast, making her sway and thread her fingers through his hair and pull him closer.

And then the marvelous man, who was out of breath and quaking beneath her hands, started nuzzling beneath her breast and kissing her ribs, her waist, traveling ever downward toward her belly.

Toward all that gathering heat, making her feel warm and ripe and wanting to open to him completely.

"Drew?" She gasped when he turned his head and pressed his cheek against her belly, his broad hands still spread across her bottom.

"Mmmmm . . . my love." He made a long, thrilling growl in his throat. It rumbled out of him and into her, loosening her knees and making her quiver all over.

"Oooohhhh, Drewwwwwww!" His steaming breath played out against her bare hip, his mouth a moist heat against her waist and then ever lower to that place where her thighs met her body.

"Yes, love?" He was kneeling right in front of her as she stood there on the upholstered stool looking down at him, his mouth just inches from—

"Ohhhhhhhh!" The amazing man was kissing the insides of her thighs, making love to them, one side and then the other, teasing, nibbling, moving ever closer as though he might—

"Drew, what are you do—" But he gripped her bottom with his hands and lifted her hips closer to him.

To his mouth.

He was nearly growling again, breathing like a stag in rut. "I'm going to kiss you, Caro."

"Oh, but—" And then he did kiss her.

And she must have died, because this feeling was heaven! Floating and pricked with bits of light.

His darting tongue seeking the depths of her, finding places she didn't know existed, brewing up a storm of sensations inside her that she had never felt before.

"You taste fine here, too, Caro," he whispered between his dizzying, plunging kisses.

Kisses that she was shamelessly thrusting toward with her hips, unable to get enough of him, of his delicious madness, until the room began to swim and her head grew light.

"Drew, I think I'm going to—" Her knees sagged but her champion caught her up in his powerful arms and carried her to the warm carpet and the firelight.

"Don't go anywhere, Princess." He left her with a smile, but only long enough to collect a nest of pillows and a counterpane from another room.

"Your trousers, sir!" she said when he returned.

"As you wish, my love." They were gone a moment later and her bronze god was lowering himself to her, smoothing his palm down her ribs and then spreading his fingers over her belly.

"Oh, Drew! I don't know how else you can torment me." And then she knew.

She met his hand with the tilt of her hips, dizzied by the throbbing sensation as he slid his fingers along her folds and then delved inside with two fingers, filling her with quicksilver, yet only making her want more of him.

"More, Drew!" She wanted him to hurry with his secrets.

"All in good time, my love." He was masterfully slow, drawing gasps from her with his fingers and his tongue and his nibbling, tugging at her pulse, sending her spiraling upward toward the sky, but never getting there.

Until he finally rose up on his elbows, his hard, hot penis pressed against her belly, a stunning, raw sensation that made her wrap her legs around his hips, want to take him deeply inside her.

"Come to me, Drew. Fill me."

"With all my heart, Caro. For all my days!" But he lingered exquisitely over her, drawing out her pleasure as though on another mission. Though she could see his own restraint tearing at him, bringing them both ever closer to the edge of something.

And then she felt the thick, pulsing tip of him against her slick heat, so near all that leashed and breathless pleasure.

He was smiling down on her, encompassing her fully, wild and dark, the goodness of his great heart in his eyes.

"No going back from here, Princess."

"Only forward, Drew." Like the rhythmic tide that pulled at her, that pushed her to finish this. She tilted her hips and took the tip of him into her, wanting more. "Oh, my husband! My dearest love!"

"Wife!" His handsome face grew taut and impassioned as he pressed more deeply, and then swiftly, surely. A rolling, riotous pleasure that seemed to have a force of its own, that grew and blossomed.

"I can't seem to stop, Drew." Her hips pushed up against his, mindlessly, taking his propelling thrusts as fiercely as he gave them.

"My love!" His rhythm changed, deepened.

"Oh, Drew, I . . . ohhhhhhhh, myyy!" And then suddenly soaring, searing explosion began where they were joined, a radiance in her belly, a splintering lushness that overtook her heart and her limbs and made her hold tightly to him, and hold and hold. "I love you, Drew! My dearest hero!"

Drew felt the beginning of Caro's release and finally let go of his own, riding the skyrocketing pleasure, the shuddering force that rocked him to the core. The crests rose and rose, with Caro's name on his lips and his mouth on her breast, her eyelids, her neck.

His princess.

His love.

His life.

And as he finally drifted with her back to earth, he gathered her fiercely against him in the flickering orange of the hearthlight, delighting in her kisses as she clung to him. She was still shuddering against him, breathless and sleek-muscled, whimpering her pleasure against his mouth.

"What a wondrous thing you do, Lord Wexford,"

she whispered as she caught his face in her hands. "I think I'll enjoy being your valet."

"Not nearly as much as I'll enjoy being your husband." Drowning every night in her warm eddies, his senses unraveling beneath her fingers, in the wake of her gentle laughter.

In the bliss of the wily grin she was wearing just now. "Kate will certainly be pleased about all this, Drew."

"*This*?" He rolled up onto his elbow. "Because you and I made love on the floor in front of the fire?"

"Because she's won a wager from Jared."

"That I would bed you, Caro?"

She laughed low in her throat and touched her fingertip to the end of his chin. "That I would bed *you*, my lord, before midnight. And I have. With two hours to spare."

"Bloody hell, woman. You mean Jared bet against me?"

Her brow furrowed. "I don't think he was very serious. The wager was for a dance with Kate in the Abasanti moonlight."

"Ah!" Drew laughed and sifted his fingers through her hair. "From what I know of the Abasanti, love, that would make them both winners. But I have a wager of my own for you."

"That I might bed you once more, before midnight, do you mean?" Her eyes glinted as she slid her palms over his backside, boldly kneading him, exploring, as wanton as the desert wind.

"I'm wagering, my love"—a wave of ecstasy rose in him again, made him rock hard and aching to plunge deeply into her sweetness—"that you'll marry me in the village tomorrow."

"You win that one straight away, Drew!" She kissed him fully, deeply, then lifted her starry-lashed eyes to his. "Now it's my turn to offer a wager, if you dare take it, sir."

Skeptical as hell, but so profoundly, madly in love with the woman that he nodded gladly. "Go on, Caro."

"I wager that you, Andrew Chase, first Earl of Wexford, and I, the Once-Empress of Boratania, will live happily, joyfully together, in a house full of children, forever and ever."

His heart filled with unimaginable bliss and the promise of a splendid future with his extraordinary wife, Drew laughed and gathered her into his arms. "Until the end of time, my love, my life."

Sometime later, in the moonlit darkness of their bedchamber, Caro heard the mantel clock strike midnight and smiled against Drew's shoulder.

Happily forever after, my prince.